# Yours to Keep or Throw Aside

## A Novel by
## E.D. Martin

SECOND EDITION SOFTCOVER
ISBN: 1622532325
ISBN-13: 978-1-62253-232-2

*Editor: Mishael Witty*
*Senior Editor: Lane Diamond*

Printed in the U.S.A.

www.EvolvedPub.com
Evolved Publishing LLC
Cartersville, Georgia

Printed in Book Antiqua font.

# Chapter 1 – Kasey (Present)

Rainbow light danced inside diamonds as I twirled my wedding ring around my finger. Despite annual cleanings and the care I took with the stones' facets, a dull sheen muted the sparkle that had shone so brightly when my husband David first slipped it onto my finger nearly a decade ago.

"Earth to Kasey."

I looked away from my ring, at my friend Ann across the bistro table. "Sorry. What did you say?"

"I said Colbie enjoyed staying at your house last weekend." Her daughter and mine were in kindergarten together, nearly inseparable. Ann eyed me. "You were real quiet at the Junior League meeting today, even for you. Problems with David again?"

Her barely noticeable enunciation of the last word was meant as friendly concern, of course it was, not an intentional slight. It wasn't as if I complained about my husband all the time, about my empty life.

Nonetheless, I chose my words carefully. No need to make myself the gossip at the next Junior League meeting. "I don't know what it is. Something feels off."

"Well, Kasey, every marriage is bound to hit some bumps every now and then." She took a sip of her sparkling water. "Tim and I are fine, of course, but lots of couples have problems."

"It's not so much problems, as we don't seem to connect as well as we used to. Ever since he made partner he's been working all the time. It seems like we never have the chance to talk or really spend much time together."

"Have you talked to him about it?"

I shook my head. "When would I have a chance? He works crazy nonstop hours, and when he gets home he pours himself a drink and then goes to bed. And if I try to say anything, he claims everything is fine and clams up."

"Maybe you should do something nice for him. Make him feel appreciated."

"I try. I do. He's just oblivious to it all."

Like this morning. I'd gotten up early to make him his favorite breakfast, eggs and bacon and waffles. Then he'd overslept, blaming it on me for not setting the alarm clock or checking on him enough, as if he were a child and not a thirty-two-year-old man. He'd grabbed his briefcase and a Pop-Tart and stomped out, barely saying a word to me or our daughter Aida.

I couldn't tell Ann this. Ann with all the answers, with the perfect marriage and family and manicure. Ann in her form-fitting velour jogging suit, getting appraising looks from men in the restaurant and jealous stares from their wives and girlfriends. Ann who loved the lifestyle that came with being the wife of a wealthy Southern doctor.

"You'll figure something out. He's such a great guy." She glanced at her watch. "I hate to dine and dash, but I need to run some errands before school gets out. Tim's out of town this week, or I'd have him do it." She fingered her bill. "Hey, Colbie and I are having a special girls' night tonight. You and Aida should join us."

"Tuesday is David's career networking night, so my mom's picking Aida up." I rolled my eyes. "I think tonight we're going to a client's house for cocktails, but I might feign a headache and stay home."

"That's the price we have to pay." She pulled her wallet from her purse, counted out some bills. "We get the fancy house, gorgeous husband, big allowance, and social bragging rights, and all we have to do is play trophy wife a couple nights a week. What's the problem?"

"The problem is, I don't want to be a trophy wife. I'd give up everything in a heartbeat if we could just spend more time as a family." I stabbed a tomato slice with my fork.

"You make it sound like we're being forced into this." She wrinkled her nose. "I'll see you at the PTA meeting tomorrow, right?"

"Yeah, unless my headache extends to that too."

"Kasey," she said with a laugh, "having to be around other people isn't a bad thing. You have the perfect life. Lighten up!"

"Except for the unhappy marriage," I muttered as she walked away.

And what was life worth without someone in it to love you?

***

After lunch I had a few errands to run too. Most people scoffed when I denied spending my days at home on the couch eating bonbons, but there really was more to being a stay-at-home mom than daytime soaps. David believed in making the best impression possible, so he asked that his suits be impeccably cleaned and pressed; that meant frequent trips to the drycleaners. I tried to get into Aida's school, if not her classroom, on a weekly basis, and PTA consumed a good deal of time as well. On top of that were numerous social obligations: luncheons for various organizations to which David belonged, meetings for clubs he'd encouraged me to join, and evening cocktails and dinners with friends and clients. Aida was currently in gymnastics and begging for riding lessons, which would mean more running around on my part. Throw in routine house cleaning, laundry, and grocery shopping, and I had little time to myself.

Today I arrived home with several hours free to spend however I wanted, for once. I'd stopped by the library and picked up a couple books, trashy historical romance novels that were as far as I could get from my mundane suburban life, but as I walked up the sidewalk to our front door, the fresh scent of lilacs reminded me of work that needed to be done around the yard. Not that I minded gardening. Today, however, I needed to know there was something beyond my Richmond neighborhood, beyond being a lawyer's stay-at-home wife, even if it only existed in books.

As I stepped onto our front porch, an envelope tucked in the front storm door caught my eye—no return address, no postage, just *Mrs. Sanford* scrawled in messy feminine handwriting. I picked it up, opened it, and pulled out the contents: a letter, wrapped around several photographs. I smiled at the quaintness; who printed out pictures anymore when they were just as easy to email?

I set the letter aside and studied the photos. Their low-quality fuzziness indicated they'd been taken with a webcam, but I could still clearly discern two people intimately engaged. As I focused on the images, my smile faded. One figure was David; although his face wasn't visible in the photos, after almost ten years together I'd have recognized his stocky frame anywhere.

The other figure, the female, was not me.

"No," I whispered, shaking my head. "No, no, no." Louder and louder, shaking my head more fiercely, it was all I could say as I backed up and collapsed onto a wicker chair on the porch. The letter in my hands trembled so badly I could barely read it.

> *Dear Mrs. Sanford,*
>
> *Your husband and I have been in love for a year now. I make him very happy, much happier than you ever did, as you can tell in the pictures. But every time I bring up ending his marriage he makes excuses. I got tired of this and gave him a final choice: me or you. He refused to leave you. I want a man who isn't too cowardly to follow his heart, so you can have your husband back.*
>
> *Sincerely,*
> *A woman scorned*
> *PS - good luck satisfying him after he's been with me.*

The words blurred through my tears. Another woman? Things weren't great between us, but infidelity was the last thing I expected from David. Ever since we started dating, he'd always said he loved me and only me. I thought he meant it, had no reason not to believe it. Things like this happened to other people. Not us. Not me.

Shaking, gasping, unsure of what to do next, I somehow stumbled into the house. I wanted to cry, to scream, to smash something, to go back in time just ten minutes and throw that letter away, never read it, never find out my husband had been with someone else. Instead, all I could do was stand in our living room, sucking in breaths, the letter and photos clutched in my hands.

Minutes passed, hours maybe, and gradually I was able to breathe again. I paced the room, the movement instilling in me a false sense of decisive action. I tried to determine what to say to David, how to handle this, the next steps to take. I tried to be rational but my thoughts wouldn't cooperate, wouldn't stay in one place long enough for me to work anything out. I shook my head occasionally, although whether it was to clear my thoughts or in disagreement with them, I couldn't say. How dare he jeopardize our family, our home, everything we'd worked so hard to create for ourselves!

Something I was certain of, however, was that whatever happened next, we'd never have our life back, never the same as it had been. Gone, all gone. I sank down onto the couch, wishing we had a pet, something soft and warm to hold for comfort, settling for a chenille throw pillow that I hugged close.

I picked up my cell phone and called Ann. It went straight to voicemail.

"Hey, Ann, it's Kasey." I paused, unsure whether I wanted to tell her about this. She always talked about how perfect her relationship with her husband was, how many men had loved her before she'd picked Tim to spend her life with. She wouldn't understand. "I—" My mind blanked. Feeling foolish, I stared at the pictures as I waited for the message to time out, then deleted it and hung up.

David was the only man I'd ever loved, who'd ever really loved me. I'd had boyfriends in high school and college, some casual and some long-term, but David was the only one who had ever meant anything. He'd always had a way of making me feel as if I mattered. Maybe at first I was just flattered by the attention of a popular attractive guy, but it quickly became more than that. He listened to me, supported me, backed up my ideas and defended me, took care of me.

I thought I was doing the same for him. Turned out I was wrong, that I'd missed something along the way.

My phone rang, probably Ann returning my call, but I ignored it. I read and reread the letter, trying hard not to stare at the pictures but failing again and again. In one the sheets were tangled around his legs, his back muscles tensed. Her arms hugged his neck, legs wrapped around his waist. In another she straddled him, long blonde hair falling to mask her face as she leaned forward, masking David's as well. All clues to her identity were carefully hidden except for the blur of a tattoo on her ankle.

It was obviously him; he wouldn't be able to deny it. Why had he done this? Was he going to leave me once I confronted him, or would we be able to work through it all? Should I even confront him? Should I leave him?

And what about Aida? Anger rushed back. We had a daughter, a wonderful little girl who didn't deserve this mess, didn't deserve to have her home broken because her father felt—felt what? Unfulfilled? Horny? Bored?

My mind raced from one scenario to another as I cycled between rage and sorrow, always coming back to the basic fact that my husband had cheated on me. Despite years spent doing everything I could to create the perfect home for my family, to be the best partner to him I possibly could, my husband had cheated on me.

\*\*\*

The front door opened and I heard David walk in, whistling a tune he'd probably heard on the way home. His briefcase thudded on the foyer's ceramic tile, and his suit jacket rustled as he hung it on the coat rack. His footsteps moved into the kitchen, paused, and then he strolled into the living room, running a hand over his short blond hair, unaware of how our lives had changed. Late afternoon sunlight streamed in from the floor-to-ceiling windows, mottled slightly by saplings in the tiny backyard, illuminating his figure.

"Hey, Kase." He came over to me and kissed my cheek.

I flinched but he didn't seem to notice. Didn't notice I'd been crying. Didn't notice everything was different now.

"Court adjoined early, so I stopped and picked up dinner on the way home. I know you've been pretty busy and tired lately. Hope you didn't cook anything yet."

I shook my head and bit my lip, still unsure how to bring up the letter, the pictures, the fact I knew he'd cheated on me. My husband had cheated on me. That sounded so harsh, so clinical, so daytime-talk-show trashy.

"Where's Aida?" he asked.

"With my parents, since we're supposed to have drinks with the Carvers tonight. I'd really like to skip it though." After an afternoon of crying, the headache I'd wanted had arrived.

"Alone time for us? I like it." He grinned and pulled me into his arms, as if everything was fine, as if he hadn't been taking another woman into his arms.

I pulled away and thrust the letter and pictures at him. Trying not to shake, I said in as level a voice as I could manage, "Someone stuck these in the door today."

His brow wrinkled, then his eyes widened as he read the letter and saw himself in the photos. Surprise was conspicuously absent; he'd known I would find out, knew of the woman's ultimatum.

That realization channeled my jumbled emotions into pure rage.

"What's going on, David?" My voice was as smooth and deadly as ice.

He glanced at me, then looked away and sat down on the couch. He was thinking hard, going into lawyer mode with himself as the defendant this time, weighing his words against the truth and what I'd believe. It meant he was hiding more.

"What the hell is going on, David?"

"Kase, I can explain." He twisted the letter in his hands.

"Yeah?"

"It happened, and it's over. I didn't want you to ever have to know about this."

"Why were you in bed with another woman, David?" I folded my arms across my chest.

"I'm telling you, babe, it didn't mean anything."

"I don't care if it meant anything or not." A lie, pure and simple. "Why were you sleeping with someone else?"

He looked down at his hands, at the letter, at his feet, still not at me. "She wanted me to leave you for her. I told her no. I guess this was her way of getting back at me."

"Yeah, that's what the letter says. What I want to know is why you were in bed with another woman to begin with." I glared at him with a bravado I didn't feel.

He glanced into my eyes and was caught, unable to look away.

"I never meant to hurt you. She was there, and I was stressed, lonely, I guess. She provided an outlet. I don't know. She didn't mean anything though. I love you and only you."

"Who is she?" My voice was still cold, my fists clenched, fingernails cutting into my palms.

"The one in the pictures? She was—"

"As opposed to who, the one taking them?" I pounced on his choice of words; after years as a lawyer's wife, I'd learned the importance of paying attention to the nuances of someone's speech. "What do you mean, the one in the pictures? There were more?"

"I swear, they didn't mean anything." His voice trembled as he stood and held out a hand in supplication.

"They? How many, David?" I backed away, out of his reach. "How many?"

He stared at me. "Kase, I—"

"How many?"

"Two," he whispered.

"Two? You slept with two women?" I pressed my arms across my body, clutched my elbows to stop the shaking in my hands as a wave of hysteria threatened to destroy my body.

"Yeah. She makes two." He nodded at the letter in his hands.

"You slept with two women who weren't me. When? Why?" I took a deep breath, then another, as my world continued to collapse around me.

"The last couple years or so." Again in a whisper.

"A couple years? This has been going on for a couple years?" Another deep breath. "Were you going to tell me? Were you going to let me know you were this unhappy, that I apparently wasn't meeting your needs?"

He came over and placed his hands on my arms. "I'm sorry, Kase. Please believe me. I don't know what I was thinking. I wasn't thinking. I was stupid, I know that. I love you, and only you. Please forgive me." I tried to pull away again but his grip tightened as he stared into my eyes, pleading for me to believe him. "Please, Kasey."

I looked at him, at the man I loved, standing in front of me, and looked away. My gaze fell on a picture of Aida on the mantel. Next to it was a family portrait, then our engagement photos, our wedding. This was my husband, my partner, the father of our child. It wasn't supposed to be like this.

The tears I hadn't realized were waiting under my eyelids spilled down my cheeks, and my frame was wracked with sobs.

David wrapped his arms around me, his tears mixing with mine.

"How could you?" I whispered, any strength I might have had to fight his touch gone. "How could you do this to me, to Aida, to us?"

"I'm so sorry," he murmured, stroking my hair. "I'm so sorry, Kase. I'm so sorry."

# Chapter 2 – Andrew (Age 34)

Metallica blared from my cell phone, jarring me from my sleep. I didn't mind. I was having the same dream I'd had for the last ten years. My unit patrolled a frozen forest and came under ambush from concealed machine guns. An explosion silenced the onslaught, sprayed us all with hot desert sand. When the smoke cleared, every soldier I'd ever lost stood facing me, staring at me with accusing eyes.

No, I didn't mind waking up at all.

The couch creaked as I rolled over and hit the talk button. "'Lo?"

"I miss you, Andrew. You know how much I hate being alone." My girlfriend, Lauren, or probably my ex-girlfriend after tonight. "And I hate fighting with you. We need to talk."

"It's—" I checked my watch, the numbers barely visible in the light coming in from outside "—three in the morning. Can't this wait until tomorrow?"

"Did you even think about what I said?"

"Babe, it's late. Can't we talk about this tomorrow?"

"We've never gone to bed angry, and I don't want to start. Come back over."

I sighed. "Fine, I'll be there in a little bit."

I hung up the phone, then sat up and stretched. I didn't fit on the small couch very well, not for sleeping, at least. I'd stormed out of our apartment after Lauren started screaming. I didn't plan my exit very well, ending up at my kid brother Jesse's place, crashing in his living room.

I got dressed and scrawled a note telling him where I was going, then slipped out the door, careful not to slam it behind me. His wife didn't like me much, wasn't fond of me crashing there. Normally I would've gone to my dad's place, but he was out of town on business, and his wife wasn't fond of me crashing there either.

The cool Kentucky air swept over me. It felt good to be outside, just me and the night. I glanced up at the full moon high in the sky as I drove. A poem I'd heard as a kid popped into my head: *I see the moon and the moon sees me. God bless the moon and God bless me.*

I laughed under my breath. God and I didn't have much to do with each other anymore.

At the apartment complex, the light in our unit was the only one on in the whole building. Lauren was a night owl, but this late was pushing it even for her. Me, I grabbed sleep when I could. In addition to working four ten-hour patrols a week, I took classes at the community college. Then there was Lauren; pretty high maintenance, she took up a lot of my time.

I hesitated outside our apartment door. When you'd been kicked out of your place, should you knock? Just go right in? Either way, she would find a problem with it.

I knocked.

The door flew open. "Why'd you knock? You live here too." Lauren's eyes glittered brightly as she grabbed my hand, pulled me into the room, and nudged the door closed with her foot. She wrapped her arms around me and kissed me as if I'd been gone for days.

I enjoyed kissing her, of course I did, but I had class in four hours and a long shift after that. I disentangled myself from her and plopped down onto the couch.

"I didn't come back to mess around with you." A yawn escaped from my mouth. "Let's talk so I can go to sleep."

She sat next to me on the couch, legs folded daintily beneath her as if to argue with my sprawl. "I want you to move to Asheville. Why are you fighting me? Don't you love me?"

"Of course I love you." Another yawn. "But moving to a new town is a big deal. I like it here."

"But there's nothing for us here."

"Our families are here."

"Yeah, but I don't like my family. And no offense, Andrew, but your family doesn't really like you."

"My dad likes me." I frowned.

"That's not the point." She sighed. "This head nursing position is a really good thing for me, for us, for our future. I'm taking it whether you move with me or not, but I want you to come with."

That woke me up. "You're accepting the job? You said you'd wait until we agreed on what we were going to do. You said we'd figure it out together."

"Well, when you told me how selfish I was and stormed out, I decided you were right. I am selfish. So I called the hospital and accepted the job. That means either you're coming with me, or you're staying here by yourself."

"You woke me up in the middle of the night to give me an ultimatum?"

"I've been worrying myself sick about this since you stomped out. I've always tried to put you first, Andrew. I didn't object when you wanted us to get this crappy apartment, or when you decided to go back to school, even though you wouldn't have much time for me." Her lower lip quivered, just enough to be noticeable. "Can't you put me first for once, too?"

I stared at her. Nine months ago, when I'd gotten back from my latest deployment, I'd resumed my job at the police station. One weekend we'd had a basketball tournament against teams from the hospital and fire station. Lauren had been there. A mutual friend introduced us, we'd started talking, and we just clicked. A lot of people assumed it was just sex, but there was more to

Lauren than her looks. She was smart, funny, and great with people. We'd been together for six months, and I liked her. A lot.

I wasn't sure if it was love, if she was *The One*, but I would never know if we ended things now. "Fine. I'll go."

She lunged forward and tackled me with her small frame. "I knew you'd say yes!" She covered my face with kisses.

"The things I do for you...." I picked her up and carried her into the bedroom, but I was asleep as soon as my head hit the pillow.

*** 

When I returned to the apartment the following night, tired from a long shift of routine patrols and endless paperwork, the door wouldn't open. "Lauren?" I pounded for her attention. "Everything okay?"

"Just a minute, hon." She grunted as I heard something heavy slide across the floor.

The door opened, barely wide enough for me to squeeze through. Half-filled boxes littered the living room and kitchen, and extended into the bedroom.

"Packing already?"

She didn't look up from the cabinet she was emptying. "Yeah. I guess I forgot to tell you I start in a week."

"A week?" I sat down on the one empty kitchen chair. "A week. How am I supposed to find a job in a week? And what about my classes?"

"I'm sure they'll transfer. And you'll find something. Cops are always in demand."

"You said last night you always put me first."

"And you said last night you'd put me first, for a change."

"What about us? Can't we decide this together?"

"I thought we did."

"A week." I shook my head. "Couldn't you have given me some warning about this?"

She paused and stared at me, a stack of Tupperware bowls in her hands, her expression unreadable. "If you don't want to be with me, just say so."

What a loaded comment. "You know I want to be with you, baby. It's just that I have to transfer units too. And the Guard's not big on that. Tons of paperwork."

"So stay." She slammed the bowls in a box and reached up to empty the next shelf. "It's only a few hours to Asheville. You could come visit me on your days off."

"I don't have any days off, not between work and class. You know that."

"Well, then, I guess either you move, or that's it."

"I can't believe how unconcerned you are about this." I stood and paced the small kitchen.

Lauren walked over to me, leaned up and kissed my nose. "You're so sexy when you're mad."

"Don't try and change the subject."

"Fine." She leaned against the counter, arms folded across her chest. "I care, really I do, and I want to be with you. It's just that this is a really big career move for me. I feel that if I don't take it, I—we—are going to be stuck in this shithole town forever. You understand that, right?"

I nodded. I'd grown up in a shithole town too, and I understood what it was like to be stuck there. I'd gotten out, but most of the people I'd grown up with were still there. Still stuck.

"And who knows, maybe this'll be a great opportunity for you too. Don't you wanna see the world?"

"I've seen the world, and quite frankly, North Carolina doesn't really count when I've been all over Europe and the Middle East."

"We could get a little cabin in the mountains." She came over and wrapped her arms around my neck, pressing her body close to mine. "We'd be all alone, able to do whatever we want, whenever we want. Just the birds and the bees watching."

Smiling in spite of myself, I leaned in and kissed her. Lauren had a way of defusing our fights, of winning me over to her opinion. Her body, warm and soft in my arms, fit comfortably, perfectly against mine.

I kissed her again. "I want to move with you, babe, really I do, but I just don't think I can be ready in a week."

"I can't postpone this. They need someone immediately."

"So what do we do?"

"I'll miss your kisses." She emphasized her words by hungrily pressing her lips to mine.

"You're not helping." Not that I was either. Her sensuality was addictive.

"No, guess not. We can figure it out later."

I couldn't argue with that.

\*\*\*

After my last final of the semester, I headed back to the apartment one last time. All the stuff I'd kept for the two months that I'd spent here while Lauren started her new job in Asheville was securely stowed in the U-Haul trailer downstairs. Time to take the plunge, to follow my girl to a new town.

"Ready to go, Lucky?"

The cat eyed me from her carrier, the only thing left in the place. She wasn't big on change either. Or Lauren. And Lauren wasn't big on the cat. I'd taken Lucky with me the first few times I'd gone to visit her, but she'd put an end to that after the feline threw up in her purse. She maintained the cat had done it on purpose. I secretly agreed. Lucky despised every girl I'd ever brought back to my place.

Lucky bitched the entire drive to Asheville. Towing a trailer through the mountains with a yowling cat wasn't the worst experience of my life, but it was pretty fucking close. I hoped I'd made the right choice, that moving to be with

Lauren was worth it, that Asheville could feel like home, maybe even be the place to start a family. Hope flared up before I could stop it. It had been fifteen years since I'd felt this way, since I'd let myself think about kids. Ever since.... I shook my head, locking down that train of thought, and focused on driving.

I made pretty good time, considering I was towing an eight-foot trailer through the Blue Ridge Mountains, and arrived in Asheville an hour early. I pulled up to Lauren's apartment building and parked beside her car, a little red Ford Fiesta. Leaving Lucky in my truck, I knocked on Lauren's door. She'd given me a key, of course, and this would be my place too now, but it wasn't mine yet. No answer, so I knocked again, pounded maybe. Her car was in the lot. She had to be home.

Nothing. She'd given me the key, so I might as well use it.

"Lauren?" I called as I let myself in. "I know I'm early and you said to call as I was getting close, but my phone was dead. You.... Who the fuck are you?"

A man had come out of the bathroom, wearing just a pair of boxers and a surprised scowl. "Who the fuck are you? How'd you get in here?"

I struggled to keep my fists at my sides and not in his face. "I'm Lauren's boyfriend, that's who the fuck I am. And I used my fucking key, because today's the day I move in."

"Boyfriend? I don't think so. She never said anything about a boyfriend."

Lauren came into the hallway. A man's t-shirt fell halfway down her tanned thighs.

"Right, baby?" he said.

"Well, actually...." She bit her lip.

"What the fuck, Lauren?" I stared at her, pleading for this not to be happening. Not another relationship ending this way. Not after I'd just given up everything in Kentucky for her.

"So this guy is telling the truth?" The other guy stared at her too. "I don't believe this." He stormed past her into the bedroom, then stomped past me with a handful of clothes. "I don't fucking believe this."

I couldn't take my eyes off Lauren.

"You can hate me, if you want," she said to me as she fidgeted with the hem of her shirt. "I wouldn't blame you, but he was just fun in bed. You're the one I want to be with, Andrew."

She took a step towards me, but I shook my head.

"I don't fucking believe this." I turned and walked towards the door.

"If you're leaving, can I at least get my key back? It's a huge hassle having to make copies all the time."

"Fuck you, and fuck your key. After today, I am glad to inconvenience you."

I pulled her door shut behind me and calmly walked down the hall out to the parking lot; calmly pulled out my keys and carved "WHORE" into the driver's side door of Lauren's car; calmly got into my truck and drove off.

I was in a new town, with no place to live and no job for another week. Just me and a cat and a trailer full of all my shit. What the fuck was I supposed to do now?

# Chapter 3 – Kasey (Present)

The days after I found out about David's infidelities passed in a blur. With Aida still in school, I spent my time at home, curled up alone on a couch in the living room, thinking through my options. Trying *not* to think through my options. I needed details, but I was afraid of what I might discover.

First, of course, I wanted to learn the identities of the two women. His secretaries? Neighbors? My heart seized up every time I realized they could be women I saw on a daily basis. Women who were probably laughing at me for being so unaware and naive as to think that, despite my problems with David, he wouldn't find resolution in someone else's bed.

What about the second woman? Maybe they'd only spent one afternoon together, instead of engaging in something that played out again and again. Or should I expect a letter in the mail from her too?

I desperately wanted to confront David, but look what happened before: I'd ended up crying in his arms. No, I didn't want that to happen again. I needed someone to talk to, a confidante to hash out theories and make plans with.

Several times, I tried to dial Ann's number, but each time I stopped and hung up halfway through. I knew exactly what she'd say. "If only you'd kept him satisfied.... Something like this would never happen to Tim and me.... It's only an affair, just the price we pay for having the big house and social status...."

I hadn't realized just how alone I was. I used to have close friends in college and during the first years of my marriage, but contact with them became sporadic after kids and careers took over, and we'd drifted apart. David always made new friends for us, other lawyers and community leaders and their wives. They were always his friends, though, not mine.

There wasn't anyone else, not really. Sure, I went to lunch with women in the neighborhood and chatted with other mothers at Aida's gymnastics classes if I didn't have a book with me, but we always kept our conversations light, superficial. If I brought this up, my situation would become fodder for the bitchy women who delighted in this kind of juicy gossip. David cheating was bad enough; the whole world discussing our private lives for entertainment would be unbearable.

My parents wouldn't be of any help either. I knew exactly how our conversation would go.

"Hi, Dad, I'm not sure how to tell you this—"

"Kasey? It's not Sunday afternoon. Is everything okay?"

"That's what I'm calling about."

"Let me get your mother." He'd pause, his hand over the mouthpiece. "Helen? Kasey's on the phone.... Yes, I know we talk on Sundays.... I don't know what's wrong."

"Hello, dear." My mom would be on another extension. "You know it's not Sunday, right?"

"Yeah, Mom, but I don't think this can wait until our usual chat." Deep breath. "David... David's been having an affair."

"A what?"

"An affair, Dad. He was with another woman."

"Nonsense, dear. Did you hear what she said, Tony? David's too nice a boy, Kasey."

"No, Mom. Really."

"No, Kasey, you must be mistaken. Things like that don't happen to people like us."

"Mom, listen to me—"

"Kasey, don't upset your mother. We'll talk to you on Sunday."

Affairs, like alcoholism and out-of-wedlock children, remained taboo in my family. Anyone so uncouth as to fall short of the family's values should at least have the decency not to exacerbate the situation by speaking of it.

My lack of close confidantes hadn't bothered me. Not really. At least not until now, when I needed someone but there was no one to turn to. I'd always talked to David when I had a problem, or fixed it myself, or ignored it until it went away. But this? No. *He* was the problem.

David said he loved me, and he probably did. Deep down, I felt the truth behind his words. But how could he have hurt me so deeply? He understood the importance I placed on our family, that I valued the home we shared more than anything else. If he'd lied to me about this for so long, was our whole relationship a lie as well? Was it possible, or worth it, to rebuild a lie?

I needed answers, concrete actions. I had to keep my mind off the pictures, off David's pale thighs brushing against that woman's tan ones, so I made lists that I later tore up so he wouldn't see them: pros and cons of staying or of leaving; possible outcomes of counseling, divorce, or killing him and hiding his body in a dumpster behind his office.

\*\*\*

As I lay alone in bed a couple nights after the confrontation, thinking through those lists, my mind wouldn't quiet enough to sleep. After several hours I gave up and headed downstairs to the kitchen.

I took a carton of orange juice out of the fridge and reached for a glass. My husband's cell phone lay charging on the counter. I paused, ears alert. Snores drifted in from the living room; David slept on the couch, a wise move on his part. In the distance a car drove through the late spring night, and closer, a neighbor's dog barked. All clear.

I grabbed his phone, but hesitated. Lies and secrets had brought us to this point; would I be any better if I went through his phone without his knowledge? But of course I was better than him. How could this compare to what he'd done?

I flipped open the phone and scanned through his list of contacts. After the first hundred or so, the search seemed futile. If her name were listed, she wouldn't be recognizable; David wouldn't be so stupid as to label her "Girlfriend" or "Mistress" or whatever some such nonsense. His text messages all seemed to be from business contacts or his brother, nothing asking him to meet up somewhere for a quickie or demanding he leave his wife. His pictures were equally innocuous.

I sighed and put the phone back on the counter, drank a glass of juice, and made my way through the dark to the stairs in the foyer. David's briefcase sat on the floor, the outline of his laptop glinting in the street light coming through the glass at the top of the door. I snuck a glance into the living room; he sprawled comatose on the couch. Bag in hand, I darted upstairs to the master bathroom and locked the door behind me.

His email password was the same as always, ADIAYESAK123, but his personal and work accounts were clean. Either he'd gone to great lengths to erase everything, or he had a secret account.

A creak outside the door brought my attention back to my surroundings. I shoved the computer into the linen closet and pressed my ear to the door. Nothing. I flushed the toilet, giving myself an alibi, then washed my hands. Dark blue eyes stared back at me from the mirror, red and ringed by swollen dark circles. I searched them for clues as to what I should do next, but mirror-Kasey appeared just as confused and troubled as the real life version.

I opened the door a crack. Nothing out of place, so I grabbed David's laptop and returned it to his briefcase.

I lay in bed, staring at the ceiling, running through possibilities in my head, for at least another hour before falling asleep.

\*\*\*

I was listening to music while on hold the next morning, three days after I received the letter, when David came into the kitchen, startling me. I slammed down the phone.

"Shouldn't you be at work?" I positioned myself with the island of cabinets between us. "Or at a hotel, or that woman's house, or wherever you were meeting her?"

"Kase, don't be like this." Although he was his usual put-together self, the dark circles around his eyes revealed that the last few days had worn on him as well. We hadn't exchanged more than a few words since the afternoon I'd discovered his betrayal.

"What did you expect, David?" I drummed my fingers against my thigh, out of my husband's sight. This was my time to plan, and his unexpected appearance didn't help. "How am I supposed to react? Should I tell you what you did was okay?"

"I think we need to talk." He moved around the cabinets towards me but stopped as I shook my head at him. "Yeah, we need to talk about this."

"Fine. Talk."

"I'm sorry for what I did. I'm sorry you found out. What can I do to make it up to you?"

"I don't think you can do anything." I took a deep breath and made a decision. "I'm leaving. Aida and I can't stay here with you. We were a team, a family, and you destroyed that."

His eyes widened. "You can't leave. I need you here, and you need me. We love each other. We can work through this."

"No, I don't think we can." I blinked back tears, not completely sure of my decision. "We're going to stay with my parents until I can get on my feet. I'm calling divorce lawyers. I can't stay here with you, David, not in this house with the memories of what we had together. I can't. Not after this." I swallowed hard, my cheeks wet.

"Kasey." He walked over to me and took me in his arms.

I stiffened and tried to pull away, but he held me tightly, taking my chin in his hand and making me look up into his brown eyes.

"Kasey. I love you. You and only you. We can work this out. Please?"

I shook my head, unable to speak, crying openly now. "I don't know, David."

"Please?" His hand brushed my teary cheeks. "Please, Kase."

"I don't want to give up on everything we had," I admitted, ending my resistance and sagging into his embrace. "But how can I trust you?"

"I'd do anything for you. Just tell me what you want."

"I want to move." This came to me suddenly. It wasn't on my lists, but it made sense.

"What?" Now it was his turn to pull away. He frowned. "Move? Where? Why?"

"I want a fresh start, somewhere far away from that woman. Far away from all your women. If we're going to get through this, we need new memories, together, somewhere else."

He studied my face. "Okay."

***

That night, after Aida was in bed, David came into the living room where I was balled up on the couch, trying to read a book to escape my thoughts.

"Will Asheville do?" he asked.

I put my book down and looked up. "What?"

"You said you wanted to move. I called around this afternoon, and an old friend from law school offered me a spot at his firm in Asheville, contingent upon me passing the North Carolina bar, of course. It's about a six-hour drive, far enough to get away but close enough so we can still see family when we want. Will that work?"

"When?"

"I'll need to wrap up my cases here, as well as prepare for the bar. We'll have to get the house on the market and find somewhere down there. It's gonna be a lot of work. Are you sure this is what you want?" He downed the contents of his glass and moved to the liquor cabinet in the corner.

"You're willing to do all that just to fix our marriage?"

He poured himself a shot, threw it back, and then poured another. Without turning to look at me, he replied, "I told you, I'd do anything for you."

\*\*\*

The next step was to explain to Aida we'd be moving, and convince her to buy into the idea. She'd lived here in Richmond her whole life. Her aunts and uncles, cousins and grandparents all lived here. I'd moved away from my relatives when I was her age, and never really felt like I belonged in my adopted city. Could I do the same to my own daughter? More importantly, would she forgive me?

Our lives had carefully set routines. It hadn't started out as anything intentional, but over the years, as David's career required more of his time, those patterns and traditions had grown in importance. No matter what happened between me and David, no matter where we lived, those routines would stay the same.

On that Saturday, as on every other Saturday, I planned on taking Aida to the Richmond farmers' market. She stood out front, chatting with the flowers while waiting for her father and me to join her. Her nose would be covered with pollen, something that set David to sneezing when she invariably gave him butterfly kisses, but he never seemed to mind.

Inside the house I checked my watch; I'd already been waiting ten minutes. I went to the foot of the stairs and called up, "David! You coming?"

No answer. He knew our routine.

I headed upstairs, wondering what his attitude would be. Penitent husband? Long-suffering martyr? Angry victim? Maybe I'd luck out and get all three.

"David?" Water ran in the master bath, so I knocked on the door. "Aida and I are having a girls' day out. We'll see you later."

No reply, but I had a cell phone if he needed us.

Once outside, I looked around but couldn't find my daughter. "Aida?"

No reply from her either. It wasn't like her to wander off. Worry choked my mind, despite the knowledge that we lived in a safe neighborhood, with neighbors always watching from behind nearly-closed blinds. Something might happen at any time, and eyewitness accounts always bumped someone pretty far up the queen-of-the-neighborhood list.

"Aida?" My voice trembled as I checked my car in the driveway, a blue BMW 528 David bought me for a birthday present last summer as yet another unnecessarily extravagant token of his love.

She wasn't hiding in there. Perhaps she'd gone back inside. As I fished my house keys out of my purse, the sound of giggles drifted out from the front flowerbed. Huge hydrangea bushes lined the front of our house, the pale blue blossoms perfuming our yard. Tulips in vivid reds and pinks overflowed in front of them, adding their fragrance.

And their laughter. I smiled as my heart rate dropped.

"Looks like my hydrangeas ate a little girl," I said in a loud voice. "I wonder if I can buy another one at the farmers' market?"

"Here I am, Mommy!" Aida popped up between the house and the bushes, petals scattered in her long blonde hair and on the straps of her sleeveless sundress.

I pretended not to notice her. "My flowers *talk*, too?"

She popped back down, then crawled out onto the lawn. "I was investigating."

"Investigating what?"

"Hayleigh said pirates always bury their treasure, so I was investigating to see if I could find any back there."

Hayleigh was Aida's best friend. Their imaginations fed off each other, which was something I encouraged. Hayleigh's mom was more cautious, especially when it involved potentially ruining an outfit, so our house usually became the site of exploration and experimentation.

"Did you find any?"

"I think I need a shovel."

"We'll find you one later. I need to dig around in the garden anyways, and I'd love your company." I pulled her to her feet and squeezed her into a hug.

"Mom-mee," she squealed, pulling away.

I laughed. "Ready to go?"

"What about Daddy?"

"Today it's just you and me, sweetie." I headed towards my car, pulling her by the hand.

"But Daddy always comes with us."

"I know, but he's not coming today."

"Why not?"

"He has work stuff to do."

"Oh."

I glanced at Aida in the rearview mirror. Her lower lip stuck out slightly, her eyebrows furrowed. Staying together for the sake of the children might be the wrong thing to do, but my daughter loved her father every ounce as much as she loved me. I owed it to her to at least try to fix things.

After we'd visited the farmers' market, I suggested we grab lunch. David had texted to tell us he was heading to his office to catch up on some briefs, which was just fine with me; I was determined to enjoy my time with Aida.

We ordered sandwiches from a downtown café and sat at an outdoor table to eat. The sunshine warmed my skin, promising summer and hope and leaving me in a good mood for the first time all week. As I sat watching my daughter try to hold conversations with hungry birds awaiting sandwich crumbs, I almost forgot about what David had done. Almost.

I set my sandwich down on my plate. "Aida, Daddy and I have decided we're going to move to a new town. What do you think about that?"

She stared at me with wide blue eyes; my eyes, everyone always said. Her hair was blonde like her father's, and her features resembled his more than mine, but she had my slender build. A good mix of both her parents. "I won't see Hayleigh anymore, will I?"

Guilt bubbled up inside me. "You can see her when we come back to visit your grandparents."

"We won't have to have dinner with Grammy and Pop-Pop every week? And no more church with them?" She eyed me, as if this would be the issue that decided it for her.

I tried to hide my smile. I disliked the weekly church service and dinner with David's parents as much as she did. "Nope, they'll stay here."

She popped a chip in her mouth, the wheels turning in her head. So much like her father. "It's a deal."

I heaved a sigh of relief and hoped our parents would take the news as well as Aida.

*** 

Sunday morning, David was impatient to get to the service. Normally, we both dragged our feet. Neither of us was religious or felt at home at our church, but his parents insisted we attend with them, and I'd learned over the years to pick my battles. The service wasn't bad, really, as long as I tuned out the bits about the decline of civilization due to the current progressive social agenda. I often used the time to make grocery lists or to think through a schedule for the upcoming week.

The bad part came after the service, followed by the worst part. David's mother insisted we stand around and chat with the other church members, and we couldn't avoid this. Most of their conversations were thinly-veiled insults, bragging, and gossip. Today was even harder to endure, knowing we'd soon be free. I chided myself for thinking that way, but I couldn't help it. The move had taken hold, a magic solution for my marriage.

After we'd reached our social interaction quota, we caravanned to David's parents' house, where his mother, sister, and sister-in-law prepared a large dinner. Every week I offered to help, but every week they rebuffed me, claiming I didn't know the family recipes, as they reminded me often, "on account of you being a Yankee 'n all."

David's father was also a lawyer, as *his* father had been, and *his* father before him. His mother had stayed home to raise her three perfect children, support her husband, and do her civic duty by hosting luncheons for her chapter of the Daughters of the Confederacy. They'd never considered me, a Northerner by birth whose family had only been in the country since the Civil War, good enough for their son. They'd never embraced me as a member of the family, no matter how hard I tried to please them.

With the impending move fast approaching, I shouldn't have to put up with this. "I lived in New York for five years," I wanted to declare while we ate. "I've been in Virginia for twenty-six, so I'm not a Yankee anymore. I've been married to your son for nine years, and Carol's been married to Jake for three years, yet she knows all the recipes. Why is she family and I'm not?"

It was pointless to argue with them. David wouldn't come to my rescue; he never did. I still hadn't figured out if he was a mama's boy or just terrified of her. If the latter, I didn't blame him; she intimidated me too. Her cheerful cattiness, hitting when I least expected, kept me off guard, unable to think of retorts.

"Aida, dear, eat your asparagus," David's mother said as we sat at the dining room table.

"I don't like asparagus, Grammy."

"Nonsense. Everyone likes asparagus. Your cousins are eating theirs, but they probably eat well at home too."

Aida glared at her cousins, who weren't eating their asparagus; they were throwing it on the floor for the dog. "Mommy, do I have to eat my asparagus?"

"Not if you don't like it, sweetie."

"Nonsense, Kasey. Of course she should eat it. Everyone in this family eats asparagus. My goodness, what do you feed the poor child?"

I glanced at David, but he was staring intently at his plate as he chewed. I kicked his shin under the table.

He coughed, choking on the bite in his mouth, but still said nothing.

"We're moving to Asheville," I announced, changing the subject.

My in-laws' mouths dropped open.

"David, you didn't tell them?" I asked sweetly. Since he'd thrown me to the wolves, I'd do the same to him.

"David, is this true?" asked his father. He didn't talk to me, and barely even acknowledged me if David was present. "How could you do this to your mother, to your family, without discussing it with us first?" He gestured at his wife, who was hamming-up her role of victim by dabbing at her eyes with her napkin.

"Well," David said, fidgeting with his fork, "Kasey decided we needed a change."

I kicked him under the table again. "And please, dear, tell them *why* we need a change."

He glared at me, the same look Aida had given her cousins. "Well, I've been working a lot of overtime at the office and haven't been spending as much time with Kasey and Aida as I should be. A friend in Asheville offered me a job at his firm. It'll be less stressful. And haven't you always said that family comes first?"

"I'm proud of you, son." David's father raised his glass in salute. "To David, who always knows his priorities."

I smirked as we raised our glasses. They'd spin this so I was to blame, but I couldn't wait to see their reaction when they discovered the truth behind our move. Family first, indeed.

\*\*\*

My glee was short-lived as word of our upcoming move, and its true reason, spread like wildfire. David was a well-known and respected member of the community and, by virtue of being his wife, I was too. Or, at least, I had been. Everywhere I went, patronizing smirks, pitying stares, and derisive laughs greeted me.

While choosing peaches at the grocery store one day, a middle-aged neighbor who, like me, stayed home while her husband was at the office, pushed her shopping cart past me.

She laid a hand on my arm. "I'm so sorry about you and your husband." She said it loud enough for the entire produce section to hear, possibly the whole store.

I stiffened. My circle devoured gossip, but this was fast, even for them. Maybe the woman who'd sent the pictures had spread word about the affair too? "Yeah, it was quite a shock."

A woman across the aisle froze, obviously listening to our conversation. Couldn't they mind their own damn business?

"Well, for him to carry on like that for so long, and with two different women.... Could it really have been that great a shock?"

"What are you saying? I let him cheat on me?" My hand tightened on the peach I held, leaving slight indentations in the fruit.

"That's not what I said at all, dear." The woman patted my arm. "Such a pity, bless your heart."

As she moved away, and the woman across the aisle finally selected the perfect bag of carrots, I stared at the fruit in my hand, unable to move. Was my neighbor right? Should I have expected him to cheat? Was David's infidelity my fault? What had those women offered him that I didn't, that I couldn't?

\*\*\*

As I went through the checklist from the realtor and prepped the house for the market, I had plenty of time to contemplate those questions. They ate me up. Why had David cheated, and with whom?

I asked him one evening after Aida was in bed. "Who were they?"

He sighed, as if everything would go away if I'd just leave it alone. "It doesn't matter. I realized you're the one I love, the one I want, and I'm here with you."

"Was it the sex? Were you bored with me? Did you want someone with a better body than mine?"

"You're beautiful and sexy, Kase. It wasn't the sex."

"So you wanted more of a relationship?"

"Dammit, Kasey. It happened. It was a mistake, but it's over. Let it go so we can move past this."

David left the room, a tumbler in hand as he went to his office in the basement, presumably to sulk for the night. I brought the subject up twice more, but both times it ended with him taking off for an hour or two, returning inebriated but in a better mood.

I didn't know how to react. What did it say about our marriage, and our likelihood of fixing it, if I looked forward to his petulant silence?

\*\*\*

Two weeks after we made the decision to move to Asheville, I attended a PTA committee meeting at Aida's school, the last one of the year, meaning the last for me at that school. General meetings were held at night, when working parents could attend. The committees, however — the important ones, at least — were carefully crafted to contain stay-at-home mothers like myself, all of similar social and economic backgrounds. While we waited for the chairwoman to arrive, the dozen or so of us present made small talk, and the conversation quickly turned to my misfortunes.

"It's too bad you're moving," Ann said from her spot across the circle from me.

"We think it's for the best." I forced a smile and hoped that was enough. Maybe she would change the subject.

"I can't imagine how I'd react if Tim ever did something like that," Ann continued. "To have to go through that? Well, bless your heart. And then for everyone to know? Why, you must be absolutely mortified."

My hands tightened on the notebook in my lap as I fought to keep a smile plastered on my face. "It's difficult, yes. When I found out, I wanted to—"

"Angela Robinson's husband cheated on her," interrupted another woman who lived in the neighborhood. "Did y'all hear? He was sleeping with his secretary, and when she found out she kicked him out. Turns out she forgot they'd signed a pre-nup, and she ended up losing the house and having to move in with her parents. Poor woman, bless her heart."

The others murmured their agreement.

"Cindy Godwell had the same problem," said a woman I was acquainted with only from the meetings. "Except when she found out, she went out and slept with the pool boy. Turns out she'd hidden an infidelity clause in her pre-nup so she was able to kick Eli out. She was smart enough to make sure she never got caught with the kid either."

"I think she paid the kid off," said Ann.

"Have you thought about cheating to get back at David?" someone asked, smiling wickedly. "Maybe with the pool boy?"

It took all my concentration to keep smiling, to not scream at these women to shut up and mind their own business. "We're trying to work things out, hence the move."

The women nodded. "Well, we'll keep you in our prayers," said Evangeline. "And be thankful our own husbands would never do the same to us."

Before I could respond, before I could do something completely out of character like slap Evangeline across the face for her rude comment, the chairwoman arrived and the conversation shifted from me to PTA-related business.

I couldn't focus on the meeting as I sat in my chair, fuming. This was the last meeting. I could jump up and scream at them to shut up, tell them if it could happen to me it could happen to them, but I sat silently, decorum and precedence holding my tongue. If I said anything, showed any annoyance, it would only cement me as the center of conversation this summer. One month and we would be in Asheville, away from all this. I could last a month.

As we walked down the hall after the meeting, I pulled Ann aside. "That was brutal. Want to grab lunch?" Although we frequently met during the week to chat over food, I'd been too busy with the house to spend much time with her.

"I'm pretty busy today." She looked at her shoes, at the posters on the walls. Not at me. "I have a bunch of errands to run, and I'm watching my nephew this afternoon. Another day?"

"Sure. I'm just feeling a little lost, what with David being an ass and the stress of the move, and it'd be nice to have someone to talk to, you know?"

"Sure." Her smile didn't quite meet her eyes. "I'll see you around then, okay?"

And so it went with most of my so-called friends: neighbors, former coworkers, and other women in my social circle. I wasn't an open person, but when the move or the affairs came up in conversation they changed the subject to something safe and mundane, or they told me horror stories about people they knew who'd either cheated on their spouses or been cheated on. Their smugness, their pity, and their fervent, naive belief that their own husbands would never stray made it all worse.

I began a countdown to the day of the move. "When we're in Asheville," I told myself, "everything will be better. When we're in Asheville, David and I will fix things." Maybe, just maybe, if I told myself that enough, I'd actually start to believe it.

\*\*\*

As the day of the move approached, David's outbursts increased in intensity as well as frequency. I finally confronted him one night in his office. He spent a lot of time holed-up down there, studying hard to pass the North Carolina bar. If he didn't pass this summer he'd have to wait until the following February to take it again, but more than anything his chief motivator was pride.

I leaned against the door frame, arms folded against my chest, watching him pore over an old textbook from law school. David always had to be the best at whatever he did, always had to have the best of everything. It hadn't been as noticeable when we first dated, or even early on in our marriage, but his vanity increased right alongside his status in the community.

He traded in his Cavalier for an Escalade. I wasn't happy about that; the vehicle was too big for two adults and a small child, a gas guzzler to the point he could barely afford to drive out of town. More than that, though, I worried about safety, about him rolling the damn thing. He claimed the Escalade demanded admiration and refused to budge.

The next thing to go was my job. I was working as a copy editor for *Women of the South,* a regional magazine. It wasn't glamorous by any stretch, but I liked my coworkers and the material we printed. I even wrote the occasional article, a nice way to put my journalism degree to use. David thought I should stay home with Aida instead. Sometimes I missed working, even though spending my days with my daughter more than made up for it.

Finally he upgraded our home. I loved our first place, an older two bedroom house with a huge yard, old oak trees I envisioned Aida climbing someday, a sunny spot for a garden, and beautiful rose bushes I spent hours tending. But when David realized he could realistically become a partner in his firm, he decided we needed a house that matched his ambitions, so we moved into a cookie-cutter house in a gated community. I tried my best to make the house ours, but it always seemed so impersonal, so generic.

It seemed only logical that I'd be next. Maybe the woman at the grocery store was right; maybe I should've expected affairs.

"I'm busy, Kase." David took a gulp from the glass in front of him but didn't look up from his desk.

I didn't realize he'd seen me standing there. "If we're going to make this work, we need to talk."

"Fuck, Kase, I said I was busy."

"I know, but you've been studying every night. We never spend time together anymore. Maybe if we went out for dinner we could figure this all out. I could find a sitter for Aida and we could —"

He spun around in his chair, bloodshot eyes flashing. "Fine. You want to talk? Talk."

I swallowed hard. I'd thought about this conversation for a while, planned out every word, but with him glaring at me with such intensity, it all vanished. "I guess I just want to know why you cheated. What did I do wrong, and how can I trust you're not going to do it again?"

He took a deep breath before answering. "I told you, I was stressed. And you never cared how I felt. You were too busy with all those fucking committees and keeping up with the neighbors."

"I did that because it's what you wanted! It was your idea to move to this house. It was your idea I quit my job to stay home. This was your dream, so I made it mine too. That's what happens when you love someone, when you're part of a team."

"So this is all my fault?" He clenched his jaw.

"This is the life you wanted, David. You just forgot to tell me it included girlfriends on the side." I wrapped my arms more tightly around myself. "I love you, and I want you to be happy, but I want you to be happy with me."

"You were happy being poor? I worked my fucking ass off to get to this point. Look what we have to show for it—a huge beautiful house, a great kid going to the best school in town. We're at the top of the social ladder. We've put so much work into this life. I'll do whatever you want, but I hate to throw it all away."

"I don't consider giving everything up to save our marriage 'throwing it away,' David."

"Do you realize what I'm willing to give up for you? I've lived in Richmond my whole life. All my family and friends are here. Everything I know is here, in this town. I'm leaving all this because you asked me too. I'm sorry if I can't be as happy as you are about this every single fucking minute."

I stared at him, my mouth agape. "You slept with other women, yet I'm the bad one? I can't believe you."

"This is bullshit and you know it, Kasey." He stood up, slamming shut the book he'd been reading. "I love you and Aida. I want to be with you. I said I was sorry, but I'm not going to put up with these constant recriminations."

"All I want is a promise that you won't do it again." As he brushed past me, I reached out to take his hand. "Please, David, I've worked so hard to give you the perfect family, the perfect home. I just want a promise in return."

"I told you, I love you and I'm sorry. Now fucking drop it already." He pulled his hand from mine and stomped upstairs, leaving me in the doorway wondering if our marriage was salvageable, or even *worth* salvaging.

\*\*\*

Several nights later, I broached the subject with him again. Rather than confront him in his office, I waited until he prepared for bed. He'd moved from the couch to the guest room back to our room, but it wasn't the same. In opposite sides of our king-sized bed, we may as well have been on separate continents.

"David?" I hesitated in the bathroom doorway. "About the other night."

I studied his reflection in the mirror as he brushed his teeth at the sink. He was still the handsome man I'd married, at least on the outside, but I wasn't sure who he was on the inside, not anymore. His brown eyes stared back at me, full of questions but no animosity.

"I don't want to fight with you, but I meant what I said the other night. I quit my job when you asked me to. I moved to this new house when you asked me to. I've gone to every social event, joined all the right groups, everything you wanted me to do. I've tried so hard to make this the best home possible for you, and for Aida too. What did I do wrong?"

He rinsed out his mouth and turned to face me. "Kasey, it wasn't anything you did or didn't do."

"Then what was it?"

"I ask myself that all the time." He pulled me close and wrapped his arms around me. I leaned my head against his cheek, smelling the mint of the toothpaste and behind that, faintly, the aftershave he'd used that morning.

"What's your answer?"

"Do you remember how we first met?"

I smiled, thinking back on our college days. "Of course. I was working at the school library, and you kept bugging me until I agreed to go out with you."

"You were always so afraid you would be fired if you spent your entire shift talking to me. You were so interesting, so unlike anyone I'd ever met, that I couldn't help it."

"I couldn't believe some of the stuff you pulled in there. Remember the time you had pizzas delivered for your study group? I was so worried you'd be banned from the library, and then you'd flunk out of school and I'd never see you again."

He chuckled. "Remember our first date?"

"The waiter dropped a plate of lasagna in my lap. I was mortified, and then you stood up and argued with the manager until he agreed to pay to have my dress dry-cleaned. Everyone was staring at us, cheering you on while I just wanted to crawl under the table and die."

"I didn't realize until later how embarrassed you were. I thought you'd never talk to me again."

"But the next day you were back in the library, and you told me we were going out for a do-over date, sans messy Italian food. How could I say no to that kind of confidence?"

"I guess I just know what I want."

I looked up at my husband. "Am I still what you want?"

He kissed me softly. "I love you. I love Aida. I always will. I was stupid to do anything to jeopardize our marriage. You know I'd do anything for you two."

"Does that mean you're okay with moving?"

"This is hard for me."

"I know. I understand, but I need proof you're serious about fixing us."

He sighed. "I need you to trust me. Trust that I love you, that I realize I screwed up, and that we can fix this."

I pulled back and looked him straight in the eyes. "Does that mean this won't happen again?"

"Kasey, I'm going to do everything I can to make you regain your faith in me. I just need you to trust me."

# Chapter 4 – Andrew (Age 33)

Machine gun fire popped in the background. I paid little attention until it sounded like rubber bands snapping next to my head. Everyone in this damn city, in this damn country, had a gun, and they wanted us to know. Someone, somewhere, was surely taking note of it all, but an NCO like me just focused on those snapping rubber bands.

I walked along the corridor of the bombed-out factory we were using as a camp for a few days, kicking spent brass out of my way. I'd been deploying for years, and I was used to the sound of gunfire and angry civilians and screaming dead. To the smells of spent ammunition and blood and shit. To the sight of mutilated bodies and burnt shells of vehicles. That didn't mean I was happy with it or liked it, but it didn't matter, not anymore, because next week we'd be going home.

Only some of us, though. Some of us were already home, shipped back in flag-draped wooden boxes. They said I was one of the lucky ones, going back to my family alive, but sometimes I envied those guys. You couldn't hear someone screaming when you were dead, couldn't see the blood or the pain in their eyes.

Guys like Taylor Nelson, nineteen. Car bomb went off while we were on patrol, and he was closest. Part of a door sliced him nearly in half. I was the first one there and I held him in my arms as he died, poor son of a bitch trying valiantly to hold his own guts in, both of us trying to be brave. We used to give him grief because he was just some fresh kid who'd never even kissed a girl. And thanks to a fucking IED he never would.

I tried not to think about my dead boys, tried not to think about life back home, about lost friends and lost girls. I tried not to think at all while in country. If you weren't careful, your mind led you astray real quick. Better to focus on my surroundings, on my boys.

My unit had some downtime as we waited for our next patrol of the neighborhoods. It wasn't much when you compared it to our free time inside the wire, but outside most of the boys took advantage of the break to get some much-needed rest. Not all of them, of course, not when they were young and bored in the middle of a foreign desert.

As I walked past one of the rooms, filled with army cots and discarded desks, a soldier called out to me. "Hey, Sarge!"

I paused in the doorway. Several soldiers were gathered around a cot heaped with clothes. "What's up, Reyes?"

He grinned at me, a grin that boldly proclaimed he was up to no good and proud of it. "This is the best one yet!"

I walked over to the cot and looked down. What I'd mistaken for clothes was a sleeping soldier—Butch, a short skinny guy who was anything but. "Is that...? Where the fuck did you find yourself Saran wrap in the middle of a desert?"

"My girl sent it to me," Reyes giggled. "Isn't this awesome?"

They'd securely attached Butch to his cot with plastic wrap. Judging by its opaqueness, there had to be at least a dozen layers.

"Watch this." Reyes grabbed a bottle of water and poured it over Butch's face.

Butch jerked his body up but the plastic held. I had to admit, they'd done a great job. Butch's sputters quickly changed to a profanity-laced tirade against his fellow soldiers, their mothers, and the US military in general. I shook my head, grinning, and left the room and continued down the corridor.

I stopped at a window at the end of the hallway and lit a cigarette. A bad habit, but I only smoked over here. Everyone did. Something to help us unwind, to relax and forget about everything. Being a soldier you had to be able to turn yourself off, put your boys and your mission first, and I'd gotten good at that.

My boys were everything when I was over here. They relied on me to keep them alive. Their training, their survival, their deaths—if something went wrong it was because I fucked up. There was no one to blame but me—not God, not Fate, not their own damned stupidity. If they did something stupid, it was because I let them think it would be okay. They suffered for my mistakes, for my lack of judgment.

That was why I was the one talking to the mamas when we got home, like after our last deployment.

*\*\**

We'd flown into Fort Campbell and walked onto the parade grounds. As soon as the first guy stepped out, the place exploded with shouts and tears. All the soldiers found their families, hugged their girls and kids and parents, but not all the families found their soldiers.

I walked over to a woman at the crowd's edge. She was crying quietly, her hubby's arms around her. It took a lot of courage, a lot of strength, to come when the troops were getting in and your son wasn't one of them, when you'd already buried him but still wanted to support his unit.

"I'm Sgt. Adams," I told them.

"Pam Nelson," she replied, her voice strong despite the tears flowing down her cheeks.

"Kent Nelson." Her hubby held out his hand.

Taylor Nelson's parents.

"Taylor was in my unit," I told them. "He was a great kid. He was quiet but every time he said something we all listened. Real friendly." I rambled on some more about him, I think. I wasn't sure what else to say but I knew I needed to say something.

"Were you with him, when...?" His mama couldn't finish.

"Yes, ma'am, I was right next to him, holding him for his last moments. He was real brave. I'm sorry I wasn't able to do more than that for him." My voice shook, and I found myself blinking rapidly.

She threw her arms around me, a tiny little woman about half my size. Her voice was muffled against my chest. "Thank you, Sergeant. It means so much that you were there for Taylor when he...."

"I'm sorry I couldn't do more for him," I said again as I awkwardly patted her on the back, and then her hubby took her in his arms and they stood there and wept together, for the sons lost and the sons who made it back, and I moved on to the next grieving set of parents.

Even though I'd done that my last few deployments, I never knew how they'd react to my approach. Sometimes they'd thank me for talking to them, thank me for doing my best, even though I hadn't, of course; if their son didn't make it back alive with us, I'd failed. I never understood what they were thanking me for, not really. Maybe they didn't see it as my fault for getting their kid killed; maybe they thought anything I'd done was enough. Maybe they were just relieved their boy hadn't died alone.

Sometimes they'd just stare all empty-eyed at me, accusing, silent. All I could do then was offer apologies and condolences that weren't enough, because I'd failed them, failed their son. I honestly didn't know which reaction was worse—they both made me feel like shit—but how I felt didn't matter. I'd failed, and now I was the one telling a mama her son wasn't coming back, would never give her grandbabies. Even worse, the grandbabies wouldn't ever see their daddy again.

***

I tried to push those thoughts out of my head, to focus on the here and now. I looked at my watch; time to gear up for patrol. I stubbed out my cigarette and headed back to my cot.

Old Dog was lying on his cot next to mine, reading a letter from home. Most of our family kept up a steady stream of letters, cookies, silly string and Saran wrap, whatever we needed over here. Most of them.

"Anything good, Old Dog?"

"Suits are a bitch, man. There was some hiccup in the system and my old lady didn't get one of my paychecks deposited on time so she missed a couple bills and now the bastards are harassing her about it. But on the upside, Shanna lost another tooth and Jimmy is going on his first official date."

He grinned at me but I could sense his frustration.

I didn't have Old Dog's family problems. I'd gotten a letter shortly after we got over here, but didn't save it; no need, because it always read the same, every deployment. I'd get back to civilian life, find a good one that maybe someday could settle down with me and raise a family, and then I'd be shipped out again. I'd get over here, and shortly after get a letter saying she "has needs" and I wasn't meeting them. *It's been nice but fuck you I'm gonna find someone else.*

What about my needs? It was enough to make anyone swear off relationships altogether.

***

We headed out on patrol, trading the relative safety of our temporary accommodations for the streets of a once upscale neighborhood. We'd been tipped off that one of the houses had a cache of weapons and possibly served as a meeting place for a local group of insurgents. It was a routine patrol, but we never knew what we would find.

Our humvees rattled down the wide pockmarked avenues as the drivers wove their way around civilians and animals and other vehicles. It was chaos compared to back home, but there was a sense of planned beauty in it if you sat back and observed. Not that we had time for that, of course; one wrong step, one moment of letting our guard down, and that chaos could erupt into some nasty violence.

"You ever been shot, Adams?" Butch in the back was full of questions for me. He acted as if simultaneously in awe of and scared shitless of me.

"Yeah."

"Did it hurt?"

"A bullet ripped through my leg. What do you think?"

"Did you get a cool scar?"

"What kind of stupid dumbass are you?" asked Scotch. "Of course he got a cool scar."

Butch ignored him. "How'd you get it?"

"I took a bullet on patrol about ten years ago. Took a year of physical therapy until I could walk without limping anymore." A gulp of water from my canteen tried to wash away the image seared into my mind of a charred boot. "My other scars ain't as bad though, just little ones all over, from shrapnel mostly. I been shot a few other times too but mostly just grazed, thank God. And some concussions from being knocked out by nearby explosions, but I made it out of those okay." Even if not everyone else did.

"You know what Adams did, when he was over here before?" Old Dog called down from the turret above.

"Pay attention up there. Your stories don't mean anything if we end up dead from you not doing your job."

"We were under pretty heavy fire and one of our boys went down," said Old Dog, ignoring my command. "Without thinking, Adams ran over to him, picked him up, and brought him back to safety behind a humvee. None of us knew how he made it through that alive, but he did. He always does."

"That's awesome, man." Butch punched me on the shoulder. "Fucking awesome."

Yeah. Me, the one responsible for all these guys dying over here, and I was the one who made it out with just some scars.

"Chicks dig scars," said Reyes. "Butch, you need to get your ass shot up so all the girls will want you when you get home, instead of just your mom."

"What's wrong with Butch's mom?" Scotch asked. "I want Butch's mom."

"Shut the fuck up about my mom."

I didn't mind the scars. I'd gotten off lucky, and they reminded me daily of those I'd lost, that I'd failed those boys as a leader, as a brother in battle. Even one soldier not coming home alive meant that I'd failed, somewhere, somehow.

\*\*\*

We arrived at the house, a three-story structure riddled with bullet holes and surrounded by a courtyard full of weeds.

"Open up!" Old Dog shouted through the locked door. "U.S. Army! Open the door!"

Of course no one opened the door for us, a dozen heavily armed men in full body armor, so we kicked it down and carefully made our way inside, spreading out to check all the rooms. We'd done this enough times now to know who went where and did what. Me, I stayed in the main room, kicking through the furniture. Not that they usually hid anything out in an open room like this one.

Reyes returned first, pushing a woman ahead of him. She looked to be about twenty-five, eyes wide but surprisingly calm. Reyes pushed her to the floor and stood above her, gun pointed at her head. Like most women in the city, she wore the traditional hijab and abaya; God knows what was hidden under it so we weren't taking any chances.

A moment later, three small children busted into the room, followed by Scotch. They ran to their mother, who hugged them close and began muttering in Arabic. Probably a prayer.

Reyes's gun never wavered.

As the rest of the boys searched the house, I found myself thinking, what if this woman were my sister? My wife? How would I react if my family or my girl were threatened like that? For a brief moment, I realized that we weren't doing ourselves any favors over here by busting in like this, by threatening a mother and her kids.

Then I thought of my boys who'd been killed over here already, boys like nineteen-year-old Taylor Nelson, killed by men with masks, and by women like this one who didn't hesitate to strap bombs to their babies and who hid uzis under their damned dresses. Those young soldiers were killed, their only sin trying to protect their country and the freedom of everyone back in the States.

"I fucking hate these insurgents," I said to Reyes and Scotch. "I fucking hate them so much for putting us in harm's way, and I especially fucking hate them for putting their families in harm's way."

If only we could make these people understand that me and my boys were a team out here, no matter what branch we were in, and that we looked after our own. They killed one of us, we killed fifteen of them; we killed their family.

I looked at the woman kneeling on the floor, at her dark eyes watching us. I looked at her kids gathered around her. I really wished there was a way to make them understand.

*** 

We didn't find any weapons, nothing but that mama and her kids. Probably just another case of a neighbor reporting the family as part of some stupid feud, wasting our time when there were real enemies out there, trying to hurt us and anyone else who got in their way.

We arrived back at our temporary camp without incident, something I was grateful for. It didn't always happen that way. It was such a rush in battle, that adrenaline surge that came with knowing someone was trying to kill you but you were gonna get the bastard first. Nothing compared to it, but it was also good to make it back safe. We'd lost too many boys already, seven from our unit killed and at least half of us wounded during this tour. One more week, I told myself. One more week and we'd be home safe.

Several of us sat around on our cots, shooting the shit.

"As soon as we get back, I'm gonna haul my ass to Wal-Mart and stock up on Twinkies," declared Butch.

"That's only 'cause you ain't got yourself a girl!" giggled Reyes. "Poor little Butch, gotta rely on Twinkies to meet his needs 'cause he ain't got himself a girl!"

Butch threw his canteen at Reyes, much to the amusement of the other boys.

"What about you, Adams?" Scotch asked. "Got any big plans for when you get home?"

"Nope, just gonna find me a job somewhere and wait to be sent back, I guess."

I'd been in and out of the military for fifteen years, and it was getting harder and harder to move back and forth between here and civilian life. They trained us to kill, to not think, and that's what I did over here. Then they took us back to the States, said thanks and good luck and pushed us into so-called normal life, and expected us to be just fine. Like that was even possible.

Coming back from my first tour had been a real shock to my system. I'd just gone through hell for my country, and I was ignored. I expected to have girls throwing themselves at me, but instead they ridiculed my scars. I expected people to thank me, but instead they wanted to talk about why what I'd been doing—doing to keep *them* safe—was the wrong thing. My pain and my losses were entertainment for them, amusing stories to hear about at parties and in the grocery store, and then to forget about as they went back to their daily lives. Soldiers were dying so they could go to fucking Wal-Mart without worrying about someone trying to blow them up.

They could forget, but I couldn't. I could never forget our sacrifices.

***

Orders soon came down to move out, off to another temporary camp somewhere. We had everything together, ready to go, when Butch came tearing over.

"Old Dog," he asked, "you seen my helmet? I can't find the bastard anywhere."

"How the fuck did you lose your helmet?" Old Dog had been in the service longer than me and had a hell of a lot less tolerance for the younger guys.

"I don't know. It was here and then it wasn't."

I checked my watch. We had three minutes to find the helmet. I walked over to Reyes and Scotch. "Where's Butch's helmet?"

"What helmet?" Reyes asked. He glanced at Scotch and giggled.

"Where the fuck is the helmet?"

Scotch quickly eyed the ceiling tiles above us, then looked back at me. "I don't know anything about a missing helmet."

"For the fucking love of God, you put his helmet in the fucking ceiling?" I took a deep breath, tried to restrain myself from punching them both in the head.

"A ceiling, perhaps. Not necessarily that ceiling." Reyes giggled again.

Another deep breath. I checked my watch again. "We leave in two minutes. You have one minute to return Butch's helmet, or he gets both of yours. You wanna be out on the streets without a helmet?"

They exchanged glances, then looked at me, decided I wasn't joking, and dashed from the room.

I took another deep breath and stalked out. I understood the boys liked their jokes, but there was a place for them. Hiding someone's gear was just irresponsible. So fucking irresponsible. Did they have any idea how important a helmet was, when that IED went off and there was shrapnel and concrete raining down on everyone's heads?

The more I dwelt on this, the angrier I got. How could they be so fucking stupid? I saw an abandoned trashcan in the corner of the hallway and kicked it as hard as I could, scattering its contents, mostly cigarette butts, down the hall.

Old Dog must've heard the crash because he popped out into the hallway. "For fuck's sake, you act like a five-year-old sometimes. Did kicking that make you feel better?"

It hadn't, but his comments did. "Growing up, my stepdad always said to me, 'Andy, real men don't show their emotions.' You know what I told him?"

"I can probably guess."

I grinned at him. "I'd say to him, 'Fuck that.'" Real men didn't play mind games. And real men didn't hit women either, but that was a whole other issue.

"I'm surprised he didn't beat the shit out of you for that."

"Yeah, well." I shrugged, and my grin faded as memories of my childhood tried to surface.

I shook my head to clear my mind. We were about to move out, and I needed to calm down. I was a soldier first and foremost, and for me and my boys to stay safe, I couldn't think about anything else, not my asshole stepdad, and not the actions of the dumbfucks I was leading through a war zone. No more thinking about the families back home that I was fighting for, for my family that was never gonna happen if I didn't make it back.

\*\*\*

That night, inside another abandoned factory, I made the rounds, checking on my boys to make sure they were doing okay, to see if they needed anything. More machine guns popped in the distance, not close enough to worry about, not yet, but you could never tell. That was the thing with this war, and with relationships, and with life in general; you could never tell.

# Chapter 5 – Kasey (Present)

David and I rode down the interstate locked in a tense, uncomfortable silence. I stared out the passenger window at the kudzu that had taken over the wooded hills, while my stone-faced husband focused on the road ahead, his hands clenching the steering wheel. We'd spent the last three hours in a battle of wills. David reached over to turn on the radio, and I retaliated by snapping it off.

He sighed. "Look, Kasey," he said, his voice defensive. "For weeks now I've told you I'm sorry. I'm going along with your stupid plan. Why are you still being like this?"

"You're right, dear." My tone dripped with venomous sweetness. "Saying you're sorry makes it all better."

He unclenched his jaw. "What the hell else do you want from me?"

"How about a promise to keep your temper under control?" I turned to face him. "Is that too damn much to ask?"

"Don't you dare curse at me." His voice rose in volume and pitch; his face reddened.

"Oh, so you're going to be the one taking the moral high ground now?" I deliberately tried to provoke him.

"I swear to fucking God, if you don't fucking drop this passive-aggressive bitchiness—"

"You'll what? Sleep with our new neighbors? Leave me for your new secretary?"

"Fucking-A, Kasey!" He pounded the steering wheel with his palm, hitting the horn by accident. Aida stirred in the back seat but didn't wake, and he drove on, knuckles white on the steering wheel.

I turned back to the window, eyes closed, head pressed against the glass, remembering what a mess the morning had been.

The movers had arrived promptly at seven. Everything was boxed up, labeled, ready to go. They quickly devised a plan to pack everything neatly and efficiently into the truck. David, with his complete lack of experience, tried to supervise, to the point where the team manager took me aside.

"Ms. Sanford, I hate to be rude...." He twisted his cap in his hands.

"Yes?"

"Well, ma'am, we're at the point that if your husband doesn't remove himself from the situation, he's gonna get a dresser dropped on his head."

"I see."

"Accidentally, of course."

"Of course." I smiled. "I'll talk to him."

"Thanks, ma'am."

David was in the dining room, supervising a couple men as they wrapped padding around the buffet mirror.

"The tape should go on the blanket, which needs to be wrapped tighter." He pulled the tape out of the mover's hands. "Here, I'll do it."

"David, can I have a word with you? In the kitchen?"

"I'm kind of busy, Kase."

"Now?"

The movers shot me a grateful look as David handed the tape back and followed me into the other room. "What is it?"

"You're in the way, and the movers are about to seriously maim you."

"Kase, don't be stupid." He glared at me.

I took a deep breath, held it, exhaled. "Why don't you and Aida go on ahead? I can wait for the movers to finish up, then drive down myself. If you want, you could stop in Raleigh, go to a mall or park or something. I could catch up with you, or just meet you at the new house."

"They need me here."

"No, David, they don't. Your hovering is making them angry. Angry movers break stuff. Our stuff."

"No, *movers* break stuff. Our stuff. If I'm watching, they won't."

I folded my arms across my chest and leaned against the counter. "According to our contract, insurance only covers broken stuff if they pack it. If you help them, you could actually cost us money." Maybe the financial argument would work, or the legalese; David usually responded well to that.

He huffed and shook his head.

"Tell you what," I said, crossing over to him and taking his hands in mine. "Take Aida over to your parents' place to say goodbye one last time. I'll supervise here. By the time you get back, they should be about done."

He smiled. The physical contact was having an effect on him. "Fine. But if you need anything, call."

He returned three hours later, just in time to see the bottom fall out of one of the boxes. Papers from his law school notebooks scattered across the lawn.

"What the fuck are we paying you to do?" He marched across the yard.

"I'm sorry, sir. The contents were too heavy, and the tape gave out. You must not have taped it well enough to...." The mover trailed off under David's withering stare.

I hurried over, put my hand on David's arm to calm him. "It was just an accident. Have Aida help you pick up the papers."

"This is ridiculous." He ignored me. "How much are we paying these incompetent assholes, and they're already ruining stuff before it's even on the truck?"

"David, enough." The sharpness in my tone made him pause and look at me. I lowered my voice so only he could hear. "I know you're stressed, but you're not helping the situation. The movers are almost done. If you so much as talk to a single one without being spoken to first, I'm not letting you in the house in Asheville."

"Kase—"

"You think I'm joking? Try me."

For whatever reason, he gave in and went with Aida. They watched videos on his laptop in the backseat of his SUV until the truck was sealed. However, he didn't say much to me either. At the time that wasn't a problem, but three hours later the silent treatment made being stuck together on a long car ride about as fun as a root canal. I wasn't about to apologize first, though. *He* was the one who needed a lesson in civility and compromise.

I turned from the window to steal a quick glance at my husband, wondering what he was thinking about and when we'd stopped asking each other about those thoughts. I opened my mouth to ask but let my breath out instead. It would only lead to another argument.

"What?" David's voice was now calm. He took his eyes off the road long enough to look over at me.

As his head turned, a whiff of his aftershave drifted over to me. I sighed. "Nothing."

***

We spent the next few weeks settling into our new house. I enrolled Aida in a summer camp so she could meet some kids before she started first grade in the fall. David disappeared to his office every day, leaving me at home to unpack. I threw myself into my work, making the place ours. I'd selected the house without any input from David, and he'd wisely gone along with my choice.

Our new home was on the edge of the revitalized downtown area, in an older part of the city. Stately trees filled the large yard, a porch wrapped halfway around the house, and gabled windows looked out onto the Blue Ridge Mountains. I loved its old charm and delighted in choosing new paint and carpet for each room, making it into the best home for our family.

The move wasn't fixing our marriage as fast as I'd hoped. David and I talked to each other, were civil, but we walked on eggshells, afraid to say anything that might set the other off. At least, that's how I saw it, and how I hoped David saw it. The alternative was too painful to consider.

A month or so after we'd moved to Asheville, David, Aida, and I sat out on the porch after dinner. Aida and I sipped sweet tea while David nursed a scotch on the rocks.

"How was school today, sweetie?" David asked. They sat on the porch swing, Aida snuggled up at his side.

"It's not school, Daddy. It's camp."

He smiled. "Okay then, how was camp?"

"Camp was fun. Meredith and I made BFF bracelets today."

"BFF?"

"Best friends forever," I explained.

"Gotcha." David took a swig of his drink. "So does that mean you're making friends here?"

"Yeah, a few. There's Meredith and Connor and Lou and Abigail and Samantha and Jonathan." She paused, ticking the names off on her fingers. "And Allen and Annabelle. They're twins."

"What about you, Kase?" He turned his gaze towards me. "Make any new friends here yet?"

I scrunched a little tighter in the Papasan chair. "No, not really. Not yet. I've been busy with the house." Truth be told, I wasn't ready to jump into the social scene. I liked being able to do what I wanted all day, without committee and meeting obligations. But my deeper fear was that as soon as people learned why we'd moved here—and they would eventually, no doubt about that—they'd treat me like a leper. It was irrational, but it didn't stop me from thinking it.

"The senior partner's wife is thinking about starting a weekly cocktail hour. It would be a great way to meet people."

I shrugged.

"You always loved those things, back in Richmond."

"No, David, I went to those things. There's a big difference."

"Yeah, well, you'll love this one. His wife apparently loves history. She's head of the local Daughters of the Confederacy chapter."

"I can just imagine it. 'Why, you're a Yankee, bless your heart.'"

"It'll be fine." David stood up, came over to me and kissed the top of my head. "I'll just tell her it's proof I know how to pick a winner."

I shook my head, smiling. "I still don't want to go."

"Then you better come up with something better to do. It's a week from Thursday. That gives you exactly nine days to get yourself a social life." With that, he walked inside.

***

The next morning, I stood in the living room, surveying the scattered boxes that still needed to be unpacked, and thought about what David had said. "You boxes can wait," I said to the mess before I went upstairs, changed into a wide-strapped tank top and flowery cotton skirt, grabbed my purse, and headed outside.

I paused in the driveway before getting into my car. Our house wasn't far from downtown, and it was a beautiful summer day, free of the humidity that made most of the South unbearable this time of year. Pulling my hair into a loose ponytail, I set off down the sidewalk.

Like many metropolises around the country, Asheville had recently poured millions into restoring its downtown area. The city center now bustled with gourmet restaurants, specialty boutiques, and plenty of tourists eager to dine and shop in such beautiful surroundings. The town had made it to the top of many quality-of-life lists, leading a number of retirees to move to the area in search of opportunities to spend their pensions. As a result, Asheville was flourishing, supporting a vibrant arts scene and many independent retailers and restaurants.

I strolled along, taking in the streetscape. Tantalizing aromas wafted out from little restaurants and cafés. I stopped to examine the menus posted at some of them, making a mental list of ones I'd like to try. Musicians decorated the street corners, ranging from Mongolian pipe players, to drummers using plastic buckets, to simple acoustic guitarists. Bright flowers overflowed from planters, giving the sidewalks an old world charm.

One store in particular stood out. The display in the front windows of McKay's Books and Coffee featured a variety of what appeared to be robots assembled out of books, coffee mugs, and spoons. I paused to examine them, reading the titles and marveling at the creativity of their construction.

After a few minutes, I sensed someone staring at me and looked through the window into the café section of the store. A dozen or so people dotted the tables, some sitting alone and others grouped together. Near the back, three people clustered around a table. A balding man and a plump woman had their backs to me, and facing them, facing me, an attractive blond-haired man, maybe mid-thirties, watched me intently.

Most people would have the decency to look away when they'd been caught staring, but not this guy. Our eyes met. He took a drink from his coffee cup and laughed at something but didn't break eye contact.

I dropped my own eyes back to the robot in front of me, my face on fire, then glanced back at the stranger. He was still watching me. I swallowed hard, unsure why I felt so uncomfortable, and hurried off down the street.

A block later I stopped at another storefront, this one displaying kitschy arts and crafts. No one inside watched me, and I laughed at myself for even checking. So what if some guy had been looking at me? This was a new town, a chance to be whoever I wanted. And I wanted to be a person who visited a bookstore, regardless of who might be in it.

*\*\*\**

For the rest of the week, I left the boxes alone and explored the town. The mall offered nothing special, but downtown and the shops that made up Biltmore Village provided a fun opportunity to browse, as did the artists' community at Black Mountain. Each day, I found an excuse to visit McKay's.

But he wasn't there. I didn't know why I expected him to be there, or why I felt disappointed that he wasn't. Maybe he was a tourist already onto his next destination. Or perhaps he was a local but married. Like me. I'd moved here to fix my marriage to David, not fawn over some guy I'd seen once.

I should've stayed away, if one chance encounter had knocked me this out of sorts, but the place was exactly what I needed. Despite the dozen or so assorted bookstores in town, including a couple standard chain ones, McKay's didn't lack for customers. It carried both new and used books on a wide range of topics. The cozy little shop had crowded aisles and shelves overflowing with books, and overstuffed armchairs and couches hidden among the stacks. An attached coffee shop provided customers with a place to relax while reading their new materials, or to meet with friends.

By the following Monday, I'd exhausted the rest of the town. Aida and I had emptied the last of the boxes the day before, leaving me free of any commitments. A trip to McKay's would be the perfect reward for all my hard work.

Sipping a glass of sweet tea, I flipped through a magazine on Southern culture, similar to the one I'd worked for in Richmond before Aida was born. The blond man had returned, sitting at a nearby table with the same middle-aged couple and a college-aged guy. I did my best to ignore him and my racing pulse, to not stare at his handsome face, his well-defined muscles easily visible through his t-shirt. If he'd been staring at me, then he could be the one to start the conversation.

The café was quiet, for the most part. Not library, everyone-whisper quiet, but respect-my-space, let-me-read-in-peace quiet. Until raucous laughter burst from the blond guy's table. I looked up from my magazine, frowning slightly at the unexpected interruption, and told myself I was showing my disapproval, not using this as an excuse to memorize the lines of the man's face.

"So what did you end up doing?" asked the college-aged guy, looking up from the laptop in front of him.

"This is the best part." The blond man leaned in, ran a hand over his crew cut. "I ended up following this drunk-ass woman down the road to a church, middle of the night, going about five miles an hour, because she wanted to marry that goat first, 'just in case.'" He slapped the table for emphasis as his companions roared with laughter.

Amused by the man's exuberance but baffled by the punchline to a joke I hadn't heard, I shook my head at the disruption and tried to focus on my magazine.

"Another time, we busted a party next to the university and confiscated a couple donkeys. They claimed everything they were doing was legal and consensual, and even tried to show us videos of what they planned to do. We watched them, to build a case against them, of course. I didn't even know half those positions were possible." His friends howled with laughter, and others around him chuckled.

I closed my eyes, let out a deep breath. Didn't they know people came to a bookstore to read, not to listen to raunchy stories? I'd wanted to see the blond guy again, but his audacity was beginning to irk me. First he stared at me for no discernible reason, and now he was interrupting the tranquility of the café with no regard for someone who might want to read without disruption, without hearing crude stories.

Perhaps sensing my annoyance, he looked over and caught me watching him.

I dropped my gaze to the magazine in front of me, but not before getting a good look at his pale blue eyes. The look in them left me feeling like he had some kind of x-ray vision that allowed him to see into my heart. *Great. Now I'm a cliché.* I swallowed hard. It was just the light in the café, nothing more.

He launched into another story, an off-color tale again involving women and farm animals.

I wondered if it was to spite me but just as quickly chided myself for the thought. We didn't know each other; why would he go out of his way to make me angry or uncomfortable, to get my goat? I smiled at the pun, then shot him another glance.

He was still watching me with those piercing eyes. Evaluating me.

My breath caught in my throat. I gathered my drink and purse and hurried out of the bookstore, leaving the magazine on the table.

*** 

"Let's play a game," said Aida. She lay on the floor of the living room and had just finished coloring a picture of a pony.

David, watching a ballgame with a drink in hand, grunted from his spot on the couch.

I looked up from my position in the corner armchair, setting aside a romance novel I'd read several times before. "What game, sweetie?"

"Trivial Twister Land."

"Trivial Twister Land?" repeated David, still watching the game. "I'm afraid I'm not familiar with that one, kiddo."

"That's cuz I made it up!" Aida grinned.

David and I exchanged glances and smiled too. Our daughter preferred to create her own entertainment.

"So how do you play?" I asked.

"It's real easy. We use the Candyland board. When you land on a color, you answer a question that's the same color. If you get it wrong, you have to put your hand or foot on the Twister mat. The first person to fall over loses."

"Where do the questions come from?" asked David.

"From Trivial Pursuit, of course!" Aida had a child's version of the game, and while her reading and knowledge levels kept her from answering many of the questions, she still enjoyed playing it.

"Of course." David nodded. "I'm up for it. How about you, Kase?"

"How can I say no to a game of Trivial Twister Land?" I smiled at my daughter.

The game quickly degenerated into giggles. I pretended not to know the answers to simple questions, and David made a big production out of repeated attempts to cheat by reading the answers off the cards. The game ended with the three of us tangled in a pile on the Twister mat.

"I win!" declared Aida as we disentangled ourselves.

As I tried to stand, David pulled me on top of him and kissed me. Caught up in the family fun, unable to remember the last time I'd enjoyed myself so much, I closed my eyes and returned the kiss. But all I could see was a pair of pale blue eyes staring back at me.

***

For the next few days, my mind kept returning to the eyes of the man at the bookstore. Even after that quick glimpse, they still haunted me. That *man* haunted me. For some reason, I was simultaneously intrigued and put off. We'd never spoken to each other, never interacted. All I had to go by was a glance, an overheard conversation. That was no reason to—to what? To think about someone? That's all it was; no need to overreact. For God's sake, I didn't even know his name.

Even if he occupied more of my thoughts than he should, it was only fair. David had cheated on me, and those pictures of David's naked body pressed close to another woman's never left my mind. No harm in me staring at an attractive man, not after what my husband had done.

Several days after family game night, days spent exchanging smiles with David, days filled with positive feelings about our future, I went back to the bookstore. I couldn't spend all my time there, and told myself, and David, that when school started I'd join the PTA, find somewhere to volunteer, start up the never-ending routine of cocktails and dinners. My efforts to get out of the house and get to know the town had appeased him, meaning he'd been fine with me avoiding his coworker's Confederate-friendly wife. For now, I'd enjoy the anonymity and freedom that came with having no responsibilities, no connections to my new town.

While browsing McKay's history section, walking backwards reading the titles, I bumped into the blue-eyed man, who was engrossed in the military history section.

He scowled at me for a brief moment, but as recognition dawned in his eyes his expression softened.

"I'm so sorry." Heat rushed to my face. "I wasn't paying attention. I didn't mean to disturb you."

"No harm, no foul." The corners of his lips drew back into a smile, or perhaps a smirk. "You come here a lot, right? I've noticed you around."

"Yeah." The warmth spread throughout my whole body. "You too."

"I'm Andrew."

"Kasey."

I tried to think of something witty to say, or quirky. Something that would make him laugh, make him want to get to know me. He regarded me with a mixture of polite boredom and expectation.

I gestured toward the section behind him. "So, you like military history?"

"Yep."

"I think it's interesting, but I always get frustrated by the policy decisions. We go in and do whatever we think is best for a country, without consideration for what they want. No wonder they hate us so much, if all we do is use violence to enforce our will." I paused, realizing I might be ranting, and gave him an apologetic smile. "My dad fought in Vietnam, so I grew up exposed to all this. I'm a pretty strong pacifist."

"Career military." All traces of the smirk, or smile, or whatever it had been, were gone.

"Oh." My face was definitely on fire.

"If you'll excuse me?"

I nodded, and Andrew walked past me to the counter where a tall, thin woman was standing. She grinned and punched him in the arm, and he responded by pinning her in a bear hug. She squealed, and the short plump woman who regularly shared his table came over and tickled his side. He set down the first woman in order to free his arms to defend himself. All three laughed, and when the second woman motioned towards the door, they all went out together.

I watched in envy. There were social cues everyone else seemed to intrinsically understand but, try as I might, I just didn't see them. As a lawyer's wife, at the top of the social ladder, I'd become good at faking exuberance, but always felt bad afterwards, almost guilty for betraying my true self. My true self didn't make small talk, or giggle whenever someone of the opposite sex said something, or punch a guy as a sign of affection. My true self, it seemed, was incompatible with the guy whose eyes wouldn't stop watching me.

I sighed, put my book back on the shelf, and headed home.

\*\*\*

Over the next couple weeks I walked to the bookstore nearly every weekday. I told myself it was to escape the boredom, not to make a better impression on Andrew. It had been one brief interaction that he probably didn't even remember, that he had no reason to remember.

That *I* had no reason to remember. Why couldn't I stop thinking about him?

I learned more about him through conversations overheard in the café. Sergeant Andrew Adams of the Asheville police force worked mostly evening shifts, but remained continuously on call. He'd been in the Army and currently served in the Reserves. Single, and with no immediate plans to change that, he drank a lot, swore a lot, knew a lot of people in town, and was rarely alone at McKay's.

As I watched him, almost always surrounded by people wanting his opinion and attention, I wondered how I'd ever be able to compete with them, and *why* I wanted to compete. Things had improved with David to the point that we were talking again, at least as friends, if not as a married couple. Yet every time I kissed my husband, I imagined how Andrew's lips would feel. Why? Nearly everything that came out of them irritated me. I'd also learned from my observations that the man was crude, arrogant, self-absorbed. But those eyes, and the way he'd looked at me the first time, promised there was more to him.

It was curiosity that drove me to McKay's every day. Curiosity, plain and simple. I wanted to know how he could look at me and, with one glance, make me feel so flustered, so not myself. Nothing more than that. Certainly no kisses, no touching. Just because David had cheated on me didn't mean that I'd cheat on him. No, it was only curiosity.

\*\*\*

Again in the bookstore, I sipped my sweet tea and observed the people around me, glad for the air-conditioning after my walk on the warm July day. Despite my better intentions, my gaze repeatedly settled on Andrew, who today sat by himself in a corner.

"Hey, Andrew, I got a question for you," said a college student sitting nearby. He was enrolled in summer classes, I'd learned, trying to save some money and graduate early.

"Not today, Mike." Andrew scowled as he flipped through the medical guide book in front of him.

"It's for a class, man. Can't you help a brother out?"

Andrew sighed loudly, made a big production of marking his spot and shutting his book. "What is it?"

"It's for a poli-sci class. What's your take on the current anti-war sentiment in this country?"

Andrew stared hard at him. "How do you think I feel? Our troops are dying over there, and no one gives a damn."

I surprised myself by speaking up. "I think you're wrong about that."

"Oh, really?" Andrew focused his angry piercing blue eyes on me. "What would lead our resident pacifist to say that? What do you know about our troops?"

"I know that there's a difference between supporting our troops and supporting the policies that send them over." I licked my lips. "I think really examining whether our troops need to be over there is as patriotic as you can get. Why put them in harm's way unnecessarily?"

Andrew looked at me as if reevaluating our prior encounter. *God, those eyes.* "Sometimes you have to hit hard, Kasey. The world's a cruel place."

He remembered my name.

I swallowed hard. "I realize that. I just want to make sure we're hitting the right targets, for the right reasons."

The radio on his belt squawked out a string of numbers. He stood up, pushed in his chair, and directed a small smiling smirk my way. "Duty calls, but I want to continue this conversation with you."

I narrowed my eyes at him, not sure if he was serious.

He met my gaze. "Okay." His smile widened slightly, and then he headed out of the bookshop.

"What's his problem today?" asked Mike.

"Rumor has it he's about to be put on standby to head to Afghanistan," said the middle-aged man who usually sat with Andrew. "Half the guys in his unit were either wounded or killed during his last deployment. He carries a lot of scars around with him."

"That would be a lot for anyone to deal with," Mike said, shaking his head as he resumed typing on his laptop. "Had I known specifics of what he went through, I wouldn't have brought it up."

I tried to go back to my book but couldn't focus. All I could think was that he wanted to keep talking to me, that he knew my name, knew who I was. We'd introduced ourselves, of course, but people rarely remembered names the first time, especially not weeks later. Maybe that meant he'd been paying attention to me just as I had been to him. Maybe he'd thought about my eyes, my lips, like I had his?

I gave myself a mental shake. I was married and wanted to stay that way. He knew my name, that was all, and he wanted to continue an impersonal conversation that had been cut short. No need to read too much into this.

*** 

The next day, all the tables at the coffee shop were full, occupied mostly by a large group of boisterous teenagers. I ordered a sweet tea to go. There was still a lot to do around the house, and it wasn't getting done with me spending so much time at the bookstore.

I was weaving my way through the students towards the door, focused on not spilling my drink, when a hand grabbed my wrist.

"There's a seat here if you want to stay for a bit," Andrew said.

He didn't let go of me, and his touch sent shivers up my arm. I hoped he didn't notice.

The couple who usually sat with him was at the table. The woman moved her purse off an empty chair, and I sat down.

"It's busy in here today," she said. "I've seen you around a lot recently, haven't I? I'm Erica, and this is my husband Ron." The man nodded at me while his wife continued. "We run an art studio nearby and stop in here on breaks. And, of course, it's always nice to chat with Andrew when he has a free moment. They have good coffee here too, don't you think?" She brushed a crumb off her lap, not skipping a beat in monologue, not giving anyone a chance to answer. "And pastries and snacks in general. Not as good as that little café around the corner, but this place is cheaper, at least, which is nice when you have your own business to think about. Can never be too careful with money."

She paused to take a sip of her latte, and I murmured my agreement.

"Ron here handles all the business stuff, and I create," Erica continued. "I'm a very creative person, a very free soul. I get inspiration from everywhere—trees, clouds, rainbows, rainstorms, flowers, animals, nature, the people around me, the mountains, sex, everything I see and do." She fluttered a hand at her surroundings. "I try to experience as much as I can. I want every moment to fuel my passion for creating."

"Sounds tiring," said Andrew, that smug sarcastic smile of his playing across his lips. "I know all that passion would probably wear me out pretty quickly." He winked at me, and my pulse quickened.

"Oh yes, it is," Erica said. I couldn't decide if she was oblivious to the intended meaning of Andrew's remark or just ignoring it. "Such exuberance and passion is exhausting, but it's worth it. God has blessed me with this gift, and who am I to defy His wishes by not sharing it with everyone I encounter? This is just another chance for me to spread His glory to others. And, speaking of God, what church do you attend, Kasey?"

"I don't." After our experience in Richmond, I wasn't eager to join a church here if I could avoid it.

"Oh." Erica's brow furrowed, and then she brightened. "Well, I invite you to come to ours if you need a home, which it sounds like you do. We go to Christ's Liberty Praise New Evangelical Church. Bible study at seven on Wednesdays, and service at eleven on Sundays. It's a community of creative people such as myself, all trying to find a way to use our gifts to further Jesus' good news in our troubled world."

"In other words, one big God-loving orgy," Andrew said, and Ron and Erica laughed.

My eyes widened.

"Speaking of God, we should get back to the shop if we want to finish those Bible school posters by Monday." Ron stood up. "It was nice meeting you, Kasey."

"Yes, it was." The dozen or so bangle bracelets on Erica's arm jingled as she stood. "I just love getting to know new people. Bye, Andrew dear. Bye, Kasey." The scent of her perfume hung in the air as they left, a mixture of patchouli and something floral. Whatever it was, it was strong.

I stared after them. "Wow."

"Yeah," Andrew agreed, leaning back in his chair. "They're fun, aren't they?"

"They're something, all right." I might have used "exhausting" to describe them. "Other than lots of 'love,' apparently, what kind of stuff does she create?"

"Paintings, ceramics, designs on clothes, jewelry. A little bit of everything. She has a shop right down the street."

"Nice stuff?"

"Yeah, I guess. They seem to be doing pretty well with it."

"You have interesting friends."

"I like being around interesting people. Imagine how much the world would suck if everyone was as mopey as you all the time."

"Me?" I frowned at him. "I'm not mopey. I prefer to observe my surroundings before I jump in."

"You need to loosen up." He gave me that half-smirk smile of his. "Learn to relax. Get that stick out of your ass."

"Screw you." I grinned back, surprised by how comfortable I felt with him.

"See, there you go. Good response." He took a sip of his coffee, but the cup was empty. "I need a refill if I'm going to make it through tonight's shift. You want anything?"

"No thanks."

"Sure you don't want anything? I'm offering." He smiled, a genuine smile, not sarcastic or teasing or anything.

The tingles I'd felt when he'd touched my wrist were jumping all over my body. I motioned towards my nearly full glass. "I'm good."

"Next time, then."

He wanted a next time? I tried to wipe the idiotic grin off my face before he returned.

He sat down with his coffee and looked at me, that arrogant half-smile playing at his lips. I tried not to stare at him, at his lips, his pale blue eyes in his tan face, choosing instead to play with the straw in my tea.

"So," he said, sipping his drink, "what brings you back in here to mope day after day?"

"Boredom." I ignored his attempt to annoy me with his word choice.

"Oh?"

"Yeah, my daughter's at summer camp all day, and my husband's at his office. I don't really know anyone in town yet, so I come here."

"You're new here then?"

"Yes."

"Where'd you move from?"

"Richmond. My husband got a new job here." Best to leave it at that for now.

"So you're a housewife."

Usually I bristled at the label, but the way he said it implied that it was completely natural, acceptable. Almost noble. I nodded.

"Nothing wrong with that." He smiled. "You take care of your hubby, he takes care of you. That's how it should be."

My hand tightened on my drink, thinking of how David had repaid me. If Andrew noticed, he didn't say anything.

"What about you?" I asked, changing the subject away from myself.

"Cop here in town."

"Your girlfriend doesn't mind you spending all your free time here?"

"No girlfriend, no one at home but a jealous cat. So I come here instead."

We fell silent. I considered continuing our conversation from the other day but thought back to the first time we'd spoken, how he'd reacted to my comment about being a pacifist. I didn't want to upset him, or jeopardize the warmth I felt sitting there with him, so I quietly sipped my tea. Andrew didn't say anything either, just watched as I fiddled with a straw wrapper. I shifted in my chair, dropped my eyes to my drink as the silence lengthened.

"Well," he said finally, pushing his chair back from the table, "I should get ready before my shift starts. I'll see you around."

"I hope so," I blurted out, then blushed.

He smiled at me, that real smile again, and left the shop.

I stared at his muscular back as it retreated, wondering what it looked like under his t-shirt. *Stop it*, I told myself, but for the rest of the day I walked around in a distracted daze, thinking about his shoulders, his lips, his smile.

# Chapter 6 – Andrew (Age 14)

I slouched at a folding table in the back of the big tent, my tie loosened and shirt untucked, watching the celebration around me. The scowl on my face seemed to be working because no one came near me. I took a drink from the half-full cup of beer in front of me. It had been sitting at an empty table; no one seemed to notice it was gone. No one seemed to notice me. Of course not. This was Dad's special day, Dad and wife number three.

"Andrew, you're not supposed to be drinking that." My kid brother Jesse came over and pulled out the chair next to me.

I put my foot up on it. "This spot's taken."

"I'm gonna tell on you." His eyes shot wide as he stared at my drink.

"So?" I took a big swig, even though the warm beer left a gross taste in my mouth. "The worst that'll happen is I'll get grounded. Big deal."

Jesse sat down in the chair next to my foot. "Karen looks real pretty today."

I shrugged. "I guess."

"Do you think she's nice?"

"What's it matter? She's not our mom, and you ain't gonna see her but for a few weeks in the summer when you come to visit."

"Nope, I just live across town. I see her and Dad every week." He wrinkled his nose. "She's not a very good cook."

I forced myself to take another gulp as I studied my brother. At seven he was already tall, skinny, blond—just like me. "Your mom's a good cook though, right?"

"Yeah." He turned and watched Dad swing Karen around on the dance floor. "Andrew, can I ask you a question?"

"It's a free country."

"Why did Mom and Dad get divorced?" He continued watching the couple dance.

"I dunno."

"Dad was married to your mom too, right? And they got divorced?"

"Yup."

"Do you know why they split up?"

"Nope." I drained the rest of the beer, hoping he didn't notice my disgust, then stood up.

"Where you going?" He stood as well.

"Dunno."

"Can I come too?"

I rolled my eyes. The last thing I wanted was my kid brother following me around. Ever since I'd gotten to Dad's place last week, it was like Jesse and me were attached at the hip. "Go get me some chips."

"Okay, Andrew." He smiled and took off towards the buffet.

As soon as he moved a couple tables away, I walked towards the lake behind Dad's house. Once I was far enough that no one would notice, I pulled a cigarette from my pocket, lit it, threw the match in the yard, and took a drag.

For wedding number three, this was a pretty big celebration. It was Karen's first marriage, so she probably wanted something special. I'd thought about telling her not to bother, because the marriage probably wouldn't last long, but who knew? Maybe third time would be the charm for Dad.

***

Later that evening, after all the guests had left and the tents and everything in the backyard had been taken down, Jesse caught up with me as I sat in the den playing Contra on the Nintendo.

"Can I play too?" He plopped down on the couch next to me.

"Nope." I kept my eyes on the screen. Sometimes, if I didn't make eye contact, he'd give up and leave me alone.

"Please?"

"No."

"Can I just sit here and watch?"

"Fine," I huffed. "Just don't say anything. And don't breathe on me."

"Okay," he said happily.

I rolled my eyes and did my best to ignore him.

I'd been playing for maybe fifteen minutes when Dad came into the room, leaned against the door frame.

"How's it going, boys?"

"Andrew and me are playing Nintendo," Jesse informed him.

I grunted.

"There's been a slight change in plans. I know you both wanted to stay all week, but Karen's mom had a nasty fall, and we need to be there in the hospital with her. Jesse, you're going back to your mom's. Andrew, we're going to drop you off at your uncle Stu's house for the night. He'll take you to the bus station tomorrow so you can head back home."

"Don't like Stu." I scowled. My uncle was a jerk, real rude and stupid just like my stepdad back home.

"I know, but we don't really have any other options."

"Why can't he stay at my house?" asked Jesse.

"Because your mom and sister hate me."

"Andrew," Dad said, but didn't finish because he knew it was true. My ex-stepmom had never liked me.

As much as I disliked Jesse following me around, it was still a million times better than being at home with my stepdad. An idea popped into my head. "Why do we even need a stupid babysitter? I'm old enough to take care of Jesse for a couple days just fine."

Dad frowned. "I don't know if that's such a good idea."

"What's not a good idea?" Karen asked as she walked into the middle of our conversation.

"Please, Dad?" Jesse pleaded. "Andrew'll take real good care of me, I know he will."

"Andrew suggested he stay here and look after Jesse."

"That's a great idea!" Karen clung to my dad's arm and smiled real big at us all. "It'll give the boys a chance to spend some time together. Make us feel like a real family."

"We're not though," I said.

"Andrew," Dad said sharply.

"What? We're not. I live with my mom and never see you. Jesse lives with his mom and probably never sees you either. And Karen and you'll probably have kids too, right? They'll be your family, not me and Jesse."

"That's not true." Tears sprung to Karen's eyes. "I want you to think of me as your mom, Andrew, when you're here."

"I already have a mom." I stood up, threw the controller on the ground. "So does Jesse. We don't need you." I strode past her and towards the door.

"Andrew, get back here," Dad yelled after me, but I just kept walking.

Once outside, I headed towards the lake and sat down at the end of the dock, dangling my feet in the water. With the sun down the air was chilly, especially on my wet feet and legs, but I didn't mind. I lit a cigarette and leaned back to watch the stars come out. The Big Dipper was the only constellation I could find, but it didn't matter. Wherever I was, looking up at the stars always made me feel better, like God was watching out for me. Didn't seem like anyone else was.

After awhile, the wooden dock vibrated with footsteps. I didn't move.

"There's a list of instructions and phone numbers on the fridge," Dad said. "There's some money on the counter if you want to get a pizza or take the bus into town tomorrow."

"You really trust me?"

"I know Jesse bugs you, but he looks up to you. Take care of him, okay, kiddo?"

"Yeah, I will, Dad."

***

The next day Jesse woke me up bright and early. "I want breakfast, Andrew."

"Ummp." I buried my head under my pillow and went back to sleep.

He returned several hours later. "Andrew, I'm hungry."

The extra sleep had left me more alert. "Fine. Gimme a few minutes and I'll make you lunch."

I heard him bounce away as I lay in bed a few extra minutes, enjoying being able to sleep in. Back home I was out of the house as soon as possible on the weekends. Anything to get away from my stepdad.

I sat up and stretched, pulled on a shirt and headed to the kitchen.

Jesse was at the table in front of two plates sitting on the placemats Karen insisted we use. "What's for lunch, Andrew?"

"Pancakes."

"For lunch?" He giggled.

"Yeah, for lunch. And then what do you say we go hang out at the mall for awhile?"

"Just you and me?" His eyes lit up, and I couldn't help but smile.

"Yeah, just you and me."

The kid devoured his pancakes, in a hurry to go to the mall.

I made him load up the dishwasher while I showered, and then we walked down the road to the bus stop.

"I've never taken a real bus before," he told me after we'd boarded.

"Yeah?"

"This is fun, Andrew."

We got off the bus at the mall.

"Let's go to the arcade," suggested Jesse.

The tiny arcade sat off the food court, with maybe a half-dozen or so video games, an air hockey table, and a couple of those claw games filled with rip-off prizes. Not great, but it was something to do.

"Let's play Rampage," Jesse said.

"Isn't that too violent for you?"

"It's just a game." He stuck his tongue out at me. "And besides, all you do is punch buildings and eat people."

I lightly slugged his arm. "Sure it's not punch people and eat buildings?"

"I'm so gonna beat you!"

"We'll see about that."

Fourteen quarters later, I had to admit my kid brother was pretty good at the game. Better than me, actually. "How'd you get so good?"

He shrugged. "Dunno, just am. Wanna try something else?"

"Sure, what?"

"Double Dragon?"

"Okay, but I gotta pee first. Stay here, okay?"

He nodded.

The restrooms were across the food court, next to a comic book store. I'd pretty much outgrown comics, and reading in general, but I still liked to check in on Superman and see what he and Lex Luther and Lois were up to. This store had a pretty good selection, and I got caught up in thumbing through them.

"Hey, kid, this ain't no library," the guy behind the counter finally said. "Buy something or get out."

"Yeah, whatever." I rolled my eyes and left the store. Everyone always thought just because I was a teenager I was some kind of punk kid. No way I'd spend any money in his store, with his attitude.

I walked back to the arcade. A group of boys, maybe ten years old or so, clustered around the Double Dragon game. I pushed through them to the players.

"Hey, what's the big deal?" one of the kids asked. "We were here first."

Jesse wasn't there. I looked around, but the room wasn't that big, not big enough that I'd miss seeing him. "You seen a little kid? Blond hair, real skinny?"

The kids shook their heads, focused back on the game.

"Seriously, I'm looking for my brother, Jesse Adams. He goes to school here. Second grade, I think. Any of you know him or seen him?"

The kids shook their heads again, but I didn't even know if they'd heard me. *Fuck.* I tore out of the arcade, stood at the edge of the food court, and swept my gaze over the tables. No blond-haired boys by themselves. I walked along the edge, by the restaurants. No sign of him there either. My heart thudded in my chest. What if he'd been kidnapped, or gotten lost? Or wandered outside and gotten hit by a car? He was just a kid. How could I have been so stupid to leave him by himself?

I ducked outside and looked around. No ambulances, no people huddled around a body on the ground. Back inside I scanned the tables again. Still no Jesse. Adrenaline surged through my veins, leaving me jumpy. Adrenaline and panic. I took a deep breath. The kid was smart, and knew better than to go outside, to wander away.

I started down the main corridor of the mall, looking into each shop. He couldn't have made it too far. I turned around and headed back. Once he realized he was lost, he'd most likely look for me around the restrooms or arcade. *Fuck fuck fuck.*

I returned to the arcade, but still no Jesse. I could go to mall security, but what if Dad found out Jesse got lost when I was supposed to be watching him? No, better to find him first.

Maybe *he* had to pee, too. I raced over to the restrooms. Just before stepping inside I caught sight of a little blond head in the comic book store.

"Jesse!" I called, actually running now. When I reached him I pulled him into a tight hug. "Fuck, kid, I was so worried about you. Why'd you wander off?"

"You didn't come back. I thought you left without me."

I knelt down in front of him, hands on his shoulders, and looked him straight in the eye. "Jesse, you might bug the shit out of me sometimes, but I'm your big brother. I ain't never gonna leave without you."

"You mean it?" He looked back at me, his look full of admiration and love.

"Yeah." I stood, tousled his hair so he couldn't see how wet my eyes were getting. "Moms might come and go, but you and me got something special. We're family."

# Chapter 7 – Kasey (Present)

The next Saturday, I awoke to a beautiful summer sunrise. David snored softly beside me. We'd been sleeping in the same bed since we'd moved, although I kept to my side, and he did the same. I quietly wiggled out of bed, stretching as I made my way to the window. Bright sunshine illuminated the mess that was our backyard.

"We really need to get some landscaping done," I said to my husband's sleeping form.

David muttered something and pulled his pillow over his head. He was not a morning person.

Grinning, I padded down the hall to check on Aida. Still sleeping. Guess I'd be weeding by myself.

After changing into a stained t-shirt and shorts, I headed outside. An uneven brick patio jutted into the grass, with weeds sticking up through the cracks. It would be a challenge, but I envisioned the space filled with azaleas and roses tucked into strategically-placed beds, maybe a wisteria-covered archway leading to a large garden overflowing with fruits and vegetables. It would take years to achieve the desired effect, but I didn't mind. Gardening relaxed me.

Today I'd tackle the beds lining the back of the house. Weeds had choked their way around everything and would need to be removed before I could plant anything of my own choosing.

The repetitive motion of pulling weeds soon cleared my head of all thoughts. No Andrew, no David, no cheating. Unfortunately, it was too good to last for long.

"Mommy," Aida called, bounding out of the house in her nightgown. "Daddy says you should come in and make us breakfast."

I leaned back on my heels and wiped my forehead. "Daddy can make his own breakfast. I'm busy."

Aida scurried back inside, and I returned to the weeds.

She was back outside a moment later. "Daddy says he's really hungry, and will you please come in and make him breakfast?"

"Please tell Daddy I'm still busy."

"Okay."

I rolled my eyes. Granted, I usually made breakfast for the three of us on the weekends, but how hard was it for him to pour a bowl of cereal or pop a couple slices of bread into the toaster?

"Why do you always insist on playing out here in the dirt?" David stood above me, arms folded across his chest. He too was still in his pajamas, a faded t-shirt and flannel pants. "We could pay someone to do it, and then you'd have plenty of time to spend with your family."

"You mean, to make you breakfast."

"You're a great cook."

"I'm busy, David, and I like gardening. You know that." I yanked up some dandelions, the motions emphasizing my words.

"Remember the first time you spent the night at my place? I woke up to the smell of waffles. Waffles." He laughed. "I knew you were a keeper when you made me breakfast."

I smiled at the memory. "Yeah, well, no waffles today."

"Does that mean I get something else for breakfast? Because you're just what I had in mind." He pulled me to my feet, leaned in to kiss me, but pulled back and wrinkled his nose. "Damn. You need a shower first."

"Jesus, David, you sure know how to ruin a moment."

"Fine." He leaned in and pressed his lips dispassionately against mine. "Better?"

"Forget about it."

I turned back to the flower bed, but David grabbed my hand. "I'm sorry. We can go out for breakfast, okay?"

I stared at him, not saying anything.

He pulled me towards him. "Don't be like this. I'll make breakfast for you."

"You're a horrible cook."

He grinned. "See, that's another reason why I need you around. You keep my ego in check."

I couldn't help but grin back. "Let me shower and change, and then we can get breakfast at the farmers' market."

***

Since moving to Asheville, we'd continued our tradition of Saturday morning trips to the farmers' market. Aida loved looking at the bright flowers for sale, as well as charming the merchants into giving her free samples of whatever was in season. Berries, melons, fresh cheese — she loved them all.

At the edge of today's market, David recognized someone he knew, and they became deeply engrossed in lawyer talk. I could tell it was going to be a long discussion.

"We'll meet up with you later, okay?" I told him as Aida jumped from foot to foot next to me.

He nodded and waved us away, and we strolled towards the center of the market. Aida studied the booths around us as we walked, trying to determine which would be most likely to give her samples. I waited next to her, making my own list of what to purchase, when I felt a hand on my elbow and jumped.

"Did I scare you?" Andrew asked, a grin on his face. He looked delicious in civilian clothes, a t-shirt that clung slightly to his muscular chest and a baggy pair of cargo shorts.

"No. Maybe." I tried to frown at him, but it didn't work. "You don't come across as the farmers' market type."

"I'm full of surprises." He crouched down so he was eye level with Aida. "And who's your helper?"

"I'm Aida." She held out her hand for him to shake.

"Nice to meet you, Aida," he said, taking her hand in his. "I'm Andrew. I'm friends with your mama." He studied her face a moment, then looked at mine as he stood. "She looks just like you. I think it's the eyes."

I blushed under his scrutiny. "Is that a good thing?"

His eyes didn't leave mine. "Of course."

I looked away, but could feel him still watching me, which drove any response from my mind.

Fortunately, Aida broke in. "We're going sample hunting, Mr. Andrew. Would you like to come with?"

"Sample hunting?" Amusement crept into his voice. "I'd love to, if it's okay with your mama."

I shrugged. "Sure, if you want."

We walked along the row between the stands, our senses overwhelmed by the vibrant colors of the wares, the perfume of the peonies and tulips and fresh bread, the chatter of the crowds around us. As we paused for Aida to approach a stall, Andrew leaned close, his mouth near my ear.

"Your kid looks like she's having fun." His breath tickled, suffusing my body with a happy warmth I hoped he didn't notice.

"We do this every week. It gives her a chance to burn off some energy."

"And gets you out of the house too?"

I nodded.

"Shouldn't your hubby be around?"

"Why?"

"You don't seem like the type whose hubby would let her just wander around when she should be spending time with him instead. And talking to strange men? Bet he won't like that."

I turned to face him, the warmth gone. "You don't know anything about me or my husband." I glared at him. "I choose to spend time with him, or whoever I want. He doesn't force me to do anything."

He held up a hand in defense, as if to shield himself from my anger. "That's not what I meant."

"Oh, really? Care to explain, then?"

"The whole feminism thing is overrated. There's nothing wrong with needing to be taken care of, or taking care of your guy."

I rolled my eyes. "I'm my own person, Andrew. I don't need anyone taking care of me."

He stared at me hard, then broke into a grin. "You are impossible to talk to, you know that?"

I stared back, brow furrowed. "What?"

"Picking a fight about everything." His grin turned into that half-smirk of his. "How long has it been since you got laid?"

My jaw dropped. "That is none of your damn business."

"Yeah, that's what I thought." He chuckled.

Before I could offer a retort, David approached. His eyes narrowed as his gaze fell on Andrew, and he threw his arm around my shoulders. "Making some friends, Kase?"

"Yeah." I slipped my arm around David's waist, snuggling close to him. "This is Andrew, from the bookstore. Andrew, this is my husband, David."

David's grip on me tightened. "Nice to meet you."

"Likewise."

Neither man smiled.

Andrew turned his pale eyes to me. "I've got some stuff to do. See you around, Kasey." He nodded at me and walked away.

He passed Aida as she returned from a stall. She said something to him, the market too loud for me to hear, and offered him a handful of cherry tomatoes. He responded by popping a couple into his mouth, ruffling her hair, and continuing on his way.

I stared after him, my eyebrows still drawn together. Had that been an argument? I'd pissed him off, he'd pissed me off, but then he laughed it away. I wished my fights with David always ended like that.

"Just a friend?" David asked, his fingers digging painfully into my shoulder.

"Ow, David. Yes." I tried to shrug off his arm, but he held tight.

"He's a good-looking guy. You know what he does for a living?"

"Cop. David, you're hurting me. Let go."

"Probably doesn't make much." David stared after Andrew, by now at the other end of the market.

"Let go!"

"Sorry, Kase." David shook himself, eased his hold on me, and kissed my cheek as Aida approached. "You and Aida get some goodies?"

"Nothing yet." I rubbed my shoulder.

"Figures. Aida, what do you say we skip breakfast here and go get some lunch instead? It's getting pretty crowded."

I trailed behind them as we headed back to David's car, lost in thought. Why did Andrew even care about my sex life? I barely even knew the guy, and it wasn't as if he could do anything to change it. It wasn't as if I wanted him to do something to change it. *Right?*

***

Monday afternoon, back at the bookstore, a uniformed Andrew darted in for a cup of coffee and left without saying anything. He was on the clock; I understood.

Tuesday, however, he was at a table with Ron and Erica when I arrived. They all smiled, nodded at me, but there was no invitation to pull up a chair, no sliding over to make room for me, no fingers on my wrist when I walked by, no acknowledgment that we'd seen each other over the weekend. Maybe I'd pissed him off more than I'd realized.

The rest of the week continued like that, leading me to believe I'd imagined everything between us. It made sense; I was lonely, in a new town where I didn't know anyone. Perhaps I was subconsciously looking to make David jealous? Andrew was just being friendly.

I repeated that to myself on my way into McKay's Friday morning. I spent an awful lot of time in there, but today I had a purpose: to find a book on backyard landscaping and figure out a big project to focus on, something constructive to do instead of wandering around town developing one-sided friendships with single men.

After picking several books off the shelf, I dropped into an overstuffed couch in the back of the store. The first step was admitting I had a problem when it came to Andrew. Now to avoid said problem.

Engrossed in the books' bright, glossy pictures, I jumped when hands covered my eyes.

"Guess who."

"Will you stop sneaking up on me?" I leaned forward to free myself from Andrew's hands.

He let go, came around, and eased his tall frame onto the couch next to me. We weren't touching, but he was close enough I could smell his aftershave.

He flipped through one of the books lying next to me. "So, Suzie Homemaker's trying her hand at construction this weekend?"

"Something like that." I stared down at my book, tried not to encourage him.

"I miss doing projects like that. I've lived in an apartment so long, I'm losing all my man skills."

"Man skills?" I couldn't help but giggle at this.

"Yeah, man skills." He chuckled too. "Mowing the lawn, using power tools. Hell, I don't even have a grill." He let out an exaggerated sigh. "I'm an embarrassment to the male race."

"Buy a house."

"No point. Who knows when I'll get called up and sent over again."

"I thought you were getting called up?"

"Nope, false alarm. They really jerk you around. It's never certain until you're on base with all your gear, saying goodbye...."

I watched as he stared at the book in his lap, his pale blue eyes unfocused. Reflexively, I laid my hand on his arm. "You okay?"

"Yeah." He smiled, a sad smile that didn't reach his eyes. "Every time I ship out, I think it'll be better this time, but it's not."

"Stop going."

"Can't." He shrugged. "They need me over there more than anyone needs me here."

What could I say to that? I barely knew him, couldn't reassure him without it sounding false or patronizing. So I just left my hand on his arm.

"Enough about that." He patted my hand. "What're you building?"

"I don't know. Maybe a new patio, or just some flowerbeds. It depends how energetic I feel."

"Your hubby going to help?"

"Maybe. I think he'd rather pay someone to do it."

"Where's he work?"

"He's a lawyer."

"No wonder you can afford to sit around all day."

I glanced over at him, ready to fire off a response, but his smile took the sting out of his words. I smiled back. "And you said I'm the one who tries to pick fights?"

"Just making conversation." He looked down at his sand-colored watch, probably a standard-issue army device. "And, speaking of actually working for a living, I should get ready for my shift." He let go of my hand and stood up. "See ya around, Kasey."

"Yeah, see ya."

So much for avoiding the problem.

*\*\*\**

I spent the afternoon browsing through landscaping centers and greenhouses, ending with a trip to the Biltmore Estate gardens in search of further inspiration. When I finally returned home, David was there and in a jovial mood. He'd spent the last couple days taking the bar exam and was relieved to have finished, confident of his success. After having a few drinks with his new colleagues to celebrate, he'd left me a message saying he'd picked up Aida, a task that usually fell to me. I arrived home to find them playing Candyland in the living room.

"Where ya been, baby?" He stood up to give me a kiss.

I wrinkled my nose at the strong smell of alcohol on his breath. "How much have you had to drink?"

"Don't be mad, dear. I'm celebrating. I know I aced the bar, which means that in a month I'll be able to start taking cases in North Carolina. And when that happens, you know what I'm gonna do?"

I shook my head.

"Will you get me a pony, Daddy?" asked Aida.

"Yes, I most definitely will. A pony for my dear sweet daughter, and a big, long cruise for Mommy and me. How's that sound, Kase? Just you and me, reconnecting, living it up in a tropical paradise for a week or two?"

"Really, Daddy?" Aida squealed. "A pony?"

"Cross my heart. Scout's honor." He drew an "X" over his heart, then held up two fingers. "I promise."

"Really, David, a pony? Isn't that a bit much?"

"What? She's a good kid. She deserves a pony. And how can you say no to a face like this?" He pulled Aida over to his side, and they both stared at me with big sad eyes and exaggerated, pouting lips.

I kept a straight face as long as I could, then laughed and hugged them both. "I just want it known that I'm not taking care of it."

"Fine, fine," said David. "We all know you're too busy at that bookstore, anyway, to do much around here." I opened my mouth to protest, but he shook his head. "But let's not get into that tonight. How about dinner instead?"

"Let's go to Mac's," exclaimed Aida. Mac's was a local diner specializing in burgers as well as a variety of traditional Southern dishes, and it had quickly become Aida's favorite.

"I was thinking of something a little more upscale," said David, "someplace where we can celebrate in style."

"Please, Daddy?" Aida bounced on her heels. "Please? Please please please?"

"You and your mother decide. I'm getting a refill before we go." He got up, grabbed his tumbler, and left the room.

I looked down at my daughter. We'd named her after David's grandmother, but the name—from Italian for happy—fit her perfectly. No matter what happened, she always seemed able to adapt and maintain her sunny disposition.

"Of course we can go to Mac's, sweetie, if that's what you want." I pulled her into a hug, and she squirmed away.

David returned to the room shortly, full glass in hand. "Did you decide?"

"Mommy said we can go to Mac's, Daddy."

"Again? We always eat there. There are a million restaurants in this goddamned town, and we always eat at the same place."

"We can stay in for the night, if you'd prefer." I smiled at him, although I didn't feel it, not when he was drinking and bringing out the profanity. "You want to celebrate, right, David? Let's please not turn this into an argument."

"Who said anything about this turning into an argument?" He knocked back his drink in one large gulp. "I'm tired of staying in. We always eat here. You might be out all day meeting people at that fucking bookstore, but I'm stuck in the office and want to go somewhere for dinner."

"We don't have to go there if you don't want to, Daddy." Aida's eyes widened as she stared at her father. "I just really like it."

David looked down at his daughter and squeezed her shoulder with his empty hand. "No, it's okay, sweetie. We can go there if that's what you want."

"Aida, go get your shoes." After she left, I turned to my husband. "Everything okay?"

"Fine, fine. I'm just tired. Too much studying lately."

"Are you sure?" I put my arms around his neck and kissed his cheek. "If you want to talk about anything, anything at all, I'm always here to listen."

He scowled. "I said I'm fine. Jesus, Kase, just drop it, okay?"

I took a deep breath, held it a moment, then let it out. My thoughts flickered to Andrew, so eager to patch things up, wanting a family of his own to be around. "Fine."

***

The restaurant was busy for a Friday night, it being one of the few family-friendly, locally-owned restaurants that served alcohol. Aida kept up a running monologue of her day's events, and David half listened while scanning the crowd for people he knew. He hopped up a couple times to go over and say hello to acquaintances, and people approached our table several times.

I nodded and smiled, knowing all the right things to say after years of practice. "Nice to meet you, lovely family, yes, thanks, we're very proud of him, nice meeting you too."

By the end of the meal I was tired, worn out from constantly being on display. A headache had been growing all evening, David had tossed back several glasses of wine with dinner, and all I wanted now was to leave quietly.

It was not to be. Walking out of the restaurant, we passed a table full of police officers enjoying some burgers, Andrew among them. He was sitting farthest from me, and greeted me in typical Southern fashion as I passed—head nod, raised palm—and then, to make sure that I noticed him, he called out, "Hey, Kasey."

David swung back to the table, hands clenched into fists. "Leave my wife alone," he slurred loudly.

"David." I put my hand on his arm to calm him, to restrain him if necessary, while Aida watched with wide blue eyes.

"Excuse me?" Andrew said, clearly taken aback by David's overreaction to a simple greeting.

"You better back off," David continued, shaking off my hand. "She's married. To me."

"David," I said more loudly, firmly. "Andrew is just saying hi. Let's go."

"Everything okay, Kasey?" Andrew frowned, eyes narrowed.

"Yes, fine. We're just leaving." I pulled on David's arm, but he held firmly rooted in place, his bulk and his anger giving him an advantage.

"You hear me? She's married."

"Yes, he knows. Now come on, please. Let's go home before you do something stupid."

"Something stupid, eh?" His voice was still too loud for the situation, louder than I liked. "Are you insulting me?"

"David, please. Not here, not in front of everyone," I said in a voice only he could hear. "Let's just go, okay?"

He eyed Andrew up and down, still not moving.

Andrew watched him carefully, tensed and ready to leap up at any moment.

David nodded once to himself, as if satisfied with the situation, then took Aida's hand in his and headed towards the restaurant's exit.

I shot Andrew an apologetic look and hurried after my family, catching up with them as David was unlocking his SUV. "Give me the keys, please."

"Why?" He smiled at me, the same smile I imagined he used in court when he knew his client was guilty and tried to convince the jury otherwise.

"Aida, climb on in." I waited for our daughter to get in. "Because you're drunk." Because you're being an asshole, I wanted to tell him.

"Kase, don't be ridiculous." His smile grew. "I'm just fine."

"No. You had most of a bottle of wine, as well as God knows how many drinks before dinner." I reached over, tried to grab the keys from his hand. "Give me the keys."

He grabbed my wrist with his free hand, squeezing until I winced. Still smiling, he said, "I'm fine. Get in the car."

"No." I stared hard at him.

"I'm fine. Watch." He dropped my wrist, then heel-to-toe walked about ten paces with his arms out. He laughed. "See?"

"David—"

He walked back and kissed my forehead. "I'm fine. Stop worrying and get in the car."

Through the slightly tinted windows, Aida's eyes followed our every move. She must've been scared out of her mind.

I sighed, walked around and got in.

Once the car was in motion, David turned to me and asked cheerfully, "You close to that guy, dear?"

"I told you, he's just someone from the bookstore."

"He doesn't seem like your type."

"He's just a guy at the bookstore." I clenched my fists in my lap. All I wanted was to get home before this got any worse.

"Adams, right? He's been a witness in a couple of the cases I've observed. From what I understand, he has a lot of issues. Stay away from him."

"I barely know him, but he seems okay."

"Well, he's not." He stared straight ahead, concentrating on the road. Then, quietly, so that Aida wouldn't hear from the backseat, he asked, "You fucking him?"

"What?" I tried to keep Aida from hearing. I felt guiltier than I had reason to feel; thoughts weren't the same as actions, and whatever feelings I had for Andrew wouldn't be acted on. "Jesus, David, of course not."

"Good," he said, in a low, calm voice, "because if I find out you are, I'll kill you both. He so much as touches you, I'll kill you both. Understand me?"

"Oh my God, David." Fury and frustration edged out any fear I might feel at his threats. "What the hell is your problem tonight?"

"That asshole wanting to fuck my wife is the problem." He pounded his fists on the steering wheel and slammed on the brakes so hard I was thrown towards the dash. "You stay away from him, or, so help me God, you'll both regret it."

In the backseat, Aida cried out and began sobbing. I turned around to console her, and David chose that moment to floor the gas, knocking me back into my seat.

Before I could react, he told Aida in a soft, cheerful voice. "It's okay, pumpkin. Mommy and Daddy are just working out some problems. No need to cry, okay?"

Aida sniffed. "I don't like it when you yell."

"I won't yell anymore, kiddo. Mommy almost made a very bad choice, but everything's fine now, right, Kase?"

I took a deep breath, fuming at his behavior, and tried to smile. "Everything will be just fine, sweetie," I reassured her.

As soon as we arrived home, I scooped up Aida, even though she was big enough to walk, and rushed into the house, a messy mix of anger, embarrassment, fear, and guilt. I needed some time away from David to calm down. Perhaps realizing he'd gone too far, he stayed in his SUV and drove off; whether to drink in a bar, sleep with some random woman, or drive off a cliff wasn't something that concerned me at the moment.

We sat on Aida's bed, leaning against the headboard, my arms around her. I didn't know what to say, how to reassure her. Tonight my husband had revealed a side of himself I'd never seen before. Had it always been there, tamped down, controlled? Or had it developed over time, part of the new David who valued status and image over all else? More importantly, was this a permanent part of him, something we'd see again?

"Mommy?"

"Mmm?"

"Why did Daddy get mad about Mr. Andrew?"

I thought for a moment. "Remember back in Richmond, how Colbie got mad when you played with Hayleigh, instead of her?"

"Yeah?"

"Well, this is the same kind of thing. Daddy is like Colbie. He thinks I should spend more time with him than Mr. Andrew."

"Why can't you all just play together? That's what me and Colbie and Hayleigh did."

Imagining David's reaction to that made me smile. "That would certainly fix everything." I kissed her head. "Now put your pajamas on and brush your teeth, and don't worry about Daddy and Mr. Andrew."

She hopped off the bed, then turned back to me. "Will Daddy stop yelling?"

"Yes, Daddy's done yelling." I hoped I was right.

***

After Aida was in bed, I allowed myself to think back on the evening. I stomped around the master bedroom, hurling dirty clothes into a laundry basket, and then practically kicking the basket out of the room. How dare David get upset with me for merely saying "hi" to another man! He'd never been the controlling type, not really. Sure, maybe he'd encouraged me to befriend the other stay-at-home mothers in our gated neighborhood, and he'd pushed me to join committees and attend social events with his colleagues' wives, but that was only because he knew of my shyness and wanted me to fit in. At the very least, he'd never flat-out forbidden me to talk to someone.

And what audacity, to accuse me of cheating. To accuse *me*, after what he'd done? My mind flashed to the figures in the pictures I'd received, pictures I'd never be able to forget. David — my perfect husband and partner — had slept with someone else. He'd been so unhappy with me, with our lives together, that he'd turned to someone else.

Those pictures.... My anger disappeared, and I sank down to the floor, back against the bed. I just wanted David to be happy, for both of us to be happy together. I'd done everything he wanted, and it hadn't been enough. My everything hadn't been enough. Head in my hands, sobs wracked my body as I released all the pent-up frustration, anger, and grief from the past few months.

"Kase?" said a voice from the doorway.

I looked up at David, wiping my cheeks with the back of my hands. "Yeah?"

"You okay?" He came into the room and sat down on the floor next to me.

I looked at him, my face streaked with tears, and didn't say a word.

"I'm sorry for what I said. It was unfair."

"Yeah, it was."

His breath reeked of alcohol. "I just don't want anything to get in the way of fixing us. Or any*one*. You understand, right?"

"Yeah." That was my husband, always looking out for my best interests.

"I won't yell again. I promise."

I stood up. "I'm tired. Goodnight, David." Before he could respond, I walked out the door and down the hall to the guest bedroom.

He didn't follow.

Sleep was a long time coming for me. My mind raced, thinking of what David had said, what he'd done to me, and especially what could be so wrong with Andrew that my husband would react so strongly to him.

# Chapter 8 – Andrew (Age 17)

"Quick, quick, get in the car," TJ shouted.

We piled in, me and Mark in the backseat and Dale up front with TJ, and as soon as the doors were shut the car peeled away with a screech of tires. We raced down the narrow road in the dark, headlights off.

"What happened?" Mark asked.

He and I had been best friends longer than I could remember, always egging each other on to pull increasingly stupid and dangerous stunts.

"I thought I heard someone coming," said TJ. He could've been our voice of reason except he was just as fucked up as the rest of us.

"You ass." Dale smacked TJ in the back of the head. The car swerved slightly as TJ tried to avoid the blow. "There wasn't no one. Fuck, we was almost done, too." Dale leaned back, lit a cigarette and took a drag.

Our project for the night was vandalizing our principal's house. He was away for the week at a conference or something, so we took it upon ourselves to spray paint some messages on his siding, TP his trees, bust out a few windows. Fun harmless stuff.

"I thought I heard someone," TJ insisted. "I don't wanna get caught."

Dale leaned over and smacked TJ upside the head again. "Stop being a pussy. Ain't no one gonna catch us."

TJ glared at Dale but didn't say anything. Didn't wanna get smacked again, and I didn't blame him. Dale was a mean son of a bitch, probably the most fucked up and uncaring of all of us, and that was saying a lot.

Just another small town Mississippi night, stuck in a little shithole town with jack-nothing to do. Weren't no jobs here but people stayed because of their families, and family was everything when you ain't got nothing, even when you hated them. All us kids growing up here knew life would suck. Sure, you could try to get that American dream of a nice car, a girl you loved who loved you back, kids and a dog, a decent house and a job that paid the bills— but it was hard to come by.

Chances were you'd marry someone you argued with and who cheated on you, working a job that didn't quite pay enough for an asshole boss, ending up with a kid who was just like me. We were all heading that way anyways, me and Mark and Dale and TJ, if we didn't end up in jail first. Hell, Dale even had a kid already, a cute snot-faced little girl who stayed with her mama. That helped explain why Dale was how he was, because he knew he'd fucked up royally, fucked up at least three lives so far; a lot of pressure when you were only seventeen.

We drove around for a while, smoking cigarettes and talking about girls we wanted to fuck, before heading home. Dale lived with an aunt who couldn't care less if he was dead in a ditch, so he could stay out as late as he wanted, but the rest of us had a curfew. TJ's was set by his parents and mine and Mark's by the courts, so most nights we were all home on time. I wasn't ready for jail yet, not for a few underage drinking incidents, at least.

They dropped me off and TJ said he'd see me tomorrow at school, but I wasn't sure about that. I wasn't big on school; didn't see how a bunch of teachers could really show me anything useful, and besides, what good was an education? There was a factory here, a few of them I guess if you didn't mind driving, that hired just about anyone. I'd probably end up there; hell, we probably all would. Lots of truckers around here too, since everyone wanted to get the hell out of this place, but that wouldn't be an easy job to get, what with me having a DUI on my record.

I got home just a few minutes after eleven so I snuck in real quiet, hoping no one noticed. No such luck. Gary, my asshole stepdad, was sitting in the kitchen waiting for me.

"You're late, Andy," he said, putting down his magazine and looking up at me.

I hated being called Andy, always had, and he knew it. I could feel myself getting angry.

He noticed it too.

"Where you been tonight, Andy?" he asked while I was trying to edge past him to my room.

Damn it, he was trying to make me mad on purpose. I tried to stay calm but I wasn't very good at it. I didn't answer him.

"I asked you a question, boy," he said, getting up from the table and coming towards me.

A couple empty coke cans sat on the counter. He didn't drink coke plain, so he was probably pretty wasted. This wasn't gonna be pretty. I still didn't answer him.

I moved away from him, but he was faster than me. Bigger than me, too. I was 6'2", muscular but wiry, and no match for him. He was several inches shorter but he had about seventy-five pounds on me.

Gary threw me up against the wall. My head cracked against it so hard little specks of light danced in front of my eyes for a moment. We glared at each other with pure hatred. I'd never been able to do anything right according to him, so I stopped trying.

"Where you been?"

I could smell the whiskey on his breath. My head hurt, I was tired, and I didn't want to deal with this. "None of your damn business," I told him, knowing exactly how he'd react.

Sure enough, *crack*. My head hit the wall again and blood spurted out my nose. Pain raced outward from the center of my face.

Something inside me snapped. Gary had broken my nose one too many times. I made a fist and punched him in the gut. Then real quick I got him in the face. Now it was his turn to bleed.

At this point Mama came into the kitchen. She looked at us both, me standing above my stepdad with blood dripping down my face, him lying on the floor holding his own nose. She sobbed, of course, her reaction whenever I disappointed her, which happened a lot.

"Sorry, Mama." I looked at Gary on the floor. His stomach was exposed as he lay there so I kicked him, not hard but hard enough.

"Don't you ever fucking touch me again," I said, and walked out the door.

The night was cooling off but it was still sticky. I loved the humidity of the South. I loved everything about the South, actually: the weather, the history and culture, the food. As much as I complained about being here, I couldn't imagine living anywhere else.

I hopped in my car and drove off into the night. My car was crappy as hell, just a twelve-year-old Pontiac Grand AM POS, but it ran and had an awesome stereo and that was what mattered. My dad bought it for me last summer, and I was real grateful to him for it. Things got bad at home a lot and it was real nice to be able to leave when I needed to. Like tonight.

I headed towards Carly's place, listening to a Megadeth tape blasted real loud. I needed something so loud that I couldn't think. Me and Carly had been close since we were little. Gary had a huge problem with our friendship, on account of her being black and him being a racist asshole, but I loved her to death and wouldn't give her up for the world. We'd messed around some, but she was a friend first and foremost. We knew each other too well to be anything else. I'd say she was like a sister to me except she looked real good naked, and sometimes my thoughts were less than brotherly.

When I got to her trailer, a dull light shone in her window even though it was late. She was probably still up studying. She liked school and got mad when I skipped it. She was a good kid, and sometimes I wondered why she even put up with me. Like tonight.

I parked in front and walked around to look in her bedroom window. Her mama worked two jobs and Carly had a couple little sisters who were probably asleep. I always tried to be real quiet and respectful when I was over, especially late at night. Sure enough, she was lying on her bed reading a textbook. I tapped on her window, soft enough to not wake her sisters.

She jerked her head up, real scared for a second, but then she recognized me and relaxed. She came over and opened the window.

"Dear Lord, Andrew, what happened to you?"

"I got home a few minutes late." She'd seen this happen enough times over the years that I didn't have to explain more. She looked like she was about to cry though, and I felt real guilty for bothering her with this.

"Go around to the front and I'll let you in."

I met her at the door and she led me inside to the bathroom. I sat on the toilet as she wet a washrag and gently wiped the blood off my face. Even though she was being real careful, it still hurt and I winced, which caused big fat tears to roll down her cheeks.

"I'm sorry, Carly." Sorry that I couldn't control my temper and stuff like this happened. Sorry I disappointed everyone. Sorry I couldn't fix her problems like I wanted to. Sorry my life sucked and she was the one stuck straightening it out. But all that came out was sorry.

She nodded. We'd known each other long enough that she knew what I wanted to say but couldn't.

"I love you, Carly Ann Jefferson," I told her. I meant it, too.

She just smiled at me, this great big wonderful pretty smile, and went back to cleaning my face up. She wanted to be a nurse some day. I always told her she could be a doctor if she wanted to, but she always just shook her head and said a nurse was good enough for her.

"You need to stay here tonight?" she asked.

I nodded. No use telling her what I'd done. No use making her worry.

"I'll fix up a spot on the couch for you."

"Can't I sleep with you?" My nose throbbed like hell, definitely broken, so I didn't feel up to messing around with her tonight, but it sure would feel good to fall asleep cuddling her.

She shook her head. "Mama'll be home late tonight, and she wouldn't be too happy about that."

Ms. Jefferson liked me, tolerated me at least, but Carly was right that she wouldn't be too keen on me in bed with her daughter, even with both of us clothed.

***

I woke up in the morning to the smell of coffee and bacon. I got up, stretched, and followed my aching nose to the kitchenette. Ms. Jefferson was sitting at the table drinking coffee. Carly's younger sisters were there too, chowing down on bacon and cereal.

"Morning, Andrew," she said to me, then looked up and gasped. "Lordy, boy, what happened to you?"

I hadn't looked in the mirror yet so I didn't know how bad I looked exactly, but I got an idea based on how bad I felt.

"My stepdad was drunk." I didn't need to say no more; she'd been through this enough times with me over the years to hear what I left out.

She nodded, stirred coffee that was just slightly lighter than her skin. "Well, help yourself to some breakfast."

I liked being at Carly's house. Her family'd been through a lot—her dad got picked up for selling drugs when her youngest sister was a baby and had been out of the picture ever since—but instead of reacting to it by arguing and fighting like most people would, they were all as close as could be, a real family, taking care of each other. I hoped to have that some day, if I ever got straightened up enough.

Carly didn't ever skip school, so I ended up going too. I felt horrible and looked worse, and spent most of the day sleeping. I was a smart enough guy, sure, but didn't see the point of these classes for the most part. It was early in the semester and I was already failing all my classes. Failed them all last year too, and if I didn't like them enough to pass the first time, you could bet your ass I wasn't going to like them the second time. Most of my teachers didn't care if I slept, as long as I wasn't disruptive. For those that did yell at me, well, I just didn't go to their classes. Problem solved.

During fourth period someone knocked on the door. An assistant principal and a sheriff's deputy walked in, looking for me. I wondered how they knew it was me last night at the principal's house, but I didn't wonder too hard. It didn't matter. I was too tired, too worn out with life to care about much of anything.

They escorted me down the hall to an empty office, walking on either side of me like they expected me to take off. Which I couldn't do, because they were walking on either side of me. My mama was waiting in the room for me, which was a real bad sign.

It turned out to be some kind of intervention program. Either I signed up for some alternative school thing, or they kicked me out of this school, which meant I'd be violating my probation for stealing a car a couple years ago, and that would mean some real jail time. They also hinted that if I didn't cooperate I might be facing some assault charges for last night, but that bullshit wouldn't fly because any fool could see by looking at me that it was self-defense.

I asked for a day or two to figure it all out, which surprised them I think. My mind was already racing with my options, like heading out that night to Kentucky to live with my dad, or flat-out burning down the school.

They said I had until the following morning.

Mama didn't look at me much or say anything. She'd been crying again.

I didn't say much to her either. What could I say that I hadn't said a hundred times before? She'd made her choices and we lived with the consequences. About time maybe I did the same.

After school I spotted TJ and Mark in the parking lot; Dale dropped out a year or two ago and wasn't allowed on school grounds.

Mark whistled and said, "You look like shit, man."

"Fuck you."

"I saw you and Carly getting here together this morning," he said. "You hit that last night?"

"Hell yeah. Fucked the bitch all night long. She's a real nice piece of ass."

I expected laughs but got nothing. I turned my head and Carly was standing right there, looking at me with eyes so full of hurt and betrayal that it about broke my heart.

"I was just playing," I told her. "Joking with the guys."

"Fuck you, Andrew!" She fought hard not to cry in front of everyone, a real private person. "Fuck you." She turned and stormed off.

"Carly, I was just joking around!" I followed her, but she gave me the finger and kept walking.

"Guess he's not getting any tonight," I heard Mark say, and TJ laughed.

Everything went white with rage. I turned back and punched Mark hard. He went down but scrambled to his feet, angry.

"What the fuck is your problem, man?" He rubbed his jaw where I'd hit him.

I responded with another punch but he dodged this one. I swung again and still didn't connect. He was a solid guy but he wasn't fighting back. A crowd gathered around us, cheering us on. I swung again, made contact. He finally swung and got a direct blow to my nose, right where Gary got me last night. I fell to my knees, unable to stand because of the pain. The crowd, sensing that the fight was over, quickly broke up.

Mark looked at me and shook his head. "You got problems, man." He and TJ walked away, leaving me sitting on my knees in the parking lot.

I stayed there, kneeling, unmoving, until the lot was empty except for a few teachers' cars. Then they too were gone. Everyone drove around me, ignoring and avoiding me.

I felt lonely, empty. I'd fucked up again, and this time I didn't know how to fix it. Maybe it wasn't even worth fixing. I sure could've used a drink right now, or a cigarette. I needed to fix things with Carly but I didn't know how, didn't know if I should even bother. She didn't need me messing up her life anymore.

I didn't get up though. I stayed there and asked God what I should do, asked Him to forgive me, asked Him to cast out the demons that tempted me. I asked Him for a sign.

I stayed there for a while, sitting back on my heels in the school parking lot, talking to God. He'd been the one constant in my life and I hated to disappoint Him, but it seemed like I just couldn't do anything right. Most of the time I didn't care, or at least pretended not to care, but not right now. Not today.

After awhile footsteps crunched in the gravel towards me. I ignored them, figuring it was just someone gonna yell at me more, and I'd get mad and do something and make things worse. I wished whoever it was would just go away.

They didn't though. A pair of brown feet in dusty white flipflops stopped in front of me: Carly, with her usual green toenails. She knelt down in front of me and wrapped her arms around me, not saying anything.

I leaned my head on her shoulder and, before I knew it, started crying, sobbing like a baby right there in that empty school parking lot. She didn't say anything, just let me cry.

My tears stopped and still she held me.

After awhile she let go, stood up, and pulled me to my feet.

"Mama said to tell you that you're welcome to come to dinner tonight."

I knew then I was gonna stay here in this shithole little town, gonna do that alternative program and graduate, gonna be someone some day, because I had someone right here was worth being someone for.

# Chapter 9 – Kasey (Present)

"All you intellectuals are the same," Andrew declared one early September afternoon as he sat at a table in McKay's, sipping his coffee.

"Erudite?" Mike, the college student, said without looking up from his notebook.

"Sagacious?" I suggested from my seat next to Andrew.

"Sophic, perhaps?" Mike grinned at me.

"Recondite?"

"How perspicacious of you to pick up on that."

"See, that just illustrates my point," said Andrew.

"And what is your point?" I exchanged a smile with Mike.

"Y'all think y'all are better than everyone just because y'all are so smart and know so much. But what good is that if you haven't experienced life any?"

"Who said we haven't experienced anything?" Mike asked indignantly.

"And who said we think we're better than everyone else?" My brow furrowed in hurt confusion.

"You're what, eighteen? Nineteen? What have you experienced in life?" Andrew asked Mike. "Have you watched your best friend die, with nothing you could do about it?"

"I watched my mom die of cancer. There was nothing I could do about that."

"Yes, but that's different. You could prepare for that. You don't prepare for your best friend to be alive, laughing with you, and then suddenly not."

"It's always about the wars with you, isn't it?" Mike sat very still, his breath steady and controlled. "Poor Andrew, the war hero."

"That's low, man." Andrew's eyes unfocused slightly, staring at the coffee mug in front of him. "I saw a lot of bad shit over there."

"We're not saying you didn't." I leaned in towards him. "But you need to recognize everyone's experienced loss. Everyone has problems, and while they might not be the same as yours, might not be as intense, people still feel just as strongly as you do."

Andrew watched me as I spoke. "You don't know what I've been through."

"You don't know what I've been through, or what Mike's been through. And it's insulting for you to accuse us of assuming we're better than everyone when you do the same thing."

"I don't think I'm better than everyone."

"Yes, you do," Mike said under his breath. Andrew shot him a withering glance, and Mike ducked his head back to his notes.

"Yes, you do." I repeated Mike's words firmly, more loudly. Andrew stared hard at me, and I met his eyes, not willing to back down.

Over the past month Andrew and I had spent more and more time together at the bookstore. While sometimes our chats were friendly, joking about superficial subjects, more often they were small sparring matches over politics and our views on the world. Neither of us held any thoughts back; when one was wrong, or out of line, the other called him or her on it immediately. Sometimes other patrons joined in the discussion, interjecting their opinions when pertinent, but often it was just the two of us.

Andrew stood up, drawing himself to his full height as if to use that as another point against me. "That's it. You need a time-out."

Before I could react, he picked me up and threw me over his shoulder.

"Put me down, you idiot!" I laughed in spite of myself, my cheeks burning, as I felt everyone's eyes upon me, watching my feeble struggles to free myself. Andrew was strong, however, and his grip on my legs never wavered.

He dumped me onto an overstuffed armchair among the stacks. "You can come back when you're able to play nice," he said with a straight face, then strode back to his table.

I popped back up and followed him.

Not giving me time to sit down, he grabbed me, slung me over his shoulder, and threw me into the armchair again. I struggled to get up, but he hovered over me, pinning me with his presence.

I willed my breath to even out, my heart to stop pounding. Andrew was so close, practically lying on top of me, and it would be so easy to bend my neck, kiss his lips....

"That wasn't a very long time-out." He stared down at me. Was he aware of how close we were?

"Let me up, Andrew."

"I meant what I said, Kasey. You're real smart, but that doesn't count for much in life."

"I disagree. Being smart is a good thing."

"Your husband's a smart guy, but you're still having problems."

"Where is this even coming from? What's bothering you today?"

He studied me, and I flushed under his scrutiny. Finally, he stood up. "You think too much, you know that?"

"You make no sense sometimes, you know that?"

"You ever give your mind a vacation, just let yourself feel instead of overthinking all the time?"

"I don't overthink."

"Yes, you do. Right now, for example."

"What am I overthinking?"

"Everything." He smiled and walked away.

I remained where he'd left me, marveling at the man. He was never what I expected, full of constantly shifting moods: sometimes playful, sometimes angry, but never apologetic, never explaining himself.

And what was it with him about David? I hadn't told Andrew anything about our problems, about why we'd moved to Asheville, but he knew we were having some kind of issues. He didn't bring them up, just dropped them into conversation as a dig on David. Why was he so envious, so angry about my marriage? It wasn't as if he expected me to leave my husband for him. *Right?*

Andrew and David were so similar. Both were confident—overly confident, most of the time. Both were opinionated, decisive. Both needed to be in control. So why, then, was my reaction so different? When Andrew irritated me, I fought back. When David irritated me, I rolled over and gave in. Why did I feel Andrew and I balanced each other out, while with David I wasn't a partner so much as a supporter?

It hadn't always been like that. When we'd first started dating, he listened to me, my opinion just as valid as his, just as relevant. Then it all changed. He needed someone to help him, to back him up. It was romantic, the wife taking care of her doting husband, until life got in the way. My opinions led to arguments, and, tired from chasing after Aida all day, it became easier for me to give in.

Maybe I needed to fight back with David, go after what I wanted, say what I thought. I smiled. Maybe my friendship with Andrew could be a positive thing for my marriage, after all.

I stood and walked back to the cafe. A dozen or so patrons sat at the tables, singly or in pairs, sipping their drinks, flipping through books or magazines, and chatting quietly. A routine day.

Andrew looked up from his own magazine as I approached. "Think you can behave yourself now?" His face revealed no hint he'd done anything out of the ordinary.

"I think so," I said, equally earnest.

"Good, because next time you misbehave you're getting a spanking." Still the straight face. He went back to his magazine. At the next table over, Mike snickered.

My eyebrows shot up, and a shiver of warmth permeated my body. "Excuse me?"

"You heard me." He didn't look up, continued reading his magazine.

"Guess I'd better be good then." I sat down across from him and flipped through my own magazine, trying to focus on an article about school fundraising ideas, but my mind took a different track. Andrew and me in bed, naked bodies pressed together, kissing, touching....

A hand rested on my shoulder, and I jumped.

"Sorry to startle you, Kase." It was David.

I turned around and looked up at him. "Hey, hi! What are you doing here?"

"Nice to see you too." He grinned at me and sat down in the third empty chair at the table.

Andrew continued to read his magazine, but I sensed him tensing, listening.

"Sorry, it's just that you've never been by here before." It was difficult keeping the frown off my face. McKay's was my place, my world, somewhere I could be myself, or whoever I wanted to be, without any expectations or pressure from David. I reminded myself of my decision to be more assertive and amended it to include being myself, being whoever I wanted to be, around David too.

"I got some great news today, and thought I'd tell you right away in person. I assumed you'd be here, since you're always at this place."

I ignored the slight barb. "What's the news?"

"I passed the bar. I'm a North Carolina lawyer!"

"That's wonderful, David! When do you start taking cases?"

"Immediately."

"That's great news." I smiled at him.

"So I thought, to celebrate, we could go out to lunch now. That is, if I can get you away from this place."

I again ignored his comment. "There's a PTA meeting this afternoon, but I can definitely fit in lunch." I stood up. "See ya, Andrew."

Andrew glanced up at me, regarding me for a moment with his piercing blue eyes. I had no idea what was going through his mind. "See ya."

David held the door for me as we walked out into the bright late summer sunshine. I slipped my hand into his as we walked down the sidewalk.

"Where to?" I asked.

"Do you always sit that close to him?" David stared straight ahead as he spoke.

"Who?" I knew exactly to whom he was referring.

"That guy, Adams."

"We weren't close. Jesus, David, can't I even sit at the same table as someone?"

"I told you to stay away from him."

From the corner of my eye I saw a muscle tighten in his jaw. I stopped and dropped his hand. "And I've told you, we're just friends."

"Damn it, Kasey." He grabbed my hand and continued walking, jerking me along behind him. "Why do you have to be like this today?"

"Like what?" I glared at him.

"So negative, so argumentative. Why can't you just be happy for me today?"

"I am happy for you. Why can't you be happy that I'm making friends?"

"Those people aren't friends, they're acquaintances. They're people you see and say hi to, but not people who care about you." He stopped, took both my hands in his, and looked into my eyes. "They're not at our level."

"Our level?"

"I'm a lawyer. I might not be as important as I was in Richmond, but I'll get there. You need friends who are important too, friends who understand what it's like to be important. Friends that matter."

"Like your colleagues' wives."

"Exactly."

I jerked my hands free again. "None of that matters, David. I don't want to be friends with people like that. I want friends who care about me because of who I am, not because of who I married."

"Now, Kasey, I'm telling you this because I want you to be happy. You know that, right? And usually we're happiest with people we have the most in common with, that's all." He smiled at me, a smug patronizing expression.

"I'm happy with the people at the bookshop." Realizing that I sounded petulant instead of assertive, I took a deep breath. "Look, I understand your concern, but please keep in mind —"

His cell phone rang, and he held up a finger as he checked who was calling. "I have to take this." He spoke into the phone while I stood there, arms folded across my chest. "Yeah...yeah... now? I had plans.... Yeah, I understand. Okay." He hung up and turned back to me. "They need me back at the office. We'll talk tonight." He kissed my forehead and started off, leaving me standing by myself on the sidewalk.

"You can't just walk away in the middle of a conversation," I called after him.

He turned and came back. "That was a partner at the firm. I told him I had plans, but he still needs me to come in. I can't exactly say no."

"Why not? Tell him you're taking your wife to lunch."

He sighed and rubbed the bridge of his nose. "I can't. It just doesn't work that way."

"Right. Work always comes first." I started to walk back the way we'd come.

"Kase, wait." He grabbed my arm. "I need to make a good impression on these guys, and if that means I have to skip lunch with you, well, I'm sorry. Right now, yeah, work does come first. Once I'm established, we'll have time for us again. Promise." He looked into my eyes. "Promise."

I sighed. "Fine."

The muscles in his jaw ticked. "I'm doing this for you. I'm putting in long hours trying to establish myself here, for you. I'm missing out on time I could be spending with you and Aida, because you wanted to move here. Let me remind you, this was your idea, and I'm the one making it work. So I'm sorry if I can't spend all day sitting on my ass like you can."

"Let me remind you of the reason I wanted to move. Should I have just moved out? I was so close to taking Aida and leaving, David, but I thought we could make this work. That means both of us making the effort."

"I'm making a fucking effort!" His face turned red. "Really, I am, but I need a little understanding from you. I swear to God, you get like this and —"

"And what?"

"I need to get back to the office."

"And what, David?"

"Forget it. I'll see you tonight." He turned and walked away.

I let him go this time, unsure of what exactly had just happened. Recently, it seemed as if every little thing between us escalated into an argument, despite my best intentions. If I ignored David's snide comments, his condescending tone, he continued to make them until he got a rise out of me. If I attempted to defend myself, he attacked back, then ended it by leaving in a huff.

Had moving to Asheville been the right choice? At least in Richmond I'd had friends, although they hadn't exactly been friends. Fair-weather friends was a more apt description, friends when I had been one of them, when I hadn't needed them for anything.

Andrew would still be at McKay's, so I considered going back. Maybe I could talk to him about this, since he was the closest thing I had to a friend here. It wasn't hard to imagine his reaction; he'd tear David apart either verbally or, God forbid, literally. No, best to let it go for now. David was right: we'd definitely talk about this tonight. I'd see to it.

*** 

I thought more about it all at the afternoon's PTA meeting. True to my word, I'd joined the organization as soon as school started. And, as expected, the women were identical to those in Richmond: same husbands, same haircuts, same attitudes. They engaged in the same false sincerity, the same vicious attacks on the members not present. Sitting there, listening to the women pretend to flatter each other with thinly-veiled insults and comparisons, I wondered why I'd even joined an activity I disliked so much. Maybe I should resign, find something else. There had to be people I could relate to somewhere in this town.

My phone beeped, and I glanced down at a new text message from David: *sry abt erlier. lts do dinner mk it up to u. luv u.*

His abbreviated message made me smile. At thirty-two, David was young enough to be on the cutting edge of technology, yet old enough to appear silly following the latest trends, including his text message spelling.

*sounds good. luv u 2*, I responded.

After the official end of business, the PTA members milled around, chatting and making plans for the weekend. I tried to slip out without anyone noticing, wanting to avoid the hated small talk. To others, it may have come across as selfish, but I didn't care to hear the small details of someone's background, to listen to anecdotes about her family, to search for a common acquaintance, especially if my conversation partner was someone I would only see again in a superficial setting. And if I didn't care to get to know someone, chances were she felt the same way about me, even though she was probably too polite to ever admit it.

"I don't think we've met yet." A blond woman in a gray velvety tracksuit approached me, effectively blocking my exit route. "I'm LuAnn. Capital *a*, no *e*."

"Kasey. Lowercase *a*, one *e*."

LuAnn chuckled as if this was one of the cleverest things she'd ever heard. "Welcome to the PTA. I meant to welcome you at our last meeting, but you slipped out before I had a chance to introduce myself."

"Well, you caught me this time."

"What brings you to the PTA?"

"My husband forced me to get involved in the community. It was either this or read to blind inmates."

"You are so funny, bless your heart." LuAnn chuckled again. "Just wait until the Girls meet you. They'll love you." She waved over a couple women who had been standing by the door. "Kasey, this is Krista and Monica. Girls, this is Kasey, our new member this year."

I pasted on a smile as I faced the Girls. Krista and Monica wore outfits similar to LuAnn's, and I bit back a comment about the Three Stooges. "Nice to meet you."

"So, tell us about yourself," said LuAnn.

"Well, I'm new to town."

"And what does your husband do?"

"He's a lawyer."

"My husband's a doctor, but Krista is married to a lawyer. And Monica's husband is an architect."

I nodded. David would be pleased; these were definitely our kind of people.

"And tell us about your children."

"Aida is in first grade and about as normal as they come."

"Bryson—that's my son—is in second grade and loves to read," said LuAnn. "I'm so proud of him."

"Cole loves to read too. He always has his nose in a book," said Krista/Monica. I wasn't sure who was who and equally sure it didn't really matter.

"Nairobi does too, except when she's at soccer practice. She's a great athlete," said the other Krista/Monica.

"Bryson's coach said he's the best Little Leaguer he's ever seen."

"Your husband is the coach!"

"He's had a lot of experience coaching, though. I believe him."

"Cole is good at sports too. And Jillian has a lot of potential."

"Jillian is three! How could you even tell at this point?"

"Nairobi could read by the time she was three."

"So could Bryson. But it was expected, since he was walking at nine months."

"Jillian was walking at eight months. We were so proud of her."

"Nairobi was signing at four months."

I couldn't help it; I laughed, which quickly turned into a cough as I felt the Girls' eyes on me.

"What about Aida?" asked LuAnn.

"Like I said, she's about as normal as they come. I, of course, think she's wonderful, but don't we all think that about our kids?" I smiled at them innocently.

"Well, yes, of course." LuAnn was clearly taken aback by my refusal to get into the bragging competition.

I checked my watch. "It's been lovely chatting with you ladies, but I should really get going. It was nice meeting y'all!" I moved towards the door as fast as I politely could.

Halfway there, however, I stopped and looked around for the chairwoman. She was standing in a corner, surrounded by a handful of women.

"Excuse me." I pushed my way next to her. "You're the chairwoman, right?"

"Yes?" Her eyes flickered over my jeans and t-shirt, and she sniffed slightly. "Can I help you?"

"I'm Kasey Sanford. I'm new this year."

"Nice to meet you." The disdainful look in her eyes said otherwise.

"Yeah. Well, you see, I hate to go back on my commitment, but the PTA just isn't working out for me."

"Oh?"

The other women watched us, their faces registering various levels of surprise.

"Yeah, so consider this my resignation."

"But why would you want to quit? The PTA is a very worthwhile organization."

I nodded. "It's just not working out."

Before she could say more, before any of the women could say anything to me, I turned and left, trying hard to keep the grin off my face.

On my way back to the house, I detoured through downtown and parked outside Erica and Ron's art shop.

"Kasey!" Erica squealed when I came in. She was in a corner of the cluttered shop, arranging a jewelry display. "What brings you in today?"

"I quit the PTA and need something to get me out of the house. I was thinking maybe art classes, or a book club. Can you recommend anything?"

"Oh, sure. There's a gallery around the corner that offers drawing and landscaping classes, and a studio on the south side of town does pottery. Some of the local craft stores do knitting and crocheting and all that. The colleges offer various classes too. And you could always head over to Black Mountain. They always have something going on."

I nodded as she paused for breath.

"As for book clubs, the library usually has several, depending on what genre you're interested in. The colleges probably have stuff too. And McKay's used to, but I think they've all died out. I bet you could easily get one going again, if you wanted to."

"Thanks, Erica."

"And now that I think about it...." She went behind the counter and rummaged around in a stack of binders and folders. "Aha." She handed me a piece of paper. "Here's a list of some art studios around Asheville. If the other avenues don't pan out for you, you can always go around and ask these guys."

"Thanks." I smiled and touched her shoulder.

"What are friends for?"

I thought about that on the drive home. Erica was right. Friends encouraged you; they didn't force you to be who you weren't. I'd made the right choice to quit the PTA, and I hoped David would see that too.

At home, a note from David lay taped on the large mirror hanging on the foyer wall.

> K -
> *Sorry about earlier. I arranged a little treat for you. Enjoy it and come straight home after because I have another surprise planned for you.*
> *Love,*
> D

Tucked to the back of the note was a card for Asheville's luxury spa. I smiled and shook my head. When David set out to impress someone, he didn't hold back. I just wasn't sure if it would work how he wanted this time.

*\*\*\**

Try as I might to prevent it, throughout the massage and pedicure my thoughts turned to Andrew, as they did more and more frequently. We had days like today, full of joking and arguing and physical contact. But then he might go a week without so much as looking at me.

Was I reading too much into his behavior? Overthinking, as he put it? Did he want more than friendship? To be fair, he acted that way with all the women to whom he was close. Did I want more than friendship? Why did I want more than friendship? Sure, things with David were still bumpy, but they were mostly improving. Wasn't this spa treatment, and whatever surprise he had planned for later, proof of that? I loved David, and wanted to keep our family together, make it stronger than it had been before, make my marriage the partnership it had been at the beginning.

Then there was Andrew. Always Andrew. Whenever I went to McKay's, I hoped he'd be there, hoped it would be a good day and he'd pay attention to me, hoped he'd find an excuse to brush his hand against mine, to smile at me. Just thinking about him now sent a shiver of warmth through me. His eyes, his lips, his athletic physique....

I gave myself a mental shake to stop those thoughts. I was married. My relationship with my husband, whom I loved, was getting better, despite today's lunchtime argument. There could be no room in my heart, in my life, for anything beyond friendship with Andrew.

Besides, my mind continued, pushing its way down a path that needed to be avoided if at all possible, if my own husband had cheated on me, why would a stranger like Andrew be interested? David knew my every thought, my habits, my quirks, and that hadn't been enough to keep him faithful. I would be entering any new relationship with baggage: a child, a broken marriage, a distorted sense of self. Andrew could have his choice of any woman he wanted. Why would he want me?

But David still wanted me, didn't he? Wasn't this massage proof of that, proof of his love? Why did I even need proof?

\*\*\*

I returned to a darkened house.

"David?" I cautiously walked inside. "Aida? Hello?"

"Aida's at a friend's house tonight," David called from the direction of the kitchen. "Go upstairs and get changed, then come on down."

My earlier frustrations melted away, replaced by intrigue at his instructions. As I walked into the bedroom, I gasped. Lying on the bed were a new slinky black dress and a small jewelry box. I quickly changed into the new garment, then opened the box. Inside, a small diamond pendant necklace glistened. I fastened it around my neck and glanced at myself in the mirror.

I sighed. Going to the gym was part of my daily routine in Richmond, but since discovering David's infidelities I'd been too busy to exercise. No, I corrected myself, there'd been no point in exercising. The woman in the pictures had been fit, sexy, alluring. Not words I would use to describe myself. I inhaled, sucked in my stomach, stuck out my average breasts, regarded my reflection, and sighed. Even if Andrew and I were somehow compatible mentally, I doubted he'd consider me his type physically.

David walked into the room wearing a black sports jacket over a crisp white shirt and a coordinating black tie. His brown eyes widened when he saw me standing there. "Wow. You look beautiful."

"I guess." I frowned at my image in the mirror.

"No, really. I hoped the dress would fit, but wow. Wow."

"The necklace is too much, David. It must have cost a fortune."

"You're worth every penny." He came up behind me, wrapped one arm around my waist and, with the other, pushed my long, thick hair out of the way so he could kiss my neck. "Pull your hair up," he whispered, "put on the diamond earrings I got you for Christmas last year, and meet me downstairs." He kissed my neck again and then left the room.

As I moved to do as I'd been told, mirror Kasey frowned at me. I stopped and studied her. Mirror Kasey stared back, accusations darkening her blue eyes.

"Fine," I told her, brushing out my hair, tossing my head to feel the thick silkiness graze my shoulders. I yanked out the earrings David had chosen and put in a small pair of gaudy ladybug studs Aida had given me when she was three. Mirror Kasey smiled.

Satisfied, I headed downstairs. The house was still dark, except for a faint glow coming from the dining room.

I stopped short in the doorway. Candles of various sizes adorned the table, which was set for two. A large vase of white and red roses sat in the middle of the table.

"You did all this?" The candlelight blurred and shimmered as I dabbed at my eyes with the back of my hand.

"I told you, I'd do anything for you." David entered the room carrying a small platter heaped with pieces of meat and cheese.

"Yeah, but this is...." *Too much. Perfect. Not enough.*

"I was a jerk today. I shouldn't have been. I want you to trust me, so I need to trust you. Right?"

My face flamed, and I hoped that David didn't notice in the low light. Of course David should trust me. There was nothing between me and Andrew. *Nothing, right?*

David set the platter down, walked over to me, took my hands in his. "Right, Kase? We can trust each other, right?"

I looked up into his eyes, which searched mine. He seemed so sincere. I kissed him. "Right."

His lips lingered on mine, and then he pulled away, took my hand, and led me to the table. "I figured we could get some more use out of that fondue set we got for a wedding present."

I laughed and sat down. "Remember how we had fondue so often right after we got married?"

"All week long I forced down hot dogs and ramen, dreaming of our Friday night fondue."

"I hated doing dishes. If we had fondue, we didn't need to worry about silverware."

"So, finally, the truth comes out! I thought you were just a culinary snob." David let out a small laugh, then grimaced. "I hate that we had to live like that for as long as we did."

"Live like what? I was so happy our first years together."

"Really? But we never had any money to do anything. When we did have time together, it was just...." He shrugged. "I don't know."

"I liked our time together. We'd go for drives and just talk, remember? Late nights cuddling, baring our souls. What's wrong with that?"

"We can still do that."

"No, we can't. Whenever I voice an opinion, I feel like I'm under attack if you don't agree with me. There's never any debate, just you being right and me being wrong."

"When have I ever done that?"

"Today?"

"Jesus, Kase, I said I was sorry for that. I had to get back to the office."

"I know. It just seems like it's always about work with you. There's never any us."

"I said I was sorry. I got you that spa package, that necklace, and now this dinner. Doesn't that count for anything?" He reached across the table, poured himself a glass of wine and downed half of it.

"It's not about money, David. It's about time, and the quality of that time. It's about listening to each other."

He sighed. "Okay, fine, I'm listening. Bare your soul."

"I quit the PTA today."

"What? Why?" Even in the low light, his clenched jaw was visible.

"I don't like those people. They're so fake."

"Did you even give them a chance?"

"I can't take all the barbed compliments, the constant attempts to outdo each other. It was the same back in Richmond. I need to be around real people."

"Like that Andrew guy."

I looked up, caught off guard by the flatness of my husband's voice. "Like the people I've met at McKay's, yeah."

"I've told you—"

"Yeah, I know. I'm better than them."

"Exactly." He finished his glass of wine and poured another.

"I'm not, though. I don't even know who I am anymore. And I don't know who you are, either. I need to figure that out." I took a deep breath. "And I'd like your support, because if you're not along for the ride, I honestly don't think we're going to work it out."

"Of course," he said softly, coming around the table to my chair. He pulled me to standing and wrapped his arms around me.

I buried my face in his shoulder, breathing in his aftershave, the stronger aroma of the alcohol on his breath.

"Fixing our relationship will take time, and there are bound to be hiccups along the way, but I promise I'll be there with you every step of the way. You mean so much to me, you and Aida. I don't want to lose either of you."

I nodded, not trusting my voice enough to speak without shaking.

He tilted my head off his shoulder. "I love you, stupid earrings and all," he murmured, kissing me.

Closing my eyes, I melted into his kiss. His hands drifted down and across my body, and I shivered at his touch.

He pulled away. "Forget the fondue. Go upstairs while I blow out the candles."

I nodded again and went upstairs to our bedroom. I sat on the edge of the bed, nervous as if it were my first time. It was, sort of, my first time with David since I'd found out about his affairs. When had he found time for sex with the other women? Had it been during the day? On business trips? And where? His office? Our bed?

David bounded into the room, knocked me back on the bed and kissed me, his hands picking up where they'd left off downstairs.

Motionless beneath him, I closed my eyes, and those damned pictures appeared. I clenched my eyes shut, but they wouldn't go away.

He hitched my dress up around my waist and slowly slid my panties down my legs.

"No," I said, barely audible.

David's hands didn't stop.

"No," I said louder, shaking my head. "No."

He paused, looked at me with his head cocked slightly to the side.

"I can't, David. Not yet."

His jaw tightened.

"I see those pictures. When you touch me this way, I see those pictures." I swallowed hard. "I'm sorry, but I just can't. Not tonight. Not yet."

"I understand." His voice was flat as he rolled away from me, stared at the ceiling.

"David?"

"Yes?" His voice seemed a million miles away.

"Could you just hold me tonight? Like you used to?"

"Are you sure?" Voice still flat.

"I want to, but it's going to take time." I inched over and laid my head on his shoulder.

"Yeah, I know." He kissed my head and sighed.

# Chapter 10 – Andrew (Age 12)

There comes a point in every man's life when he realizes God is speaking to him and pointing him towards a higher calling. I'd recently reached that point. It was clear to me that God put me here on His great green earth for one purpose: to kiss Megan Ashford, the most beautiful girl He ever created.

Megan was spectacular. She had these amazing brown eyes with flecks of gold in them, eyes you wanted to look into forever. Her smile put angels to shame, even with her braces. She scrunched her nose real cute when she laughed. Her light chocolate skin was flawless, and her braids were always in neat, even rows. And her body, already in the sixth grade... wow.

Her personality matched her looks. She was funny and nice to everyone, even the unpopular kids. She was smart too, but not so smart you felt stupid in comparison. She was perfect in every way, and I loved her.

I wrote her notes in class most days, although I'd never worked up the nerve to give them to her. Today I was working on a poem.

> Megan, you're so beautiful,
> I love you so much.
> If you would be my girlfriend,
> I would

I wasn't good at poetry and couldn't think of anything that rhymed with *much* except *such* or *Dutch*, and those didn't fit.

I spent all math class trying to figure it out, so absorbed in it I wasn't paying attention when Mr. Spencer came over to my desk and picked up my notebook.

"Notes in class, Mr. Adams?" he asked. Everyone snickered.

"No, sir." I glared up at him.

He quickly read the note. I was afraid he was gonna read it out loud this time, but he just looked at me through dusty glasses and said, "See me after class."

I breathed a sigh of relief. If anyone knew what I'd written, I'd be dead. Love notes from a guy like me to a girl like Megan were social suicide.

After class I stayed at my desk while everyone else left.

My friend Dale smacked me in the back of the head on his way out. "I love you, babycakes!" he said in a high-pitched voice, then laughed.

I scowled at him. If only I wasn't already in trouble, I would've jumped up and hit him right back.

After the other students had cleared out, I walked over to Mr. Spencer's desk. "You wanted to see me, sir?"

He shuffled through papers and didn't look up. "How many times have I caught you writing love letters in class, Andrew?"

"Dunno." I looked down at my feet, hands shoved deep in my pockets, face burning.

"This'll be the sixth time this year. How many have you actually given to Megan?"

"None." My face burned brighter as I traced the cracks of the floor tiles with my sneakered foot. This wasn't the kind of conversation I wanted to have with a teacher.

"This has got to stop." He put down the papers and stared hard at me. "Your grades have really taken a nosedive in the last few months. You're a bright kid, Andrew, but if you continue to goof off in class you're headed for trouble. So no more notes. Homework in on time. Passing test grades. The next step is a conference with your parents. Understand?"

"Yes sir." The last thing I wanted was for Mr. Spencer to talk to my mama and stepdad. Gary would beat the crap out of me if he knew my grades were slipping. "I'll try to do better."

"No trying. Do it."

"Yes sir."

As I turned to leave, he called after me, "Oh, and one more thing, Andrew."

"Yes sir?"

"Try talking to Megan. Girls don't have cooties, you know."

\*\*\*

Math was my last class of the day, so I headed to my locker and grabbed my bag. I walked outside into the warm fall sunshine and found Carly, Mark and Dale waiting for me. We all lived fairly close to each other so we usually walked home together, unless one of us guys had detention. Carly never got detention.

"How'd it go, sweetie pie?" Dale crowed in that loud voice.

I glared at him. "Shut the hell up."

Carly frowned. "What'd you get in trouble for today, Andrew?"

"Writing another love letter to Megan, I bet." Mark grinned. "I wish Mr. Spencer would've read it out loud!"

"Why don't you just talk to her if you like her so much?" Carly asked, as we set off towards home.

"I would, but what if she doesn't like me? I don't wanna look like an idiot."

"And writing her stupid love letters is any better?" Dale adjusted the filthy old baseball cap he always wore. He claimed his dad had given it to him, but none of us believed him. My stepdad said Dale's mama didn't even know who his dad was, but we didn't bring it up; most of us was missing a parent.

"She goes to me and Carly's church," said Mark. "Maybe we could talk to her, test the waters for you."

Carly's frown grew. "I don't know. She's, well...."

"Wonderful? Perfect? Everything I want?"

"I don't want you to get hurt."

"Carly loves Andrew," Dale shouted. "You're jealous that he doesn't like you."

"Am not!" Her lower lip trembled.

"Shut the hell up," I told Dale, punching his arm hard.

"Screw you all," he said, and stomped off towards his house.

We watched him go. I felt kinda sorry for the guy, in his clothes that didn't fit right, that his mama got for free from his church. It was just him and her, and she was gone half the time, out doing drugs and partying and bringing a different boyfriend home every month. But that was no excuse to be rude to Carly.

"Will you talk to her?" I asked her. "Please?"

"What would I even say to her? We're not really friends. Heck, I barely know her."

I thought for a moment. "Tell her you got a friend who wants her to watch him in next week's football game and get a snack afterwards."

"What a romantic first date," laughed Mark. "You're gonna be all sweaty trying to make out with her."

I punched him on the arm too, but not as hard as I'd punched Dale. "Please, Carly, will you do it?"

"What is it you like about her so much anyways?"

"She's smart, and funny, and nice, and really, really pretty."

"I'm smarter than her."

"Yeah, but you're my best friend. It's different with Megan."

"Okay, I'll do it." Carly's lip trembled again.

I gave her a big hug, then turned off towards my house.

*** 

A week later I was sitting on the bench watching my teammates run the ball down the field. I'd failed a math test and missed a history project, so I was on probation until I pulled my grades up. That was okay, though; I didn't feel like playing football today. Sure enough, Gary had let me have it when I failed that test, and I wasn't up for getting tackled on the field, not until the bruises faded.

I turned around and scanned the bleachers behind me. Megan sat at one end by our opponents' goalpost, surrounded by a group of friends. I turned back to the game before the coach could yell at me for not paying attention, and tried to think of a plan for how to approach her. I needed her away from her friends, somehow.

We ended up losing, 17-12. If I'd been playing we probably would've won. I was pretty good at football, better than anyone would probably expect considering I was benched so much for my grades. Gary always asked me why I even bothered to be on the team if I didn't get to play much. Him and Mama didn't ever come watch, so what did it even matter if I played or not?

After the game I climbed up onto the bleachers next to Mark and Carly. There was another game after mine, another local middle school playing, and most everyone watched both games. There wasn't much else to do on weekends.

Mark nodded in Megan's direction. "Your girlfriend is here."

"She ain't my girlfriend."

"And she never will be either if you don't talk to her."

"I will, I will. I'm just waiting for the right moment."

Mark reached into his pocket, pulled out a crumpled dollar bill and some coins, counted the money. "I bet you one dollar and forty-seven cents you won't talk to her."

"I will too." I grabbed the money from his hand. "Watch this."

I walked over to the concession stand and bought a bag of popcorn and a coke. Then I took a few deep breaths and walked over to Megan. "Hi, Megan." I tried to say it all smooth but my voice squeaked a little.

Her friends giggled.

"Hi, Andrew," Megan said, smiling at me.

That gave me the courage I needed. "You staying for the next game?"

"Yeah."

"Wanna share some popcorn?" My heart pounded so loud she could probably hear it. What if she said no? Her friends were watching us closely.

"Sure." She smiled again, real big this time, and I was so relieved I about dropped the coke.

"We can probably see the game better if we sit at the top of the bleachers." Away from her friends, just me and her, I didn't add. Would she realize why I wanted her to move?

"It's pretty hot up there. Why don't we move under the bleachers, into the shade?"

*Did she just say what I think she said? Go under the bleachers with Megan Ashford?* I nodded, barely able to keep from shaking with excitement. "Okay."

She climbed down from the bleachers and took the coke from me. "It sure was nice of you to buy me a drink."

"You're welcome," I stammered, feeling a little put out. I know I didn't play but I still sat in the hot sun for a while, and I was thirsty too. Next time I'd get two cokes.

I glanced back at Mark and Carly. Carly had a huge frown on her face, and Mark looked like he was trying to calm her down. What was she so upset about? Carly was my best friend and always would be, but I loved Megan. I didn't wonder too long though, because as soon as Megan and I were under the bleachers she kissed me.

My first kiss. Megan's lips were soft, impossibly soft, and cherry-flavored. I closed my eyes and pressed my mouth against hers, my tongue darting out against those cherry lips, tasting her. Her mouth parted and my tongue brushed against hers. It dawned on me I was a lot taller than her and she was on her tiptoes, so I wrapped my arms around her. She pressed herself tight against me and I could feel her hard nipples on my chest. My trembling hand awkwardly moved down her back. She didn't protest so I kept moving it until it was on her butt. Still no protests, so I squeezed a little. She just kept kissing me with those cherry lips. I imagined this was what it must be like in heaven.

Too soon, though, she pulled away. I tried to pull her back but she laughed at me. "I gotta go, Andrew. See you at school Monday!" She picked up the coke and popcorn and ran off.

In a daze, I remained under the bleachers, eyes closed, still tasting cherries on my lips.

***

Monday morning, sitting at the table eating breakfast, I still couldn't get Megan off my mind.

"Andy!" my stepdad growled.

"Huh?"

He set down his newspaper and glared at me. "I asked you if I should be expecting any phone calls this week about your grades."

"Dunno." I shrugged.

"Sweetie," Mama said from the sink where she was washing dishes, "what Gary is trying to say is, did you get your homework done this weekend?"

I grunted. I'd been too busy fantasizing about Megan to do anything else, but I knew better than to tell him that.

"What was that?" Gary asked.

"I said, 'Yes sir.'"

"You better not be lying to me, boy. 'Cause if I find out....'"

"Gary, Andrew knows better than to lie to you."

"Stay out of this, Judy," he said in a low voice.

I looked over at Mama. Her back was to me, her head bent low towards the steaming water. She always stayed out of it.

"What do you care?" I asked Gary. "They're my grades, not yours."

"You getting smart with me?"

It wasn't worth a fight, not before school. "No sir." I stood and took my cereal bowl over to Mama.

As I walked past Gary, out of the room, he reached over real quick and smacked my head. I almost fell over but managed to stay upright, without reaching for the wall or a chair or anything. That always made him mad, when I didn't show no reaction.

"You better keep those grades up, Andy."

As I left the room, I thought I heard Mama let out a little sob, but with the water running it was hard to tell.

***

I was late for school, of course. All Gary's fault. Walking too fast made me dizzy. I would've cut completely but I couldn't wait to see Megan. Thinking about how her cherry lips tasted, how they felt, helped push all thoughts of my stupid stepdad out of my mind.

I didn't have a chance to talk to her until lunch. Dale, Mark, and I were sitting together eating our nasty cafeteria pizza, when she came up to our table.

"Got a minute?" she asked me shyly.

"Sure." I jumped up.

"Can I have your pizza?" Mark asked. He was one of seven kids at his house and ate whatever he could get his hands on.

"Sure," I told him. "Who knows how long this'll take?" I grinned at him and followed Megan into the hallway.

"This way," she said, and led me to an empty science classroom. She pulled me into a closet in the back, shut the door behind us, and kissed me. Cherries again.

That became our pattern. By Wednesday, her shirt was off. By Friday, her hands were down my pants. And always the taste of cherries.

***

Carly, Mark, Dale and I walked home together from school Friday afternoon. I hadn't seen much of Carly all week; she'd been avoiding me.

"So you gonna be under the bleachers with Megan this weekend too?" asked Dale. He winked at me.

"Her lips taste like cherries." I didn't think I'd ever be able to smell cherries again and not think of Megan.

"So I've heard."

"What?" I stopped on the sidewalk. "What do you mean, 'So I've heard'?"

"Nothing, man." Dale made a big production of adjusting the straps on his backpack, and wouldn't look at me.

"No, I wanna know!" Mark and Carly exchanged glances. This made me nervous, suspicious. "How would anyone know what Megan's lips taste like, besides me?"

"Andrew," Carly said, laying her hand on my arm, "maybe this is something you should talk to Megan about tomorrow."

"Y'all are just jealous," I yelled. "None of y'all have ever kissed anyone and y'all are trying to make me feel bad about it. Well, fuck that."

Carly stared at me wide-eyed. She never swore.

"Listen, man," Mark started.

I cut him off. "No, you listen. Megan likes me. *Me.* I'll talk to her about this tomorrow. You'll see!" I turned away and stomped off towards home.

***

I spent that Saturday's game on the bench too. I'd been too excited about Megan all week to do any homework or studying or anything, so my grades once again weren't good enough to play.

After the game, which we lost again, 21-18, I spied Megan sitting on the bleachers with her friends again.

Before I could go over and talk to her, Coach Johnson pulled me aside. "Listen, Andrew, I know this is a difficult age, and you have a lot on your mind: sports, school, family, girls...." He smiled at me, like he was my best friend and we shared some kind of secret.

I scowled at him.

"And you're a great asset to this team, don't get me wrong. But rules are rules. And the rule is, if you're suspended due to grades more than three times in a season, you're off the team. You know that, right?"

I scuffed at a clump of grass, thinking about Megan. "Yes sir."

"This is week three for you, Andrew. That means if you don't get those grades up, you're done. You understand?"

"Yes sir."

"So you going to pull those grades up? Make an effort?"

"Yes sir." I didn't care. All I could think about was Megan and cherries.

When he was finally done lecturing me I looked around for her, but I didn't see her anywhere.

I walked over to her friends. "Where'd Megan go?"

"You're too late, Andrew," one of them said, and they all giggled.

"What do you mean?" My chest tightened.

They giggled again. "You were replaced," another girl said. "By someone who deserves her."

"What do you mean?"

"You think someone like Megan would really go out with someone like you?"

They all laughed, and my hands tightened into fists. I ran down the steps, their giggles ringing in my ears, and dove under the bleachers.

At the far end was Megan. She was kissing Ben King, a guy a year ahead of us in school, a good-looking guy who got good grades, played football, had two parents and money. Someone not at all like me.

My world went silent, numb, as I watched them. I felt like throwing up.

Then the rage hit. Her friends were lying. Megan was my girl, not his. "What the hell do you think you're doing?" I walked towards them, shaking.

Ben looked up as I approached.

"Get away from her," I growled at him.

"What?" Ben was confused.

He was a good guy, but that didn't matter because he was kissing my girl. Mine.

"I said get away from her."

"Look, man, I don't know what the problem is." Confusion filled his green eyes. "She asked me to come down—"

Before he could finish, I punched him square in the mouth. "That's a lie," I yelled as I punched him again. "Megan likes *me*! She'd never do that."

Ben stood up and took a swing at me. I punched him again and Megan screamed. Soon adults were down there, pulling us apart, and Megan wouldn't even look at me.

Since I didn't have parents or anyone at the game, I was given to Coach Johnson to deal with. I sat with him for most of the second game, and then during a timeout he got up to use the bathroom. I looked around, noticed that no one was watching, and slipped away.

I wasn't sure where to go. I'd be in big trouble when I got home, big painful trouble, and I wanted to put that off as long as possible, so I just walked and walked.

I thought about Megan, about her cherry lips. About how her hands felt down my pants. About how if she was so willing to kiss me and then Ben King, she'd probably kissed a lot of guys. Of course she'd kissed a lot of guys, if she was willing to kiss me. How could I have been so stupid?

I ended up in front of Carly's trailer. Her mama was out front, digging in her flower garden. She always made sure their place looked real nice.

She looked up and saw me. "Well, hello there, Andrew," she drawled. "Carly's inside in her room. You can go on in, if you like."

"Sure thing, ma'am. Thanks." I was always real polite to Ms. Jefferson, the one adult in my life who'd always been nice to me.

Carly's two sisters were watching TV in the tiny living room. I patted their heads, which always made them giggle, then headed to Carly's room. It was real tiny, made smaller with three girls sharing it. She was lying on her bed, reading. She read a lot. I knocked on the open door.

She looked up. "I'm surprised to see you here. I thought you'd be at the game, making out with Megan again."

I sat down next to her. "She decided to make out with Ben King today instead."

"Oh, Andrew." She sat up and gave me a big hug.

"I guess you're happy about this?" I asked bitterly. "Gonna tell me 'I told you so'?"

"No." Her arms were still around me, and I leaned my head on hers.

"Your braids are nicer than Megan's."

"I'm smarter than her too."

We sat there next to each other on the bed, her arms around me, not saying anything for a while.

"Hey, Carly?"

"Yeah?" She pulled back a little to look up at me.

"Thanks."

"For what?" Her eyes had specks of gold in them too.

I leaned in and kissed her. Her lips tasted like peppermint.

# Chapter 11 – Kasey (Present)

After our failed date night, I'd tried to be more affectionate with David; a healthy emotional connection required a strong physical component. Hugs, kisses, and brief or lingering caresses were no problem, but the idea of being intimate, of sex, when he'd been with other women, conjured up those pictures: the sheets tangled around his feet, the muscles in his back tensed, the woman's legs wrapped around his waist, her arms around his neck. Her face was obscured in all the pictures, that cowardly bitch. Protected by her anonymity while she ruined my life.

David dropped Aida off at school one morning, letting me sleep in. He was all about little courtesies now: picking up dinner on the way home from the office, giving me bouquets of fresh flowers, not even a hint of further displeasure over the PTA.

I took a long shower, giving myself a chance to think about my marriage, about what I wanted. About the other woman. She'd *tried* to ruin my life, and *did* destroy the Richmond life, but how fulfilling had that life really been? David and I were practically strangers, residing together, but not living. Maybe the affairs were a warning signal that we were off the path we'd intended to follow. I laughed to myself. Maybe I should tell David to send the woman a "thank you" card.

"I'm glad to see you in such a good mood today," David whispered in my ear.

I jumped and let out a small scream. David grabbed my elbows, helping me regain my balance on the slippery surface.

After pulling loose, I turned to face him. "What the hell are you doing in here?"

"I'm not meeting clients until later this morning, so I thought I'd come home and spend my free time with you." He grinned and leaned in to kiss me. Water glistened on his naked body. "Scrub your back, wash your hair. You know, the usual."

"The usual. Yeah." Smiling, I turned back to the water and lifted my face to the showerhead.

He reached around and gently placed his hands on my breasts, pulling me against his chest. He pushed my hair aside and nibbled on my neck. I ducked my head, and a spray of water hit him in the face.

"Oh, you're getting it now!" He chuckled as he leaned forward and turned the faucet as cold as it would go.

"You are such an ass!" Laughing as the chilly water hit my body, I backed up quickly to get out of the spray.

He wrapped his arms around me. "We used to do this all the time."

"David, I'm freezing now." I extended my foot to turn the water hot again.

"Just turn it off. I'll warm you up."

I did what he said, as he grabbed a towel hanging next to the shower and draped it around my shivering shoulders. With a second towel, he gently dried my legs, then looked up at me. "Warmer now?"

"Yeah." I smiled at his thoughtfulness. "You're still all wet, though."

He quickly toweled himself off and wrapped the damp cloth around his waist. "Better?"

"Now what?" I studied my husband, taking in his short blond hair, his brown eyes, his broad chest. Still as attractive as the day we'd met.

He pulled the towel from my shoulders, then, with one arm under my knees and the other supporting my back, he carried me into our bedroom and gently deposited me on the king-size bed.

My pulse quickened. The memory flooded in: David's back, those legs around his waist. I swallowed. "I can't. I told you, not yet."

"Stop thinking and relax." He kissed my neck, my collarbone, my breasts, my belly button. "You are the most beautiful woman I've ever seen."

I lay on the bed, trying to focus on what David's mouth was doing, rather than on the pictures. He'd probably followed this same routine with the other woman, all the way down to the tattoo on her ankle. That tattoo. The pictures danced before my closed eyes. There was something familiar about that tattoo, a small red blur on the left ankle. Lots of women had tattoos like that. Of course I'd seen it before, seen it in a hundred different places. And one, in particular.

I gasped and pushed David away from me.

"What?" he asked, startled. "I know it's been a while, but I don't think I'm doing that bad."

"That tattoo." I jumped up, ran over to the closet where I'd stashed the pictures, and pulled them out. "I know I've seen that before."

"Kase, let it go." Worry filled his voice. Guilt. "Please, just let it go."

My mind flashed back to Richmond, to PTA meetings and evening cocktails and chatter-filled lunches. That tattoo. How had I missed it? My speech was ragged. "That bitch. That bitch! Does Tim know?"

"No." David remained on the bed. "As far as I know, he never found out."

"Ann was my best friend!" I collapsed against the closet doors, sank to the floor as the weight of my words hit me. "How could she? How could *you*?"

"I told you, it was a mistake." His voice quavered. "It was a huge mistake, on both our parts. And I realized it. I realized I only loved you. Please, Kase, you have to believe me."

"I don't have to do anything," I spat at him. I tried to slow my racing heart, tried to think. My shallow breaths left me lightheaded. I tried to calm down, to stay in control. "Ann? Of all people, it was Ann?"

"It was just going to be a one-time thing, I swear. It was a mistake. We were drunk, not thinking. It shouldn't have happened. None of it should've ever happened."

"You took pictures? You knew I'd figure it out. Why?" None of this made any sense. Ann, my best friend, with David? "And for her to say this would never happen to her? What about her daughter? What about Aida? Why'd Ann send that letter?"

"She didn't." Spoken in barely a whisper.

"What? This doesn't make any sense."

"Ann didn't send it."

I stared at him, willing myself to breathe, tears streaming down my face.

"I told you there were two women. Sue was always friendly around the office, wanting to go to lunch and get drinks after work. I didn't mean for anything to happen, really, I swear. She was so sympathetic, so understanding of the stress I was under, and one thing led to another. I knew it was wrong, Kase, that it was so clichéd to sleep with my secretary. I broke it off with her, and she flipped out."

I shook my head and took several deep breaths. "This still doesn't make any sense. How did she get pictures of you and Ann?"

He looked at his hands, and in that small voice, barely audible, he said, "Ann and I used Sue's apartment a few times. She must've suspected something, must've set up a camera to catch us." He stared at me, his brown eyes wide. "It was wrong, all of it. I know it. I'm sorry, so sorry. Please believe me."

I remained on the floor, not sure what to say. Then it dawned on me that I was naked, sitting on the floor completely naked. David was seeing me naked, just like he'd seen his secretary, just like he'd seen Ann. Ann with the tattoo. Ann who'd said she was glad her husband would never cheat on her.

The secretary was a cliché; he was right about that. And that hurt. God, it hurt so much that he'd slept with her, that she'd gone after him knowing full well he was married. But it didn't hurt as much as Ann's betrayal. Ann with her sanctimonious views on cheating. Ann with a daughter of her own. Had she even thought about the effects on our kids?

I stood and dug through my dresser drawers, and put on the first things that came to hand, not caring what I looked like. Caring only about David's lies, his betrayals.

"Please, Kase!" He continued to beg, still sitting on the bed. "It was wrong. I didn't want you to find out it was her, didn't want to hurt you more. I love you. I care about you. I was wrong, and I want to fix us." He stood and came over to me as I tore a brush through my drying hair. "Please, say something to me."

I took a breath and stared at his reflection in the mirror as I continued to untangle my hair. "Did you love them? Why would you protect them? Protect that bitch? Do you have any idea how much this hurts, in light of everything she said to me? Do you still love her? Still love them?"

"I never loved them, Kase." His voice broke. "I love you, and only you. I had Sue fired, just to get away from her. It just... it just all got out of hand." He placed his hand on my arm, but I shrugged it off. How dare he touch me.

"That's an understatement."

"We've gotten so much closer since moving here." His voice was almost a whisper. "We can work through this too. It's all in the past. This doesn't change anything. Please."

"No." I set my brush down. "I need time to think."

\*\*\*

I ended up at McKay's. I'd been there for about twenty minutes when Andrew came in, dressed in jeans and a t-shirt, off-duty. After getting a cup of coffee he sat down at my table, not saying anything. I didn't say anything to him either, staring at a magazine, but thinking of David and his secretary and Ann. Thinking of that tattoo.

Andrew cleared his throat, but I ignored him, not feeling like talking. When that failed, he tore a napkin into small pieces, wadded them up and threw them at me.

"Stop it." My gaze flickered to him, then back down at the magazine. No makeup, tear-stained face; I probably looked horrible.

He continued, now making the pieces bigger.

"I said stop it."

"Nope." Still throwing pieces of napkin.

"Andrew, I mean it. Stop it."

"What's the magic word?"

"Knock the hell off, because I'm not in the mood."

"Jesus, what's your problem today?"

"My problem is I'm trying to read, and I don't appreciate you throwing stuff at me."

"Fine, I'll sit somewhere else. Is that what you want?" He stood up, jarring the table with his leg and toppling my glass of sweet tea. The cold liquid quickly poured into my lap.

"Damn it, Andrew!" I jumped up, but my pants were already soaked.

"Oops," he said with a laugh.

"Oops? Oops is all you can say?"

"Here." He laughed again and handed me half a napkin, all that was left.

"Fuck you." Deep breaths as tears welled up in my eyes, threatening to spill over. Not this, not today.

"Hey now! So your pants got wet. They'll dry. What's the big deal?"

"The big deal is my pants got wet. The big deal is you didn't say sorry for spilling my drink. The big deal is I asked you to stop throwing stuff at me, and you wouldn't. The big deal is I'm kind of a huge mess today, and you didn't even notice."

I plopped down on a dry chair, head in my hands, my eyes squeezed shut to keep the tears in. I shouldn't have come to the bookstore, should leave before things got worse. I didn't need Andrew, the closest friend I had in Asheville, mad at me.

He didn't get mad though. He knelt down in front of me and placed his hand on my knee. "You okay?"

"You are so damn inconsistent." I didn't look at him, couldn't if I wanted to keep from crying.

"What? I was just joking around, and you got upset."

I shook my head. "It doesn't matter."

"So why bother bringing it up?"

"I don't know." Nothing made sense — not my marriage, not my reactions, not Andrew. One day, one moment, he was joking around, the next he was callous, and then immediately concerned. I wanted to simultaneously punch him and kiss him.

"Fine, then," he said, obviously frustrated by my mood.

Several people were staring at us, at how strange we looked: me with wet pants, and Andrew kneeling in front of me.

He glanced around and stood up. "C'mon." He took my hand and led me towards the door.

"Where are we going?"

"Somewhere more private."

He led me down the street, still holding my hand, which calmed me immensely. He seemed unaware he was touching me. "Maybe if you talked to me about what's going on, you'd feel better?"

"I'd like to talk to you, but whenever we talk about anything serious I piss you off, and I don't know why."

He ducked down an alley, pulling me after him. About a hundred feet down was a half-empty lot, completely hidden from the street by the narrow building at the front. It was filled with grass, trees, flowers, and several scattered park benches. I had no idea anything like this existed here.

"Kasey, I'm always here," Andrew said. "Maybe if you just ignored that part of you that needs to fight me? Or maybe I need to be less defensive?"

"I don't know. All I know is that we argue. I don't want to, but we do, and I don't know why."

He led me over to a bench and sat down. "We'll find a middle ground."

I sat next to him, and he put his arm around my shoulder. I leaned against him, and he pulled me close. The events of the last few months and of that morning jumbled through my mind: my husband, his affection and temper, constantly fighting, hypocritical Ann, David's jealous secretary, Andrew's behavior.

"I'm just so confused about everything right now. My marriage is a mess, and you're not helping any."

"Kasey," he said softly, "we'll figure it out."

We sat there not saying anything for a moment.

"Growing up, my family wasn't close," I said, speaking to mask my nervousness at being so close to Andrew. "When David and I first met, first started dating, I saw the potential for us to make the life and the family I always wanted but never had. And, together, we made that." I paused, thinking of everything we'd had together. "My family is everything to me. I'm just not sure where my husband fits in anymore."

He nodded and looked down at me. "Where do you want him to fit?"

"I don't know." For the last ten years it had been me and David, a team, taking care of each other. He provided for me, sheltered me when I was too passive to fight back, and I provided a strong foundation from which he could launch himself into the world each day. A team, but somewhere we had gone wrong. I didn't want to be that passive person who needed to be taken care of anymore, and David obviously didn't need my support. "I don't know."

"Nothing wrong with that. Some people know what they want, and some need time to figure it all out."

"What do you want?" I wasn't sure I wanted to know his answer, but we were here, his arm around me. I hadn't expected this to happen, even though I'd thought about it. Didn't expect it to happen again, so I may as well ask.

"I want—" He broke off, and when he spoke again his voice was heavy, tired. "I want to do it all over again. Everything."

"Your life isn't that bad, Andrew."

"There's no room for anyone else, Kasey, no matter what I want. I'm unreliable, always shipping out again, coming back with baggage. My past doesn't leave much room for a future."

"You could stop enlisting."

His fingers tightened on my shoulder. "Fighting seems to be all I know."

"David and I fight a lot." I swallowed at the thought of that tattoo. "Today was particularly bad."

"I thought so."

We sat in silence, his arm still around me. He didn't ask for details, leaving me both relieved and slightly annoyed. I didn't want to talk to him about what had happened that morning, but I at least wanted him to ask. The tears returned as, even now, one-on-one with Andrew, I was ready to argue with him; I couldn't help it.

"Where do we stand, you and me?" My heart pounded, hoping he didn't notice how nervous I was to hear his response. "I annoy you a lot, I know. You ignore me half the time. Should I just stop trying?"

"Trying to what? What is it you want?"

What did I want? There I sat with a man, not my husband, who had his arm around me, and it felt so natural, so right. But just because David had cheated didn't mean that I could, that I would. And who knew if Andrew even wanted to.

I didn't want to tell him any of that. He'd led me there, was holding me close, but maybe it was just to calm me down. He probably did this with all the women he knew. It didn't mean that there was anything between us.

Finally, I said, "I don't know."

"You and me, we're very opposite creatures," he said, his voice matter-of-fact. "You'll never see through my eyes, and I won't see through yours, so what else is there?"

It wasn't what I'd hoped to hear, but no worse than expected. I should never have even brought it up, and just nodded.

"I like you," he said. "I—"

His cell phone rang. He pulled it from his pocket and checked the incoming number, then got up from the bench and walked a few feet away. He spoke low into it, so low I couldn't hear what he said.

I sighed. Always the interruptions.

He returned shortly. "I'm sorry, Kasey, but they need me to cover a shift right now."

I just nodded again, trying not to cry in frustration, not trusting myself to speak.

He pulled out his wallet, extracted a card and handed it to me. "Here's my number. We'll talk later. I promise." He bent down, kissed the top of my head, and walked away down the alley.

I watched him go, wondering what he'd been about to say before his phone rang. I'd found that, with Andrew, once the moment was gone, that was it. He didn't ask for things to be repeated, and he wouldn't bring something up again unless he felt strongly about it.

My mind cruelly filled in the blanks. *He likes you, but you're just a random woman who needs to grow up and move on. He likes you, but you're married, so what exactly do you intend to get out of this? He likes you, but you annoy him all the time, so leave him alone already.*

Yet he'd taken the time to calm me down. He hadn't admitted he wanted more, but he'd hinted at it, danced around it. Maybe he needed someone who knew what she was getting into.

I knew. Hadn't I spent countless hours with him over the past few months? Didn't I know him as well as anyone could?

Except I was married, with a child. Despite my problems with David, we were still bound together. No matter how good Andrew's arm felt around me, how right and natural, I was still David's wife. Despite my husband's faults, despite the present, we'd had a good life together overall. He was sorry; wasn't that obvious? He wanted to try to fix things. Didn't I owe it to him to at least calm down, talk to him, before moving on to someone I wasn't even sure about?

\*\*\*

"Kasey!" David's voice was thick with exasperation as we sat in the dining room that evening.

"What?" I asked, startled from my thoughts.

"I've asked you four times now to pass the peas. Everything okay?"

"What do you think?" I stared at him.

He hadn't said much to me since he'd arrived home after work, and nothing about the morning's revelations. Instead, he'd retreated to his office with a bottle of gin and closed the door.

I'd left him alone. What was there to say?

"I have a surprise for you."

"I don't want any more of your surprises."

He ignored my comment. "Remember how I said we'd go on a cruise to celebrate me passing the bar?"

"David," I started, but he held up a hand to cut me off.

"I booked it today. Two weeks in the Caribbean, just you and me for Christmas."

"What about me, Daddy?" Aida's lower lip trembled slightly. "I wanna go too!"

"I have a surprise for you too, sweetie." He smiled at her. "It's not the same as a pony, but you and Grammy and Pop-Pop are spending those two weeks at a ranch where you get to take riding lessons."

"David—" I tried again but was interrupted by Aida's squeals of happiness.

"Riding on a real horse, Daddy?"

"Yup, a real horse."

"Aida, are you done with your dinner?" I asked.

"Yes ma'am."

"Okay, then can you please go play? Daddy and I need to talk."

I tapped my fingers on the table while waiting for Aida to leave the room, then turned to my husband. "Were you going to let me have any say in all this?"

"It's a surprise, Kase!" His smile faded as he saw the look in my eyes. "Remember our honeymoon?"

"I wanted to spend a week in the mountains, but instead your parents paid for us to spend two weeks in Fiji."

"And it was wonderful, wasn't it? Just you and me, spending our days in the sun on a secluded tropical beach."

"Yeah, it was nice, I'll give you that. But—"

"Consider this an early tenth anniversary present. A second honeymoon."

"David, it's too much. It's too expensive. I don't want to be away from Aida for two weeks. And—" I stopped, unsure of how to finish my thought without angering him.

"And?" His eyes narrowed as he took a gulp from his ever-present tumbler.

"And... and I don't want to spend two weeks with just you."

A muscle in David's jaw clenched. "I told you, I'm sorry. A million fucking times I've told you that, and now I'm trying to make it up to you, to treat you like you deserve. Why can't that be enough?"

"And how is it that I deserve to be treated? Cheated on, then bribed until you're back in my good graces?"

His hand tightened on his glass, knuckles white. "The first time I saw you, you were crying. Do you remember that?"

I shook my head, puzzled at where he was headed.

"I was in the library, getting ready to leave, and someone was at the counter chewing you out." He stared into his glass. "You kept apologizing, even though it was obvious the guy was a fucking jerk, and he kept yelling at you. It was at that moment I decided to get to know you, because you looked like you needed someone to take care of you." He looked up, his brown eyes meeting mine. "And I've tried to do that, Kase. I've tried my hardest to take care of you, to give you everything you deserve. Yeah, I've fucked up, but can't you at least give me the benefit of the doubt?"

"I'm trying to." The tears were fast approaching. "But you know how important this family is to me. And, let's be honest, you fucked up pretty bad."

"At least I'm trying to fix things! I agreed to move, to start over, even though it meant leaving my family and friends behind. What have you done to help our marriage? You won't even let me touch you!"

He had a point. He was trying, even if it wasn't helping much, and, other than this morning, I'd avoided talking about his affairs, avoided intimacy. I thought of that morning with Andrew, how good it felt to have his arm around me.

Then my thoughts turned to Ann, to my best friend in bed with my husband. "So now it's my fault everything is fucked up?"

"You're a big part of it, yes. What effort are you making? You spend all your time at that fucking bookstore, wasting your time with people who don't even matter."

"They matter to me."

David reddened, downed the rest of his drink. I'd lost count of how many he'd already had tonight.

"Well, they shouldn't." He stood and walked into the kitchen to fix himself another drink. When he returned, he came over to me rather than returning to his seat across the table. "I'm just trying to take care of you. This is what's best for you."

"Sleeping with my best friend... was that best for me too?"

"Damn it." He slammed his glass down on the table, sloshing the contents over the side. "Fine, you wanna know why I slept with her? Why I really slept with her?"

I looked up at him. Did I really want to know the truth? Finding out he'd cheated had been bad, but finding out it was with Ann was worse. How much more painful could this be?

I nodded. "Yeah."

"You didn't change. Almost ten years together, and you were the same person I'd married. You were happy with the same dreams we had in college." He finished his drink in one gulp. "Me, I want more. My secretary was stress relief, didn't mean anything. But Ann, she understood me. Tim is worthless, no ambition. Ann got me, understood what I want from life, because she feels the same way."

His words froze me to my chair. This was worse than I'd anticipated. If it had been just about the sex, that would've been okay. No, not okay.

Understandable, at least; Ann was attractive. But for him to say she understood him better than his own wife?

That was a punch in the stomach, leaving me without the means to breathe, able to focus only on the pain. "If she was so perfect, then why'd you stay with me?"

"Because I love you. Because you and Aida need me." He clumsily brushed my cheek with his hand. "No matter what, you need me."

"Like hell I do." I jumped up, knocking over my chair.

David stared at me, startled.

"I *have* changed! Changed enough to see that I was a fool to stay with you. I don't need you. I don't need your protection, or your presents. I don't need you, if this is who you are now."

"Kase." He reached out, but I spun around and left the room. He chased after, grabbed me roughly by the forearms. "Don't you walk away from me."

"Let go of me," I hissed, struggling to free myself.

"Mommy?" Aida stood there next to us, her eyes wide, her voice fearful.

David looked at her and let go of me. "Everything's fine, sweetie. Mommy and Daddy are just talking."

"C'mon, Aida." I glared at David. "Grab your shoes. We're leaving."

"What's going on, Mommy?"

"Do as you're told, please." I grabbed my purse and keys, and turned back to David. "I'm not talking to you when you're drunk."

"Where are you going?" He watched me, eyes narrowed. "Why don't you just calm down, and we can talk now?"

Aida returned, and I ushered her out the door, ignoring my husband.

He stood in the doorway. "Kasey, where are you going? Where are you taking Aida? Don't leave. We need to talk this over."

Still ignoring him, I settled Aida into the backseat and buckled her in.

David followed us onto the lawn, over to my car. "I'm sorry. I love you. Don't go. Don't take Aida."

I got into the driver's seat and locked the door behind me.

"Kasey, don't go!" A note of rage crept back into his voice. "I'll forgive you if you agree to come inside right now. Don't do this. We can talk about this, okay? Be adults about it?" He tugged on my door handle. "Get out of the fucking car."

His voice was so low I could barely hear him through the rolled-up window. His cool tone and the rage in his eyes were something I hadn't experienced before, and that scared the hell out of me. I shook my head wordlessly, staring at him with eyes probably as big as Aida's.

"Get out of the fucking car, Kasey!"

A porch light came on across the street, as did a couple down the block. Maybe my neighbors were concerned, or were looking to be entertained. Either way, I wasn't staying.

I started the car while Aida cried softly in the back seat, trying not to draw attention to herself. I didn't blame her.

"Get-out-of-the-fuck-ing-car!" David punctuated each word with a blow to the driver's window. With the last word the window shattered, spraying me with glass.

I shrieked, threw the car in reverse, and peeled out of the driveway.

David jumped back, still screaming after me. "I love you, Kasey. Come back! Why are you leaving?"

Leaving the neighborhood, I ducked down side streets and took a random path in case he tried to follow. No thinking, just focusing on breathing, on getting away.

"It's okay, sweetie," I repeated over and over, not knowing which one of us needed reassurance. Poor Aida. I could barely make sense of this myself; how would I explain it to her?

I guided the car out of town, the night air coming in chilly through the open window. After a while, Aida's cries quieted into the soft sounds of sleep. I tried not to think about David's words, about my smashed window, about anything at all, and instead just drove with no destination in mind. Eventually, I looped back into town, yawning, to find a hotel for the night. Sorting out what to do about David and our marriage could wait until tomorrow.

Flashing blue lights behind me interrupted my daze. I pulled over to allow the police car to go around me, but, to my surprise, it stopped behind me. Just what I needed tonight.

I rolled down what was left of the window as an officer walked over. "Evening, ma'am," he said, shining a flashlight on me, then into the backseat, the beam lingering on the sleeping Aida for a moment.

I nodded, focused on digging my license out of my purse.

The flashlight beam was shining right into the car now, making it impossible for me to see his face in the darkness. "Kasey?"

"Andrew."

"What a nice surprise." He smiled at me, then became serious. "What's so important that you're going sixty in a thirty-five?"

"My husband—" I stopped, unsure of how much to tell him. "We had another fight tonight, and I guess I'm just distracted right now. I'm sorry." I offered him a weak smile.

He studied me, and I hoped he couldn't see what a mess I was in the dark. He leaned over to look at Aida in the backseat, but recoiled when his arms touched the broken glass littering the edge of the window. "What happened to your window?"

"It broke."

"Your hubby do this?"

I stared at him.

"Where you headed now? Not home, I hope."

I shrugged. "I don't know. Hotel, I guess."

"Unless you have your own credit card, I suggest you don't do that. He could easily check and see where you are. Have a friend or relative you could stay with?"

I shook my head. There was no one in the area that I knew well enough, especially at this time of night.

"Well, then, that leaves you no choice." He frowned. "You'll have to stay with me."

"You?" My pulse quickened, despite my current situation.

"Sure. I have room." I opened my mouth to protest, and he continued, "No, really, I insist. I want you to be safe."

"Why the concern? You barely know me." I immediately regretted my bluntness.

"Because I consider you a friend, and because I keep people safe. It's what I do." He shrugged.

My heart sank. I was a friend to him, that was all. Despite our conversation earlier, I was nothing more than a friend. He'd do the same to help anyone. I was nothing special to him. A small voice inside me whispered insidiously, why would I be anything else? I swallowed hard and nodded.

Andrew didn't seem to notice. "My shift isn't done until midnight. I'll take you over to my place and let you get settled in, then come back when I'm done. Sound good?"

I nodded again, not trusting myself to speak.

"All right, follow me then." He returned to his car and pulled back onto the road.

I followed closely behind, and we soon stopped outside an apartment building on the southeastern edge of downtown, the opposite side from where I lived.

I got out of the car, then carefully extracted my sleeping daughter, moving slowly so as not to wake her.

Andrew walked over to us. "Got any stuff?"

I shook my head.

"Then let me take your kid." Before I could object, he gently took Aida from my arms and draped her around him, her head on his shoulder. She stirred slightly but didn't wake. "I live on the third floor, and there's no elevator. This way."

I nodded and followed him up to his apartment, watching the way he tenderly and nonchalantly carried Aida, admiring his broad shoulders and muscled backside. My mind was a jumble of emotions and feelings. I was tired, first and foremost; arguments with David always seemed to sap all my energy. I was disconnected from the scene too; it was such an unexpected turn of events, it seemed surreal, a dream from which I would wake up any moment and find myself back at home calmly eating dinner, no shouting or broken car windows, no Andrew. Finally, slowly overpowering everything else, came desire. I again thought of how his arm had felt around me earlier that day, thought of his lips and kissing him, of sleeping next to him in his bed, of things we'd do to each other's bodies.

I was so preoccupied with these thoughts I almost ran into him when he stopped outside his apartment.

"Keep in mind, I'm a bachelor." He opened the door and gestured for me to enter first. "Y'all can have the bedroom, and I'll take the couch."

"No, you can't do that. We can take the couch. Or the floor."

"I've slept in a lot worse places than on a couch." He grinned. "I insist. It's easier this way."

Too tired to argue, I nodded, and Andrew carried Aida into the bedroom and gently laid her on the bed.

"I need to finish my shift. Make yourself at home, and I'll be back in a couple hours." Another quick grin, and he was gone.

With Aida fast asleep, I walked around the living room, taking in the details: a picture of an older woman, most likely his mother; a large American flag hanging on the wall, its edges tattered; a collection of mainly action DVDs; a homemade crocheted afghan draped on the back of the couch. Not much insight into his life, into him.

A glance at his kitchen revealed a coffeemaker and microwave on the counter, several speckled bananas and some old mail. I opened the refrigerator: milk, a bag of shredded cheese, some condiments and carrots, a couple six-packs and a half-full bottle of wine. Andrew definitely lived alone here.

I used the bathroom next, a room just as clean and empty. Inside the medicine cabinet, however, pill bottles lay in disarray; blood pressure medication, sleeping pills, antianxiety drugs. He apparently worked hard to portray himself as cool and collected, as functional.

His bedroom had as much personality as a cheap hotel room. Aida was fast asleep where Andrew had laid her, curled into a tight ball. I slipped off her shoes, eased her under the blankets, and kissed her forehead. Poor girl. I still didn't know what to tell her, still didn't know what to tell myself. I sighed, removed my jeans, folded them neatly on a chair in a corner of the room, and slid under the covers myself. The bed smelled of Andrew's aftershave, of his deodorant. While I'd dreamed of being in his bed, I never thought it would happen. Certainly not under circumstances like these.

Dead tired but free of distractions, my mind refused to calm down. I tried to think about David, about what to do the next day, but kept coming back to Andrew and his lips, being held close in his arms while he kissed me, feeling his powerful body under my hands. I lost track of the time as my mind went back and forth between the two men, caught between the uncertainty of my bond with my husband and the thrilling unknown possibilities with the strange man to whom I was so powerfully drawn.

After some time, the front door creaked open. Andrew entered, so comfortable in his surroundings that he didn't need any light other than that coming in from the streetlights. I lay still in bed as he paused at the bedroom doorway and leaned against the frame. My eyes had adjusted to the darkness, and I could see him watching me, his expression unreadable. After a few moments, he left. The bathroom door opened and shut, and the sound of running water was the last thing I heard before drifting off to sleep.

A noise awakened me, and I opened my eyes, momentarily disoriented in the dark. I glanced quickly at Aida, still sleeping soundly beside me. The noise came again, a low moan crossed with a whimper. Again I glanced at my daughter, but she wasn't the source. The noise came from beyond the bedroom.

I got out of bed and walked into the living room towards the noise, only vaguely aware I was half naked. The sound came from a large, dark shape on the couch.

"Andrew?" I whispered, cautiously approaching him.

He lay on his side, facing me, eyes tightly closed, body tensed. He moaned, whimpered, and shook his head.

I crouched down next to his head and gazed at his troubled features, fascinated by his vulnerability, wondering what could disturb this man's sleep so deeply. Without hesitation, seemingly involuntarily, I lightly stroked his cheek, felt the sandpapered texture of a day's worth of stubble. As my fingers touched his skin, he sighed softly but didn't wake. I left my hand resting gently on his face, and the tension melted from his body, his features calming, becoming more relaxed. It crossed my mind that I wouldn't be able to explain this if he woke, but I pushed the thought away.

Once he was breathing slowly and rhythmically, once I was certain the dream had passed, I leaned forward and lightly kissed his sleeping lips, then stood and returned to bed.

***

"Mommy?"

I opened my eyes to bright sunshine streaming onto the bed — Andrew's bed. So last night hadn't been a dream after all.

"Mommy, where are we?"

"We're at Mr. Andrew's apartment. Remember him? He's my friend we met at the farmers' market."

Aida stretched, yawned, and pushed her tousled blonde hair from her face. "Why are we at Mr. Andrew's place?"

"Daddy...." I hesitated. "Daddy and I had a fight last night, and Daddy's in time-out right now."

"He tried to hurt you." Her lip quivered as her eyes filled with tears.

"But he didn't." I pulled her close and gave her a big hug. "And—"

"And he won't," Andrew said from the doorway, his face unreadable.

"Promise, Mommy?"

"Promise." I kissed her forehead as she snuggled up next to me.

"Y'all hungry?" Andrew asked.

"I am!" Aida wiggled away from me.

Andrew smiled. "C'mon out to the kitchen, and we'll get you something."

She hopped out of bed and followed him into the other room. I quickly dressed and ducked into the bathroom, then joined them.

Aida sat at the kitchen table, her back to me, and Andrew leaned against the counter, arms folded across his broad chest, watching her. He looked over and smiled at me as I entered the room.

"Mr. Andrew has a gun," Aida announced as she shoveled cereal into her mouth.

"He's a police officer, so of course he has a gun."

"Have you ever shot somebody?" Aida asked, cocking her head and looking at him critically.

"Yes."

"Was it a bad guy?"

"Something like that."

"Did you kill him?"

"Aida!" I tilted my head and gave her that universal that's-not-a-nice-thing-to-ask look. "Enough questions. We need to get you ready for school."

"Do you feel comfortable enough with her being there?" Andrew asked.

I nodded. "She'll be fine. He's mad at me, not her." Until I knew what would happen with David, it was best to keep her routine as normal as possible.

"You can't drive her around with a broken window, and besides, you're a mess right now. I'll take her to school and explain what's going on. You stay here and get showered, and then, when I get back, we need to talk."

"I'm going too."

"You're a mess, Kasey. I know the counselor at her school. I'll explain everything."

"I'm going. She needs me."

"Mommy." Aida wrinkled her nose. "You kind of are a mess right now. I'll be okay with Mr. Andrew."

"See?" Andrew's half-smirk was back. "Ever ridden in a police car, kiddo?"

Her eyes shot wide. "Can you turn on the sirens? And the lights?"

"Sure, why not?" He grinned, and turned to me. "She's had breakfast. Does she need anything else before going to school?"

I shook my head, the surreal feeling from the day before returning. This should be my family — Andrew and Aida and me, happy together, loving, disagreements but no fighting, no hatred.

"All right, then let's roll out."

Aida came over and hugged me. "Bye, Mommy."

"Listen to Mr. Andrew, okay? He'll take good care of you." I held my daughter tight, long enough for her to squirm. "Everything's going to be okay, I promise. I love you."

"I love you too, Mommy." She pulled free and walked out the door, her small hand slipping into Andrew's larger one.

Surprise etched across his face, followed by a smile, a small, soft genuine expression that seemed to light up his whole being.

"I'll be back in a bit," he said over his shoulder. "Stay here."

I nodded, thinking of the kiss last night, of our conversation the day before, wondering what he wanted to talk about, but mostly focusing on the kiss. *And what about your husband?* a small nagging voice asked. *You're still married, and you have a daughter to think about.* I frowned, concentrating hard. *Stay or go, yes or no?*

After a moment, I picked up my purse, dug out pen and paper, scrawled "sorry" across the scrap, and left Andrew's apartment.

# Chapter 12 – Andrew (Age 24)

I sat in the recliner in the living room of my mama and stepdad's house, watching TV. It was a typical stupid sitcom, one where the mama is a bitch and the dad is an idiot and the children — there are three of them, always three, and one is a girl who dresses all slutty and one is a rebel and one is super smart — are rude, spoiled little brats.

I would've flipped to something else but it was all the same mindless garbage. How could people watch this crap when there were soldiers being killed overseas and barely a mention of it on the news? My best friend died so people could have one hundred channels of shows like this?

I thought of Matheson. I always thought about him — his round face, brown shining eyes, short black hair; his foot lying on the ground about three meters from a smoking hole in the ground; his helmet hanging from a tree five meters in the opposite direction, hanging from a branch as if placed there by a kid playing a game. But there weren't any children in that forest anymore. They were all hiding or dead. Probably dead, like Matheson. Just a hand left to remember them by, or maybe a foot, like Matheson.

It wasn't just his foot though. It was still in the sock and boot, of course, and a good chunk of leg remained attached to it. Some of the fabric of his pants too, which had been tucked into his boot per regulations. Surprisingly, very little blood covered everything. The blast had cauterized his wound when it blew his leg off, when it blew him apart so that all that remained of him was that foot.

My mind kept jumping around, from his smiling face to his foot to his helmet. Face foot helmet, face foot helmet. I closed my eyes and saw them, opened my eyes and they were still there. Face foot helmet. I turned back to the television, tried to focus on that instead. It didn't work. Face foot helmet.

Mama came into the room. She'd been extra cheerful since I got home a couple weeks ago, making all my favorite meals and babying me in a way I couldn't remember her ever doing before.

"What are you watching, Andrew?" She fluffed the pillow under my leg.

I'd taken a bullet in my shin, luckily through just the right spot to avoid amputation; the reason I was back home. With therapy I'd be fine, able to walk without a limp some day, but in the meantime I didn't mind. At least I still had a leg. All Matheson had was a foot.

"Stop fussing over me, Mama." Her constant attention made me nervous, irritable.

She paused, tears welling up in her tired eyes. "I'm worried about you, is all, sweetie. All you've done since you got home is sit in here and watch TV. Why don't you go hang out with your friends?"

"I don't have any friends anymore. They're all gone or dead."

"Oh, Andrew, that's not true. Don't say such things." She stood there a moment, then left the room to cry or make me a snack or something.

It was true though, what I said: hard to be friends with just a foot. Did they bury it, just a foot in a coffin, or did they throw it in a dumpster with other medical waste, or maybe take his foot out and reuse the boot? Everyone I'd known back here had moved on, either gotten married and had kids or left the area. Matheson's foot would never need to worry about moving on.

My stepdad came into the room, Mama a step behind him. "Enough bullshit, Andy," Gary bellowed. "Get off your ass and go find yourself a job."

"He can't walk," Mama exclaimed. She argued with him a lot more, I'd noticed. And he argued back a lot less. "How is he supposed to get a job if he can't walk?"

"He can't just sit here all day, Judy. He needs to get out and do something."

"I can walk, Mama." I raised myself out of the chair, wincing, grabbed my crutch and hobbled a couple steps. It was hard, painful, but manageable.

"See?" Gary crowed. "Stop babying him so much."

"He can't drive though." She put her hand on my arm. "Andrew, sit back down. Don't push yourself so hard."

"It's fine." Not really, but I was sick of sitting at home with her hovering over me and him yelling. I pushed past them to the front door. "I'll take the bus."

I got outside and made my way to the bus stop, pausing pretty often to rest my leg. I wanted to stop, to go back home, but I had to do this. I needed to prove I wasn't broken.

When the bus came, it took me longer to climb the stairs than everyone else. They all watched me, probably judging me. Matheson's foot didn't have to worry about stairs anymore.

I sat down in an empty seat towards the front and leaned my crutch next to me. Two girls sat across from me, one blonde and the other brunette. Their makeup was heavier than I preferred but their lack of clothing made up for it. Both wore low-cut, skin-tight t-shirts and shorts that left most of their tanned thighs exposed. I smiled at them.

The blonde eyed my bandaged leg. She whispered something to her friend, and they both looked at me and giggled.

I turned and looked out the window.

I got off downtown, feeling everyone staring at me as I limped down the stairs. Downtown didn't have much to offer: empty storefronts with run-down apartments above them, a few discount stores selling stained furniture and hand-me-down wedding dresses, law offices and county political party headquarters, a half dozen bars. The same generic face of shithole towns as when I'd left. I picked a bar and headed in.

It was mostly empty, not surprising for the middle of a weekday afternoon. It'd get busy around four or five o'clock, as everyone got off work and came over for a drink or five before going home to wives and girlfriends who nagged about rent money spent on booze, to whining children who didn't understand why they couldn't get the latest trendy shoes and video games. The guys gave in, of course, trying to make their kids happy because they remembered what it was like growing up and being the kid without, and sank deeper into debt. The drinking didn't help, but it was an hour or two of postponing the inevitable, at least.

I didn't want this life for myself, never had. Matheson's foot would never have a family to disappoint.

I sat down at the counter and ordered a beer. The bartender eyed me, maybe because I was someone new. I'd changed a lot in the last five years, more muscular, sporting a military crew cut, although mostly people said it was my eyes. When I looked at my reflection in the mirror, the same old blue eyes stared back at me, but apparently everyone else could see something more in them. Not me. All I saw was Matheson's foot. His brown eyes were gone, thanks to a land mine in Bosnia. Just his foot.

I recognized the bartender as a classmate a couple years ahead of me. His sister had been a year behind me. We went to the same parties. I couldn't remember his name. Matheson's first name was Brad. His helmet they found on the tree had "Rad" written on it, but no one ever called him that. As far as I knew they never found his other boot.

I finished my beer and ordered another. And another. And another. I drank the cheap stuff that tasted like piss, because my disability didn't add up to much. My stepdad was right; I needed to get a job, but with my leg all gimped–up, there wasn't much I could do. The idea of working in an office, stuck behind a desk all day, made my head hurt. I hated the idea of working in a factory too, and those were pretty much my only options if I stuck around here.

I decided to re-enlist.

Walking got even harder after four beers, but at least the pain wasn't as sharp. I pulled out a bottle of painkillers, which went everywhere with me now, and downed a few. Matheson's foot wasn't on the edge of my mind as much either. Part of his tibia stuck out, charred on the end, but I blinked it away.

I limped down the street towards a recruitment office a couple blocks away, aware of people staring at me as I leaned my full weight on the crutch. They made me increasingly pissed off, judging me without knowing my story, without knowing what I'd been through.

A car drove past honking like crazy. I ignored it and kept walking, but the rusty gray sedan pulled up next to me. The driver leaned over and, rolled down the window to reveal a white smile in a dark face. "Holy shit, Andrew, is that you?"

Mark, from high school. We'd been close, but then I got caught vandalizing our principal's house and he didn't. I entered the alternative school program and we grew apart. After enlisting and shipping overseas for five years, I didn't really keep in touch with anyone, especially kids from school who knew my life story. It was just too painful.

At that moment I decided to move to Kentucky near my dad, where no one knew me.

"Hey, man," I said.

"What happened to your leg?"

"Got shot."

"No shit! Where?"

"Bosnia."

"What the hell were you doing in Bosnia?"

"Getting shot in the leg."

"Real funny, man. No, I mean, why's our army in Bosnia? I don't even know where that is."

Matheson's foot floated across my mind. "Because there are some bad motherfuckers over there trying to kill all their neighbors. We were trying to prevent a genocide."

"No shit," he repeated, apparently amazed by the history lesson. "So I guess you saw combat?"

"Yeah."

"Kill anyone?"

I thought of Matheson's foot, and Matheson himself. We were out on patrol through a patch of forest near our base. Routine shit, did it everyday through the same spot. Matheson wasn't paying attention, stepped on one of the bouncing betties that littered the landscape, and froze.

"I'm fucked, guys," he said real quiet, eyes wide.

We all froze too, five of us plus him, guns at the ready.

"I stepped on a live one and can't move my foot!" Panic crept into his voice.

"Just stay calm," barked Rosenberg, our squad leader, with panic in his voice too. This was bad. "We'll radio back and get you help."

Everything probably would've been just fine, except that an ambush erupted out of the woods around us. My leg all of a sudden felt like it was on fire, and Rosenberg lay on the ground with half his head gone.

"Get down!" someone yelled, maybe me, I don't know, and we all dropped to the ground.

All except Matheson. "I can't move!"

What the fuck could we do, except shoot in the direction of our attackers?

Miraculously, Matheson was still standing. He took a deep breath. "There's a brush pile at your seven o'clock, about ten meters away. Gimme Rosenberg's gun and get over there to call this in."

"What about you?" Lee demanded. "We can't leave you."

"Go!" Matheson screamed, already firing into the trees.

We made it to the brush pile, me and Lee and Stutsman and Erickson. Stutsman hopped on the radio while I tried to shoot and not pass out from the pain in my leg.

Back out in the open, Matheson wore a scared but determined expression as he just kept firing into the trees, where the shots were already slowing. Then he took a hit in the chest and toppled. An explosion rocked the trees and our brush pile, and all fell quiet. Our attackers were dead or gone, we were bleeding from shrapnel wounds, and all that remained of Matheson was his foot, and his helmet in a tree.

"Andrew?"

I shook my head, bringing myself back to a humid sidewalk in Mississippi, away from the cold forest in Bosnia, a forest with dead bodies and a foot. "Yeah?"

"You okay?" Mark looked at me funny, a mixture of pity and confusion and fear and exasperation.

My temper flared. I deserved his respect, not his pity. What the fuck had he done with his life that made him think he was better than me? I saw my friends killed, young guys who had their whole lives ahead of them. And he'd been here instead, living a cushy pain-free life. I hated him, hated the whole fucking town. I needed to get out of here.

"I'm fine."

He wouldn't understand my feelings. No one did.

"We should grab a drink sometime, catch up on life," he suggested.

I didn't think he meant it. "Sure."

"Need a lift?"

"No, I'm just heading back to the bus stop." I'd re-enlist in Kentucky; no sense doing it here if I was leaving.

"Nonsense. Hop in, and I'll give you a ride. Staying with your mama?"

"Who else?"

He didn't respond, just watched as I maneuvered myself into his car, careful not to jostle my leg.

I noticed a car seat in the back. "You have kids now? You don't strike me as the family type."

"I've changed, man." He grinned at me, a big dopey grin full of pride. "We got a little boy, eighteen months old, and another one on the way."

"Congrats!" I meant it, glad to see him straightened out. "Who'd you end up with? Anyone I know?"

His smile faded a little. He glanced at me, then back at the road.

"Who?" My hands curled into fists.

"Carly."

The world stopped around me as his words sunk in. "My Carly?"

"What the fuck do you mean, *your* Carly? You left her, man!"

"Like hell I did!"

"Yeah, you did, Andrew. You went off to the army and didn't bother to keep in touch with her."

"She could've written me."

"She was busy with school. You had to have expected that. And then her mama passed away, and you were too busy with that other girl. Carly needed you and you weren't there. I was, so she turned to me. I love her, man, and you bet your ass I treat her good and don't take her for granted."

I remained silent, thinking about his words. True, I'd gotten a letter from her saying that her mama had died, leaving just Carly to take care of her younger sisters. I'd meant to write, meant to call, but I'd had my own problems with Jenna and our baby. Not that Carly had seemed to care about any of that.

I rubbed the bridge of my nose, let out a breath I didn't realize I'd been holding. "You're right. I fucked up and dropped the ball with her."

"Damn straight you did," Mark said, angry but calming down. "You should come by and see her sometime. Meet our kid."

"I will." I didn't know if that was the truth or not.

\*\*\*

That night, as I tried to fall asleep, Matheson's foot just wouldn't go away. Face foot helmet. I got up, went into the kitchen, and had a few shots of scotch. My leg was killing me so I downed a handful of painkillers too. If only they worked on more than just physical pain. At least the combination knocked me out quickly.

\*\*\*

*Me and Carly walked along a beach. The copper sunlight, filtered through layers of dust and smoke, cast long shadows on the sand. Burned up husks and parts of humvees and tanks and helicopters were washed up on shore, along with their dead crews. Carly tried to pull me away from the carnage, pleaded with me to walk above the high-tide line, but I fought her, looking for the rest of Matheson's body to reconnect with his foot. She must have realized her attempts to stop me were pointless, because she came over and helped me search.*

*She was digging through the corpses when they came back to life and tried to drag her away. She didn't scream, didn't resist, didn't fight back.*

*I grabbed my rifle and started shooting them, stabbing at them with my bayonet, but there were too many of them. As they dragged her into the water, I realized Matheson was the one holding her.*

*"I'll trade you," he said with a horrible grin. "Your girl for my foot."*

*I was frozen and couldn't run into the water. "I don't have your stupid foot!"*

*"Too bad....."*

*He pulled Carly under the water. She still didn't struggle, just watched through sad brown eyes filled with a quiet acceptance of her fate, watched me as if to say, 'what's the point in fighting when the outcome will be the same either way?'*

\*\*\*

I bolted upright in bed, drenched in sweat. Matheson's foot was again before my eyes. Face foot helmet.

I got up and limped back to the kitchen for another drink. I poured a shot, threw it back, then sat at the table with the bottle. I was glad Carly had found happiness. I was glad Mark was taking care of her. I threw back another shot, then a third.

Face foot helmet.

# Chapter 13 – Kasey (Present)

I left Andrew's apartment and drove home slowly, full of apprehension, not sure what awaited me. Would David still be there? Should I start packing? Where would I go? What about Aida? David's temper was all too familiar, but he'd never turned violent before, had never displayed so much rage.

The thought of bringing Andrew along had briefly crossed my mind, but he and David hated each other so much his presence would probably enrage David further, as would bringing along any other law enforcement. Better to chance it alone.

The house was quiet as I pulled into the driveway, the broken glass littering the concrete the only sign something disturbing had occurred last night.

I rested my hand on the door handle, ready to get out and face the aftermath, when the weight of what had happened hit me; not its effect on me, but on Aida. If he wanted to argue with me, to scream and get violent, that was one thing. But to do it all in front of our daughter?

He'd been attached to her, doting and devoted, since the day we learned I was pregnant.

We'd been married a couple years. I worked at *Women of the South* magazine, mostly copy editing but with the occasional writing assignment, supporting us while he wrapped up law school. We'd started discussing a family soon after we first started dating. David often joked that I was obsessed with the perfect family, but he understood why.

David came from a close family, had a brother and sister he saw at least once a week when we lived in Richmond. They shared everything, conquered everything together.

My family was the complete opposite: only child, distant parents. I didn't want that for my children, and neither did David. We wanted our kids to know they came first; family came first.

Maybe I was naive, but that spring before Aida was born, I attributed my fatigue and aching back to work-related stress, to apprehension over David's upcoming bar exams, and not to pregnancy. I'd never had a regular cycle, so when David forced me into my doctor's office to get my symptoms checked out, pregnancy was the last thing I'd expected.

\*\*\*

I was so excited I went straight from my appointment to the University of Richmond School of Law building, where David was finishing up an afternoon class. I sat on a bench under the stately trees that dotted campus, smiling like an idiot at everyone who walked past.

David came bounding out of the building, and I hurried over to him, trying to keep my face neutral.

"Kase!" He gave me a big kiss, then pulled away, worry in his brown eyes. "Everything go okay with the doctor?"

"Better than okay." I broke into a grin. "I'm pregnant."

"That's wonderful! Better than wonderful. Incredible. Amazing. Perfect. Wonderful. Did I say that already? Because it is. Absolutely wonderful!" He picked me up and spun me around. Not a moment's hesitation, fear, regret in his voice. Just happiness. Pure happiness.

As the pregnancy progressed, he spent nearly as much time talking to my belly as he did to me. In addition to telling the baby how excited we were to meet her, how happy we were to have her as a part of our family, and how much we loved her, he told her about all the plans he had for our future. He told her he'd personally see to it she was the most spoiled, well-loved child who ever existed, that she'd always come first, me and her, no matter what.

The day Aida was born, a cold, dreary December day, might have been the happiest day of David's life, more than when he proposed and I said yes, more than our wedding. The nurse laid her on my chest, a tiny squalling ball of flesh, and I couldn't help but marvel at her. Our perfect baby.

David stroked my cheek, then turned his attention to our daughter. "Hey there, Aida," he whispered. "Welcome to our family." He reached for her hand, and her tiny fingers curled around his. He smiled at her, tears glittering in his eyes. "I love you. You and your mommy both, and I promise nothing is ever going to change that."

\*\*\*

Now, sitting in my car and staring at the mess in the yard, his words from almost seven years before echoed in my head. I swallowed down my tears, my memories and regrets, and opened the car. I owed it to Aida to straighten this out, one way or another.

I clutched my keys tightly in my fist, ready to strike and defend if necessary. The front door was unlocked. Slowly, cautiously, I entered the house. Broken dishes lay scattered everywhere, and a glimpse into the living room showed at least one bookshelf had been overturned, with papers and pages coating every surface.

I sagged against the wall. Whatever I'd expected, a tangible sign of our broken marriage wasn't it.

"Hello?"

No answer.

"David?"

Still no answer. I moved into the living room, cringing at the reckless destruction. In addition to the bookshelf, several lamps were knocked over, and a window overlooking the side yard was broken out.

Sprawled on his stomach in the middle of the mess on the floor was my husband, snoring loudly. Snoring as if everything were okay, as if nothing had happened last night.

Seeing him there strengthened my resolve. I owed it to Aida to protect her from all this, and so did he. I nudged him in the ribs with my foot.

No response.

I nudged him again, so hard it was almost a kick.

"What the fuck?" he muttered in a thick, slurred voice. "Leave me alone."

I kicked him again, nowhere near a nudge. "Get up."

His eyes fluttered open, then closed again. "Leave me alone."

"Get up." Another kick, keeping my voice impassive, focusing on his promise to Aida.

"God, Kasey, what do you want?" He still didn't move.

"Get up." Kick.

"Stop kicking me!" He tried to grab my foot but failed, probably because he was lying on the floor with his eyes closed.

"Get up." Kick.

"Fine, fine." He opened his eyes, winced at the light, and rolled over, his expression pained from the movement. He caught sight of the room. "Holy shit, what happened?"

"You don't remember?" I tried to keep my voice even, but disbelief crept in. How could he not remember?

"Remember what?" He lay on the floor holding his head in his hands, as if the room were spinning and he could keep himself straight if only he held tightly enough.

"Last night."

"What happened?" The man was genuinely baffled, honestly couldn't remember a thing. "This mess — did I do this, Kasey?" His voice wavered, the gravity of the situation sinking in.

I nodded, trying not to cry, not trusting myself to speak. I wanted to scream in frustration, wanted to kick him and run out the door and never see him again, wanted to hold him and tell him that everything would be okay, wanted him to hold me and make everything better and magical again. Mostly, I wanted to sink down and cry until the events of the last day, of the last few months, were washed away and forgotten.

I did none of that, however. Instead, I looked at him until I felt able to speak, and said in as icy a voice as possible, "Yes, David, you did this."

He struggled to his knees in front of me and grasped my hand, his bloodshot eyes bright with tears. "I am so sorry, Kasey. I don't know why I did this, because you know I love you, right? You and Aida are my life, and I would never do anything to hurt you." He paused, horror in his eyes. "Oh my

God, where's Aida? Did I—" He stopped and looked at me with eyes begging me to lay his fears to rest.

"She's at school. We left before you could throw things at us."

He took a breath, nodded, and pulled himself up using the couch as a crutch. "Did you go to a hotel?"

I hesitated. If he knew the truth, chances were he'd blow up at me. On the other hand, he'd most likely find out anyway, so perhaps it was best to tell him now.

Despite being hungover, probably still drunk, he noticed my hesitation. "Where did you go?" Eyes narrowed, voice cold, remorse for his actions disappearing.

"Andrew's."

"Did you fuck him?"

"What?" My jaw dropped. "Of course not!"

"Really."

Anger surged through me. My husband had admitted to connecting better with his mistress than with his wife, smashed up my car and our house in front of our six-year-old daughter, and yet he felt the need to level accusations at me? "What if I did?" I asked, deliberately provoking him. "How many times did you screw someone behind my back? Don't I get a turn?"

David's eyes bulged in rage, teeth clenched. Wordlessly, so quickly I didn't have time to react, he slapped me hard across the face.

I crumpled to the floor, hand to my stinging cheek, eyes gleaming with tears I struggled to hold back. But the tears weren't of sadness, not anymore. They were of rage, pure and simple. Rage and disgust. Any sympathy I'd had for him, any desire to fix our marriage, vanished.

He dropped down and crouched on the floor next to me. "Oh my God, Kasey, I'm so sorry. I didn't mean to hit you. I don't know what came over me!" He put his hand on mine, and I flinched.

"Get out," I told him in a low voice.

"But I love you!"

"Get. Out," I said again, each word a punch in the air.

"I said I was sorry!"

"Get. Out."

"But Kasey—"

"Get out!"

"You can't kick me out. I paid for this house. You don't even have a job." He sneered.

"So?" I stood, making sure to face him. My last remaining trust in him now gone, I backed towards the door. "I want you out by the time Aida's done with school, or I'm filing assault charges."

"You wouldn't." He took a step towards me.

"Wanna bet?"

He took a deep breath. "Kasey, let's discuss this rationally." He used what I considered his "courtroom voice."

"Rationally?" I laughed. "We're beyond rationality at this point." I placed my hand on the doorknob behind me. "By the time Aida's home from school, David."

I walked out the door.

He didn't follow.

I didn't want to be in my car with the broken window, yet another reminder of what had happened, so I walked down the sidewalk with no destination in mind. I tried to sort through everything that had happened in the last twenty-four hours, but it was so far from my normal life, so different from anything I'd ever expected to happen to me, that I had a hard time wrapping my mind around it.

Disconnected scenes surfaced and sank: David's slap, flashing red and blue police lights, Andrew's arm around me, the shattering of my car window, kissing Andrew's lips. Always back to the feel of his lips on mine, the feel of his cheek under my hand, amazement at my ability to soothe his nightmares.

With everything that had happened, why did my thoughts always come back to him? Hadn't last night shown me we were friends, nothing more? We could've moved Aida to the couch so he could share the bed with me. Was he that much of a gentleman, showing restraint, or did he truly not want more?

Tears stung my eyes, and I angrily, clumsily, wiped them away. Meaning nothing to him hurt me more than the dissolution of my marriage, than the slap, than all David's angry rants. I tried, for the hundredth time, to decipher why exactly I felt so strongly about Andrew, but once again there was nothing I could concretely put my finger on. He simply felt right, right in a way David never had despite all our years together, despite everything we'd shared.

Not that it mattered. I could either love Andrew or hate him as intently as I wanted, but if he had no feelings for me, none of that mattered. How ironic, tragic even, that Andrew was the one who respected my marital status. David didn't, and I certainly didn't, as evidenced by my inability to get Andrew out of my thoughts.

If only I could talk to someone about this. Before I moved, Ann would have been my confidante. Ann, who'd slept with my husband for God knows how long. Ann, who'd listened to me complain about my marriage, about David, and agreed her husband was the same way. No talking to Ann now. Punching her, maybe, or clawing her eyes out, but not talking.

David was so blind with jealousy over Andrew, so in denial of his affairs' effect on us, there was no point in even talking to him. Better to make him leave. Better for me and Aida to move on without him.

*Aida.* I squeezed my eyes shut and willed away the tears, needing to focus for her sake. I hated David so much right now, wanted him gone, but what was best for Aida? Did I owe it to her to try one more time to work things out?

David's words from last night came back to me. He'd tried to lay the blame on me for his affairs. Would it have made a difference if I'd been open with him about my feelings, about what I wanted from life? I'd gone along with whatever he wanted, trying to keep the peace, to make him happy. I'd thought that was what he wanted, but that wasn't what he'd wanted at all, although he hadn't told me that either. Our lack of communication went both ways.

Andrew had said we needed to talk, but we weren't much better at communicating than David and me. At least Andrew and I held nothing back, speaking our minds instead of trying to keep the peace. We were open about everything except the things that mattered, like my feelings for him and his for me.

As I saw it, there were only two possible outcomes of confiding in him: I open up, and just like David he thinks I'm too passive, my situation too messy, and he wants nothing more to do with me; or, even worse, he returns my feelings and I become dependent on him, just like I'd depended on David, and then he'd want nothing to do with me.

I thought of the previous night's stolen kiss, pointless and wonderful, and wanted to go to him now, but couldn't. Not until I knew where we stood.

***

I approached McKay's, wiping at my wet cheeks with the backs of my hands, only mildly surprised to find myself there. Outside the door, hand on the knob, I paused with the realization that I didn't want to be there, didn't want to be around people.

I turned away and continued down the street, unsure of where to go but needing to go somewhere. Less than a block later, a voice behind me called out my name, so I stopped and turned around.

Andrew quickly approached, in uniform and holding a to-go cup.

I waited for him to catch up.

"Hey," he said when he reached me, his eyes showing concern as they searched mine.

"Hey."

"Everything okay?"

I glanced down at my clothes, the same ones from last night and that morning at his apartment. Did he even notice? "Sure."

"Really?"

"David and I had another fight." Simple, to the point.

"Your husband is an ass."

I nodded, teeth clenched to hold back the sobs I didn't want Andrew to see.

He took me by the hand and again led me to the secluded park hidden within the block, and we sat down on a bench. "You left this morning."

"Yeah."

"Why? I told you to stay."

"And I have to do everything you say?" A half-smile was all I could muster at the moment.

"You should, yeah."

"Why?"

"Why don't you trust me?" He turned towards me and our knees touched. His pale blue eyes studied me.

I looked away, knowing that if I didn't I'd tell him everything. "I trusted David. Look where that got me."

"Great love involves great risk." He took my hand in his. "Sometimes you roll the dice and pray the other person is investing the same." The sadness, the regret in his voice, caused me to look back at him. "Sometimes all you can do is pray, Kasey."

"I rolled those dice, and lost."

"I've lost too, more times than I want to remember, but you have to keep a little faith." He looked at me again, straight into my eyes. "You're married, you have a kid, but you're not happy."

"No." My marriage, my husband, my current life—none of it made me happy or content, and it hadn't for quite a while. My mind darted back to the feel of Andrew's lips the night before; that made me happy.

"I shouldn't say anything," he said. "I'm just an old soldier. What do I know about your life, about anything?"

"No. Sad to say, right now we're so far apart, I don't know what will happen. But whatever happens, I'm not going to deliberately hurt my husband." *Even though he's deliberately hurt me.*

Andrew said nothing, again looking at my hand while running his fingers over mine.

"You hide behind that soldier argument a lot." I tried to change the subject back to something more comfortable.

He shook his head. "It's not hiding so much as a fact. I don't expect to live a long life. I accepted it a long time ago. So, what I learned is, no matter how brief, follow your heart. Matter of fact, I'm amazed to still be around after some of the stuff I've been through."

"Maybe God has something else in mind for you."

He shrugged. "Who's to say?"

We sat quietly for a moment. Andrew's eyes were unfocused, probably thinking hard, but I couldn't tell about what. He was so unpredictable, just as likely to lean over and kiss me as he was to stand up and walk away.

*A kiss.* I knew I should focus on David, on what I was going to do if he didn't leave, on what I'd do if he actually did, and what I'd tell Aida, either way. But sitting there, Andrew's hand warm and comfortable in mine, it was hard to focus on anything but the man next to me.

"The way I see it," he said, breaking the silence, "if you love someone, and they love you, you take care of each other no matter what. That's the way it's supposed to be, right?"

David had wanted to take care of me too. "What if she doesn't want to be taken care of?"

"Don't mistake wanting to protect someone as a sign of weakness," he said, bemusement playing across his lips. "Man and woman were given strengths and weaknesses. Together, we fill each other in to make a solid whole."

"As long as you accept she's still her own person."

"Of course, but every woman has different needs, wants, and desires. It's hard to try and figure out what they are."

"It's not hard to figure someone out if you care enough about them to do so."

"True, but it helps if they return it. Sometimes you go for the wrong person."

"That hardly matters," I argued, my heart racing. We'd never really discussed relationships before, and I wasn't sure how hypothetical Andrew was being. "Sometimes you just care about someone, and helping them is enough of a reward, no returned feelings necessary."

"If you end up where you give more than you get, after a time, you're sucked dry, and there's nothing left." He shook his head. "My mama told me something once. She said love isn't fifty-fifty, like in the movies. Sometimes your partner may be down or whatever, and it may be seventy-thirty, where you give more than you get. But, after that, when you're dealing with more, your partner will be there for you to give you what you need."

His words hit home. Maybe that had been the problem with me and David, that give and take. We'd been so busy trying to give each other what we thought was needed that we'd missed the mark, burned ourselves out on our relationship. David had reacted with affairs, with drinking, while I'd—

What had I done? Thrown myself into a life I didn't want? Focused more on meeting Aida's needs than David's? Maybe the problem was I hadn't found an escape.

"Have you been in an equal, give-as-necessary relationship like that?" I asked.

"No," he said bitterly. "Usually the girl I'm with is great until I deploy, and then she has 'needs' and breaks up with me when I need her most. Every time, it's been the same thing."

I nodded. I had no experience with the military but imagined that deployment would be hard on everyone.

"Have you ever just given yourself to someone, trusted he'd take care of you, without worrying about being hurt by him?" he asked, changing the subject away from his past.

"Yes." I thought of David, of him and Ann. "It wasn't enough."

"Maybe he wasn't the right one."

"He was the right one in the beginning, but now...." I shrugged and closed my eyes. In the midst of our destroyed living room had been a broken frame holding our wedding picture. Had it been intentional? "Now I'm not sure. I thought I still loved my husband, but after last night, after today, I just don't know. Part of me wants to leave, but part of me still wants to try to work things out."

"Well, there's not much I can say then." Andrew's fingers traced the lines of my palm. "If you're this conflicted, I think we both know what your choice really is. Seems like you've given up on the possibility of anything better."

I thought of all that was lost: my home in Richmond and everything and everyone that went with it, my dignity as David's affairs had been revealed to the community, and now possibly my home in Asheville as well. Most importantly, during my marriage to David I'd lost my sense of self, and as my world continued to crumble around me, I didn't even know where to begin to look for it. "I've given up on a lot."

"Maybe I can help." He raised my hand to his lips and kissed it softly.

"I'm making excuses, I know." I tried not to show how the feel of his lips on my skin thrilled me. "But it's difficult to put yourself first when you have family depending on you."

"Kasey," he said, voice low, "a personal dream now and then isn't so bad, is it?"

"I guess not."

Andrew leaned in and gently, lightly, pressed his lips against mine. The world froze, just the two of us hidden away together. Could he actually be kissing me, be feeling what I'd felt for months now? This was the perfect moment, only....

"I'm married." I pulled back from him, my body screaming at me not to.

He stared at me, his pale eyes blazing with emotion. "Who knows what lies ahead, but for now maybe we could take care of each other."

To back up his words, his hands drifted across the jeans covering my thighs, his fingers leaving a burning desire in their wake.

Despite what my body and my heart were crying out for, what was happening, what could happen, wasn't something I'd do. Despite what David had done, despite not knowing myself anymore, I still couldn't cheat on my husband.

"Andrew, I don't know—"

"Just trust me." He kissed me again, this time so deeply my body melted against him.

I couldn't help giving in, forcing away the turmoil in my mind. There'd be plenty of time to sort through it all later, decide what to do. Someone, who didn't feel like me, leaned in and kissed him again. I shivered, not so much from the cool fall air but from the delicate pressure of his hands as they slid over my body. I wanted this moment to never end, to stay here in his arms forever. There were no problems here, just the safety of his lips.

The radio on his shoulder squawked and, reluctantly, he pulled away. "Duty calls." He kissed me again anyway, just a small one that left me wanting more. "We'll talk later, okay?"

I nodded, not sure of my ability to form a coherent sentence, or what words or feelings I even wanted to convey.

"Dreams, Kasey." He smiled, a superior, conquering smile that gave a hint of what could be between us, then walked away down the alley.

I remained on the bench for awhile, deep in thought. No matter what Andrew said, I didn't need protection. I needed a partner, an accomplice, not a savior. I didn't belong to anyone but myself; not to David, not to Andrew. I wasn't some property to be owned, and would give myself to whomever I chose. No one could take that from me.

Now I had to decide who got me. My lips twisted into a sideways smile. If only it could be that simple.

It used to be, though. It had been for David, at least. We'd been on a handful of dates when we went to a party at a friend's frat house. The atmosphere had been raucous, overwhelming for someone like me who was used to quiet evenings curled up with a book. David had taken charge, his arm snugly around me as he introduced me around. "This is my girlfriend, Kasey," he told everyone.

It was the first time he'd said those words. Technically, I was his girlfriend at that point, as much time as we'd spent together, but he hadn't asked, hadn't said anything about it. He just declared it, right there in front of everyone. While a part of me was annoyed at his presumption, an even larger part of me was flattered: David wanted me, didn't want anyone else to have me.

Looking back, that night set a pattern for us, a relationship that wouldn't change for over a decade. Because I was his girlfriend, his wife, his, because he was the one who chose me, I let him take the lead. I clung to his side at social events I wouldn't have gone to otherwise. I let him pick our house, our vacations. Once that pattern was set, it was easier to follow than to change. Over time, I became who he wanted me to be.

Except I wasn't anyone, at least not anyone I recognized, not anyone I wanted to be. Not anyone he wanted either, as his actions clearly illustrated.

I wouldn't make the same mistake with Andrew, no matter what happened between me and him, between me and David. Moving to Asheville had been a wake-up call for me, an opportunity for me to be the person I'd always wanted to be, whoever that was.

I remained on the bench, idly watching the squirrels chase each other through the grass. The questions floated in my head: Who was I? Who did I want to be?

First and foremost, I was a mother.

I jumped up. *Aida.* What kind of mother was I to have sent her to school after what happened last night, sent her with a near stranger? I hurried out of the alleyway, pausing on the sidewalk. My car was back home, and I didn't want to drive it with a smashed window. Besides, David would probably still be there, and I definitely didn't want to see him right now.

As I glanced around, trying to decide what to do, my eyes fell on Erica and Ron's shop. I hurried over, an idea forming in my mind.

The bell jangled as I opened the door. A couple women, both retirement age and wearing glasses with brightly-colored jewels on the rims, browsed through racks of earrings and necklaces.

Ron looked over at me from behind the counter. "Kasey! You look...." He frowned. "Everything okay?"

I ignored his question. "I have a huge favor to ask you. My car's in the shop, and I need to pick up my daughter. Do you think I could get a ride?"

He reached down under the counter. "Take my car. I'm manning the shop today and don't need it. We'll come by and pick it up tonight." He tossed me a set of keys. "It's the green Civic parked behind the building."

"Are you sure that's okay? You don't really know me that well."

"Yeah, just don't wreck it or anything." He smiled at me, his grin not reaching his eyes. "And know that, if you need anything else, even just someone to listen, Erica and I are here for you, okay?"

I blinked rapidly and pushed a smile onto my face. "Yeah, thanks."

First things first: I stopped at Walgreens and bought some toiletries, just enough to freshen up in the bathroom and let me feel human again.

Next I went to Aida's school and pulled her out for the afternoon.

"Mommy!" she squealed as she walked down the hallway towards me. She broke into a run, threw her arms around my waist and buried her head in my stomach.

I knelt down to her level and hugged her close, breathing in the faded, yet familiar, scent of Johnson's baby shampoo.

She pulled back after a minute and eyed me suspiciously. "Is everything okay?"

"Yeah." I took her hand and led her outside. "I figured, after the last day or so, we could use some girl time together. I know you really like school—"

"Mommy, I'm playing hooky," she said in a loud whisper. "Mr. Andrew won't arrest me for it, will he?"

I laughed. "No, not if we don't make a habit of it."

Aida eyed Ron's car, so different from my own BMW, and her nose wrinkled. "You got a new car?"

"No, I'm borrowing a friend's while mine gets fixed."

"'Cuz Daddy broke yours, right?" Her lower lip trembled.

I hadn't meant to bring that up so soon, and quickly changed the subject. "Want to go to Mac's for lunch?"

Her lower lip relaxed and she nodded; meltdown postponed.

I kept the conversation light, focusing on innocuous subjects like school and Barbies. After Aida had finished her fried okra and mac 'n' cheese, and I'd polished off my own barbecue, we visited the Western North Carolina Nature Center, a zoo-like place filled with native Appalachian species. The combination of the sunshine and the still-warm late September temperatures made it the perfect spot to wander around, talking about what had happened.

"Why did Daddy get so mad?"

I sighed. How to explain to a little girl that alcohol turned her father into a raging asshole? "Sometimes, when Daddy's had too much to drink, it makes him mean."

She turned away from the wolf enclosure she'd been studying and stared up at me. "But Daddy's not a mean person. He's a good guy, right?"

"Well, yeah, most of the time. It's just that sometimes—"

"I don't want him to be mean anymore." Her big blue eyes regarded mine. "Is he going to leave now, Mommy?"

"What?" I hadn't expected this from her.

"Kayden said his parents yelled at each other all the time, and then one day his daddy left and moved to another house and doesn't live with them anymore." Her lip quivered again, big tears welling up in her eyes. "I don't want Daddy to leave, Mommy."

I took her into my arms. "Sweetie, it's not that easy. Sometimes it's better if mommies and daddies don't live together."

"What'll happen to me?" She sobbed into my shoulder.

I swallowed hard. "We'll always love you, Aida. No matter what happens, we'll always put you first. Promise."

She pulled away from me and wiped at her runny nose with her hand. "Maybe we can make him nice again."

"Aida, sweetie—"

"Please, Mommy?" She shook her head, tears running down her face. "I don't want Daddy to leave."

"We'll see."

\*\*\*

Aida calmed down, and we wandered around the park until the time she would've been out of school, taking in the antics of the otters and black bears, feeding the farm animals.

As we headed home in Ron's borrowed car, my thoughts were a mess. I didn't know what I'd find there, didn't know what I'd do if David was gone, if he'd passed out drunk again after destroying more of our possessions. I'd thought I was done with him, especially after Andrew's morning kisses, but my conversation with Aida left me undecided once again.

When I turned onto our street, my jaw dropped. At least half a dozen vans and trucks were parked in front of our house: construction company, carpet cleaner, glass company, and a couple florists. I parked as close as I could to the house and walked inside.

The mess from earlier was gone, including the broken window and the food and alcohol stains on the carpet. Floor-to-ceiling bookcases replaced the ones David had toppled, filled with books and the random knickknacks that had previously decorated the shelves. The house smelled of new paint and fresh flowers.

Walking into the dining room, I involuntarily gasped as Aida squealed and clapped her hands together. The room was filled with probably hundreds of roses in bright pinks, pale whites, and vibrant reds.

David heard Aida and hurried into the room. Before I could demand an explanation, he said, "Kasey, I know I'm supposed to be gone, but after you left I thought long and hard about us, about how much you mean to me, and I realized I can't keep getting mad at you. I'm going to change, Kasey. I have already. I promise: no more drinking, no more yelling. You and Aida mean the world to me, and I'd be lost without you. So, please, I'm begging you, let me stay."

He dropped to his knees in front of me and pulled out a small box. "I love you, Kasey. I want to be married to you. I want to be with you, just you. What do you say? Please? You're so good for me. You balance me out. I need you. You need me. I love you." He opened the box to reveal a small ring, a simple band with alternating diamonds and sapphires set in it. "Will you take me back? Will you marry me again? Stay married to me?"

I looked down at my husband, feeling nothing for him — no hate, no love, nothing. He'd done something similar when I'd tried to leave him before, and look where that had gotten me. I thought of his shouted abuse, his slap, my terror when he broke the car window. I thought of Andrew, of how it had felt to kiss him. I thought of how much the ring and flowers had most likely cost. Finally, I thought of Aida, crying in the park over the idea of losing her father.

"I don't know." I looked him directly in the eyes. "I don't know."

"What?" His smile faltered slightly. Clearly he hadn't expected this.

"We've gone through this before. I don't know if I want to do it again."

David's jaw clenched, and I waited for the explosion. He surprised me, however. "I can respect that. I've hurt you, and it's not fair for me to expect you to immediately take me back, but I've changed. I want to make this work."

"You've said all this before."

"Can I prove it to you?"

"I don't know, David. And that's the best answer I can give you right now."

"I can live with that," he said, smiling. "Will you at least wear the ring?"

I looked at it. "I'll think about it."

***

David was charming, sweet, funny the rest of the night. He'd gotten rid of all the alcohol while I was gone, but no telling how long his repentance would last this time.

I didn't want him back, but I didn't want to start a fight, not with Aida still so upset, so I kept quiet and played along, civil but not affectionate.

After he was in bed — sleeping in the master bedroom while I was back in the guestroom — I climbed out of bed and stood outside his door. His soft snores drifted out.

Quietly, I left the house. David had fixed my car window, part of his Great Cleanup, so I drove it to Andrew's apartment building. The porch light shone outside his place. Heart pounding, I walked up the outside stairs and knocked on his door.

He opened it, wearing only a pair of sweatpants. A Chinese character was tattooed above his heart, and a small dragon chased itself around his right bicep. My heart beat more and more quickly as, wordlessly, he took my hand, pulled me into his apartment, and shut the door behind us.

"Andrew," I whispered, "I—"

He cupped my face with his hand and kissed me, silencing me as his tongue brushed against mine. His other hand found the small of my back and pulled my body towards his.

"Andrew," I tried again.

"Don't talk," he murmured between kisses. "Don't think. Just feel."

I nodded and focused on the feel of his lips. Finally, his lips on mine, with no interruptions. His mouth drifted to my neck, eliciting a sighing moan and suffusing my body with a happy warmth. He slipped my jacket off, then carefully, but quickly, unbuttoned my blouse, and tossed them both to the floor. Staring into my eyes, he took my hand again and backed into the bedroom, pulling me behind him.

My breath came in shallow, controlled sips of air. Thoughts popped into my head, of David and what I was doing, but I pushed them aside. Andrew was right: tonight, right now, I just needed to feel.

His bedroom was illuminated only by the glow of the streetlights, but neither of us moved to turn on a lamp. He sat on the edge of his bed and gently pulled me in front of him, his lips parted slightly, his breath as shallow as mine. This was yet another side to him, a nervous, uncertain side. Feeling the same as me, it seemed, although why he was nervous I couldn't guess. Wasn't this what he'd been trying to get for a couple months? Wasn't this what I'd been trying to get too?

Heart pounding in my chest, I unfastened my jeans, slid them off my hips and stepped out of them.

Andrew's gaze left my eyes, deliberately drifting down to my thighs and lingering there. He reached around and unhooked my bra, and his breath grew even shallower.

"You're beautiful, Kasey," he said in a low voice. His fingertips brushed my breasts, trailed across my belly to my navy panties and between my legs.

I closed my eyes, concentrating on his hands.

"So beautiful."

Then his touch was gone. I opened my eyes and looked down at him. His own eyes were closed, and his expression was hard to decipher. Fear, perhaps? Sadness?

I placed my hands on his bare shoulders, delighting in the way his muscles felt. "Andrew? Everything okay?"

He studied me, his face still a mix of emotions, while I traced a barely-visible scar on his chin, then ran my finger lightly across his lips. He smiled, that half-smirk lighting up his face. Before I realized what he was doing, he flung me on the bed and slipped off both my panties and his sweatpants.

I closed my eyes, heard a wrapper crinkle, and then he was inside me.

I gasped, moaned and squirmed underneath him, clawed at his back and pulled him close enough to fuse our bodies together. I begged him to stop because the feelings inside me were so intense, begged him to never stop for the same reasons. Finally, after an eternity that was over in a blink of an eye, he tensed and sighed out my name, then collapsed on top of me.

I lifted his face and kissed his lips, trying to give him back just a fraction of the happiness and satisfaction coursing through my body at the moment. He smiled, rolled over and pulled the sheets back, and I crawled underneath them and snuggled next to him, completely and utterly content.

# Chapter 14 – Andrew (Age 29)

The door slammed, the sound echoing in my already aching skull. I opened my eyes and saw Aimee's older son was home. Eric was ten, old enough to do whatever he wanted in the afternoons. Normally we watched *Jeopardy* when he got home from school, but today I just wanted to lie on the couch in the darkened living room. I'd had a long day at the station, full of pointless paperwork, and the official letter waiting for me when I got home hadn't helped my mood any.

A few minutes later the door slammed again. Without opening my eyes I knew it was my girlfriend's younger son. Sam was seven and not nearly as self-sufficient as his brother. I wasn't in the mood for the requests that would be coming my way.

"Andrew, I'm hungry."

"So get something to eat." I didn't open my eyes, didn't move.

"But Mom said I'm s'posed to ask first!" he whined.

"You did, and I told you to go find something." I still didn't open my eyes.

He ran off to the kitchen, and then came a large crash, breaking glass, crying.

*Fuck.*

I was working my way up to getting off the couch to check on Sam when the door opened again. This time it was Aimee.

"Hi, boys!" she called out, sounding tired as hell but still cheerful. "I'm home!" Upon hearing Sam crying, she dropped her purse and rushed to the kitchen.

I heaved myself up from the couch and followed her. The kitchen was a big mess. It seemed Sam had pushed a chair over to the counter to climb up and get a snack. He slipped and knocked over the chair—the crash—and a jar of spaghetti sauce had somehow broken and splattered all over the kitchen. He wasn't hurt, just scared.

Aimee scooped him up into her arms even though he was too old for that. She stroked his hair, murmured to him that everything would be okay, and then turned accusing eyes to me.

"You were supposed to be watching him, Andrew," she said, as if it was my fault her kid was a klutz.

"I was trying to take a nap. He's seven, for God's sake. I figured he was capable of getting a snack by himself."

"He's seven, for God's sake!" she shot back. "Seven! He can't do everything by himself."

"You baby him too much." I turned back towards the couch. The late afternoon sun reflecting off the yellow kitchen walls wasn't helping my headache any.

"So you're going to just leave this mess?"

"Yes." All I could think about was the couch and that letter.

"What about dinner?" She wouldn't leave me alone. "It was your turn to cook. You haven't even started."

"I'll order us a pizza."

"And where are we going to get the money for a pizza?" Her voice was tight, shrill.

"Don't go out drinking with your slutty friends this week."

Her whole body tensed, hitting me with regret for those words. Money was tight, even with both of us working, and she sacrificed a lot for us, rarely went out.

"Sam," she said, "go play in your room."

The boy ran out of the kitchen and slammed his bedroom door shut, but if we looked, he and Eric would probably be standing in the hallway trying to listen to me and their mama.

Growing up, when my mama and stepdad would fight, I'd always go to my room and crawl under my bed, head buried under a pillow trying not to hear the shouts and slaps, but then again the fighting was usually about something I'd done that he was trying to blame on her. It was hard to be in a house where everyone fought, with someone who wasn't your real dad, who you knew didn't care about you like he would his own kid. Me and Jenna's baby would've been the same age as Eric; how would I feel if it was my kid living like this?

I grabbed some paper towels to clean up the mess.

Aimee leaned against the counter, watching me. She looked great even though it was the end of the day and she had to have been tired and frazzled and I'd disappointed her yet again.

"You look beautiful." I dropped the paper towels in the garbage and walked over to kiss her.

She turned her head away from me, frowned and bit her lip. Looking down at her hands she said, "Andrew, we need to talk."

My stomach dropped. We'd been together for two years, living in the apartment for over half of that. I didn't know if I loved her, but I knew she was a big part of me and I liked having her around.

"This just isn't working, hon." She stared into my eyes, daring me to agree with her but pleading with me not to, to reassure her that it really was working.

She was right, though: this *wasn't* working. We argued a lot, and did petty stupid little things to purposefully piss each other off. We had different goals and priorities; she had her kids to think of, and I had me. We could make it work if we really tried, I had no doubt, but that wasn't fair to either of us. I wanted true love, the perfect partner for my own perfect family, and Aimee wanted — well, I didn't know what she wanted, but it wasn't me.

I didn't say this to her, though. I wasn't ready for our relationship to end, not today, not after that letter. She wasn't the one I needed, but I needed *someone* right now.

"I'm sorry," I said, because it was what she wanted me to say. "I'll make dinner right now, okay?"

She shook her head slowly. "Sorry doesn't work this time. I know you work all day and you're tired when you get home, but I'm tired too. Sam and Eric aren't your kids, but if you can't help me with them then we're done. You knew that coming into this."

Again she was right. She needed a partner, someone who could support her in all the ways she needed, not the ways I thought she needed. She hadn't had an easy life—although, really, who had—and yet again someone had let her down.

Yet again I'd disappointed someone who mattered to me.

"But you need me." I didn't want to give her the satisfaction of being right. "You can't afford the apartment by yourself."

It was true. Together we barely had enough. We'd had to rely on my dad to get by more times than I cared to admit. I hadn't been able to take care of Jenna and our baby, and now I couldn't even provide for my girl and her kids. How could I ever have my own family?

She nodded, acknowledging my argument, looked down at her hands. "Rob said he'll help us out."

Rob was Eric's dad. He was always trying to guilt Aimee into getting back together, then getting drunk and hitting her or cheating on her or something. She was better off without him.

Quick as lightning my anger was back. "Rob? Jesus fucking Christ! You know he's trouble."

"Not this time, baby," she pleaded, taking my hand in hers. "I mentioned we were having some problems and he offered to help. He cares about the boys, he cares about me, and just wants me to be happy."

She started crying as she said this, and the tears just pissed me off more. I jerked my hand back. "He's so wrong for you, Aimee, and for the boys. He's just using you. How could you possibly turn to him for help?"

I kicked one of the kitchen chairs, expecting her to run crying out of the kitchen, but she surprised me by fighting back.

"What did you expect, Andrew? You were never here for us. You don't care about us, just your own fucking self. You are such an asshole."

She was right, of course, and that fueled my anger. Anger towards myself, but it was easier to get angry at her. I needed her right now, needed someone, so I pulled out my trump card to get back the upper hand.

"Maybe you *are* better off with him. I got the letter today. I head out in two weeks."

She rushed to my side, her desire to end the relationship gone, for now at least. Of course things wouldn't work out, of course she'd have that guy in her bed before I was even in country, but caught up in my news she forgot all that. Probably didn't think it was true, even though that's what always happened.

"Oh, Andrew." She shook her head, crying hard, crying because *she* needed someone too, even if it wasn't me. It seemed she'd forgotten that just moments ago she was on the edge of ending our relationship. "I'm so sorry about all this. I love you, you know that."

I nodded, unable to say the words back, and hugged her close.

***

That night we lay in bed together and I couldn't fall asleep. Aimee cried for awhile, softly into her pillow so I wouldn't notice, but I did. I didn't do anything to console her, though, because then I'd be crying too, and I couldn't lose control. Not now. I needed to focus on the future.

I couldn't turn my mind off so I could sleep. Usually, I didn't think too much, just acted, but then again look where that'd gotten me. I was almost thirty, living with some woman who was so desperate for love and stability that she clung to me and made herself into what she thought I wanted, even though neither of us really wanted each other. Just two lonely people trying to make our way through life, already deciding to settle rather than going after our dreams, already giving up on finding happiness, on finding success.

The next day I called my dad to let him know I was deploying again, and asked if I could leave my stuff at his place. He paused a moment to hear what I didn't say—that Aimee wouldn't keep it because there'd be no us when I got back—but of course he agreed.

For the next couple weeks Aimee and I pretended everything was okay. We did a lot with the kids, acting as if we were one happy normal family. The boys played along too, and I felt bad I couldn't be the father they so badly wanted. Aimee cried herself to sleep every night, and each morning I pretended not to notice.

Finally, the day to ship out arrived. Standing there in the hangar at Fort Campbell, she gave me a big hug.

"I'll write every day, I promise." She sniffled, swatting at her eyes. "I'll send you cookies too, naked pictures, anything you want. Okay?"

I held her tightly, smelling her shampoo one last time. Strawberries. "If you don't want my stuff, feel free to drop it off at my dad's place. He can store it for me."

She leaned up and kissed me.

I smiled, hugged Sam and Eric, picked up my bag, and walked over to my gathering platoon. I looked over my shoulder, and she'd already led the boys halfway to the exit.

***

I got a package from her after a couple weeks: Rice Krispie treats, and a letter. It was quick and to the point, saying she was sorry it didn't work out, but her boys needed someone to be there, and she'd always love me, and most of my stuff was at my dad's but they were keeping some of it until they could afford to replace it.

In other words, 'Fuck off, Andrew. We don't need you anymore.'

# Chapter 15 – Kasey (Present)

The following Saturday, I awoke bright and early and made waffles with Aida. The night before had been spent in Andrew's bed and in his arms, as had every night in the recent past. I was always able to sneak back home and into my own bed shortly before dawn. Despite my lack of sleep, ongoing problems with David, and the tumultuous past six months, I was happy.

Spending time in the kitchen with Aida and showing her how to cook as we giggled at each other's jokes was immensely satisfying. I regretted that she was in school all week, forcing us to be apart.

"Something smells good," David said, shuffling into the room and kissing the top of Aida's head.

"We're making waffles, Daddy," she told him in a serious tone.

I scraped the last of the batter into the waffle iron. "Aida, why don't you start eating while I finish up? David, give her a hand, will you?"

"No, I'll keep helping you, Mommy." Aida's attitude towards her father had changed. She was now wary of him, clinging to my side whenever he came around. Over and over I'd tried to reassure her that his outburst had been an accident, that no matter what, her daddy loved her very much. She didn't buy it.

"Are you sure, sweetie?" asked David. "These waffles look awfully good."

Aida stared at him and stepped closer to me. "I'm sure."

David and I both sighed.

\*\*\*

After breakfast, I drove Aida to her weekly gymnastics lesson.

She stared out her window. "Is Daddy going to break our window again?"

"No, of course not, sweetie," I said, hoping it was true. "That was a one-time thing. Daddy made a mistake, and he apologized. It won't happen again."

"If it does, will we stay with Mr. Andrew again?"

"Aida, I told you, it's not going to happen again, I promise."

"He said he has a cat, but she hides from people. I want to meet her."

"Well, maybe someday." I glanced in the rearview mirror at my daughter, unsure what to tell her.

"We should get a cat, Mommy."

"Cats are a lot of work. Maybe if you do a good job with your chores we'll see about getting a pet."

"Okay." Aida looked out the window again, then frowned and glanced back at me. "Would Daddy hurt a cat if we got one?"

I bit my lip and blinked back tears. "Of course not, Aida. We're safe with Daddy, and a cat would be too."

"Why did he yell and break the window?"

I'd rehearsed my answer to the point I almost believed it. "Sometimes when Daddy drinks too much, he doesn't know what he's doing or saying. He doesn't mean any of it. He knows he did something very wrong, and he promised not to do it again."

"Mr. Andrew turned on the sirens for me. He was nice. I like him."

Her words surprised me but dissolved the lump in my throat. I grinned at her. "I like him too."
***

"Does it bother you that your daughter's afraid of you?" I asked David that night after Aida was in bed.

He was in his office, looking over some affidavits. "She's not afraid of me."

"No, she's terrified of you. Do you notice how she cringes whenever you come near her?"

"She doesn't cringe." He turned around. Dark circles had formed underneath his eyes. "Maybe she's not as affectionate, but... cringing?"

"You haven't noticed?" My eyes narrowed. "How do you expect her to act around you?"

"I...." He rubbed his eyes with his hand. "I don't know."

"Whatever happens between you and me, she's still your daughter. She should be the most important thing in your life—not your career, not your standing in society, not your bank account. Aida."

"She is!" He took a drink from the ever-present tumbler next to him. "You both are."

I took the glass from his hand.

"Hey!" He reached over and tried to take it back, but I held it behind me.

I stared him straight in the eyes, and he hesitated but returned my gaze. "David, listen to me. The drinking needs to stop. Your daughter is afraid of you. One more outburst and both of us are gone. No more chances."

He opened his mouth, then closed it and nodded.

I left the room, proud of my ultimatum but wondering if he'd buy it, and if I could follow through with it.

***

The next morning I'd been back in my own bed for about an hour when David knocked on the guestroom door and poked his head inside. He was fully dressed, and I froze, wondering if he realized I'd been gone all night. He showed no indication he knew about Andrew, so I relaxed.

"You're up early." I stretched and yawned.

"I'm gonna take Aida hiking today, just me and her. We need to talk about what I did. You're right. I don't want her scared of me."

"Good idea." I smiled and snuggled back under the covers, grateful to have the day to catch up on sleep.

"I miss us." He came hesitantly into the room. "What happened?"

I sat up, leaned back against the headboard. "I don't know, David. I'm trying to figure it out myself. Up until last spring I thought we were fine. Not great, but fine. And then I found out that couldn't be further from the truth. So you tell me. What happened?"

"I just don't know."

"I don't understand you anymore. Sometimes you're just like you always were, and then you pull this jealousy crap as if Aida and I are objects to control. What do you want from me?"

His brow furrowed in concentration for a moment, then he shrugged. "I want us to have what we used to have. I don't want to lose you."

I stared hard at him. "You lost me a long time ago, when you broke my car window in front of our daughter, when you started dictating who I can be friends with, when I ceased to be a person and became just your status-enhancing wife." *When you slept with my best friend.*

"I know. Believe me, Kase, I know I've fucked up." He scrubbed his face with a hand. "But we need each other."

"Really? Why is that?"

"Aida needs both of us. She deserves a loving family, two parents who love each other and her, and I realize I need to be here, working on that. And then...."

"And then?"

"To be completely honest, we can't take another scandal. Not many people here know why we moved, but enough that it was difficult to get established. If we had to move, I really don't know if I could rebuild again."

My eyes widened. David hadn't mentioned any difficulties to me. "Why didn't you tell me?"

"You were so optimistic about this fresh start, so relieved to get here and away from Richmond. I know you weren't happy there towards the end, and I'm truly sorry you were exposed to all that viciousness. So I didn't want to worry you with any of the details about the problems I had getting set up here."

"You should've told me."

"I wanted you to focus on us. On us working things out and getting our marriage back together."

He seemed sincere, and while I wanted to believe him, to believe at least that he meant everything he said, I wondered how long it would last. So many times now he'd repented and I'd dared to hope we could make things work, but then it all blew up again. No, he blew it up again.

"What do you suggest we do?"

I thought back to earlier last night, drifting off to sleep with Andrew's arm around me and awakening to his kisses on my neck, connecting with him in a way I never had with David. Was this what my husband had felt with Ann? I swallowed the lump in my throat as those damned pictures danced in front of my eyes. I was no better than David. The lump grew, and all I wanted was to sink down under the covers and sob like a baby.

"I'm proposing a truce." He obviously noticed my expression, though how he interpreted it was anyone's guess. "No, no, I mean it. This fighting, bottling everything up—we can't continue like this. We need to start talking. Start feeling."

I didn't want to talk to him or feel anything for him until I could trust him, until I knew what was going to happen with Andrew. How to tell him? "David—"

He cocked his head to the side. "Aida's awake. We need to do this for her."

Of course he was right. "Fine."

He nodded. "Thanks for going along with this, Kase." He turned to go.

"Wait."

He turned back towards me.

"I want to be perfectly clear I'm doing this for Aida. I'm not doing it because I love you. I don't know if I even do anymore."

His jaw clenched. "Fair enough."

"Do you still love me?"

"Of course. Everything I do, I do because I love you." His expression was unreadable as he left the room.

***

Whatever David had said to Aida apparently did the trick. When they came back that afternoon she was her usual bubbly self, slipping her hand into her father's and curling up with him on the couch to watch a video.

I remained skeptical of his transformation but was glad he had repaired his relationship with Aida.

Days passed, then a week, and another. David spent his evenings focused on Aida, practically ignoring me. He cooked dinner with her, helped her with homework, read her stories. I was impressed; he'd never taken so much time away from his case files, away from his nightly drinking.

It was almost enough to make me stop my nightly trips to Andrew's apartment. Almost.

***

A month or so after our affair started, a month filled with nights more wonderful than I could have hoped for, I arrived at Andrew's apartment at my usual time only to find the porch light off. There was no answer to my knock. No lights appeared to be on inside either. I assumed he was either working or had fallen asleep, and returned home disappointed, knowing nothing could be done.

Once home in bed, however, my mind began feeding me reasons why he hadn't answered the door. Work was a possibility, of course, or falling asleep, but if he was working, why hadn't he told me? If he'd fallen asleep, shouldn't he at least have left the light on? No, he was done with me.

But why? Was he bored? Was it the same reason David had cheated, something that made men not want a relationship with me? Whatever the reason, whatever I'd done or hadn't done, whatever quality I possessed or lacked, it didn't change the fact that Andrew hadn't wanted me that night. The rejection hurt badly.

The next day Andrew was already at McKay's when I arrived, sitting at a table with Ron and Erica and a new woman I'd never seen before. The new woman was chatting away with Erica, exuding confidence like I'd never been able to, the confidence men equated with beauty. My heart dropped into my stomach and proceeded to pound away painfully. I put on a fake brave smile, nodded in their direction, and immediately headed to a back corner to browse. After half an hour alone I left the bookstore, frustrated by Andrew's complete lack of response. Granted, he didn't owe me anything despite our nights together, despite how we felt about each other, but some acknowledgment of my presence would have been appreciated.

That night I debated going to Andrew's apartment. He'd made no mention of, nor shown any reaction to, not being with me the night before. Should I give him the benefit of the doubt, a second chance? I lay in bed trying to decide.

Finally, I got up around midnight, dressed, and drove to his apartment. The porch light was off, but a faint light shone through the closed blinds. My first thought was that it was the woman from the bookstore taking my place, that I should turn around and head home because I wasn't wanted or needed tonight. Then I thought of the peace of mind I would get knowing, one way or the other, how he felt. I thought of the way his arms felt around me, how his lips felt on mine.

No one answered my knock, but voices and explosions were audible from inside, most likely a movie he was watching, one of the many action films that occupied his shelf. I tried the door, found it unlocked, and went inside.

Andrew lay slumped on his couch, clad only in a pair of boxers, holding a half-full wine glass. A mostly-empty bottle sat on the floor at his feet, and several empty beer bottles lay scattered around the couch. The TV blared some black-and-white film with lots of soldiers marching around, apparently set in World War II, and he watched it intently.

I entered the room. "Andrew?"

"This was a good war." He didn't look up. "Distinct good guys and bad guys, and the people back home respected the soldiers when they came back from the front."

"You okay?"

"They lost a lot of good men. We did too."

I walked over, sat down, and put my arms around him without saying anything.

He didn't move, kept watching the television. "But they had someone to come back to. That helps. I have no one."

"You have me."

"No." He shook his head. "You have your own life and your own problems."

"I'd take you over my abusive husband any day."

"He's abusive?" Andrew's voice was sharp as he finally looked at me. "Physically? He's hit you?"

I told him everything—about the affairs in Richmond, the jealousy and arguments after moving here, the huge fight culminating in the broken car window, the slap and the directive to leave, the flowers and ring, David's sudden transformation and involvement with Aida—everything I'd wanted to confide in Andrew but had been hesitant to do.

"What does he want from you?" he asked.

"I don't know, and he doesn't seem to know either."

"You're safe with me."

"I know." I leaned over and kissed his cheek.

He gave me a small smile, then turned back to the movie. He said, in time with the actors, "'Well, boys, it's time to strike. Some of you won't be coming back alive, but we're all coming back together. We're a team, brothers fighting to save the world from tyranny and injustice.' Are we still fighting for that, Kasey?"

"I like to think so."

"I saw a lot of bad shit over there. It leaves you tired after a while."

"But you keep fighting."

He ignored me. "I've done a lot of bad stuff. I've hurt a lot of people. I'm a broken hero, Kasey, and who needs that?"

"I need you." I wrapped my arms more tightly around him.

"No, you don't. I'm too broken, better at hurting than healing."

"Andrew, that's not true."

He smiled, a bitter, knowing smile, his eyes never leaving the battle on the screen. "I'm scarred up and damaged. I know how to hurt and kill better than to love. What good am I?"

"You know how to help others. You do it every day as a cop." I hated to see him so defeated. "And maybe you can find a way to manage the pain enough to love again?"

"Women will fail me. It's in your nature."

"Everyone fails. We're always alone when we need someone the most." I thought of my problems with David, of having no one to turn to. "That doesn't mean you give up. Love is about giving all you can to someone, not about what you may or may not get in return. You hope for reciprocity, but that's not a reason to love someone, or to not love them."

"Yes, it is. Who wants to invest in someone who isn't in it for the whole deal as well?"

"You can't help who you love. Sometimes they return your feelings, and sometimes they don't. You can just hope it's not a lost cause. And even when it is, you still love them enough that you want them to be happy, to be content, even if it's not with you. That's no reason to stop loving them."

He rolled his eyes. "So says your vast knowledge of worthy relationships."

Tears stung my eyes. "That's probably part of why my marriage is failing, yes. My love is easy to take advantage of."

"I want nothing from you," he said plainly. "Therefore, no advantage taken."

"Nothing?"

"Nothing." The words were final.

"Okay, well, that's what I came here to find out, and you've made yourself clear." I stood and walked towards the door, willing myself to walk straight, shoulders back. I could cry in the car, not in front of Andrew.

"I knew you'd leave." His eyes were still on the TV. "I knew you didn't mean what you promised. You're just like all the rest."

"No." I turned to face him, shaking my head and blinking furiously as I struggled to keep my voice level. "No. You said we'd take care of each other, but now you say you want nothing from me. What else should I do except conclude I should leave?"

"I don't know what I want, Kasey. I want to be able to sleep at night, to not die whenever I close my eyes. I want to find meaning in something, but I don't know how to get any of that. I don't know what to do." He put his head in his hands.

I wasn't sure if he was crying, and it was more than I could take. I sat down next to him and gently pulled his hands away from his face, holding them firmly in mine. "Let me help you."

"You're fighting your own battles." He looked through me, as if he'd had this conversation a hundred times already with a hundred other women. Maybe he had. "And you and I are so different. I don't know how you could help me. You don't know what this is like."

"No, but I still want to help you if I can."

"I don't want to hurt you, but I'm going to, Kasey. I'm going to hurt you bad, and I don't know how I'll live with that." He squeezed my hand. "I won't mean to, but I always disappoint the ones I love. And, to be honest, I don't really understand it myself. Maybe I hurt to keep from hurting?" He shook his head as if trying to clear his thoughts, wipe his mind fresh. "I can't seem to control it, and loving and hurting both feel right, because both of them are part of me."

"I'm here for you no matter what you need." I stroked his cheek. "Whether you want me or not, I'm here for you and always will be, whatever you need."

"Can you just stay here awhile? I don't want to be alone right now."

"Of course."

I leaned against him and he put his arm around me. He continued to recite the movie lines, but with me next to him he didn't seem so remote, so agitated.

When the film ended, he started it over again. After half an hour or so, his rhythmic breathing indicated he'd fallen asleep.

I got up carefully and covered him with the blanket from the back of the couch. "Good night, Andrew." I kissed his forehead, then surprised myself with my next words. "I love you."

After turning off the television and lights, I headed home.

***

Despite him asking me to stay, my nights with Andrew were over. It had been fun while it lasted, but it couldn't last forever, not with the mess of a marriage I still had. We'd go back to being friends now, laughing and arguing at McKay's like usual. And, for everyone else there, it would be exactly the same, because no one knew we'd slept together. No one knew how connected we were to each other. No, how connected I was to him.

But I knew I couldn't do it. I'd see him and want to kiss him. He'd make some off-color remark about me, and I'd burst into tears. Or I'd be formal around him, unable to joke, flinching at his touch. I needed an escape from him, a way to pass my time away from him and all thoughts of him.

David wasn't helping any. He was, to put it bluntly, wonderful. Perfect. The guest bedroom, kitchen, and dining room were filled with bouquets of flowers he bought me every couple days. He helped with dinner and laundry. He asked me about my day, about the books I was reading. He sat down to watch TV with me in the evenings. He was the perfect doting husband, and it was driving me crazy.

Earlier that month, on yet another night when he'd arrived home with dinner, he'd come into the garden where I was preparing to plant daffodil bulbs.

"Hey, Kase," he called cheerfully. "How was your day?"

"Fine." I kept digging.

"What did you do all day? Anything fun?"

"Errands. More errands. Gardening."

"Sounds fun. Maybe I could help you this weekend."

I jerked my head up.

David was perched on the edge of the mosaic-covered patio table. He'd loosened his tie and removed his suit jacket, but even in grubby shorts and t-shirt David would look ready to head back into the courtroom, not a garden.

"You hate gardening."

"No, I don't."

"Yes, you do. For six years you've been trying to get me to hire someone to do all this for us."

"But it's important to you. It should be important to me too."

I turned back to the bed in front of me so he couldn't see my rolling eyes. "We can do separate stuff."

"But I want to spend time with you." His voice twanged petulantly, then brightened. "The Jenkinses invited us over for dinner and drinks tomorrow night."

Clyde Jenkins was a lawyer in town. He and his wife hosted weekly dinners at their home, and it was considered a social honor to be invited.

"I don't really want to go."

"Okay." His voice held no hesitation.

I looked at him again. "Okay?"

"Sure, whatever you want. If you don't want to do those networking social things, we won't do them." He smiled as he walked over and kissed the top of my head. "Anything for you, Kase."

\*\*\*

I waited for the yelling to start, the snide comments, but there was only a cloying husband pulling me towards him in an attempt to make up for lost time, pulling me towards him as I tried to get away from him. David, whom I didn't want, was on one side, with Andrew no longer on the other.

I needed space, needed to get away, so I decided to get a job.

The next day, rather than going to McKay's, I spent my time at home poring through help wanted ads. The fall tourism season was winding down, but early November meant stores were gearing up for the holidays, so I was cautiously optimistic about finding at least part-time employment.

After a couple days I'd accumulated quite a stack of applications. Bored of the house, I took them to McKay's to fill out. Andrew was there in civilian clothes, talking to Ron, Erica, and that new woman. I froze, but pushed them from my mind.

I hadn't heard from him in a week, since the night we'd watched the movie at his apartment. Fine. He knew my number, knew how to find me if he wanted me, which he didn't, not anymore. What had I done to make him not want me? What had changed?

The same thing that changed with David, perhaps, only more quickly. What had taken David years to realize took Andrew only a month.

Swallowing back those thoughts, I focused on the stack of job applications. No sense in dwelling on why he didn't seem interested anymore. So far it had been working, at least for the most part. As long as I stayed busy, stayed distracted, I could keep myself from thinking about him. Mostly.

I stared at the application in front of me, trying to decide what my biggest challenge in life was and how I'd overcome it, especially in the context of a seasonal retail position, so lost in thought I didn't notice Andrew come over to my table until he sat down, leaned over, and squeezed my hand.

"Hey." That half-smile played at his lips.

"Hey." I didn't know what else to say. He seemed to be in a good mood, and I didn't want to start an argument with him, something that would surely happen if I told him what was on my mind. I waited for him to say something.

He sat for a few moments, watching me watch him, taking in the papers scattered in loose piles on the table. "You mad at me?"

"No, why?"

"You just seem a bit distant. Maybe you're regretting the past few weeks?"

"No, I'm just preoccupied with getting these job apps filled out."

"Okay, just making sure." He lowered his voice. "I'd really like to kiss you right now."

My pulse quickened. Maybe it had all been a misunderstanding. "We could leave for a bit, if you want. These apps aren't so important that I can't take a break."

"No, I have company." He nodded towards the table.

"I see." I was careful to keep my voice neutral. Why had he even told me he wanted to kiss me if he had no intention of acting on it?

"She's Erica's sister. She just moved to town and doesn't know anything about the area, so they've asked me to show her around."

"Of course." It took all my resolve to keep my voice level, to not cry, to not hit Andrew in frustration. I'd chatted enough with Ron and Erica to know exactly what they had in mind.

"What's that supposed to mean?" His eyes narrowed. He was always on the defensive.

"Nothing."

"I see." He glanced over his shoulder at his friends. "You haven't been by recently."

"I've been busy, and I didn't think you wanted me around."

"Why would you think that?"

"Well, Friday night you specifically told me you wanted nothing from me."

"I did?"

"Yeah. Do you even remember anything we talked about the other night? Because if you don't, that's actually a big relief to me. It means you're not bullshitting me, just that I shouldn't talk to you when you're drunk."

"Yeah, it's probably a good idea not to talk to me when I'm drunk."

I rolled my eyes. "I'm gonna go ahead and assume you're always drunk. I think that might be easiest for me."

"Fair enough." He grinned at me, the same grin I'd kissed every night for the past month, the grin he'd given as he lay sweaty and naked beside me. There was no way I could return it today. "Is that why you haven't come by?"

"Part of it, yeah." I paused. "And part of it was to see how long before you'd notice and say something."

He frowned. "That's not fair. I get busy too."

"I see that." My gaze flickered over to the new woman who was laughing at something Ron had said.

"You're jealous!" He flashed a superior smirk.

"No." Now it was my turn to be defensive. "Maybe a little."

"Why?" Still that smirk.

"Because I want you." I stared at him and blinked. Instead of me, I saw that woman in his bed, legs tangled together like David's and Ann's had been. "Isn't it obvious? I want to be with you. I want to be the only one with you."

"Kasey," he said gently, leaning forward and taking my hands in his, "it's not that simple. I have a lot going on right now, a lot of issues to work through. And so do you. If I can be a friend and help you through whatever you're going through, then it's worth it. What we've shared has been fun but, no offense, you're not exactly a safe bet for a relationship right now."

I took a deep breath, and another, and glared at him through watery eyes. If he didn't want me, didn't care about my feelings, he didn't deserve to see me cry. "You couldn't have mentioned that a month ago? That what we did was just 'fun'?"

"That's not how I meant it."

I swallowed hard. "So you really are done with me now."

"No, I'll always be a friend. I'll always be here whenever you need me."

My mind flashed to the night David had broken my window and Andrew had rescued me. To David's slap, and how Andrew had calmed me down. "I always need you."

Before he could respond, before he could reassure me or break my heart further, Erica's sister came over to our table. "Hey, Andy," she said, cracking her gum, "you said you wouldn't be long, and I'm getting bored with Ron and Erica. You about ready to go?" She put her hands on his shoulder, leaned in slightly so that her large breasts were eye-level with him, and smiled at me.

I shot her a weak smile, feeling sick.

Andrew had the decency to look embarrassed. "Almost done." He gave her a smile that seemed slightly forced. "I want you to meet Kasey, a good friend of mine. Kasey, this is Alexis."

"So nice to meet you," Alexis gushed with another crack of her gum.

I nodded. Friends, he said.

"Okay, ready to go now? I'm hungry."

"Yeah, just gimme a sec, okay?"

"Sure." She stood next to him, not moving.

He frowned at her. "Give us some space. Go back over to Ron and Erica."

"Oh, okay, if you insist." She pouted, an unflattering look on a grown woman, and patted his cheek. "Don't take too long."

Once she was gone, I looked at Andrew with as little emotion as possible. If this was how he wanted it to be, I could play his game. I wasn't new to the whole being-replaced feeling. "I get the point. If you're chasing her, I am so far from your type I don't think there's anything more you need to say."

"Kasey," he said as if talking to a young child.

"No, I mean it." My voice was cool, level. He didn't get to see how much this hurt. "You're right. I am pretty unstable right now with all my marital problems. What we had was fun, but you gotta do what's best for you. And if she's best for you right now, then so be it. I wish you both the best."

"Kasey, don't be like this." Half remonstration, half plea.

"Would you rather I cry, maybe throw something? It's like you said the other night, not that you seem to remember. What's the point of pursuing someone who doesn't feel the same about you? We're friends, and I'll always—always—be here for you if you want me." I took a deep breath, unsure how much longer I could keep up the act, and forced a smile. "I mean it. Go have fun with your new girl."

He looked torn. Perhaps he knew as well as me what a mistake this was. "You sure?"

I nodded.

"Thanks for understanding, babydoll." He squeezed my hand, got up and walked over to Alexis. As they left, she slipped her hand into his, but he quickly pulled his away.

I watched them go, heart in my stomach, then gathered up my papers to leave, not wanting to become hysterical in a public place, and noticed Ron watching me. When I made eye contact with him, he got up and moved to my table.

Erica followed behind. "So you met my sister. Charming, isn't she?" She rolled her eyes.

I was unsure how to respond. Like her or not, the woman was my friend's sister. "She's very outgoing."

"We thought Andrew would be a good match for her energy," Erica explained.

Talking about Andrew and another woman was the last thing I wanted. I continued to pack up my papers, hoping they'd take a hint.

"He's been so moody lately. I thought maybe she could get him out of his funk, cheer him up, if you know what I mean." She winked.

"Yeah." I smiled weakly, wanting to leave, wanting them to go away and not talk to me about this.

"You love him," Ron said suddenly.

"What?" Erica and I replied together.

"You love Andrew." It was a simple statement, not a question.

"We're friends, and I care about him." I hoped Ron would leave it at that.

"No, it's more than that." He shook his head in emphasis. "I've watched you two interact. You love him, and he loves you."

"That's ridiculous," Erica interjected. "I would've noticed something like that."

"I wouldn't say he loves me." I ignored Erica, thinking of what Andrew had said to me. "We kind of had a thing, yes, but we're just friends. No one needs to know I told you, especially Andrew."

Erica's jaw dropped and her eyes bulged. "Why didn't he tell us? We're his closest friends!"

Ron also ignored his wife. "Had?"

I picked my words with care. "I'm married, and he's going through a rough time. I'm not what he wants or needs right now."

"But you love him and care about him deeply," Ron said. "You have for a while, am I right?"

"Since about the first time I met him." I smiled at the memory of our first exchange. What an auspicious start that had been.

"I'm so sorry," Erica said. "If I'd known I wouldn't have forced Alexis on him." She punched her husband in the arm. "Ron, why didn't you tell me?"

I shook my head. "No, it's okay. We decided it was best to just be friends. I want the best for him, and if that's Alexis, so be it."

Ron studied me, disbelief clouding his eyes.

I gave him another weak smile; it seemed that was all I could manage today. "Listen, sorry to run, but I need to get these applications turned in."

"Getting a job?" Erica asked. "Where?"

"Wherever will hire me. I'm getting bored being here all the time—no offense—so I thought I'd get a job, give me something to do with my time."

"And now that Andrew is occupied elsewhere, you need a distraction," Ron said.

"Yeah. Now that Andrew is occupied elsewhere, I need all the distractions I can get."

***

The next morning I felt nauseous, almost hungover when I woke up, likely due to crying myself to sleep the night before. Crying alone, because although David had hinted about sleeping in the same room, I couldn't do it. Wouldn't. Didn't want to give him false hope that everything was back to normal between us, although he acted like he believed it already. I brushed off the nausea, focusing my energy on finding a job, not on my rejected feelings for Andrew.

For the next week I woke up feeling sick, but by midmorning, after showering and filling out and returning job applications, I felt fine.

I avoided the downtown area unless specifically dropping off an application; I didn't want to run into Andrew, with or without Alexis. He seemed to be avoiding me as well, though I wasn't sure if it that was a good thing. Perhaps we needed to talk about what had happened between us, but if he really was done with me, then maybe it was best to just move on.

It was more difficult than I'd thought it would be. If I managed to stay occupied during the day, he'd vanish from my thoughts until I saw something or heard a song that reminded me of him, and the memories would overwhelm me—his kisses, his touch, even the sound of his voice when he said my name, when he'd sighed it in bed. It took all my willpower at these moments to keep from crying, to keep from calling him.

As a week passed, and then another, it didn't become easier to forget him. I missed him and wanted him just as much as I ever had.

***

A week before Thanksgiving, a local gift shop hired me. It wasn't the best job, but at least it was something to keep me occupied for a few hours each

- 147 -

day, away from the bookstore. I was to start the following Monday. Based on how I'd been feeling recently I decided to spend that Friday in bed.

David had been tense all week, working long hours at the office, and was less than sympathetic before he left in the morning. "Just go to the doctor already, for Christ's sake. Get some medicine so you can be Ms. Independent Woman on Monday."

I glared at him through bleary eyes. "I'll be fine in a while. And what's wrong with having a job?"

He softened his tone. "I promised myself I'd take care of you. You don't need to work."

"We've had this discussion, David." Ad nauseam. "I want a job."

"Well, at the very least, get checked out. You won't be that great an employee if you're sick, right?"

He made a good point. My doctor was able to get me in early that afternoon.

"So," said the doctor when she came into my exam room, "you've been feeling sick in the morning, but it's gone by late morning or early afternoon?"

I nodded.

"Any backaches or headaches?"

"I have been sore all over recently, now that you mention it. And more tired than usual."

She smiled at me. "You're going to be a lot more tired for a while."

"Is it mono? My throat doesn't hurt, so it's not the flu, is it?"

"Let me be the first to say congratulations. You're pregnant!"

# Chapter 16 – Andrew (Age 31)

"Oh, Andrew," my mama said to me for probably the thousandth time in the past three days. Then she hugged me again, something I was still coming to terms with after a lifetime of little physical affection.

I awkwardly patted her shoulder. "It'll be okay, Mama."

She nodded, let go of me, and went back into the living room with my aunts and cousins.

I was in town for my grandma's funeral. I'd barely known the woman, and any obligatory sadness was overshadowed by my anger at Grandma's denial of the abuse that had filled my childhood. I hadn't wanted to come back to Mississippi, to drive the five hundred miles from Kentucky, but she was family, and my mama needed my support right now.

That didn't mean I had to sit around the house the whole time though, listening to my aunts reminisce about what a good woman their mama had been. But it wasn't polite to hole up in my old bedroom either.

I popped my head into the living room. "Mama, I'm heading to the store. You need anything?"

She looked up and wiped her eyes. "No thanks. Don't be gone too long, okay?"

I nodded, even though we both knew it would be hours before I returned. Things were weird between me and my stepdad, uncomfortable. I think he was afraid I'd tell everyone about how he'd treated us, even though the physical abuse had ended nearly fifteen years ago. Mama had forgiven him, made peace with the past, but I hadn't. I wouldn't. How could anyone forget something like that, forgive it?

I pushed it down, refused to think about it most of the time, had no intention of riling everything up right now, but Gary didn't know that. He didn't know when or if I'd bring it up, so he tiptoed around me, careful for the first time in my life not to piss me off. It was nice, this power over him, but Mama didn't like the tension, so it was better if I was gone. Better for us all.

I pulled up in front of a little diner on the edge of town. There was more than enough food at the house, casseroles and cookies and pans of God knows what, but I wanted something without cream of whatever in it, something made without death and misplaced sympathy.

I sat down at a table and looked over the menu: burgers, sandwiches, deep fried just about anything you could imagine. I didn't want any of it. I wanted a beer; several, enough to wash away the memories of that house, of Jenna and the baby and this town, of my past.

I hadn't ordered yet, so it was no problem to just leave. On the way out I held the door for a woman coming in, a woman who looked remarkable familiar.

"Carly?"

She stopped in the doorway. "Andrew! I didn't know you were back in town."

"I'm just here a few days for my grandma's funeral."

"I'm sorry to hear that."

"Thanks." I couldn't get over how good she looked, how good it felt to see her, probably the one person in town I cared about. "You here for lunch?"

"No, my sister works here and I'm dropping off some clothes for her." She gestured at the grocery bag in her hand. "We're always passing along hand-me-downs."

I tried to remember back to my last time here, running into Mark years ago. "You have two, right?"

She smiled, shyly and proudly, just like when she was little and had gotten the highest grade in class but didn't want to call attention to how happy she was. "Three. And one more on the way." She patted her belly.

"Wow. Congrats! I'm sure you're a great mama." Her smile widened, brightened, making her even more beautiful to see. "We really need to catch up."

"The kids are at my sister's tomorrow night, and Mark's working a double shift. I don't go in till ten. How about you come over for dinner? Will you still be in town?"

"I'd stay just to see you." I gave her a big hug. "I can't wait, Carly."

As I walked to my truck, I couldn't get the big stupid grin off my face. It occurred to me that I didn't want to.

As sat in a downtown bar and drank beer after beer after beer, my happiness faded. It had been fourteen years since Carly and I last talked, and we hadn't left off on the best of terms. Had she forgiven me for not being there for her when her mama passed away? I hadn't forgiven myself. My childhood mixed with my present and became a jumbled mess in my mind: Jenna's mama and Carly's mama, my first kiss with Carly and my last kiss with Aimee, punching Mark in high school and shooting my first haji in Iraq, my baby with his ever-shifting features and Carly's unborn kid.

I stopped at the liquor store on the way home and picked up a case of beer, which I drank until finally my thoughts disappeared and I passed out.

***

The next night I was nervous as hell. It was just Carly, I told myself while sitting in the driveway outside her little ranch house. Growing up, we'd never had a problem talking to each other. Why should tonight be any different?

I finally made myself get out of my truck and walk up to the door. I'd barely even knocked when it flew open and revealed Carly's big smile, still as beautiful as ever.

"Come in, come in." She pulled me inside. "Sorry the place is such a mess."

"No, it looks great."

Toys were scattered across the floor, folded laundry lay piled on the couch, and a shaggy mutt slept in a corner. And everywhere were pictures, either handmade by small kids, or of the kids themselves, smiling and playing and happy. The house proudly declared it was a well-loved home, full of well-loved people.

I almost left right then.

Carly noticed my hesitation. "Let's go in the kitchen. Dinner's almost ready. I hope you don't mind pork chops and mac and cheese."

"It sounds great." I followed her into the kitchen and sat at the table. "Number four, you said?"

From the stove, she said, "Yep. Two boys, followed by a little girl, and now whatever this one is. Space'll be tight, but we're excited to have him or her join the family." She stirred a pot. "What about you, Andrew? Any kids?"

"No." It came out more sharply than I'd intended. "After... I guess I just haven't found the right girl yet."

"Oh, Andrew." She came over and hugged me. "You will."

We kept up a running conversation through dinner, mostly talking about her kids, her job as a nurse and mine as a cop, my mama and her sisters. I tried to keep it light, off anything that might upset her, like my deployments and how I felt after getting back, or my string of failed relationships. I was pretty sure she did the same for me.

After dinner we moved into the living room.

"You want a drink?" She moved a pile of laundry so we had a place to sit.

"No." I did, though. I always wanted a drink, it seemed.

She sat next to me on the couch, hands folded in her lap, still all proper like when she was a kid.

"How's Mark?" I asked. She hadn't said hardly anything about him all night.

"He's good." She nodded to herself. "He's a good guy. So excited about this baby." She opened her mouth as if to say more, then closed it, a slight crease to her brow.

I could still read her as if it'd been days instead of years since we'd been close. "What's wrong?"

"Nothing's *wrong*. Everything's right. He works extra shifts at the factory so we can save for college. He plays with the kids, reads to them, changes diapers with a smile. And he's so good to me too, always making sure I have everything I could need or want. He's wonderful. My sisters are always so jealous because I have the perfect husband."

I hesitated. "It sounds great."

"Well, it's not! He loves me, I know. He tells me, shows me every day, but...."

I waited for her to go on.

"I like him, Andrew. He's always been one of my best friends and I like him a lot. He's so good to me, always has been, so how could I not?"

I reached over and squeezed her hand.

She looked up at me. "I don't love him, Andrew. I like him but I don't love him. And I feel so guilty about it. I try to love him, I do. Really. I keep telling myself, 'give it time.' But how much time? I hate that he's wasting his life on me, when he's such a good guy and deserves so much more." She bit her lip, the same as she'd always done when she was trying not to cry, and even now it still about broke my heart.

"Oh, Carly." I leaned over and wrapped my arms around her.

She fell against me and started to sob.

After her tears quieted, she said, "I've never admitted this out loud before. Does it make me a bad person?"

"No," I said into her hair. "You're the goodest person I've ever known. You're happy with Mark, right? With your life and kids?"

She nodded.

"Then how can this be a waste? You have three-and-a-half beautiful children, growing up with two parents who love them more than life itself. You're sharing your life with one of your best friends. So you have doubts. We all do. That doesn't make you a bad person."

She let out a deep breath. "I guess I just wanted more. I'm happy, but I always thought...."

"I did too."

We sat on the couch like that, arms around each other, thinking about what could have been, what was instead, until it was time for her to go to work.

She invited me to come back the next day, to see Mark and meet the kids, but I declined. I could tell she was relieved. We exchanged numbers, but we both knew we'd never call.

As I left my mama's house the next day to drive back to Kentucky, one thing became clear: I would never be back to Mississippi.

And that felt just fine.

# Chapter 17 – Kasey (Present)

I gaped at the doctor. "Are you sure? There have to be other reasons I feel like crap. I can't be pregnant."

"Your urine specimen came back positive. You're definitely pregnant."

"I can't be pregnant," I whispered. My disbelief was the same as when I'd seen those pictures. "I can't. No, I can't. I can't!"

"It's a shock sometimes when you're not trying." The doctor's voice was kind. "We'll have a nurse come in and set up a sonogram. Again, congratulations."

I stared at her retreating back, my mind racing. How could I tell David about the pregnancy, when we hadn't had sex since before we'd moved to Asheville? How could I tell Andrew, when he wanted nothing more than friendship, and wasn't even doing a good job with that?

I half staggered out of the clinic. Pregnant. How would David react? He'd know immediately it wasn't his, and just as quickly he'd suspect it was Andrew's. Would he throw me out? Would he kill me first, or go after Andrew? Or maybe use this as an excuse to cheat openly?

Assuming I even kept it, of course.

No one knew I was pregnant. I could find a clinic, end the pregnancy without anyone knowing. I'd always wanted another child, but not like this. A voice in the back of my mind whispered that this was the easy way out, but I ignored it. It wouldn't be easy, but maybe it was best.

I dropped my purse into the back seat of my car, next to Aida's booster seat. Aida. I imagined sitting down with her in ten, twenty, fifty years, telling her she could've been a big sister. Would she hate me? Would she forgive me?

Would I forgive myself?

No.

I'd made a lot of mistakes in the last few months, in the last few years: acting on my feelings for Andrew, staying in marital limbo with David, not sticking up for myself or being true to myself.

But this baby wasn't a mistake. Unplanned, definitely, but not a mistake. Even if I had to raise him or her alone, it wouldn't be a mistake.

My mind made up on the baby's immediate future, my thoughts shifted to the paternal issues. How long could I put off telling David? Was it even worth it to tell Andrew, now that he'd moved on? There were so many questions, so many choices, and so few good answers or options.

That night, David didn't ask about the doctor's appointment, and I didn't bring it up. I'd put off telling him as long as I could.

\*\*\*

A couple weeks before Christmas I spent a day off running errands, finishing up some last-minute shopping at the mall. My morning sickness had subsided shortly after Thanksgiving, but I still had very little energy, something I tried to downplay as much as I could, especially around David. I strolled past a toy store and happened to notice Andrew inside, looking baffled in an aisle filled with pink. Smiling, I went in and tapped him on the arm.

He jumped, frowned, then smiled when he saw me. "Hey."

"Hey."

"I haven't seen you in a while. How are you?"

"Busy. Tired. How're you?"

"About the same."

Dark circles stood out under his eyes. His skin was paler than usual, and his brows were slightly furrowed in a worried expression.

"Everything okay?" I asked.

"No. Yeah. I don't know. I've got a lot going on right now." He stared at the dolls, clearly out of his element.

"I'm here if you need me."

"I know." Again staring at the dolls. He wasn't cold but not overly polite either. He was dismissive, distracted, and I didn't think it was just because of the overwhelming selection.

"Need some help?" I asked.

"There are so fucking many! How the hell are you supposed to know what to get?"

"Who are you buying for?"

"My niece."

"How old is she? What does she like?"

"I don't know. She's about this tall, I think." He gestured with his hand, about waist level. "She likes.... I don't know what she likes." He shook his head.

I laid my hand on his arm. "You okay?"

"I'm... yeah, I'm fine." He took a deep breath, then slowly exhaled the faint scent of alcohol.

"Get her a gift card. That way she can get what she wants."

He nodded. "Yeah. Thanks. I think I will." He turned to go, moving as if in a fog.

"You sure you're okay? You don't look like you're doing so well."

"Yeah. I don't know." He turned back just enough to talk to me.

"Do you want to get a bite to eat? Maybe talk about what's bothering you?" I stopped myself before mentioning my pregnancy.

"Look, I gotta go. I'll see you around, okay?"

With that, he was gone.

I considered chasing after him, but why? He knew where to find me. I'd told him I was there for him. What more could I do?

Nonetheless, my concern for him gnawed at me as I purchased a Barbie for Aida, then a wallet for David. I finally decided I had to do something for Andrew, so I stopped by Erica and Ron's shop to find out what exactly was bothering him; they were his closest friends in town and would be the most likely to know what the problem was.

Erica was out, leaving Ron to tend the store. I breathed an inward sigh of relief, not up to dealing with Erica's exuberance today.

"I think the uncertainty of deployment's been hitting him hard lately," Ron said when asked. "He's on possible stand-by to get sent over, but it keeps getting postponed, and all the emphasis on it is bringing back memories of past deployments."

"Is there anything I can do to help him?"

Ron shrugged. "Just let him know you're there if he needs you. I think that's all any of us can do. He'll talk to us when he's ready."

I nodded. Be there for him. How was I supposed to do that when he didn't want to talk to me, didn't even seem to want to be around me?

***

I managed to talk David out of the holiday cruise, citing fatigue and not wanting to be away from Aida for Christmas.

I didn't hate my husband, but I didn't love him either. I just didn't care anymore.

I was working on not caring about Andrew either, at least trying not to think about him. I avoided McKay's, avoided anything that reminded me of him. Sometimes I saw Ron and Erica, and they'd give me updates. It hadn't worked out with Alexis, and no one seemed to know why. Secretly I hoped it was because he still had feelings for me, still wanted to be with me as much as I wanted to be with him. But if he had these feelings, he didn't act on them, didn't tell me about them. In fact, other than a few words exchanged politely whenever we ran into each other, Andrew didn't tell me much of anything.

My apathy and confusion did nothing for my relationship with David, either positive or negative. I went through the motions of being a good wife. When he arrived home from work I asked him how his day was. I picked up his dry cleaning and cooked his favorite meals. I curled up with him on the couch as we watched TV with Aida.

If he noticed anything was wrong, he didn't mention it. He was his same charming self, the self he'd been nine months ago before our lives had collapsed in Richmond. Perhaps I was the same self I'd been then too, the same happy trophy wife I'd always been.

With one growing exception.

I thought about leaving, but where would I go? And, more importantly, why? I wasn't happy, but I wasn't miserable either. Aida was her usual happy self. Why disrupt her world any more than necessary?

Everything was fine at home. No, not fine. Acceptable. With no good alternatives, I could live with that.

***

There came a day in the middle of January when I could no longer button my jeans, and I knew it was time to tell David. I'd had plenty of time to devise a plan of attack, so shortly after he got home that night, I proposed we go out to dinner. He agreed, and we went to Mac's, the Southern family restaurant Aida loved. After coming so close to losing her, David refused our daughter nothing.

Once our food arrived, when David was in mid-bite, it was time to break the news.

My heart pounded as I tried to appear nonchalant. "I went back to the doctor today."

"Oh?" David seemed more interested in his steak than my day.

"She figured out right away what's been bothering me."

"Yeah?" Still no interest.

I took a deep breath. "I'm pregnant."

David's head jerked up as his fork clattered to the floor. He stared at me, mouth open. "But—" he managed after a moment.

"I know," I whispered, looking at my hands instead of him.

He remained quiet, and I stole a glance. His face was red, jaw clenched. An explosion was coming, despite the public location. I braced myself for the worst, but before David could say or do anything, Aida saved the situation.

"I'm gonna be a big sister," she squealed, jumping up from the table and running over to hug me. She repeated the words over and over, bouncing on her heels.

People at the surrounding tables looked over with indulgent smiles. I breathed a quick sigh of relief. There was no way David could cause a scene now.

"Damn, Kasey, that's—" He shook his head. "That's just... wow. Wow. Pregnant?"

"Yeah, I know."

"When are you due?"

"July."

"You are such a fucking hypocrite," he almost whispered, so Aida wouldn't hear. "I can't believe you."

An older man and woman ambled over to our table before David could say more. The man clamped his hand on David's shoulder, beaming.

"We were just passing on our way out when we heard the news. Congratulations, young man."

"Thank you, sir," David replied, jumping up to shake the man's hand.

"This beautiful woman must be your wife. And what an angelic daughter!" He patted Aida's blonde head.

"Yes, allow me to introduce them," David said in a rush. "John, this is my wife, Kasey, and my daughter, Aida. John Kinnard is the senior partner at my firm."

"No, no," corrected the man, "former senior partner, really just a consultant now. I retired and left my son in charge. Kasey, this is my wife, Greta." He gestured at the woman leaning on his arm.

"So lovely to meet both of you." I smiled graciously.

"We're aware of David's indiscretions," John said in what he most likely intended to be a conspiratorial whisper, "and we're so glad that he's now figured out his priorities."

"And now a new baby on the way," exclaimed Greta. "How precious. You've turned a bad situation good, bless your hearts."

The smile plastered to my face felt as awkward as the near grimace on David's face looked. I hoped the Kinnards didn't notice.

"Well, we won't keep you from your food any longer." John patted Aida on the head again. "Congratulations again, all of you."

"Thank you, sir." David shook the man's hand again.

As the couple shuffled away I heard Greta say, again in that conspiratorial whisper meant only for her husband but carrying to everyone nearby, "His wife must be a saint, bless her heart."

David looked at me once they were gone. "Well, that certainly changes everything."

"What do you mean?"

"That's my boss, Kasey. Family is important to him. Very important." He sighed and shook his head again. "I don't know what to do."

"Do about what, Daddy?" Aida's small brow furrowed in confusion.

"Babies are a lot of work," he told her. "We'll just have to figure out how best to take care of it."

"I'll help," she exclaimed, voice overflowing with happiness.

The rest of the meal she chattered nonstop about her role and duties as a big sister, for which I was relieved. Maybe it would influence David's reaction, whatever it might be.

That night after Aida was in bed, David approached me as I was sitting on the couch, flipping through a magazine. He plopped down next to me. I put the magazine down and looked at him, expecting a lecture, expecting the worst.

"It's Andrew's, isn't it?" he said flat-out.

I nodded. No point in denying it.

"I suppose you want a divorce now so you can run off with him."

"No."

"No?" Judging by his facial expression, he was truly shocked.

"No," I repeated.

"Care to elaborate? Just going to use me for my money, keep him on the side?" David's voice was still level, still calm.

I marveled at his self-control.

"It was just a brief thing. It's over." I struggled to keep my voice as emotionless as his.

"What a classy guy you picked for yourself. He knocks you up and casts you aside. Great taste in guys, Kasey."

"He doesn't know I'm pregnant."

"He doesn't?" A gleam appeared in David's eye, a gleam I didn't like or trust.

"No, but your boss does, which I'm guessing means soon most of Asheville will too."

He nodded. I could see the wheels turning in his mind as he plotted, as he considered our options and what would be most beneficial to him.

"Why'd you do it?" He stared intently at me, scrutinizing me as if I were an object he'd never seen before.

"Do what?"

"Sleep with him."

I shrugged, unwilling to tell David just how intensely I felt about Andrew, even now.

"Revenge?"

"What? No!"

"You were upset about what I'd done. He came around and said all the right things, and so you fucked him to get back at me."

"No!" I protested.

"Well, the joke's on you, because now you're stuck with his kid." David grinned, a wolf's grin that left a cold knot in my stomach.

"Are you going to kick me out?"

"I wanted to, but seeing Aida's reaction tonight changed my mind. I need her, and she needs you."

I nodded, holding my breath, barely able to believe what I was hearing. I'd expected screaming, physical violence against either objects in the room or against myself, not this calm acceptance and rationality.

"I can't trust you anymore, you realize," he said.

"You cheated too."

"Yes, but to get knocked up? Fuck, Kasey, why weren't you more careful? Didn't you use protection? I at least had the fucking decency to do that."

"Yes, we used protection. I didn't do this on purpose."

"Were you going to tell me about him?"

"No."

He sighed. "I told you to stay away from him. I told you he was trouble."

I ignored his comments. "I guess now we're even."

"No," That gleam in his eyes shone more brightly now.

"You cheated on me. Repeatedly. I cheated. Now we're even."

He shook his head. "No, you owe me now."

"What? Why?" My pulse raced, a mix of anger and apprehension.

His predatory grin broadened. This would not be good for me.

"Because I have all the power here. I could kick you out, keep you from ever seeing Aida again. Where would you and your unborn bastard go? You said yourself, it's over. You think he'll want you when you have a kid?"

"That would ruin you too. You admitted as much." I glared at him, but inside I was filled with worry. Would he really try to take Aida from me?

"It would be worth it to take you down with me." His voice was finally filled with the hatred I'd been expecting.

"I would be fine without you."

"Yes, but without Aida? I'm a powerful man with powerful friends, Kasey. I could guarantee that you'd never see her again, and I could just as easily destroy Adams as well."

"Why are you doing this to me?" My voice finally broke, betraying my frustration. "Why won't you just let me go already?"

"Because you're mine. Because no one makes a fool out of me!"

"This is ridiculous." I got up from the couch. "I've put up with your bullshit long enough. I'm calling a divorce attorney in the morning."

"Sit down!" He leapt up, striking me hard against my cheek and knocking me back onto the couch.

"Don't you fucking touch me," I said in a cold, low voice as I stood back up.

David took a step back, unsure of himself now, not anticipating this reaction.

"I am tired of the threats, David," I said in the same cold voice, eyes flashing. "I am tired of you thinking it's okay to hit me. I am tired of you acting so sanctimonious, tired of your drinking, tired of your cycles of abuse, repentance, and neglect. Quite frankly, I am tired of you. I am not yours, and I haven't been for quite a while. I want a divorce."

He watched me, eyes wide, but didn't show his usual signs of anger: clenched jaw, reddening face, fists at his side. Was he trying a new approach? What would his trick be this time?

He collapsed heavily on the couch, head in his hands. "Kasey," he sobbed, "you can't leave me."

I looked at him in surprise. "What?"

"Please, I'm begging you, don't leave me. I can't be alone. I need you. You're my world, you and Aida. I don't mean to hurt you, to cause you pain. Everything I do is for you!"

I watched him, detached. "You have an odd way of showing it."

"It's the stress. It's tough being part of the top firm, fighting these big cases. There's so much at stake, and if I fuck up there aren't any second chances, for me or for my clients, from the firm. You don't seem to care about it, about what I'm feeling, so the stress just builds up until I snap. I don't want to be like this. You keep me in check, Kase, and if you weren't here I don't know what I'd do. You can't leave me. I need you so much. I need you. I need you!" He began sobbing again, repeating himself over and over.

I looked at him and sighed, filled with disgust, both for him treating me this way and for me putting up with it. I wanted to walk out on him, knew it was the right thing to do, but because of all we'd had together I wasn't sure I could bring myself to do it.

"I told you there were no more chances."

"Kase, please. I'll make it up to you, I swear. We'll take that cruise. Or a week in the mountains somewhere. Tell me what you want, and I'll give it to you."

"I don't want anything. I never wanted anything, just you. Just you and Aida and our lives together. The house, the trips, the jewelry—none of it matters. What other people think isn't important." I flung my arms out in frustration. "None of that's important to me, but it seems important to you. And if all that is so important, then no matter what you feel for me, no matter what I feel for you, it's not enough. If the appearance of a family is what's important to you, then we're through. We were through a long time ago."

"No, that's not what's important. You are. You and Aida."

"It's too late for that, David. I want you out, tonight."

"But what about Aida? She needs me. I need her."

"You should've thought about that before you hit me."

I turned and headed upstairs to the guest bedroom. I shut the door, leaned against it, and sank to the floor. With my head in my hands and knees pulled tight to my chest, I sobbed. Sobbed for my unborn baby, having to grow up with no father when there were two men who could do the job; for my marriage, which was finally over after ten years; for Aida, who would be devastated by the divorce; for what I'd had and lost with Andrew. Finally, I sobbed for myself, for letting this mess get as bad as it had.

A knock on the door jarred me from my thoughts.

"Kase?" David tried to open the door, but my weight against it stopped him.

"Go away."

"Kase, let me in. Please."

"I said go away."

"Can we just talk about this?"

"We're past talking. I told you to leave."

"What are you going to tell Aida?"

"That her father's a cheating, wife-beating asshole. That I was a fool for putting up with it as long as I did."

"Can I please come in?"

"I want you out." I pushed my hair away from my face.

He sighed. "I'll be out in the morning."

***

He wasn't. In the kitchen the next morning, David sat on a barstool at the counter, sipping coffee and reading the paper as if nothing had happened.

Aida sat next to him, munching on a piece of toast.

"Good morning, sunshine." David put down his paper and smiled at me.

"What are you doing here?" I kept my voice flat, although my mind was racing. I wanted him out, but couldn't say anything to him now, with

Aida sitting next to him. He'd planned it that way, of course, and I glared at him.

"I was thinking, should we convert the guest bedroom into a nursery? Or maybe a new addition? My office is really too small to be a guestroom. Who knew when we moved here that we'd need more space?"

"David, I asked you what you're doing here."

His smile wavered. "What do you mean?"

My gaze rested on Aida a moment before returning to my husband. "You know exactly what I mean."

"Mommy?" Our daughter watched us with eyes too big for her head.

"Go get your backpack and put your shoes on, okay, sweetie?" I smiled at her. As soon as she was gone, I turned back to David. "Why the hell are you still here?"

"I was hoping you'd change your mind." He wouldn't look at me, wouldn't meet my eyes.

"No, not this time. I meant what I said last night." I leaned against the counter, arms crossed in front of my chest. "I've put up with you too long. I'm done with you, David."

"Can't we work this out?" He stood up and came over, but I turned away. "We'll raise that baby as our own, Kase. That baby will be a reminder to us of what we almost lost, new hope for us, a new life bringing us together."

I looked down at the counter, feeling nothing. "No."

"Please."

I glanced over my shoulder at him, surprised by the worry, fear, and regret in his voice, so different from the anger I'd come to expect. "No, it's too late." I refused to look at him directly, knowing that I might give in.

"I found a therapist this morning, someone to talk to about my anger."

I spun around and met his eyes.

"Is that enough to let me stay?"

"David—"

He raised his hands to my mouth, cutting me off. "One more chance. I won't fuck it up, I promise. I can't lose you and Aida. I can't."

"No."

"Please, Kase, I love you. Even despite everything that's happened, I still love you. Don't you still love me?"

"No. I loved who you were. I loved the guy who was smart, charming, and funny, the guy who made me feel like the only woman in the world, the guy who took care of me and put me first." I shook my head. "But that's not you, not anymore. I don't know who you are. I don't know where you fit."

"Let me show you who I am. Let me get to know you again. Please?"

"I can't trust you, David."

"I'm done cheating, I promise. I shouldn't have done it, I know, but it's over. You have to believe me." His voice shook.

"It's not just that. Hell, I don't even care about that anymore. I can't trust your temper. I can't trust your promises. You say one thing, and then as soon as you get pissed you do the opposite. I'm done with that. I'm done with you. I want you out."

"You're not changing your mind on this, are you?" He studied my face, probably looking for signs of weakness, of wavering.

I met his gaze. "No."

"You've changed, Kase." He rubbed his face and sighed. "I'll go, but I want you to promise me something."

"What?"

"Promise me you'll give me a chance to win you back. You owe me that, at least."

"I don't owe you anything."

Before he could respond, I left the room.

***

Scheduled to work all day, I found enough projects to keep my mind off David and whatever steps might be necessary to get him out of the house.

Just as my shift was ending, he came into the shop.

"I got everything taken care of." His voice was light, as if he were discussing taking a car in for an oil change, or plans for the weekend, and not the dissolution of our marriage.

"Oh?"

"Yeah." He glanced around, his gaze lingering on my coworkers who were no doubt listening in while straightening shelves of merchandise. "You're off now, right? Want to grab a snack or something while we go over the details?"

I massaged my lower back. My first trimester was barely over, and I already had swollen ankles and amplified aches and pains. At least the morning sickness had stopped. "Fine, as long as it's somewhere with comfy chairs."

I followed in my own car as David drove downtown and parked near the Grove Arcade, a large restored building housing dozens of shops and restaurants. He didn't enter, however; he walked past it and stopped half a block away, in front of McKay's.

"This okay?" He held open the door.

"Fine."

As we walked in, I scanned the store for Andrew, but there were no signs of him. I hadn't seen him for a couple weeks, and even then we'd just passed on the street, exchanging a wave but no words.

David led me to a table in front of the windows, visible to everyone passing by, which I'm sure was his intention. He handed me a manila file folder, then went up to the counter.

I opened it and flipped through the contents. The first sheet read "Separation Agreement" in bold letters, followed by several pages of bullet points and dotted lines.

"In North Carolina, you have to be physically separated for a year before you can file for divorce." David set our drinks down: sweet tea for me and coffee for himself. "So I went ahead and drew up the papers. It's a legally binding contract, but it's not a court document, so it's not public record. Go ahead and look through it. If you have any changes, we can make them and get it signed and filed tomorrow."

I quickly read through the papers. David would move out and leave the house to me and Aida, but he reserved the right to spend time with her there if I agreed to it. He'd pay monthly child support and alimony. As far as I could tell, it looked pretty standard.

"Where are you staying?" I asked, waiting for the catch. There had to be one. He wouldn't give in this easily.

"I'm staying with a friend of a friend for now."

"Are you planning on getting your own place? How's Aida going to visit you if you're staying on someone's couch?"

"Well, the thing is...." And here was the catch, of course. "I don't mind going along with all this, but I don't want anyone to know we've separated, in case it all works out okay in the end."

"What does it matter if people know?"

"It matters, Kase. If we're going to fit in here, if we're going to make it here, it matters what people think." His jaw muscle twitched, and he took a deep breath before continuing. "I'm willing to go along with whatever you think is best, on two conditions. One, you don't tell people we're separated. And two, you give me another chance to show how much you mean to me."

"David, I said I wasn't promising anything."

"Please." He reached across the table for my hand. "I know you have every reason to never speak to me again, but please let me try to win you back."

A shadow from outside brushed across our table. I looked up to see Andrew walking past, his head down, giving no indication he'd seen me. I pulled my hand from David's. "You can try whatever you want, but I don't know if it'll work."

He smiled at me. "That's a start, at least."

\*\*\*

Several days later, back in the gift shop, David came over to the counter where I was sorting greeting cards made by local artists. I hadn't seen him since the day at McKay's; true to his word, he'd packed a suitcase and spent his nights elsewhere.

"Hey, beautiful."

"What do you want?"

"I want to take you to dinner and talk about your day, talk about our baby."

"David—"

"I got a sitter for Aida. Just you and me tonight. Nothing fancy, and I promise I won't try anything. We can talk about whatever you want. We don't even have to talk, if you don't want to. We can just sit and stare at each other."

I smiled in spite of myself.

"See, there you go. What do you say?"

"Fine. I'm done at four."

"It's a date." He smiled and left the shop.

***

"I miss you," he said as we looked over our menus. We were at one of the gourmet country-style restaurants that thrived in Asheville.

I didn't answer.

"I miss Aida too, and putting her to bed at night. I miss falling asleep next to you."

I nodded noncommittally. Despite everything we'd been through, I missed having him around as well. Ten years with someone was harder to get past than I'd thought.

"How's she taking all this?"

"Mostly she's excited about the baby."

"Does she miss me? Does she ask where I am?"

I stared at my plate, trying to formulate an answer that wouldn't piss him off. "You really screwed her up this past year, all that yelling in front of her. She doesn't trust you, not completely. She's scared of you, scared that you're going to blow up again and hurt me."

"Jesus." He rubbed at his temples. "Does she miss me at all? Do you tell her I love her and would do anything to be there with her?"

"I said her daddy loves her, but it's best for all of us if you live somewhere else until you can get your temper under control."

"Fuck, Kasey. You actually told her that?"

"Why not? She knows more about what's going on than you give her credit for."

He sighed. "I wish there was a way to make this easier for her."

"Me too."

Before he could answer, the waiter arrived to take our orders. From that point on, David was polite, charming, and completely platonic. He mentioned a couple of his cases and reminisced about Aida's last birthday party. He made no mention of Andrew, or the baby, or getting back together.

"I had a good time tonight," he said as we left the restaurant.

"Me too." I meant it. When he wasn't being an overbearing, jealous asshole, he was a lot of fun to be around.

"Can we make this a weekly thing?"

"We're not getting back together."

"You didn't answer my question."

"Ask me again next week."

\*\*\*

The following week, David popped into the gift shop with Aida in tow. All three of us went to Mac's. David was on his best behavior, laughing and joking with no hint of anger.

I wondered if maybe he was actually serious about winning me back, but then I remembered all the other times when he'd acted the same way. It was too early to make a judgment.

As he continued his reformed behavior into the next week, then another, I tried to re-evaluate my feelings towards my husband. I still loved Andrew, still thought about him constantly, but if he was absent, if we had no chance of being together, might it be better to repair my marriage? Better not for me, perhaps, but better for Aida, for this unborn child Andrew didn't even know was his? Those were my options: a loveless marriage with David; a loveless relationship, or whatever I might have, with Andrew; or being alone and loveless. Better the enemy I knew, perhaps, than one I didn't.

Then I would think about my broken car window, about how Aida was scared of her father, and wondered if being alone might be the best option.

\*\*\*

As Aida and I sat eating dinner one night, her playing with her peas while I contemplated the future, the doorbell rang. We weren't expecting visitors, and it was too late for a salesperson to stop by.

"Finish your dinner," I said as she jumped up to answer the door. "I'll see who it is."

I peered through the peephole and was surprised to see Andrew standing outside my door. I opened it and smiled up at him. "Hey. I don't think you've ever stopped by before. David's away, fortunately, so come on in."

He didn't move, just stood there looking slightly uncomfortable. He wore his police uniform, and a second uniformed officer stood next to and slightly behind him.

I tensed, looking from his solemn face to his companion's identical expression. "What's wrong?" A wave of hysteria fought its way through me as he bit his lip. "Andrew, what's wrong?"

"I'm so sorry, Kasey. There's been an accident."

"No, no, no, no," I whispered, frantic, cutting him off. I shook my head, realizing why two cops were outside my house on this cold, wintry evening. "Not now. He was such a good man again."

"He was killed instantly."

I went numb, unable to stand, unable to hear anything else he might be saying. Andrew caught me as I collapsed and held me as I sobbed.

"I'm so sorry," he murmured, stroking my hair. "I'm so sorry, Kasey. I'm so sorry."

# Chapter 18 – Andrew (Age 6)

"You ready, Andy?" my stepdad Gary called from the living room.

I looked around my room one last time, making sure I hadn't forgotten anything. I paused, then grabbed Wart off my dresser. Wart was a stuffed pig I'd had forever, prob'ly my best friend, and I couldn't imagine not having him with me all summer.

"What the fuck is that?" Gary asked when I came out of my room.

"Now, Gary," Mama said. She didn't like it when he cussed in front of me, but she never yelled at him, at least not to defend me. She was scared of him.

I was scared of him too.

"I want to bring him with," I said firmly.

"You gonna suck your thumb and wear diapers too?" He wore a mean look on his face.

"No!" Six-year-olds didn't do that stuff.

Gary frowned.

Had I gone too far? I never knew with him. Sometimes he got mad if I didn't answer him, and sometimes what I meant as just an honest answer he said was backtalk. I moved closer to Mama, hoping she'd protect me if he tried to hit me. Or maybe she'd let me take Wart with me, although she didn't usually go against him unless she'd been drinking; she didn't like to be hit either.

"Gimme that thing," Gary said, coming towards me.

I got as close to Mama as I could. "No."

"Give 'im to me, you little brat."

"No." I held Wart tight against my chest.

"Now, Gary," Mama said again, but she didn't sound like she meant it.

"Stay out of this, Judy!" When he sounded that angry it meant I was on my own. "Gimme that thing, Andy."

"No," I yelled.

He leaned forward real fast to grab Wart. I held him as best I could, hugging him to me, but Gary smacked my head and my grip loosed. He pulled on my arm and suddenly it felt like it was on fire.

I dropped Wart and started crying.

Gary picked him up. "Stop crying or I'll really give you something to cry about."

I tried to hold back the tears, because if I didn't he'd do something really mean, but it was hard. My arm really hurt and it was hard to move it.

"You're too old for this thing," he said.

I knew that big boys like me shouldn't have stuffed animals anymore, but Wart was different. He listened to me when I needed someone to talk to, and he never made fun of me like the other kids did. He really was my best friend.

"He's going to be in an unfamiliar place," Mama said, maybe because she felt bad Gary hit me. "Why don't we take care of it when he gets back?"

"I told you to stay out of this," Gary said real loud and mean, and he took a step towards her.

She pulled back away from him.

I was a big boy and could take whatever he did to me, but I got real mad when he was mean to her. I stepped in front of her. "Leave my mama alone!" I tried to sound brave but I didn't think he believed me.

"You the tough guy now?" He laughed, but it wasn't a fun laugh. It was a laugh that meant he was fixing to do something that'd hurt. "If you're so tough, then you definitely don't need this." He pulled his cigarette lighter from his pocket and held the flame to Wart's tail.

"No, don't," I cried, but he didn't listen.

Mama bent down and put her arms around me, and together we watched Wart burn.

When he was mostly gone, Gary opened the door and threw him on the sidewalk. "Grab your bags and let's go. We're gonna be late."

We took a six-hour car trip to meet my dad. I didn't say much in the car, just sat and stared out the window, trying not to think about Wart or how much my shoulder hurt. I thought about how much I hated Gary. Jesus and the Bible told us not to hate people and love everyone, but it was real hard to love my stepdad when he was so mean to me and Mama all the time. I thought about how much better it was gonna be when I was big enough to beat him up, and then he'd be so scared of me that he'd move out, and me and my mama could be happy together and not scared anymore. And then maybe when Gary was gone my dad would move back in with us and we'd be one happy family again. I barely remembered when we all lived together, but I knew that we did once, and maybe if Gary was gone we could again.

We met my dad at a McDonald's in Nashville. Gary wanted a place more in-between but Dad said no. My dad was real important at his job and couldn't take off much time to come get me. Plus he said that if we didn't meet here he wouldn't take me, and since my stepdad didn't want me around all summer he said okay. Dad and Gary didn't like each other very much.

We got out of the car to go inside, but Gary held me back. "Listen, you little brat. I find out you said anything bad about me to your dad or anyone here, I'll make your life hell when you get home. Understand?"

"Yes sir." I knew he meant it.

We went inside. I looked around and saw Dad sitting in a corner, and ran over to him. "Dad!"

Mama and Gary followed behind.

"Hey, kiddo!" Dad gave me a hug, which hurt my arm but I didn't say anything. "Hello, Judy, Gary."

They nodded at him. Gary cleared his throat. "We have a long drive back. You want to grab his bags so we can get going?"

We walked out to the parking lot. My dad had a big shiny car, brand new and prob'ly real expensive. My dad had lots of money and a big house too. He always bought me lots of neat stuff for my birthdays and Christmas. Gary's car was kind of old and had a big dent in the front where he hit something on his way home one night.

Mama wiped her eyes before giving me a big hug. "Be a good boy, Andrew. I'll miss you."

"I'll miss you too," I said, but I prob'ly wouldn't. I was too excited about spending all summer with Dad.

On the two-and-a-half-hour drive to his house, I told him all the fun stuff we could do together this summer: baseball games even though I didn't really like baseball, fishing and camping trips, swimming in the lake, riding bikes, staying up late watching movies, grilling in the backyard, hitting the county fair, building a treehouse and forts in the woods, all kinds of stuff.

He let me talk for a while, then said, "I hate to break it to you, kiddo, but I'm going to be working all summer. Lynne and I would like to take a vacation with you kids, but it all depends on how much traveling I'll be doing."

It hit me that I would be alone all summer, no Wart or friends or anything, and I started crying. I couldn't help it.

Dad reached over and patted my shoulder, the same one that Gary hurt.

"Ow," I yelled real loud. I couldn't help it.

Dad looked over so fast he drove halfway into the other lane. "What's wrong, buddy?"

I wanted to tell him the truth, tell him about my arm and Wart and how Gary hurt me and Mama a lot, but then I thought of what Gary said, and of what he might do to my mama too. "I fell."

"We can take you to the doctor if it still hurts in a few days. You need to be more careful, kiddo."

I fell asleep, and when I woke up we were at Dad's house. It was real big, probably five times the size of my house back home, with a huge yard and a lake behind it, a dock to jump off of, and a big deck and patio out back with a special spot for a campfire. The garage had room for four cars in it, and it was prob'ly filled with really expensive ones like the one my Dad was driving right now. There were lots of cool big old trees that were perfect for climbing, and woods nearby to play in. This was my second summer at Dad's house, and I loved it here.

We went inside and the house was empty. A note on the fridge said everyone was at the store and they'd be back soon, with dinner.

"Everyone?" I asked Dad. I thought it would be just me, him, and Lynne all summer. Lynne was his new wife. They got married last fall. They sent us a card with a picture telling us about it. I'd never met her. She wasn't as pretty as my mama, and she prob'ly wasn't as nice either.

"Shannon and Chad live with us too," he said. "They're your stepsister and stepbrother. They live here, but sometimes they'll be at their dad's house."

I nodded and tried to keep the frown off my face. I didn't even know them yet and already I hated them, because they stayed with my dad and they weren't even his real kids, and I was stuck with my mean stepdad.

Dad showed me my room. It looked just like a hotel room, right down to the flowers on the comforter and the ugly painting hanging on the wall. I hated it.

At this point Lynne and her kids got home. We went downstairs to say hi, and to my surprise she was pregnant. I didn't know why but this made me really mad. I tried to be nice to her during dinner but I didn't like her. I didn't like her kids either. Shannon was seven and Chad was four. They stuck their tongues out at me when no one was watching.

After dinner Dad told us to go outside and play. Shannon and Chad rode their bikes around the driveway. I didn't have a bike here. Dad said he'd buy me one tomorrow, so for now I just sat on the front step and watched them. They rode real close to me, almost running over my feet.

"Can I have a turn?" I asked.

"No," Shannon said. "It's my bike, not yours."

"No," repeated Chad. "It's my bike."

Shannon stopped her bike in front of me. "Your dad loves my mama more than your mama."

"No he doesn't! He still loves my mama and someday he's gonna divorce your mama and we're all gonna live together again."

"Nuh-uh. My mama is gonna have a baby so he's staying with us because he loves us more. Plus your mama is poor. Why would he love someone who's poor?"

"She's not poor," I yelled, even though it was true.

Chad came over. "You're poor," he said over and over again.

"Shut up!" I was really mad now. He kept saying it so I pushed him off his bike, hoping that would make him stop, but instead he just started crying.

"Mama," Shannon yelled real loud, "Andrew pushed Chad."

"Tattletale," I shouted at her.

"At least I'm not poor," she said back to me, so I pushed her too.

At this point I was already gonna be in trouble, so I figured why not?

She was bigger than me though, and pushed me back. I stumbled over the step and fell down, landing on my shoulder. It hurt real bad but I didn't cry. Not in front of a girl. Not in front of someone I hated.

Dad came out and saw Chad tangled up in his bike, crying; me scuffed up on the step; and Shannon yelling her head off.

"He pushed Chad and me," Shannon yelled.

"She said me and Mama are poor," I yelled at the same time.

Dad looked at Shannon, at Chad, then at me. "Andrew, I'm disappointed in you. Pushing someone younger than you?"

"But, Dad—"

"He pushed me too, Rick," Shannon butted in.

"You pushed me back."

"You started it. I was just protecting my *poor* little brother."

She said "poor" on purpose to make me mad, I could tell, so I got up real fast and pushed her again. She wasn't suspecting that so she lost her balance and fell over.

Dad grabbed me by the neck of my shirt and pulled me away from her. "Andrew, enough! Y'all will be here all summer and y'all have to get along. Now go to your room and think about what you did."

Shannon stuck her tongue out at me, making sure my dad couldn't see her.

"But, Dad," I said again. "Shannon—"

"No buts, kiddo. Go."

"That's not fair."

"Life's not fair. Now go, unless you want a spanking as well."

I thought about telling him spankings were nothing compared to what I got from Gary, but then I remembered what my stepdad said about telling anyone about it and kept my mouth shut. Besides, what was the point? Would Dad even care, since he took Shannon's side right away?

I went inside and up to my room, even though it wasn't my room. Not really. It was just a room I happened to be staying in for a few months. It really wasn't fair. They started it and didn't even get in trouble. Maybe Shannon was right. Maybe my dad did love her family better.

Loneliness hit me. Why did this happen to me? Why couldn't I have two parents who lived together, and both had lots of money, and we'd all be happy together? Why was I stuck with a stepdad who hurt me, a mama who didn't do nothing to stop him, and a dad who didn't love me anymore? It just wasn't fair.

I felt sad but I also felt mad. Real, real mad. And the more I thought about it all, the madder I got. When I got mad I always wanted to take it out on someone or something. There was nothing in here with me though, just the stupid flowery blanket and the stupid picture on the wall—some flowers at a house in the woods, somewhere prob'ly made up. I hated that painting most of all because the people who lived in that house were prob'ly happy. There was prob'ly a mama and a dad and a little boy they loved a lot. They prob'ly never fought or hit each other and they all lived happily ever after. I hated that painting.

I climbed up on the dresser underneath the painting and took it down off the wall. It was heavy in the frame, hard to move with my shoulder hurting, but I got it down okay. I leaned it against the bed and then real quick kicked a big hole in it. I kicked again and again until there was nothing left, just pieces of paper and the frame. I felt a little bit better, until I heard voices in the hallway. I shoved the ruined picture under the bed just as Dad opened the door.

He came in and sat on the bed. "We need to have a talk, kiddo."

I didn't look at him. I didn't want to have a talk.

"I know you miss your mama and stepdad, but you're here now, for the next few months, and while here you need to follow our rules. I don't know what you're able to do at home, but here we don't hit. We don't fight. We aren't mean to each other. We use our words to solve our problems. Understood?"

"But, Dad, Shannon started it by saying mean stuff."

"That may be, but keep in mind it's hard for her and Chad too. Y'all just need to get used to each other."

"Why is it okay for some people to hit and not others?"

"What do you mean, kiddo?"

I didn't want to tell him about Gary. "I dunno. The police can arrest you and put you in jail when you do something wrong. Soldiers can shoot bad guys. Why is that okay, but I can't hit someone to make them stop being mean?"

"It's all about the greater good."

"The greater good?"

"Yeah. That means you're not acting selfishly. You're doing it to help people. Pushing Shannon is not helping people, just yourself. Make sense?"

I nodded.

"Good. Now no more fighting, understand?"

I nodded again, and he left the room.

I fell asleep but woke up a few hours later to loud voices; it was Dad and Lynne arguing. I listened for a few moments. They were arguing about me, and I felt real bad. She didn't want me here, said I was a bad influence on her kids. Said my mom wasn't doing a good job of raising me. Said she hoped the summer would go by real fast and then I'd be gone. Said my dad would be better off calling me rather than me visiting.

I thought about what Shannon said, about my dad loving her family more, and I thought about what he said about the greater good. Real quick the answer to the problem came to me: I'd run away, maybe go back to Mama and Gary. Gary didn't want me there but I could protect Mama, because Dad said fighting back was okay if you were helping someone.

I grabbed my backpack and put in a change of clothes, my jacket, a comic book, and all the money I had—twelve dollars and fifty-three cents. I snuck down to the kitchen to grab some snacks, and was about to head out the door when a voice behind me spoke.

"Where you going?" It was Shannon.

"You don't want me here, so I'm leaving. Don't tell anyone, okay?"

She just stared at me, not saying anything.

I turned and left the house.

Once outside, I wasn't sure where to go, and wished I'd brought a flashlight. I tried to go back inside to grab one but all the doors were locked. It was getting late and was real dark. I needed a place to sleep, but where? I walked around behind the house and saw the boathouse in the distance. Perfect. Lucky for me it was unlocked, so I climbed into the boat inside and curled up on the bottom.

Bright sunlight woke me, and I checked my watch: six-thirty. Real fast I climbed out of the boat and walked around the edge of the woods until I was past the house and back to the main road. It was Sunday so there was no one around, but I kept next to the woods just in case. I didn't want anyone to find me. I pretended to be an army spy, and the bad guys were chasing me, and I pretended to shoot them whenever they got too close.

Being chased by bad guys made me hungry, so I stopped to eat the chips I brought, and then the apple, but it wasn't enough. Now I was thirsty too. I wished I'd grabbed a coke or something.

I kept walking even though I was tired and starting to think this wasn't such a good idea. Then I remembered what Dad said, about the greater good, and kept going. Now I pretended that instead of a spy, I was a soldier on a top-secret mission to save Mama from the bad guys who were still chasing me. They got real close to catching me and then I killed them all.

I got so carried away that I lost track of the time until my stomach started growling. It was eleven o'clock already. I decided to get some lunch, and then I'd try to find a bus station and see about getting back to Mama and Gary.

I made it into town and found a small diner. Inside I sat at the counter.

A waitress came over. "Your mama or daddy here too?"

"Nope, just me." I didn't tell her I was running away. I didn't want her to get worried or tell anyone.

"All grown up, I see," she said with a smile.

"Yes ma'am," I said proudly, and ordered a cheeseburger, fries, and a chocolate shake. It tasted real good after just an apple and chips for breakfast.

As I was eating, a cop came in and sat down next to me.

"Morning," he said, not looking at me.

I nodded at him, mouth too full of food to talk.

He ordered a cup of coffee, then, still not looking at me, said, "I need your help, citizen."

"Yes sir?" I asked, swallowing real quick.

"Yeah. Seems there's a kid that's missing, and his family is real worried about him. You wouldn't happen to know where he might be, would you?"

"They're not worried. They don't want him around, so he decided to go back to his real family and protect his mama. It's for the greater good."

"The greater good, hmm? That's a pretty big concept for a six-year-old, Andrew."

"I heard them arguing. My—I mean, his—stepmama don't want him around, and her kids don't either. They say mean stuff about my—I mean, his—mama. We can't help it we're poor. It's my mean stepdad's fault. My dad loves his new family more anyways and don't want me around. My mama needs me."

"And where's your mama?"

"Sunflower County, Mississippi."

"That's a long ways from here. You ain't fixing on walking the whole way, are you?"

"No sir. I'm fixing to take the bus."

"You got enough for a ticket?"

"Yes sir. I think so."

"Even after your lunch?"

I frowned. I hadn't thought of that.

"You know, I bet your daddy would loan you the money, if you're really fixing to go back. Why don't I give you a lift home and you can ask him? And if he says yes, I'll even give you a ride to the bus station."

I thought for a moment. "Promise?"

"I promise."

"Deal."

"Wanna finish your burger first? I ain't in a hurry. Just gotta grab something out of my car first."

I ate my burger, wondering how he knew who I was. I asked him when he came back in.

"Your family woke up this morning and couldn't find you. Your sister said you ran away, so they called us out to look for you. You had a lot of people worried, did you think about that?"

"I told her not to tell anyone."

"It's part of that greater good, Andrew. If you know someone could get hurt, you gotta do what you can to stop that. That's exactly what your sister did."

I thought about what he said. "Most people are just trying to serve that greater good, aren't they, sir?"

"I think you're right. God made people mostly good but sometimes they do the wrong thing. They might be scared, or not thinking. You just gotta remember that, no matter how bad things get. We all got our reasons."

"Even the bad guys?"

"Even the bad guys."

I finished eating and we got in his car. I asked him to turn on the sirens and lights, and he did. It was fun speeding around in a police car. He drove me home, and when I was about to hop out in the driveway he stopped me.

"Listen, Andrew, sometimes things are bad. Really, really bad. And we want to do something to fix them. But going half-cocked into action without a plan doesn't always work. Sometimes you just got to play by the rules while waiting for the right moment, and then hit hard and fast. Don't let your temper cloud your head. Understand?"

I nodded. Play by the rules until I was strong enough to hit back. I couldn't wait to get home to see Gary.

# Chapter 19 – Kasey (Present)

David was driving home from interviewing a witness when it happened. A car had attempted to pass him on an icy two-lane road and merged back over too soon. He swerved to avoid a collision, hit a slick spot, lost control of his SUV, and plunged down a steep mountainside. The vehicle flipped and rolled several times, then exploded, charring his battered body. The other driver drove off.

All the investigators had to go on was a set of tire tracks, which were mostly erased by emergency vehicles and rescue workers on the scene. The police were asking the responsible party to come forward, but they didn't realistically expect any witnesses.

That afternoon I lay on our bed—no, my bed now—and stared at the ceiling. I closed my eyes and saw David's SUV skidding off the road, flipping and rolling down the hill like a toy flung by a giant child. They'd said he was killed instantly, but how instantaneous had it really been? What had his thoughts been? Had he known that his death was inevitable? What did someone think in a situation like that, with just seconds to live?

I opened my eyes, but his SUV was still there, bright red, flashy and expensive. How could someone miss a vehicle like that? I'd hated that he drove something like that, a big gas-guzzling safety trap. Maybe if I'd tried harder to get him to drive something else, he'd still be alive. Maybe if I'd been a better wife, he never would have cheated on me, we never would have moved to Asheville, and he'd still be alive. Maybe if I hadn't kicked him out, had tried harder to fix our marriage more quickly, or.....

Aida came into the room, climbed on the bed and snuggled up next to me. I wrapped my arms around her, not saying anything, not knowing what to say. Explaining last night that Daddy wasn't ever coming home had been one of the hardest things I'd ever done. I still wasn't sure if she understood completely. We'd never lost anyone close, just distant relatives she barely knew.

I opened my mouth to say something but shut it before uncertain words came out.

Someone knocked on the bedroom door. I looked over to see my mother standing in the doorway. My parents had arrived from Richmond that morning, and David's parents would arrive soon as well.

I vaguely remembered calling them last night.

\*\*\*

Andrew waited until my sobs quieted, then asked if there was family I needed to contact. I nodded, walked into the kitchen and dialed my parents.

My father answered.

"David, he... David...." I choked.

Andrew immediately walked over and took the phone from me. "Hello, this is Sgt. Andrew Adams with the Asheville PD. I regret to inform you that David was killed in a car accident tonight.... Yes, a tragedy.... As soon as you can, I think."

I sat on the kitchen floor with Aida in my lap as Andrew called David's parents too. He then knelt down next to me. "Go to bed. Try to get some rest. Everyone will be here tomorrow."

I nodded numbly and stood up. Andrew took Aida and followed me upstairs to my bedroom.

"Do you want Aida in here with you or in her room?"

"Here," I mumbled as I walked past him and sat on the edge of the bed.

He sat Aida back on my lap, and she promptly curled up against me. He then handed me a bottle of pills from his pocket, and I looked at them but didn't recognize the drug name on the label.

"Sleeping pills, in case you need them."

I nodded again.

"You gonna be okay tonight?" He set the bottle on my dresser.

Another nod.

He smoothed my hair and kissed my forehead. "Call me if you need anything." Then he was gone.

\*\*\*

"Kasey?" My mother's voice broke into my thoughts. "David's parents are here."

They were the last people I wanted to see right now.

They, and my parents too, had all been in denial about David's affairs. My parents had flat-out refused to acknowledge that anything was wrong with my marriage, changing the subject each time I'd brought it up. David's parents, however, conceded that *if* David had indeed been unfaithful, it was because I hadn't been a good enough wife.

It was easier on me to just avoid talking to them at all.

"You and Aida should come down and see them."

I didn't move, nor did Aida.

"We need to make funeral arrangements. Have you picked a funeral home yet?"

"No," I whispered.

"What? Speak up, dear. I can't hear you when you mumble."

"No," I repeated in a barely audible voice.

"You really should come down. It's only polite."

I pulled Aida more tightly to me and closed my eyes again.

My mother sighed and walked away.

"Yes, they're both in there," she said in response to a question I didn't hear. "I tried to get her to come down, but she won't really answer."

"It's a shock for all of us," my father-in-law said from the doorway. David had inherited his father's build, and his demeanor, especially when drinking.

I'd never realized how similar their voices sounded, not that it mattered now because I'd never hear David's voice again. I pulled Aida even closer.

She squirmed. "Mommy, you're crushing me."

My only response was to lie down on the bed.

"Well, we're hurting too, you know," my mother-in-law said. "Come downstairs, Aida, and we'll get you some lunch."

Aida kissed my cheek, then dutifully got up, and they all left.

I remained still, staring at the ceiling.

***

I spent the next few days like that, lying on my bed staring at the ceiling, letting my parents and in-laws plan the funeral and distract Aida from her father's death. No tears would come, and sometimes no thoughts either. It was easier to just lie there, empty and numb, tracing patterns on the ceiling.

Sometimes I'd be flooded with memories of me and David, of our good times. Everything he'd done to hurt me—the cheating, the yelling, the physical abuse and intimidation—was now forgotten. I focused on the last few weeks, on how he'd treated me and Aida. He'd been trying to change, to be the man he thought I deserved, and now we had no chance to be happy again, no chance to be the perfect family we'd always wanted but never gotten.

And what now of the baby? I still hadn't told Andrew, hadn't even told my parents or in-laws yet. Andrew hadn't been back over, hadn't called or emailed or sent a sympathy card, since the night he held me after delivering the horrible news. His silence told me more about his true feelings than anything he could possibly say. I found myself laughing out loud, borderline hysterical over the irony that he was so afraid of being abandoned in his time of need, yet here I was needing him, and he knew it, the bastard fucking knew it, and he was nowhere to be found.

The day of the funeral, four days after David had been killed, I was lying on my bed, on our bed, wearing a black dress, laughing hysterically.

My father walked by and stuck his head into the room. "Everything okay, pumpkin?" Clearly he was baffled by my laughter, baffled that anything could be funny to me an hour before my husband would be laid to rest.

"I'm pregnant."

He stared at me, disbelief slowly replacing his confusion over my laughter. "What?"

"I'm pregnant. Three-and-a-half months, due July fourteenth. Bastille Day. That'll go over well with David's parents, won't it? Maybe I'll give it a French-sounding name?"

He just looked at me.

"I'm not looking forward to being pregnant in the summer, but I'm hoping the mountains won't be as bad as Richmond." I babbled on, nervous that my father wasn't responding, trying to fill the silence. "Less humidity, at least. The mountains here are beautiful, aren't they? I can only imagine how it'll look in the spring with the flowers, when all the ice and cold is gone. The ice...."

The ice had killed David, as did the mountains. I hated them suddenly, hated winter, hated this city. If only we'd gone farther south, somewhere flatter, somewhere warmer, David would still be alive.

My father cleared his throat. "We need to leave soon, to get to the chapel before everyone."

"Okay, Dad. I'll be down in a couple minutes."

After he left, I continued to lie there. I felt light, empty, disconnected; the same feelings I'd had the night David had broken my car window and Andrew had offered to let me stay at his place. This wasn't my life. My husband wasn't dead, and I wasn't pregnant with the child of a man who would barely talk to me. This was all a mistake, and any moment now David would walk through the bedroom door.

"Sorry!" He'd laugh and walk over to the bed to kiss my forehead, and we'd be in love like we were ten years ago.

"Sorry?" I'd get up and pretend to be mad at him, trying not to laugh too.

"It was all just a big joke. I didn't die, and there was never anyone in my life except you and Aida."

"But you cheated on me," I'd point out, confused. "And you hit me. I can never forget that."

"No." He'd still be laughing. "None of that ever happened. I love you."

"Then why are we in Asheville? Why did we move here if you never cheated? This doesn't make any sense."

"Damn it, Kasey," he'd yell. "Why do you have to go and ruin everything with your fucking questions and logic? Fine, I'm lying. You happy now? You killed me. Is that what you want to hear? We moved here for you. Everything I did was for you, and now I'm dead. This is all your fucking fault."

I bolted upright, eyes wide open. David wasn't around, of course; I must have fallen asleep. I shook my head to clear it, and headed downstairs shaken by my dream or vision, or whatever it had been.

When I entered the living room, my parents and in-laws stopped talking. They'd been discussing me. No sense in pretending otherwise.

"Yes, I'm pregnant. No, I don't know what I'm going to do."

No one looked surprised, so my assumption had been correct. I looked at them, still feeling empty. No matter how hard I tried, I couldn't get excited about this pregnancy, not without Andrew at my side. I didn't expect the baby's grandparents to get excited either, and I surely wasn't going to tell them the father wasn't my husband until I had Andrew's full support and commitment.

"That's wonderful, dearie," my mother-in-law said after a moment's lapse, a too-big smile plastered on her lips, not reaching her eyes.

Years of experience with David's parents had taught me that they both fervently believed a woman's place was in the home, raising a family and being supported by her husband, and that a family was inferior if they didn't have those characteristics. How would they react if I remarried?

My father cleared his throat, a habit of his when he was nervous or uncomfortable in a situation. "Should we get going? We don't want to be late."

"It's not like they'll start without us," I pointed out.

"There's no need for rudeness," my mother reprimanded.

I looked at her. "Aida and I will meet you there." I headed out of the room.

"Are you sure you feel up to driving?" my father asked, but I ignored him.

My daughter was in her bedroom, curled up on the window seat.

I knocked on the open door. "Aida, it's time to go."

"Daddy's not coming back, is he?"

"No."

"Why did he have to die?"

"I don't know, sweetie." I walked over and put my arms around her.

"I miss him, Mommy, but I don't miss him a lot. Is that bad?" She looked at me with wide, solemn eyes.

I studied her, smoothed her blonde hair. Blonde like David's. Would the baby have blonde hair? "No, I don't think that's bad."

"Grandma Helen said it was." She referred to my mother as Grandma Helen.

I thought for a moment before replying, careful of how to word my response. "Some people think it's better to just remember all the good stuff about someone and not the bad. Does that make sense?"

She nodded. "Do you miss Daddy a lot?"

"Sometimes. Just like you."

She nodded again, brow furrowed, digesting my words.

"It's important to remember the good and the bad about your daddy," I continued. "But no matter what, know that he loved you very, very, very much. He loved both of us, and even though sometimes he was mean, he tried to be a good person."

"Did he love the baby too?"

"I think he would've loved your little brother or sister very much."

"We can love them to make up for him not being here."

"Exactly." I smiled at my daughter, amazed and proud of her level of comprehension, and her simple compassion. "Now it's time to go to the chapel. You ready?"

"Yeah."

"Any time you need to talk, I'll always listen, okay?" I squeezed her tight and kissed her nose. "I love you very much, and I'll always be here for you."

"I love you too, Mommy."

The funeral went by quickly. I tried to appear properly saddened, even though I wanted to shout at the person eulogizing, "You don't know what it was like living with that man. He cheated, he lied, he schemed. He fooled you all!" But I stayed quiet, knowing the funeral was for the peace of mind of his loved ones and not the right place to air his faults.

I wondered, looking at the people in attendance, friends and relatives and colleagues from all over the region, how many were here because they felt they should attend, should be seen at this particular social event, and how many were here because they cared about us. Many had expressed their deepest sympathies to me at the visitation the night before, but with dubious sincerity. How many would see us again now that there was no social benefit?

Andrew, of course, was nowhere to be seen, although Ron and Erica were present.

After the funeral, as I accepted the condolences of those who'd attended, the former senior partner of David's firm took me aside.

"We're of course very saddened by your loss," John Kinnard said, "and if there's anything we can do to help you and your daughter—daughters?— please let us know."

"Thank you." I smiled at him, a smile I hoped balanced my gratitude for his offer against the pain I should display upon being widowed. "I don't actually know yet if it's a boy or a girl."

"Either way, it'll be nice to have this extra reminder of David."

I nodded, adjusting my smile to an appropriate level. What would the man say if he knew just how little this child would remind me of my late husband?

"I don't mean to pry," he continued, "but will you and your children be financially set? I believe David mentioned you work part-time?"

My smile became more genuine. I admired the man's pragmatism; no one else had asked me yet about how I'd get by.

"That's right, sir. We had life insurance for David, of course, but I anticipate getting a full-time job as soon as I can and continuing to work after the baby is born. I'd rather have too much than not enough when supporting two children on my own."

"Good woman." John beamed at me. "Of course David would marry a woman with brains as well as beauty. The reason I ask, of course, is that we truly are saddened by David's death. Although he was only with us a short time, we feel he was family, which makes you family as well."

"Thank you, sir." I dabbed at my eyes with a tissue, the first real tears I'd shed that day. "That means a lot to me."

I turned to leave, to talk to other mourners, but the elderly man gently caught my arm. "This isn't just words, Mrs. Sanford. We currently have a couple vacancies at the firm. While secretarial and administrative work may not be your first choice, if you'd like to come by as soon as you feel ready, we can set you up with something, at least until you find something in your field. Journalism, wasn't it?"

"Thank you." The tears now flowed freely down my cheeks. Impulsively, I hugged the man. "Thank you, sir, for your generous offer."

\*\*\*

David's parents left the day after the funeral. Mine offered to stay as long as I needed them, but three days after the service I sent them on their way as well, leaving Aida and me in our quiet, oversized house.

I went through the motions of living when my daughter was around — cooking dinner, reading stories — but when Aida was at school I lay on the bed, not thinking or moving. I'd initially taken a week off work, but with the new job offer I quit outright. I had nothing to fill my days now, nothing to do but lie on the bed and think about David, about Andrew, and the baby. About what could've been and about what should've been.

One evening after Aida was asleep, as I sat on the couch staring at the blank television screen, there was a knock on the door. My heart involuntarily skipped a beat, and I wondered numbly who'd died this time. I'd get a call if it was family, as they were all out-of-state, and Aida was upstairs. I sat on the couch, going through a list in my head, when the knock came again, louder and sharper this time. Almost angry.

I opened the door and was surprised, or as surprised as I could be in my unfeeling state, to see Andrew standing on the doorstep.

"Who died this time?" I asked.

"What?" He looked confused. His eyes were bloodshot, and his face unshaven.

"Are you drunk?"

"Yeah, I think so."

I looked up at him, not saying anything.

"You gonna let me in?" he asked after several seconds.

"Why?"

"What?"

"What do you want, Andrew?"

"I don't know. Can I come in?"

I wanted to say no, to tell him it was too late, that if he couldn't be there for me when I needed him most, then I didn't want to be there for him either. I wanted to scream at him, reach into his mind with mine and let him know exactly how his absence had hurt me. I wanted to remind him he'd said he wanted nothing from me after promising so much.

"Okay," I said.

"Got anything to drink?" He walked past me into the living room, and plopped down on the couch.

"There's a bar in the corner." I gestured at a tucked-away cabinet. "Help yourself."

He stood and walked over to mix himself a drink. After downing it, he mixed another and returned to the couch.

I sat down next to him, but not so close as to touch him, and watched him silently.

He stared straight ahead and sipped his drink. "Nice place."

"Thanks."

We sat, and the silence lengthened uncomfortably. Sitting so close to him, missing another person's touch, I wanted to kiss him but didn't know if that was appropriate now, didn't know how he'd react.

He took another sip of his drink, then placed it on the coffee table in front of him. He didn't use a coaster, and I cringed, then chided myself for my reaction. He was here, had come to me voluntarily, and I was thinking about water marks?

"So...." he said.

"Yeah?" He was the one who'd come to me tonight after three months of nothing. I didn't see why I should be the one making conversation, why I should go out of my way or make any effort at all to accommodate him.

Then, with lightning speed, he was on top of me, kissing my lips and neck, hands running along my body. I wrapped my arms around him and matched his intensity, surprised by his sudden desire but delighting in it. I'd missed his kisses and his touch—any human contact, really.

His hands slid along my stomach, and he stopped. His body stiffened against mine, flinching away. I tried to keep kissing him, but he pulled back.

"What's wrong?" I asked. He was hard to read tonight, harder than usual, giving off mixed signals.

"You're pregnant." He pulled my shirt up and placed his hand on my exposed belly, on the small developing curve of the baby.

"Yeah."

It wasn't a question he'd posed; he'd known somehow. Word traveled fast in this town.

"Were you going to tell me?"

"I didn't think you'd care."

He looked at me, a pained, hurt look in his eyes. They were haunted slightly, as if he were seeing someone else in front of him besides me. "I knew you'd betray me."

"What are you talking about?" Now it was my turn to feel hurt. He had abandoned me, given up on me, yet he had the audacity to accuse me of betrayal?

"You said you cared about me, but you had no intention of leaving your hubby, did you? You were just jerking me around on the side, is that it?" He sat up. The hurt look was now mixed with anger.

I realized he didn't know the true father of the child. I smiled at him, a small, trembling smile. "I would never do anything to hurt you, Andrew. The baby's yours."

He stared at me, and I tried to read his emotions, tried to gauge his thoughts. Shock, but perhaps fear and sadness as well? And then anger.

Always the anger with him. "Were you planning on even fucking telling me?" he said in a voice filled with such raw emotion that I flinched. "For Chrissake, Kasey, what the fuck were you thinking?"

I met his angry eyes. Frustration welled up in me at his accusations, but also at his long absence. "What was the point? You made it clear that you were done with me. I want you to be with me because it's what you want, not out of any sense of responsibility. And, let's face it: say what you will, but you don't want to be with me."

"I don't know what I want, to tell the truth."

"Why'd you come here tonight?"

He shrugged. "I don't know. Partly, I guess, to find out if Erica was telling the truth when she said you were pregnant. She and Ron are concerned about you, you know."

"Why else did you come here?" I pressed.

"I don't know. I feel so lost lately, like I'm at a crossroads, and I don't know which path to take, or if it even matters which road I choose because God'll just force me down another one. It's all up to what he wants, my feelings and plans be damned." He downed his drink, then got up and made himself another.

"The wars are always with me," he continued, returning to sit down next to me. "No matter what I do, I can't escape what I've been through. Drinking doesn't work as well as I want. You keep me in check, babydoll, but you have your own problems. I don't want to add to them."

I squeezed his hand. "We can still help each other."

"I don't know. Maybe it's selfish, but I don't know how. We both have so much going on right now. I think you'd be too distracted to be what I need."

My mouth fell open. "Excuse me?"

"Well, there's your hubby's death you're coping with right now, and a kid on the way as well, without him here to help you. That's a lot for anyone to deal with."

"You can't be serious!"

"What? All I'm saying is, you have a lot on your plate right now. How could you be any help to me?"

"You are the most selfish, arrogant, self-absorbed man I've ever met." I stood up, hands clenched into fists, and paced back and forth in front of the coffee table. After a week of feeling nothing but numbed sadness, the emotions coursing through me were amplified, and I relished them, relished feeling alive again.

"That is completely unjustified."

I stopped and turned to face him. "My husband just died unexpectedly, and I'm pregnant with your child, and you have the audacity to tell me *you're* the one who needs someone?"

"Well, it's not as if you loved him, and you're obviously well-off enough to be fine without him." He waved his hand at the room around him to illustrate his point. I opened my mouth to respond, but he cut me off. "You don't know what it's like to hear the screams every time you close your eyes, to relive the battles. You could never understand."

"You honestly are trying to debate whose pain is worse?" I shook my head. "There's no comparison, no need. We're both hurting, both in need of someone. Why can't you just admit we need each other, that we can help each other?"

"I don't know what I need, Kasey, but I don't think it's you. We're too similar, you and me. We're both struggling for an escape from our pain, from our experiences. You expect too much from me, and that's unreasonable. And I don't want to expect anything from you, because you'll just leave me in the end."

"No." I walked over and sat down close enough that our thighs touched.

"They always leave, no matter what I do. I always end up going it alone. The lone wolf, that's me."

"No," I said, more forcefully.

"I'm trying to find a balance, Kasey, but no matter what I do it's not enough. That's okay, because I've accepted it, but it gets lonely inside my head, and it wears down on me. I get so tired."

"I understand, Andrew." I took his hand in mine again. "You can't compare our feelings, can't compare our experiences, but can't you at least admit we both hurt, that we can help each other, and that I can help you if you give me another chance?"

He closed his eyes, sighed, then opened them and looked directly at me. "I'll just hurt you again."

I leaned in and kissed his lips, delighting in how they felt on mine. "I know."

"That doesn't bother you?"

"No."

"It should."

"Andrew, listen to me. I don't know why I feel this connection to you, but I do. I've felt it since I met you. I know you think you're broken. I know your life hasn't been easy, that you've had a lot of heartaches and bad situations. I know what you're like, and I realize that you're a difficult man to love. But I still want to try."

"Kasey—"

"I'd do anything for you, Andrew."

"You say that, but you wouldn't be happy that way. Wasn't that why your marriage was failing? You went along with what he wanted, but you weren't happy. I don't want my girl to be miserable."

"It's about choice and trust. I choose to help you, to do anything I can for you, because I trust you. I understand you. I know that, no matter what, you appreciate me, even if you can't, or won't, show it."

Andrew stared down at my hand in his. "It's not intentional. I just feel so lost right now, and that's easier to cope with alone. I know you say I can rely on you, but they always say that. And when I need someone most, I'm left by myself. It's just easier not to trust, not to rely on others. I disappoint them, and they disappoint me."

"You left me alone when I needed you."

"You don't need me, Kasey, and you never did. I was just a phase, just a distraction from your failing marriage."

"Why do you keep saying that? Do you think if you say it enough it'll make it true? If you say it enough, do you think it'll make me give up on you? Because, if it were possible to let go of you, I would've done it months ago. No matter how hard I try to forget about you, to not think about you, I always have this small voice whispering to me to have faith that you'll come back to me."

"Kasey—"

"You came here for a reason tonight." I kissed his lips again, a lingering kiss from which he didn't pull away. "You came here because you knew I could help you. You came here because you need me too, even if you won't admit it."

"You're too good for me, Kasey." He kissed me again, hard and passionate and just as hungry as me. "Thank you."

He gently pushed me back on the couch and slid my pajama pants and panties off my hips.

"Not here," I whispered between kisses as he fumbled with his own pants.

"I don't want to wait." He shook his head. "I need this, need you, now. Please, Kasey." His voice had an urgency to it I'd rarely heard, and his motions matched.

I pulled him close to me, closed my eyes, and focused on how he felt, on the sensations flowing through my body that I hadn't expected to feel again.

Finally he tensed, sighed my name, and relaxed on top of me. I maneuvered myself so he was between me and the couch back, my back pressed against his chest. He wrapped his arm around me and held me close enough so I could feel his heart beating.

As I drifted off to sleep, I knew Andrew wasn't back for good yet. Chances were when I woke up in the morning he'd be gone. I didn't care. I loved him and knew that, in his own way, he loved me too, even if I wasn't what he thought he wanted in a partner. What we shared somehow went deeper than friends, deeper than lovers, even if he didn't realize it or admit it to himself. He'd come to me tonight because he knew I could help ease his pain, knew I would do anything for him despite what he might do or say.

I woke up in the middle of the night covered with a blanket, lying alone on the couch. Andrew was gone, as I knew he would be, but it didn't bother me. He'd come back once; he'd come back again.

***

The next morning I went to David's office and talked to John's son, John Kinnard VI, a man I vaguely remembered from parties I'd attended with David during my college days. The office needed someone for basic clerical work to start with, and John hinted at increased job responsibilities when I came back after maternity leave, which they were offering fully paid.

Standing in the office lobby, watching the lawyers and paralegals buzz around, I realized I'd never really met David's coworkers or been by his office. I'd never stopped by during the day just to say hello or to drop off coffee or a snack, despite having so much free time, or asked him to meet up for lunch at any of the nearby downtown restaurants, despite spending hours just blocks from his office, or stopped by with Aida and dinner when he was working late. I didn't know how full his caseload had been, or even what types of crimes he'd handled. Most days I hadn't even asked how his day was, just avoided his foul mood while trying to bottle up my own emotions and thoughts. I realized I'd never really tried to fix our marriage after we'd moved here, especially after meeting Andrew, just shut myself off and let him lead his own life in our new town, a life without me in it, without me as a partner, without me even as a friend.

"Can I see David's office?" I asked John. "If it's not too much trouble?"

"Sure. We've removed some case files, but other than that it's just as he left it."

He led me down a hall to a room barely bigger than a closet. A small window let in the cold winter sunshine. It had a depressing view of the dirty alley below and a featureless brick wall across the narrow street. There was hardly space to move around the office. Bookshelves crammed with legal tomes and scholarly journals lined the walls, and file cabinets occupied whatever remaining wall space could be found. A desk sat in the middle of the office, remarkably uncluttered.

What caught my eye, however, was the border along the ceiling. Rather than hanging pictures on the little wall space available, or losing them among the bookshelves, David had created a border of photos of me, Aida, and himself.

"We'll box up all his personal stuff for you, if you'd like," John said.

"Yeah, thanks." I looked around. This office revealed more of David to me than I'd gotten from him during our whole time in Asheville. "Would it be okay for me to have a few minutes alone in here?"

"Sure. Take your time."

I sat down in David's chair, a monstrous thing upholstered in itchy black cloth. It creaked when I moved and wobbled in protest of my weight. It smelled of David, of his aftershave and deodorant and soap, and of ancient stale cigarette smoke. It was a horrible chair. Why had David kept it? Did he not notice the imperfections, or did he like the chair's quirks? Why hadn't he traded it in for a new one? Had he asked and been denied?

A search through his desk drawers yielded nothing interesting: pens and paperclips, case files and expense reports, a jammed stapler, a rubber band ball. Another drawer yielded granola bars, M&Ms and potato chips. In the very back of this drawer was a small bottle of whiskey. I put it into my purse; his coworkers didn't need to see that.

I tried looking at what he'd stored on his computer, but I didn't know his password. For years he'd used the same one—ADIAYESAK123—but that wasn't the case here. I briefly considered asking John, but wanted to see the rest of the office first.

I dragged the chair over to a corner and cautiously climbed up on it, wary of losing my balance; even this early in my pregnancy I was already becoming clumsy. The picture closest to me was one of me and Aida at the Virginia State Fair the year before, laughing and holding a stick of cotton candy. Next to it was a photo of me from college, in David's car, sticking my tongue out. Next was the three of us, David and me and a baby Aida playing in the sand at the beach. Then David and Aida riding a carousel at a local park in Virginia. David and me in a park in autumn, from our engagement photo shoot. Aida as a baby again, sleeping in her crib. Me and Aida cooking dinner. The pictures continued on, each a souvenir of a happier time, of a different life.

As I looked at each one, tears streamed down my cheeks. What had gone wrong? We had been so happy, such a loving family. I tried to pinpoint the moment we'd grown apart. We were both happy dating, I was sure of that. The first years of our marriage had been wonderful. And the birth of our daughter had left us in agreement that our family was now complete, that Aida provided what was needed to ensure our contentment in the future. Then David's job had become more stressful. Had the stress slowly eaten away at us until there was nothing left?

Looking at the pictures, I knew we'd still loved each other at this point, had still enjoyed being together. Yet studying their locations and remembering their narratives, I realized that most of the pictures were from our first years together. I'd quit my job when Aida was two. Was that when it had all started to go downhill? Had I lost my identity, just as David was being consumed by his? Had my unhappiness at this loss caused me to pull away from my husband, which, in turn, led him to find someone else to connect with?

"What are you doing in here?" a loud female voice demanded.

I spun around and nearly fell off the chair. I grabbed the wall for balance and looked at the young woman, maybe twenty-five or so. She had short, thick dark hair pulled away from her face, which was covered in heavy make-up. Her low-cut sweater was inappropriate for a professional office, as were her tight-fitting pants. I was wearing simple khakis and a button-down blouse, leaving me feeling unsophisticated in the woman's presence, especially after losing my balance.

"Who are you?"

"I'm Kasey Sanford. John said I could look around in here."

The woman's eyes narrowed as she looked me over. "Dave's wife?"

I bit back a sarcastic retort. "Yes."

"I'm sorry that he passed away," said the woman, her voice softening. "I'm Charlotte Robinson. I'm his paralegal, or I was."

"He never mentioned you." Charlotte's eyes glistened, and I regretted my words as soon as I'd said them.

"I'm new here. I didn't know him very well yet." She swallowed hard and wiped at her eyes with the backs of her hands. "He was a good man. I'm really sad he's gone. I mean, not as sad as you are, I'm sure, but still. I miss him a lot. He was always so nice to me. He was under so much stress with his caseload, but he always took a moment to say hi to me, or to see how I was doing."

"Yeah." I nodded noncommittally.

"It's just so hard to believe he's gone." Her voice was husky with emotion. "He'll never be in his office again, never come over to talk to me. I'll never hear his voice again. I'll never be able to get to know him better. I'm so glad you, at least, have a baby to remember him by. And I assume you'll be taking everything from his office?"

I watched the woman, watched her reaction. It was so over-the-top, yet so sincere, I immediately realized the reason for the intensity. "He cheated on me. Did you know that?"

Charlotte's eyes widened. "He cheated on you?"

"That's why we moved down here, to get away from it all."

"Was it a long-term affair?"

"I don't know. I didn't want the exact details."

"I had no idea!"

"There were two women. One was his secretary."

Guilt splashed across Charlotte's face. "Nothing happened between me and him, I swear. I was his paralegal, and that was it."

"I believe you." I pitied the poor girl, being taken advantage of by David. "He was very charming when he wanted to be."

"Yeah, he was." She smiled. "You were lucky to have him."

I ignored her comment. "I'm going to start working here. Maybe we could go to lunch and talk about him? I'm trying to find out as much about him as I can."

"I'd like that. Your husband was an amazing man."

"He was something, all right."

***

My next stop was the bookstore. It had been several weeks since I'd been there, since before David's death. I hadn't missed the place as much as I'd expected. That would make it easier to start my new job on Monday, a job that would keep me from McKay's when my friends were there. Evenings and weekends I would spend with Aida.

It dawned on me that from here on out, and even more so after the baby was born, I'd have no time for myself.

The cafe was half-full, populated with mostly regulars. Erica and Ron sat at a corner table, flipping through magazines and sipping coffee. Ron looked up as I entered, and Erica followed his gaze. When she saw me she jumped up, ran over, and gave me a big hug.

"Kasey, how are you?" she squealed. "We're missed you. Everything okay? How's the baby? Can I throw you a baby shower? Are you feeling okay? Quick, sit down. You look great, considering everything you've been through."

She led me over to the table. Ron nodded in greeting.

"So what's this I hear about you telling everyone I'm pregnant?" I smiled to take the edge off my words.

"How'd you know it was me? Do I have the reputation for being the town gossip now?"

"Andrew told me. So, yeah, I guess you do."

"Are he and you together now? Since you're free?"

"Have a little tact." Ron frowned. It was the first time I'd heard him say anything that wasn't supportive of his wife.

"It's okay," I said. "I'm still not sure how I'll react to David being gone, but being free of him is a pretty apt way of putting it. Things were, well, things were pretty bad towards the end. They were getting better, but I don't know how everything would've worked out, had he not died."

I swallowed hard. Even though he'd been gone for a couple weeks, it still felt odd, felt wrong, to speak of it in concrete terms. He had died. My husband had been killed. David was dead. None of it seemed real. The terms were too clinical, something used to describe someone else, not David. I knew he wasn't coming back, knew it rationally, but part of me couldn't accept that he was gone. He couldn't be. Other people died, but not David, not with things improving between us.

But if David and I had somehow miraculously fixed our marriage, how would Andrew have fit into that? I loved him, maybe not more than I had at one time loved David, but differently, more deeply. There was no way I could've been truly happy with David after meeting Andrew, even if I never spoke to or saw him again. I'd always have those intense feelings for him. Hadn't the last few months proved that? I hadn't wanted David to die, especially not in such a horrific manner, but maybe, just maybe, there could be a silver lining to all this, and Andrew and I, and Aida and the baby, could make something positive out of this tragedy.

Erica laid her hand gently on my arm, causing me to jump. "You okay, sweetie?" Her green eyes were filled with concern.

"Yeah." I gave myself a mental shake. "I get distracted easily. Everything seems to remind me of David."

Ron nodded, his eyes mirroring his wife's concern. "We're here if you need anything, if you need to talk."

"Thanks." I smiled and nodded. "I appreciate having friends like y'all."

"So, about Andrew then?" Erica asked. Ron let out an exasperated sigh, and his wife glared at him. "She's grieving. I get that, but that doesn't mean she can't go after Andrew, does it, if she loves him? And you do love him, right, Kasey?"

"It's not that simple."

"Of course it is. You love him. He loves you. You're both available. What's the problem?"

"That's the problem." I nodded towards the entrance of the bookstore, where Andrew was holding the door open for a giggling Alexis. "Every time we get close again, he pulls stuff like this. He withdraws, and chases other women."

"He'll come around," Erica said. "And if not, it's his loss."

"No, it's not." I watched the pair approach the counter and buy drinks. "It's my loss, just mine. If he truly missed me, truly wanted to be with me, he'd do something about it."

All my exuberant hope from the night before evaporated, replaced by doubts and insecurities. He'd come to me because he needed me, because I could ease his pain. And yet the very next day he was back with Alexis, as if he didn't share some bond, some connection with me. And for him to flirt with some woman while I was pregnant with his child? I was hurt, of course, angry at him for this rejection, but mostly angry at myself. I'd believed him again, believed he still wanted me. Granted, he'd promised me nothing last night; he'd said he appreciated what I did for him but had offered me nothing in return.

I felt used, yet I knew I couldn't place all the blame on him. I'd wanted him badly, had wanted to feel something again, anything, and had pressured him when he held back. I'd misread him, misread his feelings for me, misread his intentions. I had no one to blame now but myself for overreacting.

Maybe I'd misinterpreted David's actions during his final weeks as well. Had he truly changed, or was it temporary again? Would he have slipped into his old patterns, into his drinking and verbal debasement? Would he have taken his rage out on the baby, on me as the pregnancy progressed, forever holding my sins against my child? I wanted to give David the benefit of the doubt, to remember him as a reformed saint, but he'd repented his sins before, and that had never lasted long.

"Kasey?" Erica's voice broke into my thoughts. "Are you sure you're okay? You're spacier today than usual."

"Yeah, yeah, I'm fine."

"I asked you what you're gonna do to get him back?"

"Get who back?" Alexis asked as she and Andrew stood next to the table. She didn't wait for a response. "Andy, get us a couple chairs."

Andrew, looking embarrassed, did as he was told and grabbed a couple chairs from a nearby table. Alexis wore a smug look on her face. It was odd for me to watch the woman, being so familiar with her sister. The two looked similar, yet they couldn't be more different. Both had the same catlike green eyes in a round face framed by dark hair. Both had full, pouty red lips. Both were outgoing, yet Erica's charm lay in her warmth, her bubbly embrace of life. Alexis, however, was sophisticated, haughty; she played the ditz, but there was a hard, calculating gleam in her eye.

I didn't trust her, didn't want her anywhere near Andrew.

"Who are you getting back?" Alexis pressed.

"Andrew, can I talk to you?" I was surprised at my abruptness but didn't care. "Alone for a minute?"

"Sure." His voice matched the sharpness of my own.

I led him outside, even though the day was cold and blustery. Through the window I saw Alexis watching us closely.

"What the hell is going on?" I demanded.

He wouldn't meet my eyes. "What do you mean?"

"I mean, you came over to my house last night." "Yeah."

"And now today you show up with Alexis?"

"So?" He shifted his weight.

"So, is she who you want?"

He sighed in exasperation. "Kasey, I don't know what I want. I've told you that. Have some faith, okay?"

"You need to figure it out. I'm not going to wait forever." I leaned in and kissed him, long and deep, leaving him breathless, then turned and walked down the street.

# Chapter 20 – Andrew (Age 19)

While lying on my bunk in the barracks, relaxing away a few moments of downtime, word came that I had a phone call from Jenna, a girl I messed around with back in Mississippi the last time I was home on leave.

"Hello?" I asked when I got to the phone.

"Andrew, I'm pregnant," she announced in a flat voice. "It's yours."

I swore my heart stopped for a moment, then a rush of emotions flooded my system: fear of being a father and of telling my mama and dad; joy that my girl was pregnant even though she wasn't my girl, not really; anger that she let this happen.

"Well?" she asked impatiently.

"Well what?" I wasn't able to come up with the right words, not yet.

"Well, what are we going to do?"

I was hit again, this time by the choices: get rid of it, put it up for adoption, keep it; she raises it, we raise it. None of them sounded good.

"Are you sure it's mine?" Maybe I could prove it wasn't. I wasn't ready for kids yet, and especially not with a girl I didn't know that well.

"Of course it's yours. Did you think I'd be calling you again if it wasn't?"

*Ouch.* I liked messing around with Jenna, liked spending time with her, but the fact she never saw anything else for us pissed me off, even though I didn't either.

"Listen, Jenna," I said, more sharply than I intended, "I didn't mean to knock you up. I'll go along with whatever you think is best, but don't get pissed at me like this is all my fault."

"Excuse me? You don't really have a choice, do you?" And she hung up.

I stared at the phone for a moment, then went back to the barracks.

"Bad news?" asked Simmons, one of my fellow soldiers. We always gave him a hard time for being real soft and sensitive, but sometimes that was a nice quality to have.

"I don't know." I sank down onto my bunk. "I'm gonna be a dad."

"Congrats, Adams!" said Matheson, another soldier in my unit. "Who's the poor girl gonna raise your kid?" They knew I wasn't married, didn't have a girl right now. "It's not that blonde bitch who dumped your ass when you got over here, is it?"

"Fuck you." I threw my pillow over my head. I needed to think.

"Well, guess that's the one then," said Matheson. "We need to celebrate."

I didn't feel like celebrating, though. It was true that Jenna sent me a letter shortly after I got here, saying we were going in different directions in life and she needed someone who could support her, not someone who'd be spending the foreseeable future either in some other country or bouncing from base to base. And I of course needed someone who could support me too, someone who'd understand why I joined up and what I could be facing over here. Jenna was not that person. I'd known it when we first hooked up, but she should have been more upfront about it all before I got over here.

Now she was having my kid. I really didn't know what to do. I thought back to my childhood, growing up without a father, and didn't want my kid to have that. *My kid.* I didn't know how far along she was, didn't know if it was a boy or a girl, didn't know when I'd see it, but as I repeated it—*my kid*—pride slowly swelled up in my chest. *My kid.* I was nervous, scared—fucking terrified—but I vowed to do right by this kid. I would give it the life it deserved, the life I never had.

I called Jenna the next chance I got. "I wanna be there for you and this kid, if that's what you want."

She was silent for a moment. "And how exactly are you going to do that, Andrew, when you're oceans away and not gonna be back for a couple years?"

"Jenna, will you marry me?" Those words stunned me as much as they did her. It wasn't what I'd intended to say but it just made sense. If I wanted to do right by this kid, then I wanted to do right by its mama too, and if marrying her was what it took, then we'd get married.

No response.

"Jenna?"

"Are you sure?" she asked finally, with that same flat voice as when she told me she was pregnant.

"Yes."

"I don't know what to say. That wasn't what I was expecting to hear."

"Is there someone else?"

"No."

"Then what's the problem?"

"It's not that simple," she said. "You're in Germany. I'm over here. How would this even work?"

"I have leave in four months. I'll be back for two weeks. We can get married then. And then you can either move over here with me, or I'll—I don't know what I'll do, but we'll figure something out. I want this kid, our kid, to have a good life, Jenna. I wanna do right by it. I wanna do right by you."

"Okay."

"Okay?" I repeated. "Okay, that's nice, or okay, you say yes?"

"Okay, I say yes!" Excitement crept into her voice. "Four months isn't long to plan a wedding."

"I know, baby, but you do what you can. Just lemme know what I can help with, okay?"

My next chance to use the phone, I called my mama. "Mama, I got some big news."

"You going to see combat?" Her voice trembled.

"No, nothing like that. It's good news. Me and Jenna are getting married!"

"Andrew, that's wonderful!" She paused. "But I thought you and her broke up?"

"Well, kinda. But Mama, here's even better news: she's pregnant!"

She started shrieking. "I'm gonna have a grandbaby! Oh Andrew, this is wonderful!"

"We're gonna get hitched when I'm home on leave in March. Can you help her with wedding plans?"

I called my dad next. "Jenna's pregnant so we're getting married when I'm back in March."

"March? March is pretty full up for me, so I don't know if I can make it down to Mississippi for a wedding. But if you need help paying for anything, just let me know."

The next couple months went by in a blur. I walked around base with a big dopey grin on my face most of the time, thinking about my baby and my girl. I got frequent updates from her. She wasn't due until June, still quite a ways to go, but was excited about the wedding. She wanted to know if I was okay with her wearing white, or if I had a preference as to what color flowers we had? Would I wear my dress uniform instead of a tux because I'd look so handsome that way? She said Mama was being real helpful with the planning but could I remind her who was really in charge here? And my dad had been more than generous with what he'd given us to pay for the whole thing but could I ask him to cover an open bar too, even though neither of us or our friends were old enough to drink? The details went on and on.

She kept me updated about the baby too, which was a lot more interesting than cake flavors and what font to put on the invitations. The baby was doing fine except for an abnormal heartbeat sometimes. She had to go in every week to get checked out. I would've done anything to be there with her, but instead I had to listen to her reassurances that everything was fine. And then back to the wedding details.

We had weekend leave in January, and the boys decided to throw me an early bachelor party. We went out and hit the strip clubs, the raunchiest ones they could find. They bought me lap dance after lap dance, and they seemed to delight in telling the strippers I'd shortly be missing out on all this because I was getting hitched.

After we got back to base, I lay on my bunk thinking about that, about all I'd be missing out on. After several hours lying awake, I got up and went outside for a cigarette, even though it was the dead of winter and I'd freeze my ass off.

A few minutes later the door opened.

"Can't sleep tonight, Adams?" Simmons said.

"Yeah, I'm just too excited and nervous about the baby and the wedding."

"That's a lot of changes for someone our age."

"No more messing with other girls," said Matheson, joining us on the stairs. "No more strip clubs. Stuck with Jenna and a kid for the rest of your life."

Simmons scowled. "Don't put it like that. When you love someone, it's easy to put them first."

"Yeah," I said, "but the thing is I don't love Jenna, and I know she doesn't love me either. I thought marrying her was the right thing to do, but will we be happy together? Does that even matter?"

"Of course it matters," Matheson said, at the same time Simmons blurted out, "No, it doesn't matter at all."

As they argued over whether it was possible to marry and then grow to love each other, I thought of my parents' relationships. My mama and dad loved each other at some point, I imagine, enough to get married. My mama and stepdad must have had some connection, some affection, that'd kept them together all these years despite the abuse. My dad was on his fourth wife now, had kids with most of them. He'd loved each woman, I was sure, but love wasn't enough.

So what was the secret to a good marriage? Would Jenna and I be able to find it, when our whole reason for a wedding was a kid? Would this kid bring us together, bring us closer, or would it drive us further apart? Would we resent the kid, blame him for our choice to be together, blame him for what we gave up?

I tried to put these doubts from my mind. My childhood, like the childhoods of so many I knew, had been less than ideal, and I wouldn't allow that to happen to my child.

"No matter what," I told Matheson and Simmons, "my kid will never go through what I did growing up. No matter what happens between me and Jenna, my kid will always be loved and kept safe."

Simmons nodded. "Of course. You'll be a great father to that kid. We all know that."

\*\*\*

Still the doubts persisted, growing stronger as the wedding approached, as the baby grew and his heartbeat became more erratic. With the guys in my unit holding me up as a shining example of responsibility, I tried to put on a brave face, to show I was strong, that this was what I wanted. But underneath, inside, I was absolutely terrified that I was going to fail yet again, going to disappoint those relying on me.

Two days before I was set to head home on leave, I got an urgent phone call from Jenna's mama. "Andrew, sweetie, I don't know how to tell you this. Jenna woke up last night in terrible pain, bleeding real bad. I rushed her to the hospital but there was nothing they could do. Andrew, she... she lost the baby. It was... he was a boy. I'm so sorry to be the one to tell you. So, so sorry, honey."

I dropped the phone back onto the cradle even though she was still talking, babbling on about I didn't even know what. I couldn't say anything, didn't know how to react. I walked back to my barrack, wooden and numb. I hadn't realized how much I wanted to be a father, to have a son to do right by, until he was gone. A son, gone. A son I'd never have a chance to know, to love.

Yet at the same time, underneath that pain, a little voice whispered to me that this was a good thing. I wouldn't have to marry Jenna, wouldn't be tied down for the rest of my life. I'd been spared the chance to disappoint my baby. I tried to push the voice away—how could the loss of life ever be a good thing—but it just laughed at me.

Inside the barracks windows guys were joking around, laughing, everyone who was leaving in a great mood. I couldn't go in there right now, couldn't be around their laughter, around people, but I didn't want to be alone right now either. I just leaned against the doorway, watching without seeing, listening without hearing, chanting in my head over and over, "She lost the baby. She lost the baby. You're free."

Matheson noticed me first. "Yo, Adams, you're going home! Act like it."

I tried to smile but I couldn't. I wanted to cry, wanted to punch something, but instead I did what I'd always done when something really affected me and there was nothing I could do to change it: I pushed it down, buried it inside. Only this time I couldn't, because it was a person and he wouldn't let me.

Simmons came over to me. From the look in his eyes, he could tell something wasn't right. "Jenna call off the wedding?" he asked in a low voice, so the other guys couldn't hear.

"No." I tried to keep out the emotion, the pain, the guilt. "She lost the baby." It hurt to say that aloud, made it real somehow, as if actually saying something instead of thinking it made it true, lended it finality, and if I hadn't told him then I'd still have a pregnant fiancée, still have a child waiting to make its way into the world. I slammed my fist into the vestibule paneling. I'd get in trouble for the hole, I knew that, but the sting of my bloody knuckles helped ease the pain just a little.

Everyone looked over at me. "What the fuck's your problem, Adams?" someone asked.

"Okay if I tell them?" Simmons asked.

I shrugged, concentrated on the pain in my hand and not the pain in my heart.

"His girl lost the baby."

Cries of "Oh shit, I'm so sorry, man." made me feel worse. Most of the guys—a good group of boys, don't get me wrong—were young, single or at least not married. Just like me. Very few had kids, so what the fuck did they know about the pain of losing a child? I knew I'd be punching one of them next, so I turned away from Simmons, away from their sincere and well-intentioned but empty condolences, and took off into the cold wintry air.

I ran and ran and ran, my steps pounding in time to the words in my head: "lost the baby, lost the baby."

Finally, I was out of breath and stopped in front of the base chapel. I went in and tried to pray, but it was hard to find the words. I was angry at God for letting something like this happen, angry at Jenna for getting my hopes up, angry at myself for feeling relief that I wouldn't be a father, angry at everyone for saying they were sorry when they didn't know what this felt like. I was angry, alone, terrified, empty.

***

Three days later I was home in Mississippi, heading to Jenna's house. I hadn't talked to her since she lost the baby; she wasn't taking my calls. I got a bouquet of flowers for her, white daisies mixed with something yellow, though I had no idea what kind of flowers she liked, what her favorite color was, her favorite book, her middle name.

I knocked on the door and her mama answered. I'd only met her once before; Jenna and I didn't really get to the meet-the-family stage.

"Come on in, honey." The smile she offered didn't make it to her eyes. "Jenna's upstairs in her room, probably sleeping. She's been sleeping a lot the last few days. Don't be offended if she doesn't want to talk."

I headed upstairs and knocked on the shut door I assumed was hers. No answer. I knocked again, then went in. "Jenna?"

She was lying in bed, watching some trashy daytime talk show. Her hair was messily pulled back, unwashed. She wasn't wearing any makeup, unless you counted her smudged eyeliner which looked like it'd been there awhile. She looked so different from the proud, beautiful girl I left, the girl who spent hours getting ready to go out. She looked defeated.

She turned her head and looked at me, through me. "What?"

I didn't know what to do, what to say, so I awkwardly handed her the bouquet. "I got you flowers."

She took them from me and threw them on the floor, and just stared at me.

I walked over and tried to hug her. "I'm so sorry, baby."

She cringed away from me. "Don't you dare even fucking touch me." Her voice was shrill, scared.

I pulled back, confused and hurt. This was not what I'd expected.

"I hate you! This is all your fucking fault. I hate you, I hate you."

"I know you're upset," I said, growing angry, "but I'm hurting too. This was our baby, after all. Both of ours."

"No," she spit out venomously, "this wasn't our baby. It was my baby. You may have contributed half its DNA but that's it. You never knew him, never felt him kick, never heard the heartbeat, never felt him die. This was my child, not yours. You don't get to grieve."

Her words, the truth in them, stung me. "I did what I could! I wanted to marry you, support you and the kid. I was doing the right thing. What more do you want from me, Jenna?"

"Nothing. I want nothing from you, Andrew. Nothing now, nothing ever." She glared at me with contempt in her eyes.

"But, Jenna, I love you." It was the first time I'd said that to her. I didn't mean it.

"That's unfortunate, because I don't love you." She turned back to the television. "Please leave."

"Jenna," I pleaded.

"Please." She turned the volume up.

I stood up and kissed the top of her head, but she didn't move. "I'm sorry. I tried."

I left the room, pausing in the doorway to look back at her. She was still unmoving except for the large tears rolling down her cheeks, matching my own.

***

That night, lying in bed at my mama and stepdad's house, I prayed to God for guidance.

He was silent.

# Chapter 21 – Kasey (Present)

"Thanks again for watching Aida today," I said to Erica, who was waiting for me in the downtown pizza parlor one May afternoon.

"It's no problem. You know that." She scooted across the bench to make room for me. "Have a seat. You look tired."

I set down my purse and massaged my lower back. At seven months, I'd reached the awkward, uncomfortable stage of pregnancy. "I'll stand here for a bit longer. The baby's decided it's fun to kick whenever I get comfortable." I winced from a potent blow to my rib cage. "Scratch that. Now she's kicking just because she can. I swear, she's going to be the death of me."

Erica laughed, but her eyes were filled with concern. "Ron and I have thought about kids, but after seeing what you're going through, we might just stick to borrowing yours."

"You're more than welcome to them, whenever you want." I plopped down next to her. My large belly barely fit into the booth. "Speaking of which, where's Aida?"

"She's in the game room." Erica patted my hand. "You doing okay, Kasey?"

I sighed, thinking of what awaited me at home. While the house wasn't exactly dirty, it could stand to be dusted and vacuumed. I'd always prided myself on having an immaculate house, but now that I was working full-time, as well as adjusting to the role of a single mother, I had little time for housework. Upstairs, several piles of laundry sat waiting to be folded, with more to be washed. Beds were unmade, floors needed mopping, and all I wanted to do in the evenings was put my feet up and relax.

"I'm fine. A little overwhelmed at times, but Aida's been a huge help around the house. And you watching her after school has been a godsend."

"Well, after what happened, how can I not help? Your kids don't have a father. You can't go it alone."

Erica's words swelled the lump that seemed to always be in my throat. As far as everyone knew, the baby was David's. Why wouldn't it be? No one knew we'd split up. No one knew Andrew and I had shared a bed—no one but David, and he'd taken that secret to his grave. That lump suddenly made it hard to breathe.

"I'm so sorry, Kasey." Erica's hand tightened on mine. "I didn't mean to bring up David's—you know."

"It's okay." I swallowed, brushed at my eyes with the back of my hand and stood up. "If you don't mind, I think I'm gonna grab Aida and head home.

I have a lot of stuff to do around the house."

"Of course." As I moved away from the table, Erica called after me, "I should probably warn you—"

Her words cut off as I collided with Andrew coming out of the game room, Aida beside him. He grabbed my elbows to steady me and stared down into my eyes.

"Hey," he said, not letting go.

"Hey." I stared back, trying to read his expression. Fear, sadness, anger and guilt jumbled into a mask that rendered it all blank, meaningless.

We stood that way until Aida tugged at my sleeve, waving lines of tickets in her free hand. "Mr. Andrew helped me with Skee-Ball. Are we going home now? I haven't even had any pizza yet. And I want to get a prize too."

Her words broke the spell. "I was planning on leaving, but we can stay to eat. Go get your prize while we're waiting for the pizza."

She scampered off, and I turned to follow but Andrew still held my arms.

"How are you?" he asked.

"I'm—" I stopped. I was physically exhausted, worried about how I would raise a newborn by myself, pissed at him for not being there for me. Thrilled at his touch. "I'm okay. How are you?"

He shrugged. "I'm okay."

"You're always welcome to stop by and see me, if you want to talk about anything."

"I know."

I lowered my voice. "And we need to make plans for the baby, for what your role's going to be."

He squeezed his eyes shut for the briefest of moments, seeming to age right before my eyes. "I know, just not right now, okay?"

"This is your kid too, Andrew. I know the circumstances aren't ideal for either of us, but that doesn't change the fact you're going to be a father."

"I said I didn't want to talk about this now." He let go of my arms. "I'll see you around." He turned and walked out of the restaurant.

I walked back to the table, my thoughts a mess. My kiss at the bookstore hadn't changed Andrew's behavior; he was as aloof as he'd been since we'd stopped sleeping together. Occasionally I would bump into him at the grocery store or drive past him on the street. We were polite to each other, but he showed me little warmth, nothing that would give people the impression we'd been lovers and he'd meant the world to me.

*Had.* I didn't know what to think now. He was constantly on my mind, not only his touch but also the conversations we'd had late at night and in the bookstore. How could he expect me to easily move on when we'd connected so deeply? That was exactly what was happening, though, with encounters like this one. I wanted to love him, especially because of the pregnancy, but he made it difficult when he kept pulling away.

I sat down at the table again, wincing at the baby's kick to my ribs.

"I should've mentioned Andrew was in there." Erica stared at her hands, which were folding napkins into triangles. "I figured you could just get Aida and go without talking to him, unless you wanted to." She glanced over at me, a smile playing across her lips.

"Why would I want to talk to him?"

"Alexis said they had a huge fight last week. She wouldn't tell me the details, but she said she's done with him."

"Alexis always says that, and then they're right back together."

Erica shrugged. "That's just a sign my sister isn't right for him. You are. We all know that. It's so simple. You love him, and he loves you. You should be together."

"It's not that simple." Have faith, he'd told me, but it was hard when every time I got close to him, he ran away. I remembered how he'd described himself as a lone wolf. I'd thought I could tame him, but I wondered now if *anyone* could tame him, or if anyone should. "He knows how I feel. He needs to decide what he wants, and I can't force that."

"Well, it should be that simple."

Fortunately the pizza arrived, followed by Aida, who was clutching a small stuffed pig.

"This is for the baby." She carefully set it on the bench next to her. "Mr. Andrew said all kids need a favorite stuffed animal to talk to. I told him I didn't have one, and he said next time he'd help me get enough tickets to get one for me."

"Next time? Does he eat pizza with you often?"

Aida nodded. "Ms. Erica invites him to dinner with us all the time."

I turned to Erica, who squirmed on the bench next to me. "Why are you inviting him?"

"Well, he doesn't have anyone to cook him dinner. And if he does manage to fix something, he has to eat it alone, so I thought I'd be nice and invite him sometimes."

"Why can't you invite him on nights when I'm not around?"

Erica shoved a huge bite of pizza into her mouth.

"I don't believe you." I shook my head. "Let us figure it out ourselves, okay?"

Not that I was doing the best job of that.

***

I tried with Andrew whenever I saw him like one day in early April. It was a warm day, and I'd decided to spend my lunch hour outside, basking in the sunshine. I was sitting on a park bench surrounded by daffodils when he walked by in uniform.

"Andrew," I called out, happy to see him. "How are you?"

He came over. "Hey."

"How are you?"

"About the same."

The sunshine had left me in a great mood. I smiled up at him. "Do you want to go to doctor appointments with me?"

"No."

My smile faded. "Why not?"

"I'm really busy, Kasey." He wouldn't meet my eyes.

"With Alexis?"

"Not just with Alexis. With work, with life. Everything's kind of sucky right now, to tell the truth."

"Would it help to know we're having a girl?"

"Not us. You."

I was puzzled and hurt by his response. David had been right there for every step of my pregnancy with Aida, and I'd assumed most fathers would want to do the same. "She's your kid too."

"I fathered it. That doesn't mean it's mine."

"That's not true, Andrew." I stood up; my back ached if I sat for too long. "We can raise her together, you know." I reached over and took his hand in mine. "She needs two parents."

"Me being in your life wouldn't make things easier for you, sweetie." He stared at my hand, rubbing his thumb over my palm, still refusing to meet my gaze.

"I know life is rough for you right now. I can help you, if you'll let me."

"You have enough to worry about right now. You don't need me around to worry about too."

"I worry about you whether you're here or not, and I miss you." I took a step closer to him. "I want you around. I want you in my life, in *our* lives."

"No, you don't," he said with finality.

"You know I'm here for you. I always have been. Talk to me about what's going on. Let me in. I want to help you."

"I appreciate it, but I don't think you can help me. I don't know if anyone can."

"Please, Andrew, don't shut me out. Let me at least try to help you."

"I have to go." He kissed my cheek, disentangled my hand, and hurried away.

I dropped back down on the bench, shivering inside despite the day's warmth.

At that point I resolved to leave him alone as much as possible. I loved him, and it pained me to know he was hurting and I couldn't do anything about it, that I was hurting and he *wouldn't* do anything about it, but he was too stubborn. I would keep it simple—say hello when I saw him, ask how he was doing, remind him he was going to be a father, wish him well, and be on my way.

Which just made encounters with him, like the one tonight at the pizza parlor, so much more painful.

***

A couple weeks later, one night towards the end of May, Andrew called.

"Kasey," he said, slurring his words slightly, "we need to talk."

"Yeah."

"Really talk."

"Okay. Talk."

"No, not now, not like this."

"Andrew, you're not making any sense."

"It's such a beautiful night. Meet me at a park."

"I can't. Aida's already in bed."

"Get a babysitter."

"Who's going to babysit at eight-thirty on a Tuesday night with no notice?"

"Erica will do it. I'll call her and have her come over, and then you can come meet me at Richmond Hill Park." Richmond Hill Park was a secluded recreational area northwest of the city, surrounded by forest, mountains, and the French Broad River.

"That's in the middle of nowhere," I protested. "Why don't you just come over here?"

"Please, Kasey." His voice had a sense of urgency I'd only heard once before, when he'd come over to my house after David's funeral. "Do this for me tonight."

I couldn't say no to him, and he knew it. "Fine, if you can get Erica over here to watch Aida, I'll meet you there in about half an hour."

"Thanks, babydoll." He hung up.

I went upstairs to Aida's room and knocked softly on the door. "Aida, sweetie, are you asleep?"

"Nuh," was her sleepy reply.

I sat on the edge of her bed. "I have to run out for a bit. Erica is going to come over and stay with you until I get back." I kissed her head. "Go to sleep, and I'll see you in the morning, okay?"

"Mmm."

I chuckled. "Love you, sleepyhead."

***

About twenty minutes later there was a knock on my door. I opened it to Erica and Ron standing on my porch.

"Both of you?" I asked, bemused.

"Andrew said it was important," Erica said. "My car's in the shop, and Ron doesn't let me drive his. Since he gave me a ride over, I'm making him stay."

"Aida's in bed upstairs. TV's in the living room. Help yourself to anything in the fridge. Call me if you need me, but I really don't anticipate any emergencies."

"That's good," Ron said, "because where you're going there isn't any service."

"I'm not sure when I'll be back. It all depends on what exactly Andrew wants."

Erica put a hand on my arm. "Take your time. We'll be fine!"

***

I arrived at the park and checked my cell phone: sure enough, no reception. Andrew was already there, waiting at a bench at the edge of the woods, his face scanning the starry night. I got out of my car and walked over, not sure what to expect. He'd sounded drunk on the phone, and as he leaned over to kiss my cheek I could smell alcohol on his breath.

"Scotch?" I'd found that scotch knocked him out fastest, left him reflective and relaxed.

He shook his head. "Nope, just beer."

I nodded. Beer made him feel manly, as he put it, decreased his tolerance of other people and shortened his temper, same effect that any alcohol seemed to have had on David. What was it with me and alcoholics? David, Andrew, even my father—the men closest to me drank heavily.

"You drinking tonight?" Andrew seemed unsure of what to say, as if it hadn't been his idea to meet out here tonight.

"No." I gestured at my swollen belly. "Of course not."

"Oh, yeah. How far along are you now?"

"About seven months. Two to go."

He nodded and looked at his feet, at our vehicles in the parking lot... anywhere but at me.

I stared at him, growing annoyed. He was the one who wanted this meeting at this place, not me. My back ached and my ankles were sore. There were a million things I wanted to tell him, but he was the one who needed to go first tonight, not me. He was the fickle one, not me.

I studied his face: the pale blue eyes that so easily pierced into my soul, the lips I'd wanted to kiss the first time I'd seen them, the countless near-invisible scars covering his skin. I hated him right now, hated him for everything he'd put me through, for rejecting me, for leading me on and using me, for taking advantage of what I'd offered him without a thought for how I felt. But at the same time I loved him more than I could express, knew that he only had to say the word, and I'd do anything he asked of me.

"Damn you, Andrew," I said quietly.

That broke him from his reverie, and he looked at me through narrowed eyes. "I'm already damned, I think."

I ignored his comment. "What do you want tonight?"

"We need to talk."

"Why here? Why now?"

"I wanted somewhere quiet, somewhere away from people."

"Fine, then talk so we can get this over with and I can go home." I plopped heavily onto the park bench. The baby stirred and kicked my ribs and I inhaled sharply, winced, and rubbed the spot. Andrew sat down next to me, but I looked at my belly, at my hands on the bench, not at him.

"We need to talk about the kid," he said.

"What about her?"

"Well, about what we're gonna do about it once it's born."

"Not *it*." I shook my head vehemently. "She. The kid is a girl, your daughter."

Andrew closed his eyes for a moment, sighed, and then opened them and looked at me. "Okay, fine. What are we gonna do about her?"

"What do you mean? I'm going to raise her, just like I'm raising Aida now. I may as well stay here in Asheville because there's nothing for me back in Richmond. I have enough from David's life insurance to get by for a while if I'm careful, plus what I make at the law office. And then of course there's child support from you, but I'm not holding my breath on that." I stared at him defiantly.

"Of course I'll pay," he said shortly, a sign his temper was surging.

"As for you, I don't know what you're going to do. That's up to you."

"What do you want? What would be best for you?"

"I wouldn't think you'd be concerned about me." My temper rose as well. How many months had he ignored me, barely been there when I needed him, and now he was concerned?

"Oh, of course not. Why would I care?" He rolled his eyes. "God, Kasey, what a stupid question. I care because we're friends, that's why."

"Really."

"Really. I care about you, Kasey. No matter what, I always will, and we'll always be friends."

"I read in an article once that relationships are never equal, that one person always needs the other one more." I looked down at my hands again. "I'm not sure if I agree with that, not completely. I do think that's what went wrong with David, that he stopped needing me as much as I needed him, but then I realized if he didn't need me, I didn't need him either."

I paused, realizing the truth in my words. I didn't need David, had never needed him as much as I'd thought I did. I hadn't needed him one moment past when I'd received those pictures.

"There are lots of reasons why you think you don't need someone," I continued. "In the last year, especially, I've found that it's true you're always left alone in your darkest hour. When you rely on someone, they'll disappoint you when you need them most. If you open yourself completely, leaving yourself vulnerable and giving them everything, then there's a very good chance you'll be rejected because your everything isn't enough. Better to hurt someone than be hurt yourself, right?"

"Kasey, I—" Andrew started, but I shook my head and continued.

"I think that's your problem with me. You're keeping me at arm's length because you don't want to get hurt, don't want to depend on me and then have me fail you when you need me most."

"You are so fragile," Andrew said softly, stroking my arm with his fingertips.

I ignored him. "And you were right, always have been, that I don't need you either. I don't need anyone, because when you believe someone's bullshit promises and rely on them, and then they drop you, validating your belief you're not worth it, then what use are they? I'm perfectly capable of tearing myself down without outside help, but even if I don't need you—"

"You don't," interjected Andrew. "I was just a phase."

"Even if I don't need you," I repeated, "this baby does. Even if I don't need you, despite all my misgivings, I still want you. I'll still leave myself open and vulnerable on the off chance I'm wrong, and I do need you. And maybe at some point that will be enough, and you'll want or need me too, or at least let me in enough to help you when you're alone and damaged. Because I'm always here for you, Andrew."

"Oh, Kasey." He stroked my cheek with his fingertips.

"I'm yours to keep, yours to raise our child with, or yours to throw aside. Whatever you need me to be, you know I'll do it. You just need to make up your fucking mind." I heaved myself off the bench and began walking back towards my car.

"Where the hell are you going?" Andrew bellowed after me. "We're not done yet."

I stopped and turned to face him. "What else is there to say? The ball's in your court. You need to decide. You gonna be Mr. Tough Guy who doesn't need anyone, who's trying to prove he's strong when really he's not? Because that's what it's all about, isn't it, Andrew? You said once that being cared for isn't a sign of weakness. Well, I've put myself out there for you time and time again. That's what love is. It's opening yourself up and making yourself vulnerable to someone else. You keep casting me aside, rejecting me, and that means either I'm stupid for coming back, for putting myself in that position, or we really do need each other, and you're just not strong enough to admit it. And if that's the case, then fuck you, Andrew. You're gonna have a daughter soon whether you like it or not, and I need someone who's going to need me, need us. If that's not you, then we're done. I can't keep putting myself out there to be thrown aside because you're too weak to let me love you."

I quickened my pace back to the car as much as possible, hampered by my large, awkward belly, shaking with rage and tears and the horrible numbing fear he would call my bluff and walk off forever this time. I hated fighting with him, hated upsetting him, but I knew him well enough at this point to understand that sometimes that was the only way to get him to respond. Halfway to my car, he overtook me and roughly grabbed my arm.

"Don't you walk away from me, Kasey. I may be a lot of things, but weak is not one of them."

"Oh really? I think you are weak. You're too afraid of what might happen if you take a chance on love, so you pretend to be all tough instead. You're a coward, just like David was."

He tightened his grip on my arm, but I refused to give him the satisfaction of seeing me flinch.

"I am nothing like that man. I'm strong. I'm a warrior, not some weak intellectual bitch like him."

"You're just like him, Andrew. You say you're strong, compassionate, good-hearted, but I don't see any of that."

"I'm a soldier, a police officer. I'd give my life to help others."

"Yes, but what of the people close to you, the ones who love you and need you? David was willing to help others, but he neglected *me*. And now you do the same."

"He cheated on you, did you know that?" Andrew asked abruptly.

"Yeah, that's why we moved here."

"No, once you were here."

My heart dropped into my stomach. It had always been a possibility, of course, but to actually hear it spoken hurt more than I'd thought. In a small voice, all bravado gone, I asked, "How do you know?"

"I saw him."

My knees nearly gave out. "How? Where?"

"I had my suspicions, so I followed him before his accident. He had a little motel in Hendersonville he'd use. Always paid cash. I assume he lied and told you he was working late."

"He'd moved out, before he...." Even months after David's death, it was still hard for me to speak of it. "So I didn't know what he did in his evenings, when he wasn't spending time with me and Aida."

"I followed him for a month or so," Andrew continued. "I didn't know what I was going to do, didn't have a plan. But then I heard you were pregnant, and I guess I just couldn't take it."

"Why?"

"Because it's not right for a man to do that when his wife's pregnant."

"But he knew it wasn't his."

"He did?"

"Yeah. We hadn't touched each other since we moved here, slept in separate beds half the time."

Andrew sighed and nodded slowly. "That would explain his reaction then."

"His reaction?" I looked at him suspiciously. "What did you do to him?"

"You know I have a temper, and it got so that I couldn't stop thinking about how he was mistreating you, about how this wasn't right."

"I slept with you. That was cheating as well."

"Yes, but this was different."

"How?"

"You and I—I don't know how to explain it. We connected. But what he was doing... it seemed vindictive almost. Malicious. It just wasn't right!" He shook his head fiercely, clearly agitated by David's actions.

"So what did you do?"

"I confronted him. He was surprised to see me, of course, but he didn't seem upset about being caught. He seemed almost happy, actually, started laughing about it. He said—" Andrew stopped.

"What?" I demanded, fearing the worst. "What did he say?"

"He said—" He stopped again. "I shouldn't tell you."

"You brought it up, and it's not as if I can ask him now."

"He said you were a whore and deserved whatever you got."

Even though I had braced myself, this was unexpected. I leaned against Andrew's chest for support, for comfort.

"So I punched him," he continued. "He went down, of course, and I turned to leave, not sure what I was going to do. And then, while my back was turned, he threw a coke can at me. Such a fucking cowardly thing to do. And I'm not proud of this, Kasey, but I turned back to him. I couldn't think, just wanted to hurt him. And I did. I beat the shit out of him, Kasey. I'm sorry."

I knew Andrew had a temper, knew he would solve his problems with his fists if it came to that, but to attack David? While a small part of me was flattered he'd done it on my behalf, I was still horrified by his actions.

"I never saw him beat up," I said, trying to give him a chance to change his story.

"I know," he said quietly. "There's more."

"More?" I was frightened now, frightened of what he was going to say, frightened of being alone with this drunk man I loved, who would resort to violence so quickly. I pulled back from him, stared up into his eyes.

"This has been eating at me for months, Kasey. I wanted to tell you, but it never seemed like the right time."

"Tell me what?" My stomach contracted at the pain and fear in his voice.

"He tried to get away, managed to get into his car. I followed him. I try to tell myself it was just to make sure he got home okay, but really it was because I still wanted to make him pay for what he did. The bastard tried to cut me off, and he lost control of his SUV."

"You were the second car," I whispered, the implications of his words dawning on me. I shrank away from him, my eyes darting around for a way to escape.

"Kasey, listen to me." He grabbed my arms again. "I wasn't going to do anything, I swear! When he went down the side of the mountain, there was nothing I could do at that point to stop him. I radioed for help, ran down after him, but it was too late."

"You killed him!"

"No! No, I didn't. I tried to save him, don't you understand?"

"Don't touch me," I hissed. "Don't you dare touch me!"

Rather than let go of my arms, however, he gripped them tighter, shaking me slightly. "Kasey, you have to understand. I tried to save him. I promise. I never meant for this to happen!"

"It doesn't matter." I tried to remain calm, but I felt myself growing hysterical. "You killed my husband."

"Kasey," he said sharply. "Listen to me. I did it to protect you. He was hurting you. I did this for you!"

"For me?" I laughed shrilly, feeling myself losing control. "Why would you do anything for me? I loved you, would do anything for you, destroyed what was left of my marriage for you, and you left me. My everything wasn't enough for you, yet you think this is what I wanted? I just wanted you, wanted to be with you, wanted you to want me too. And instead you killed my husband? Don't touch me!" I tried to shake myself loose.

"Kasey, please understand, I did this for you!" He pulled me close, kissed my lips in a physical apology.

I bit his lip hard, hard enough to taste blood.

He recoiled, his hand reaching up to blot the blood. "What the fuck, Kasey?"

I backed up quickly. "Stay away from me."

He came after me and reached to grab my arm. "I just want to talk to you, make you understand."

Although pregnant, I spun around and ran towards my car. I'd only gone a few steps, though, when a sharp pain pierced my abdomen. With a loud moan, I collapsed on the ground.

"The baby," I whispered, and then all went dark.

# Chapter 22 – Andrew (Present)

When I picked Kasey up, blood was already pooling beneath her. "It'll be okay, Kasey. Just hold on."

She moaned and her eyelids fluttered, but she didn't open her eyes, didn't say anything. This was bad. Real bad.

I laid her carefully across the seat of my truck. "We're headed to the hospital, sweetie. You'll be fine." Over and over, I narrated my actions, gave her reassurances she couldn't hear, stroked her hand, her face.

I radioed ahead, so that when I pulled up at the hospital, staff were waiting with a gurney. I'd barely stopped before they threw the door open and whisked Kasey away. I parked, then busted into the ER and went up to the registration desk.

"You brought a woman in tonight, Kasey Sanford. She's probably in the ICU right now. I need to see her."

"Are you her husband?" the nurse asked, ignoring my jagged breath.

"No, I'm her...." I stopped. What was I to her? Nothing, thanks to how I'd treated her the past few months. "I'm her boyfriend."

The nurse looked at her computer screen. "She's in the OR right now, but you might be able to see her when she's out."

"The OR? What the fuck is she doing in there?" My hands curled into fists, ready to punch my way to some answers.

"Sir, I'm going to have to ask you to calm down." The nurse's gaze slid to someone behind me, probably a security guard.

I took a deep breath. "I'm sorry, it's just I'm really worried about her."

"I understand, sir." Her voice was steady, bland. She didn't understand. She didn't care.

"Why's she in the OR?"

Another nurse came over, whispered something to the first nurse, and they both stared at me.

"I'm afraid I can't tell you that. Now, if you'll have a seat over —"

"What the fuck do you mean, you can't tell me? She could be dying. At least have the fucking decency to tell me what's happening to her!"

A hand on my shoulder tried to lead me away from the counter, but I grabbed the counter and leaned forward. "Please, you have to tell me. I love her and if something happens to her...."

By now the whole waiting room was staring at me. I could feel it. Probably wondering what my problem was. Why couldn't they just give me answers, make this easier for everyone?

"What's going on out here?"

My head jerked up at the familiar voice. Lauren stood in the doorway leading to the ICU and ORs, hands on her hips, glaring at me. Lauren, the reason I'd moved to Asheville. We hadn't spoken in over two years.

I shrugged off the hand on my shoulder and hustled over to her. "Lauren, you have to help me, please. Kasey's in there, and I don't know what's happening to her. Please." I choked out the last words as my breath caught in my throat.

"He's okay," she said to the security guard next to me, then turned back to me. "You owe me a paint job."

"I'll get you new paint, a new car, whatever you want. Just please let me in to see Kasey."

"I've never seen you so worked up before. This woman must mean a lot to you."

I wiped at my eyes, struggling to keep my voice level. "Yeah, she does."

Lauren studied me for a moment, her eyes softening. "She's just finishing up an emergency c-section."

*The baby.* In my concern for Kasey I'd forgotten all about it—her. "Is the baby okay?"

Lauren nodded. "As far as I know, the baby should be fine." She kept studying me. "Is it yours?"

How to answer? As far as I knew, Kasey hadn't told anyone I was the father. Maybe she'd wanted it that way. I didn't know, but I certainly wasn't going to fuck it up for her if she wanted to keep it secret. "No."

Lauren's eyes narrowed. "When she wakes up, I'll let you in to see her. Have a seat until then, and try not to punch anyone."

I sat down in a hard plastic chair. Jenna had gone through this, fifteen years ago, without anyone by her side. Now Kasey didn't have anyone either. Just me, letting them both down. I caught myself before I slammed my fist into the coffee table next to me, trying to clear my mind.

After an eternity, Lauren came out, her face lined and tired.

I sprung up. "Is she—"

"She's awake. You can go in and see her now."

She led me down a hallway, and paused outside a closed door. "She's groggy. Try not to agitate her." She flashed me a weak smile, squeezed my hand, and opened the door.

I walked into the room and gasped. Kasey was covered in tubes and wires, and her skin, contrasted with her dark hair, was too pale. I dragged a chair over to her bed, sat down, and took her hand that didn't have an IV in it.

Her eyes slowly opened, as if by a great effort. "Andrew?" Her voice was so soft I could barely hear her.

I leaned forward and stroked her cheek with my free hand. "I'm right here, babydoll. And I'm not going anywhere. I promise."

"I hate you, Andrew," she said again in that low voice. She closed her eyes, and I tightened my grip on her hand. Her eyes opened, looked at me, then closed again. "But I still love you. Aida too. And Zoe. Always will." Her voice was stilted, hard to hear.

"I know. I—"

But I was cut off by beeping—loud, angry beeping from the machines hooked up to her. Several nurses ran in, followed by a doctor, shouting directives to one another.

"What the fuck's going on?"

"You're going to have to wait outside now." A nurse took me by the arm and led me out of the room, refusing to tell me more.

I paced the hallway, trying to honor my promise to Lauren not to punch anything. After about ten minutes a doctor came out of the room.

"We tried, but there was nothing we could do for her. I'm so sorry for your loss."

I stared at him. Gone? Kasey was gone? How many boys had I lost, and it was nothing—abso-fucking-lutely nothing—like this.

Promise to Lauren be damned. I kicked over a tray of equipment, shoved a gurney down the hall. "It's not fair! It's not fucking fair!" Over and over until security escorted me out.

Lauren must've pulled some strings to keep me out of jail, because they just left me by my truck and watched me go, arms folded across their chests.

I went straight home and drank until I passed out, and when I woke up, I did it again. And again. And again.

I would've kept on doing it until I didn't know when, except at one point I dreamed that Kasey was standing in front of me, and Jenna, and Aimee, and Carly, and every other girl I'd ever been with, even the girls I woke up next to and never bothered to learn the names of. Kasey threw something at me, a perfect pass, and I caught it like a football. Except then the football started crying, and I looked down at a tiny baby. All the women started yelling at me at this point, yelling and crying and telling me I wasn't allowed to screw up this time. I promised them I wouldn't, promised them this time it would be different, but they just shook their heads and faded away.

I jerked awake and realized they were right. I called around and found out from Ron that Kasey's parents were in town, took care of the funeral and were now looking after Aida and the baby. I hung up without answering any of his questions, feeling so fucking horrible because at this point I had a kid and already I was neglecting it.

I went to the hospital, not sure what I'd do. I'd told Lauren the baby wasn't mine. Would they even let me see it?

The hospital waiting room was mostly deserted, just a couple middle-aged women and an older man sitting uncomfortably in a corner, dark circles under his eyes—dark blue eyes that glanced up at me, through me, eyes filled with intense emotions. I recognized those eyes, realized he must be Kasey's dad.

"Sir, you can't be in here," the nurse on duty called to me.

"Is Lauren Dupont here?" I crossed over to the registration desk. "She can clear everything up."

"Sir, after the stunt you pulled the other day, you best be leaving now before I call security."

I continued to argue with her, insisting on seeing Lauren, but the nurse wouldn't budge. I turned away, racking my brains for another way in, when an older woman and a little girl walked in the door, over to Kasey's dad.

Aida saw me first. I'd spent a lot of time around her the last few months, with her and Erica, hoping I'd have a chance to talk to Kasey, an excuse to see her. She must have latched onto me, because that little girl, when she saw me, came straight at me screaming my name like we'd been parted for years.

Before I realized what was happening, I picked her up and she crumbled against me, her arms around my neck, clinging to me like a fucking monkey, tears streaming down her face. She whispered loudly, matter-of-factly, "I have a baby sister now but Mommy's not here to take care of her."

And I whispered back, "I know, sweetie. I'm sorry." And then I was crying too, crying like I did that day back in high school. Crying for how I fucked everything up and for Kasey and for myself and most of all for those two little girls without a mama.

I guess I should've held it in, should've tried to be strong for Aida, but she didn't seem to mind, just looked at me with her great big eyes—Kasey's eyes. God, she looked so much like Kasey I about lost it again.

"Why are you crying?" she asked.

"Because I loved your mama and I miss her."

"I miss her too," she said, and I just hugged her tight, hugging her to comfort her as much as to comfort myself.

But Kasey's mama was right there, disapproving, and I didn't blame her one bit. "Aida, let go of that man."

Aida shook her head, not loosening her grip.

"I'm so sorry about this." The woman turned to me, tried to peel Aida away. "I assume you're a friend of the family. Forgive me if I'm being rude, but who are you exactly and why won't my granddaughter let go of you?"

*Better come clean.* "I'm Zoe's dad."

"Who?" Her baffled expression was mirrored on her hubby's face.

"The baby." I felt myself getting pissed even though I knew I shouldn't be angry, especially not at this woman who'd just lost her daughter.

"The baby? We named her Robin. We thought it was a good name for a spring baby."

"Well, Kasey told me she wanted her name to be Zoe, so her name is Zoe."

"When did she tell you that?" Her dad had joined us and was staring at me, eyes narrowed, trying to size me up.

"The night Zoe was born," I answered. "Right before she...." I couldn't finish my sentence.

"How is it that you think you're the father of this baby?" her dad asked, analytical, to the point. Kasey had been the same way when we'd argue at McKay's. "David's the father, of course. She told us she was pregnant on the day of his funeral. She wouldn't have dated anyone before that, not Kasey.

Despite everything that may have happened, she loved her husband."

I was really struggling to stay calm now. "Kasey and I were together before he died."

Kasey's mama gasped. "That's not possible! Not Kasey!"

"I'll take the paternity test. She told me I'm the father, and I believe her."

They weren't buying it, not wanting to admit to themselves their daughter would cheat on her husband. I realized now she probably didn't talk to them about her problems, probably didn't talk to anyone but me, and I wouldn't listen, too caught up with my own demons. I realized every time she tried to open up to me, I changed the focus to myself instead. She was strong for me, never gave up on me no matter how many times I gave up on her, let her go. She needed me to be strong for her too and instead I failed her, just like I'd failed everyone else in my life.

I resolved not to fail my baby. I owed Kasey that much at least.

It dawned on me I hadn't even seen her yet, hadn't seen my baby. My daughter. The knowledge I was now a father felt strange, so foreign a concept. I'd shut that part of me down after Jenna and I lost our baby, because no matter what she said, no matter what she believed, he was still my baby. He would have been fifteen now. I hadn't failed him, not intentionally, but I failed his mama.

That wouldn't happen with Kasey's baby.

I took a deep breath. "Listen, I know this is confusing and all, and I promise to explain it all later, when Aida isn't here. But please, can I see the baby? Don't make me wait for the test results. Please."

"You must be the man who brought her to the hospital," her father said, still watching me closely.

I could tell he still hadn't made his mind up about me. "Yeah, that was me." I'd told enough mamas I lost their sons, but this would be different because I loved Kasey. I said it again to myself. Yes, it was true, I realized now. I loved her. I regretted so much we wouldn't be together, that I'd never see her or have the chance to tell her, and I about broke down again.

Maybe it was my open grief, maybe it was Aida's joy at seeing me and her trust in me, but whatever it was, for now they grudgingly accepted what I was telling them, and finally I was allowed in to see the baby.

She was in the NICU, having been born too early. While she'd survive, she'd be in there for at least a month, possibly two or three. I'd never forgive myself for her rough start in life.

"Her name is Zoe," I told the nurse in the ward. "Not Robin, like it says on the card. Her mama wanted to name her Zoe."

The nurse smiled at me, a sad smile because she must've known this little girl had no mother, not anymore. "That's a beautiful name, very fitting."

"Oh?"

"Yeah, it means 'Life'."

I broke down again; I couldn't help it. That baby would always remind me of what I lost in her mother. Briefly, I wondered if I could love her or if I'd hate her for what she took from me. No, for what I lost because I'd failed her mama.

But then I saw Zoe and knew I could never hate her, never feel anything but an overwhelming amount of love for her. She was tiny, impossibly tiny, isolated from the world in a plastic case, hooked up to all kinds of machines because she wasn't supposed to be here yet. I wanted to hold her but settled for stroking her cheek with a gloved finger. She was sleeping but at my touch her eyes opened. She had Kasey's eyes, big and blue, and she looked straight at me.

She was perfect.

*** 

It took two weeks for the paternity test results. John Kinnard V from her hubby's law firm set up a trust fund for the girls, so that no matter what happened they'd always be taken care of. Even when it was revealed that I was Zoe's father, not David, and everyone was doing the math, he made sure she'd be taken care of too. I was overwhelmed by his generosity, by his support for a family he'd only known a short time.

While I was waiting for the results of the paternity test, I spent all my free time in the hospital with my daughter, sitting next to her in scrubs, just stroking her cheek and marveling over how tiny and perfect she was. I talked to her even though I knew she didn't understand yet, even though most of the time she was sleeping. I talked to her about me and her mama, and I shared with her all my thoughts and experiences I should've shared with Kasey but never had the chance to.

"The very first time I saw your mama, well, I wasn't in love with her. Lots of people say they see someone and bam, just know that's the person they're going to spend the rest of their life with. But that's not how it was for me. There was something, though.

"I'll always remember that first time. I was sitting at the bookstore with Ron and Erica— you'll meet them eventually, once you come home—and we were talking about my luck with women. Or lack of it, I guess. And then I looked up and saw your mama, standing at the front window. I don't know if it was the light from outside, or what, but there was just something about her, something I can't describe. I couldn't take my eyes off of her.

"She was beautiful, your mama, just like your sister is gonna be beautiful someday, and you too. Beautiful like your mama. It wasn't just physical though. She had this way of just being, the way she moved, the way she tilted her head, that made you want to be around her. Made you want to protect her and beat the shit out of anyone who ever so much as thought of hurting her.

"So I saw her in front of the window, looking at a robot display they'd built." I paused, smiling at the image of her. "And I looked at her, just kind of taking her all in. She looked down real quick, like she'd been caught doing something she shouldn't. And then she looked back at me, just as quick, as if saying, 'Fuck it, I'll do what I want.' I realized at that moment she was real strong, your mama. She had this inner core of steel, but she was so easy to bruise before you got there." My voice caught in my throat. "I didn't mean to bruise her, Zoe. I was lost myself, and she was so easy to overlook. I shouldn't have."

Zoe's eyes opened, and she looked at me. Kasey's eyes. "I'm so sorry, Zoe." I stood up, knocking my chair over, and hurried from the ward.

***

The next day I was back though. Of course. I'd let Kasey down, but wasn't going to let my daughter down too.

"Let's see if I can keep this a happy story today, sweetie."

Zoe was asleep today, looked like she was ignoring me, but I knew she heard it all. She knew what I meant to say even if she missed the words.

"I have this kid brother, name's Jesse. We've had our ups and downs, like all brothers. I have a couple sisters too, but they're a lot younger. Let's see, Michelle's twenty or so now, I guess. Damn, she'll be drinking soon. And Beth's sixteen? Seventeen? Driving already, I think. I never really had the chance to get to know them.

"Anyway, Dad wanted me and Jesse to be close, even though I stayed in Mississippi and Jesse was in Kentucky, same town as Dad. Every summer I'd go to Dad's house for a few months. When I was fifteen, Jesse would've been eight or so, we decided to see if we could convince our stepmom, a woman named...."

I tried to think of it, but Dad had only been married to her a couple years, just long enough to produce Michelle. "Candace? Carol? No, Karen. We tried to convince her Dad's house was haunted. We made up this big huge story about some chick who was murdered and thrown into the lake. We'd keep mentioning it whenever Dad wasn't around. And this was before the internet, so she couldn't just Google it.

"We'd keep turning to each other. 'Did you hear that?'" I chuckled. "At first she laughed it off, but then after awhile she started to believe us. Probably because we kept it up all summer. I wasn't very good at keeping at something when I was growing up."

Zoe stirred in the incubator. "Yeah, well, don't you worry, sweetie. Being a dad is different. I ain't never leaving you." I stroked her cheek with my gloved hand. "And someday you and Aida will be playing tricks together too. She's about the best big sister you could have. You lucked out, Zo."

Except she didn't have a mama. I dropped my head into my hands and wept.

***

I spent a lot of time with Aida and her grandparents as well. They were staying in Kasey's house until Zoe could leave the hospital. I told them everything: how Kasey loved me seemingly unconditionally but how I pushed her away time after time, how David's death affected her, how I lost her that final night. I told them I wanted to be a good father but I didn't know how, didn't know what to do.

I begged their forgiveness and was surprised when they granted it. I felt relieved and free for the first time in my life, like a terrible burden had been lifted from my shoulders, from my soul.

Kasey's father had been a soldier too, in Vietnam, and we talked about our experiences. I wasn't as alone in the world as I thought.

\*\*\*

One night after dinner, we were sitting in the living room of Kasey's house, all four of us, with Aida curled up on my lap. She was warm and soft and comforting against my chest. With her there I felt at peace. It was a feeling I relished, one I'd rarely experienced.

"Are you going to be my daddy now?" she asked.

I was caught off guard. Didn't she know that I wasn't parent material? I thought of Sam and Eric and Aimee, wondered how they were doing after almost seven years, wondered what had become of them. The boys would be teenagers now. I wondered if she'd found them a good father. I decided to track her down as soon as I had the chance, to call her and see how she was doing.

"I don't know," I told Aida, because I didn't know what else to say. "I don't know if that's up to me."

"I want you to be my daddy." She gave me a big hug. "Mommy told me you'd take good care of me. Remember? I think she was right."

I looked helplessly at Kasey's parents, who seemed just as confused as me. What did we tell this little girl?

"Aida," her grandfather said softly, "we thought you and Zoe would go live with your Uncle Jake and Aunt Carol."

"I don't like them. They're mean and they smell funny, and I don't like Grammy and Pop-Pop. I want to stay with Mr. Andrew."

They both looked at me, as if seeing me in a new light. We hadn't discussed it yet, nothing concrete at least, but from their expressions it appeared I wasn't an option even to keep Zoe.

My temper flared. I'd made mistakes in my life, lots of them, but who hadn't? My parenting doubts were gone. I'd been given a chance at redemption, and I wouldn't let them take it from me without a fight.

"We need to talk about this, Aida, before we make a decision." I glared at Kasey's parents, daring them to challenge me, but they remained silent. "But now it's bedtime. Go put on your PJ's and brush your teeth."

She obediently hopped off my lap, kissed both her grandparents on the cheek, and left the room.

Kasey's mama got up to check on her, but I stopped her. "Do you mind if I put her to bed tonight?"

I went upstairs and Aida was sitting at her window seat, looking out at the sky. "There sure are a lot of stars."

"There are more if you're away from cities and people. Out in the desert you can see billions of them."

"You lived in the desert?" She gave me a look that showed she didn't believe me.

"I was a soldier in the desert." Memories from that war flooded back on me, the pain and sacrifice and anger I felt there, but I pushed it all away, and surprisingly it went. Time enough to deal with that later. Right now I needed to focus on the little girl in front of me.

We stayed there, motionless, looking out at the stars over the mountains. Then she hopped down and got under the covers. "Good night, Mr. Andrew."

"Wait, wait, wait. You're forgetting something."

"What?" Her little brow furrowed.

"You need to say your prayers."

"Why?"

I thought for a moment about how to explain it to a small child. "They're a way to check in with God, to let him know you're trying to do the right thing even though it's hard sometimes."

"Do you say prayers before you go to bed?"

That was a fair question. It'd been almost fifteen years since I'd prayed. My faith had been shaken after Jenna lost the baby, and then after my experiences in Bosnia I lost the presence of God altogether. "I don't, but I should."

"So how do we do this?" She cocked her head to one side, as if humoring me. It was how Kasey would've responded too.

"Well, God will listen to you anywhere, but I find that it's easiest to kneel down, close your eyes, and just tell God what's going on." I demonstrated as I spoke.

She knelt next to me, that beautiful little girl, and screwed her eyes closed real tight. Her lips moved faintly.

I smiled at her, closed my eyes, and thanked God for giving me this child and her sister too.

I could feel God smiling.

# Discussion Points

**1)** All Andrew claims to want is a family with a woman who understands him. Why does he sabotage each relationship he's in?

**2)** Kasey wonders if David could really change. What do you think would have happened with their marriage if he'd lived?

**3)** Describe Andrew's relationship with his father. How does his father view their relationship, and what do you think is his justification for how it is?

**4)** Kasey's father was a veteran. What effect did this have on her relationship with Andrew?

**5)** How will Andrew do as a father to Zoe? Will he get the chance to be a father to Aida too?

**6)** Compare David and Andrew. Why can't Kasey see the similarities?

**7)** Even after Kasey finds out about David's infidelities and he hits her, she has a hard time leaving. Why is it so hard for her to leave?

**8)** Andrew's mother is also in an abusive relationship. Why does she stay?

**9)** Carly tells Andrew, "I always thought...." He responds, "So did I." What do they mean?

**10)** Alexis falls out of the story, and Erica explains it as, "It didn't work out." Why do you think Alexis and Andrew's relationship failed?

**11)** David accuses Kasey of not trying to fix their marriage. Is he right, and if so, what could she have done differently?

**12)** Kasey says she doesn't want to be taken care of. How do her actions and expectations contradict this?

**13)** Why does Andrew push Kasey away?

**14)** Would Kasey have left David for Andrew, if Andrew had asked her to? Why didn't he?

**15)** Fatherhood plays a large role in the novel. Who was the best father, and who was the worst? Why?

**16)** Compare Kasey and Carly. Do you think Andrew is consciously aware of their similarities and differences? How can you tell?

**17)** What role does alcohol play in the decisions and actions of David, Andrew, and Kasey?

**18)** How will the events in the novel affect Aida, both in the short and long term?

**19)** Compare how Kasey and Andrew attempt to protect their loved ones. Whose methods are better, and why?

# A Note from the Author

A previous version of "Chapter 8: Andrew (Age 17)" appeared as "Small Town Life" in the winter 2012 edition of *Shadow Road Quarterly*.

# About the Author

E.D. Martin is a writer with a knack for finding new jobs in new places. Born and raised in Illinois, her past incarnations have included bookstore barista in Indiana, college student in southern France, statistician in North Carolina, economic development analyst in North Dakota, and high school teacher in Iowa. She draws on her experiences to tell the stories of those around her, with a generous heaping of "what if" thrown in.

Growing up, she preferred books to people, and fortunately the library down the road indulged her introversion/misanthropy. She'd read any genre, as long as the story had relatable characters and left her thinking about what she'd read days, even years later. This has stuck with her, and it's something she aims for in her own works: Love her characters or hate them, just as long as her stories leave you feeling something or seeing the world in a new perspective.

**For more, please visit E.D. Martin online at:**
Personal Website: www.EDMartinWriter.com
Publisher Website: www.EvolvedPub.com
Google+: EDMartinWriter
Goodreads: EDMartin_Writer
Twitter: @EDMartin_Writer
Facebook: EDMartinWriter

# More from E.D. Martin

*The Futility of Loving a Soldier – An Anthology*
The eleven stories in this collection explore the physical and psychological effects of combat, both on those who serve and those back home. Told from the points of view of spouses and children as well as the soldiers themselves, the stories tackle eleven different scenarios spanning five American wars. Guilt and acceptance, despair and hope, selfishness and sacrifice, and above all, love, blend together as characters come to realize maybe their feelings aren't futile after all.

*Not My Thing – A Short Story*
When The Dancing Freemasons embark on their first major tour, Jeff's dreams of being a rock star have come true – until he can no longer connect with the music. One night after a show, he meets a woman who might be the one to get the music flowing again, but is the cost worth it?

*A Place to Die – A Short Story*
When Libby spends a summer helping out at her mom's bed and breakfast-turned-hospice, she doesn't expect to spend her time babysitting someone like Mr. Calloway – a young, vibrant financial planner with a mischievous streak. But Mr. Calloway is sicker than he seems, something neither he nor his family want to acknowledge. Libby must help him accept his fate without losing her heart in the process.

# What's Next From E.D. Martin?

**A HANDFUL OF WISHES**
This magical realism novel is coming in summer 2016 from Evolved Publishing.
~~~~~

**Special Sneak Preview**
~~~~~

# Stage 1 – Obedience and Punishment, 1953
## Chapter 1

Ezekiel Archer walked along the dusty street, hands in his pockets, kicking at rocks scattered in the gutter. Months spent wandering outside had left his skin tanned, his sandy hair lightened by the sun, and his face freckled. The late August dust, a byproduct of the dry summer, permeated his clothes, skin and hair, giving his waifish frame a forlorn street urchin appearance.

Zeke checked his watch, a clunky black monstrosity that hung loosely on his thin wrist: quarter to three. That meant it was just about time for some company. He began jogging up the street. Perhaps today he could make it to a safe hiding spot and spare himself a beating.

Shouts erupted from behind. He looked over his shoulder, counting his pursuers without breaking pace: seven. If they caught him, today would be painful.

"Stop running and make this easier on yourself!" yelled Tommy Weslewski. Tommy was the ringleader, a solid 150 pounds already at age ten, and mean as hell. He was in charge by brute force, mainly; no one wanted to feel the wrath of his fists. But he was cunning too, and while he enjoyed a good old-fashioned beating, he'd often find more creative ways to make his victim's life miserable.

"Yeah, stop and we won't hurt you—too badly!" parroted a high-pitched voice, followed by maniacal giggles. That would be Frank and Mack Silverberg, identical twins with bright orange hair and freckles. They served as Tommy's lackeys and were just as mean, although both of them combined were only about half as smart as he. As far as Zeke knew, no one could tell the two apart, but no one—including the twins—seemed to be bothered by this.

Zeke chanced another look behind him. The gang was rounded out by Shel Weinstein, a tall, thin, quiet guy who avoided calling attention to himself by beating up who he was told; Johnny Ciszek, a plump child with glasses who often found himself the target if Zeke wasn't available; Mike Blake, the "catcher," the fastest guy in school, who was tasked with catching the target and holding him until the rest caught up; and Sean McInnis, another beater whose fists left bruises that lasted weeks, as Zeke's arms and torso could attest.

Zeke's head start hadn't done him much good; Mike was rapidly gaining on him.

Not for the first time, and not for the last, Zeke wondered why they picked on him the most. Sure, he was scrawny, but lots of other kids were scrawny too. His family was no different than any others in his suburban working-class town just on the edge of Chicago. True, he preferred being alone to being around people, but when his only option was to hang around with jerks like these, what choice did he have?

Another glance over his shoulder showed that Mike was about fifteen feet behind him. Zeke put on a burst of speed but knew it wouldn't help for long. Already his lungs were on fire. He needed somewhere to hide, and quick.

This part of town was older, comprised of utilitarian shops with apartments above. None would shelter him from his tormentors, and in actuality they might aggravate his problems further, as word would surely reach his parents that he'd disturbed someone's work. Covington Heights was a close-knit community, comprised of mostly Polish and Irish immigrants. The fathers worked in local meat processing factories, while the mothers stayed home to raise the children or occasionally took jobs as nurses in the nearby hospital. It was understood by all that bullies were a fact of life; either you dealt out the beatings, accepted that you were a punching bag, or found a way to avoid them. Tattling or involving adults was not an accepted method of dealing with problems.

"You're making us work, so we're gonna make this hurt!" yelled Tommy. His voice sounded weak, winded.

Zeke knew he was in for it if he was caught, *when* he was caught. He weighed his options: beating at home, or beating from Tommy's gang. Which would hurt more?

He looked over his shoulder again. Mike was almost close enough to grab him, and the others, except for Johnny, who was panting and bringing up the rear, weren't far behind.

Zeke took a deep breath and darted into the shop nearest him. He hadn't checked the sign above the door and didn't know what to expect, but it certainly hadn't been this. The room in which he found himself was filled with what he could only describe as junk—rows and shelves of junk.

In a bin in one corner, broken metal shapes were jumbled high: rusty pipes, bent bicycle frames, and broken chair legs. Shelves along the far wall contained rows and rows of toys; baby dolls stared blankly ahead out of missing eye sockets, sitting next to splintered baseball bats and teddy bears missing limbs. One row contained clothes racks, filled with what had once been beautiful apparel but by now was tattered, stained rags. Jars in the window held marbles and buttons, and bent, rusty nails. A dented suit of armor guarded a door into a back room. Chipped dishes and tarnished silverware were laid out on a table. Everywhere he looked he saw junk, once practical but now dusty, broken, useless junk.

For an eight-year-old boy like Zeke, this place was magical.

As he stood looking around, a bell tinkled behind him, signaling that Tommy and his gang were in the store with him now. They weren't nearly as captivated as Zeke, and they thundered over to him, fists clenched and ready to strike. He wanted to flinch, to hide somewhere, but instead he bravely turned to face his attackers and the inevitable.

"What are you doing in my shop?" wheezed a voice from somewhere behind him.

He turned, knowing he should never turn his back on his enemies but curious to see who would work in a place like this.

A wizened old man, spectacles precariously perched on his nose, hobbled down an aisle towards them. His face was drawn up into a scowl that would have been comical had it not been for the baseball bat clutched in his hands, propped on one shoulder, ready to strike.

"What are you doing in my shop?" he repeated, shaking the bat in Tommy's direction, identifying him as the obvious leader of the gang. "Answer me, boys, or you can explain to your parents as well!"

The boys eyed the door, knowing as well as Zeke what would be in store for them at home if their parents found out about their day's adventures, but Tommy grinned. "It's just a mistake, sir. We'll all be on our way now, right, Zeke? So sorry to bother you."

"Yeah, come on, Zeke," giggled Frank. Or Mack. "Sorry to bother you, sir."

The boys filed out as Tommy held the door for them, waiting for Zeke and guaranteeing he'd be the first to get his hands on him.

Zeke remained glued to the floor.

"C'mon, Zeke, you heard the old man." Tommy's wolfish grin spread, making his face meaner, more predatory. "Let's go. We got something just for you out here."

Heart pounding, fear etched on his face, Zeke headed towards the door, dragging his feet to slow his pace as much as he could. This was going to be bad.

"Zeke can stay," the old man said just as Zeke reached the shop's threshold.

"What?" Tommy and Zeke asked in unison, Tommy sharply and Zeke incredulously.

"I said Zeke can stay. Off with you, Tommy Weslewski. And shame on you, ganging up seven to one. No matter how horrible the boy is, there's still no need for a cowardly act such as that."

Tommy's jaw dropped upon being identified, and he glared at the man with pure hatred.

"You can't hide in here forever, Archer!" Tommy sneered as he slammed the door behind him.

Zeke and the old man were alone.

"Thank you, sir. "Zeke could barely believe his luck. "I'm not horrible, though."

"Oh really?" A smile played across the old man's lips. "Then why were they chasing you, about to give you a solid pounding that I'm guessing isn't your first from that particular bunch of ruffians?"

Zeke shrugged. "Dunno, guess they just hate me."

"Come now, lad, there has to be more to it than that. Have you ever made rude comments about them?"

"Of course. Everyone has."

"Do you consider yourself better than them?"

"Yes," Zeke said, as if it was the most obvious thing in the world.

"Smarter too, I would think, and more handsome?"

"Well, yes."

"And you let them know, I suppose, every chance you get?"

Zeke squirmed. When put this way, he did sound a bit horrible, not that he would willingly admit it.

The old man smiled. "We'll get you sorted out yet, no need to fret. But first, I was about to have my afternoon tea when I was interrupted by you and your acquaintances. Care to join me?"

"I don't know, sir. I should probably be getting home."

"You do realize, of course, that those boys are currently lying in wait, ready to ambush you upon your exit, but they'll shortly lose interest and find another hapless chap wandering by upon which to administer their affections. It's your choice to depart, if that is truly what you wish."

Zeke stared at the man, not sure what to make of him. "How do you know that? Are you magic or something?"

The old man chuckled. "No, not magic, but I was once a young boy much like yourself. Now I'll ask again. Care to join me for afternoon tea?"

Zeke followed the man past the suit of armor and into a back room just as cluttered as the rest of the shop. Books were piled almost to the ceiling, and several workbenches were covered in tools and various odds and ends. Against one wall leaned dozens of paintings, watercolors of distant lands and garish carnivals, scenes of animals with eyes so lifelike they seemed to watch the viewer, and portraits of disappointingly ordinary people.

Zeke looked around in amazement. "What is this place?"

"Please forgive my poor manners," said the shopkeeper. "My name is Cornelius Zwyklychski, and I am a repairer of dreams." He bowed, sweeping his arm out in a small flourish.

# More from Evolved Publishing:

**CHILDREN'S PICTURE BOOKS**
THE BIRD BRAIN BOOKS by Emlyn Chand:
>   *Courtney Saves Christmas*
>   *Davey the Detective*
>   *Honey the Hero*
>   *Izzy the Inventor*
>   *Larry the Lonely*
>   *Polly Wants to be a Pirate*
>   *Poppy the Proud*
>   *Ricky the Runt*
>   *Ruby to the Rescue*
>   *Sammy Steals the Show*
>   *Tommy Goes Trick-or-Treating*
>   *Vicky Finds a Valentine*

*Silent Words* by Chantal Fournier
*Bella and the Blue Genie* by Jonathan Gould
*Maddie's Monsters* by Jonathan Gould
*Thomas and the Tiger-Turtle* by Jonathan Gould
EMLYN AND THE GREMLIN by Steff F. Kneff:
>   *Emlyn and the Gremlin*
>   *Emlyn and the Gremlin and the Barbeque Disaster*
>   *Emlyn and the Gremlin and the Mean Old Cat*
>   *Emlyn and the Gremlin and the Seaside Mishap*

*I'd Rather Be Riding My Bike* by Eric Pinder
SULLY P. SNOOFERPOOT'S AMAZING INVENTIONS by Aaron Shaw Ph.D.:
>   *Sully P. Snooferpoot's Amazing New Forcefield*
>   *Sully P. Snooferpoot's Amazing New Shadow*

THE ADVENTURES OF NINJA AND BUNNY by Kara S. Tyler:
>   *Ninja and Bunny's Great Adventure*
>   *Ninja and Bunny to the Rescue*

VALENTINA'S SPOOKY ADVENTURES by Majanka Verstraete:
>   *Valentina and the Haunted Mansion*
>   *Valentina and the Masked Mummy*
>   *Valentina and the Whackadoodle Witch*

**HISTORICAL FICTION**
*Galerie* by Steven Greenberg
*Broken Path* by Ruby Standing Deer
SHINING LIGHT'S SAGA by Ruby Standing Deer:
>   *Circles (Book 1)*
>   *Spirals (Book 2)*
>   *Stones (Book 3)*

**LITERARY FICTION**
*Carry Me Away* by Robb Grindstaff
*Hannah's Voice* by Robb Grindstaff
*Turning Trixie* by Robb Grindstaff
*Cassia* by Lanette Kauten
*The Daughter of the Sea and the Sky* by David Litwack
*A Handful of Wishes* by E.D. Martin
*The Lone Wolf* by E.D. Martin
*Jellicle Girl* by Stevie Mikayne
*Weight of Earth* by Stevie Mikayne
*White Chalk* by Pavarti K. Tyler

**LOWER GRADE (Chapter Books)**
THE PET SHOP SOCIETY by Emlyn Chand:
    *Maddie and the Purrfect Crime*
    *Mike and the Dog-Gone Labradoodle*
    *Tyler and the Blabber-Mouth Birds*
TALES FROM UPON A. TIME by Falcon Storm:
    *Natalie the Not-So-Nasty*
    *The Perils of Petunia*
    *The Persnickety Princess*
WEIRDVILLE by Majanka Verstraete:
    *Drowning in Fear*
    *Fright Train*
    *Grave Error*
    *House of Horrors*
    *The Clumsy Magician*
    *The Doll Maker*
THE BALDERDASH SAGA by J.W.Zulauf:
    *The Underground Princess (Book 1)*
    *The Prince's Plight (Book 2)*
    *The Shaman's Salvation (Book 3)*
THE BALDERDASH SAGA SHORT STORIES by J.W.Zulauf:
    *Hurlock the Warrior King*
    *Roland the Pirate Knight*
    *Scarlet the Kindhearted Princess*


**MEMOIR**
*And Then It Rained: Lessons for Life* by Megan Morrison

**MIDDLE GRADE**
FRENDYL KRUNE by Kira A. McFadden:
    *Frendyl Krune and the Blood of the Sun (Book 1)*
    *Frendyl Krune and the Snake Across the Sea (Book 2)*
    *Frendyl Krune and the Stone Princess (Book 3)*

## MIDDLE GRADE (cont'd)
NOAH ZARC by D. Robert Pease:
> *Mammoth Trouble (Book 1)*
> *Cataclysm (Book 2)*
> *Declaration (Book 3)*
> *Omnibus (Special 3-in-1 Edition)*

## MYSTERY / CRIME / DETECTIVE
DUNCAN COCHRANE by David Hagerty:
> *They Tell Me You Are Wicked (Book 1)*

*Hot Sinatra* by Axel Howerton

## NEW ADULT
THE DESERT by Angela Scott:
> *Desert Rice (Book 1)*
> *Desert Flower (Book 2)*

*Nothing Fair About It* by Linda Kay Silva

## ROMANCE / EROTICA
COLLEGE ROMANCE by Amelia James:
> *Tell Me You Want Me (Book 1)*
> *Secret Storm (Book 2)*
> *Tell Me You Want Forever (Book 3)*

*Destined for Genius* by Amelia James

*Let It Ride* by Amelia James

THE TWISTED MOSAIC by Amelia James:
> *Her Twisted Pleasures (Book 1)*
> *Their Twisted Love (Book 2)*
> *His Twisted Choice (Book 3)*
> *The Twisted Mosaic – Specail Omnibus Edition 1-3 (Book 4)*

*The Devil Made Me Do It* by Amelia James

THE SUGAR HOUSE NOVELLAS by Pavarti K. Tyler:
> *Sugar & Salt (Book 1)*
> *Protecting Portia (Book 2)*
> *Dual Domination (Book 3)*
> *The Sugar House Novellas – Special Omnibus Edition 1-3 (Book 4)*

## SCI-FI / FANTASY
*Eulogy* by D.T. Conklin

THE PANHELION CHRONICLES by Marlin Desault:
> *Shroud of Eden (Book 1)*
> *The Vanquished of Eden (Book 2)*

## SCI-FI / FANTASY (cont'd)

THE SEEKERS by David Litwack:
>   *The Children of Darkness (Book 1)*
>   *The Stuff of Stars (Book 2)*
>   *The Light of Reason (Book 3)*

THE AMULI CHRONICLES: SOULBOUND by Kira A. McFadden:
>   *The Soulbound Curse (Book 1)*
>   *The Soulless King (Book 2)*
>   *The Throne of Souls (Book 3)*

*Shadow Swarm* by D. Robert Pease

*Two Moons of Sera* by Pavarti K. Tyler


## SHORT STORY ANTHOLOGIES

FROM THE EDITORS AT EVOLVED PUBLISHING:
>   *Evolution: Vol. 1 (A Short Story Collection)*
>   *Evolution: Vol. 2 (A Short Story Collection)*

*The Futility of Loving a Soldier* by E.D. Martin


## SUSPENSE / THRILLER

*Shatter Point* by Jeff Altabef

TONY HOOPER by Lane Diamond:
>   *Forgive Me, Alex (Book 1)*
>   *The Devil's Bane (Book 2)*

*Enfold Me* by Steven Greenberg

*Shadow Side* by Ellen Joyce

THE OZ FILES by Barry Metcalf:
>   *Broometime Serenade (Book 1)*
>   *Intrigue at Sandy Point (Book 2)*
>   *Spirit of Warrnambool (Book 3)*

THE ZOE DELANTE THRILLERS by C.L. Roberts-Huth:
>   *Whispers of the Dead (Book 1)*
>   *Whispers of the Serpent (Book 2)*
>   *Whispers of the Sidhe (Book 3)*

*Kill or be Killed: Under Cover* by Linda Kay Silva


## YOUNG ADULT

CHOSEN by Jeff Altabef and Erynn Altabef:
>   *Wind Catcher (Book 1)*
>   *Brink of Dawn (Book 2)*
>   *Scorched Souls (Book 3)*

THE KIN CHRONICLES by Michael Dadich:
>   *The Silver Sphere (Book 1)*
>   *The Sinister Kin (Book 2)*

**YOUNG ADULT (cont'd)**

THE DARLA DECKER DIARIES by Jessica McHugh:

*Darla Decker Hates to Wait (Book 1)*
*Darla Decker Takes the Cake (Book 2)*
*Darla Decker Shakes the State (Book 3)*
*Darla Decker Plays it Straight (Book 4)*

JOEY COLA by D. Robert Pease:

*Dream Warriors (Book 1)*
*Cleopatra Rising (Book 2)*
*Third Reality (Book 3)*

*Anyone?* by Angela Scott

THE ZOMBIE WEST TRILOGY by Angela Scott:

*Wanted: Dead or Undead (Book 1)*
*Survivor Roundup (Book 2)*
*Dead Plains (Book 3)*
*The Zombie West Trilogy – Special Omnibus Edition 1-3*

www.ingramcontent.com/pod-product-compliance
Lightning Source LLC
Chambersburg PA
CBHW060428180626
46817CB00007B/2723